IN PRAISE OF
THE ALABASTER CROSS

"When I was given *The Alabaster Cross* I was very lukewarm about reading it. I suspected it would be either a sermon or a lecture on living a righteous life disguised as a novel. Boy, was I surprised. *The Alabaster Cross* is riveting! I almost never read a book in one setting, but I couldn't put it down. Excellent writing style and character portrayal! The characters are so real I often felt like I was looking in a mirror. I want more! Is there a sequel on the horizon?"

CANDACE DOMBROSKY
Athens, Georgia

"For years as a pastor and writer, Richard Exley has proven to be a masterful storyteller. Finally Richard combines his years of ministry, writing, and incredible gifts to produce a remarkable novel that is sure to grab the heart and engage the mind of readers. *The Alabaster Cross* will draw you into worlds most have never known and will have you living alongside each character. You will hurt for them and cry with them. You will readily identify with their joy and their pain, with both their struggles and their triumphs."

DR. CHUCK STECKER
President, Founder
A Chosen Generation
Littleton, Colorado

"I didn't just read *The Alabaster Cross* I lived it! The characters were so real it seemed I could feel what they felt; anger, joy, sorrow, hurt, and love—especially the love between Bryan and Diana. It's definitely a page turner. I couldn't put it down. This is the perfect book to read with a cup of hot chocolate, a favorite blanket, and a box of tissues. It took me to the Amazon Basin, introduced me to dear friends, and softly reminded me that life is precious."

LATISHA LIMPIN
Las Cruces, New Mexico

"I am on the plane flying from Chicago to Tulsa and I just finished reading *The Alabaster Cross*. WOW! This is no ordinary novel! Yes, the story is told in a wonderful way and it certainly keeps you turning the pages, but it is so much more. It is also a collection of deep spiritual truths and nuggets of wisdom discovered as the story unfolds. I am certain it will have a profound and meaningful impact on those who read it, as it did on me."

KURT D. GREEN
Founder and President
Sequoyah Technologies
Tulsa, Oklahoma

"As a pastor who has spent a lifetime working with people, I can tell you that *The Alabaster Cross* is more than just a fascinating read. It's fast moving, exploring both the dangers of the Amazon Basin and the real-life struggles of wounded people searching for healing and wholeness. It moved me to search my own heart and confront my childhood issues as I help my elderly parents prepare to leave this world."

PASTOR PHIL NEELY
Grand Junction, Colorado

"Set primarily in the wilds of the Amazon River basin, *The Alabaster Cross* is a gripping adventure story. But more than that, it is an intriguing saga of relationships among complicated people. No cardboard characters here! The heroes and villains of this tale are multi-dimensional, so true-to-life that the reader gets the feeling he knows each one personally! The eternal struggle between good and evil, love and loss, and man's struggle for survival against overwhelming odds, plays out in the lives and characters of each person, showing clearly the consequences of the choices made by each. Dr. Exley shows his profound understanding of human nature as he crafts this riveting novel. It is definitely a MUST READ!"

EVELYN LOOPER
Counselor, Educator, and Minister
Tulsa, Oklahoma

"From the moment I began reading *The Alabaster Cross* I felt I was right there. And Richard Exley's characters and plot kept me there until the wee hours of the morning. Readers will surely be satisfied with this novel. It's an entertaining read, full of conflict, resolution, and redemption."

MAX DAVIS
Author
Baton Rouge, Louisiana

"*The Alabaster Cross* is a fascinating book combining real life struggles and profound spiritual insights. Richard Exley has a way of disguising truth as fiction and thus addressing the deep issues of our lives. Even though *The Alabaster Cross* is a novel, I gained hope for a difficult situation with my grandson. It is a book to be enjoyed and so much more."

HAZEL VESLEY
Mack, Colorado

"Having been in the Amazon basin of Brazil on a number of occasions I was intrigued by a story based on an area that I have visited and love for its vastness, wildness, and mystery. Richard Exley's portrayal of the Amazonian Rain Forest is captivating, but it is the story of human drama, childhood memories, the love between a man and a woman, and jungle adventure that makes *The Alabaster Cross* an addictive read (you can't let it out of your reach). See if you are brave enough to pick up *The Alabaster Cross* and strong enough to lay it down."

DON EXLEY
Missionary to Latin America Area Director, The Southern Cone

"*The Alabaster Cross* brings to life an amazing story of loss, love, and redemption set against the backdrop of the Amazon Basin. I cried, I laughed, and was completely captivated by the characters (especially Bryan and Diana) and the unfolding of events made so real I felt like I was there."

LINDA THOMPSON
Owner of Linda's Merle Norman
Houston, Texas

"*The Alabaster Cross* is a masterpiece! This book will help us all realize how deep and how wide is the love of God. Every parent and teenager must read *The Alabaster Cross*. I highly recommend it."

DWAIN JONES
Ministry Representative
Mission of Mercy

"*The Alabaster Cross* not only takes you on a journey into the rain forests of the Amazon Basin, but more importantly it takes you on a journey of the heart. Richard Exley provides us with characters so rich and real that at times it feels like he is holding up a mirror allowing us to peer deep inside ourselves at those inner places we try to hide even from God. Bryan, Diana, Caroline, Helen, Rob, Eurico, there is something of each of them in all of us. *The Alabaster Cross* moved me, stretched me, and it changed me. Although this is Richard Exley's first novel, we can only hope it will not be his last."

LEAH STARR BAKER
Author
Tulsa, Oklahoma

"Richard Exley is an unusually skilled novelist, bringing to life both the characters and the setting. His descriptions of the rain forest will have you swatting at mosquitoes and sweat bees while his development of the plot will have you "living the story" as you search for your own answers to life's most difficult questions. Whether you have experienced the loss of a parent, a painful divorce, a dysfunctional relationship, or a crisis of faith, you will connect with the characters and their personal struggle for answers, healing, and growth. *The Alabaster Cross* is a worthy read that picks up speed with each page as it races toward a most unexpected conclusion."

KAREN HARDIN
President
Priority PR Group

"*The Alabaster Cross* was a great read! It was difficult to put down and even when forced to, I found myself thinking about the characters and anticipating what might happen next. Bryan's struggle with anger and forgiveness is so palpable that when he finally accepts God's love and forgiveness, I found myself engulfed in relief and peace! I can't wait for the sequel. I want to know what happens to Rob, Helen, and Carolyn."

KENDA BLACKWOOD
Pastor's wife
Greensboro, North Carolina

"A great read, a real page turner! *The Alabaster Cross* rewards the reader with important life lessons communicated in an absorbing manner using the beautiful but dangerous Amazon Rain Forest as a backdrop."

KEN RUTHERFORD
Sioux City, Iowa

"Richard Exley has an extraordinary gift of painting pictures with words. Black letters on white pages became brilliant in color with emotion while unraveling the tale of the Whittaker family. When I closed my eyes after reading a certain passage, it was as if I could smell the atmosphere that had been created on the pages before me. *The Alabaster Cross* led me on a journey of emotions that I would gladly take again, through the Amazon Rain Forest. Richard is truly a gift to the body of Christ."

MARI-LEE RUDDY
Pastor's Wife
Littlestown, Pennsylvania

"I found *The Alabaster Cross* almost impossible to put down. It takes you on a captivating journey of mystery, intrigue, hope, and destiny as Bryan searches the Amazon jungles in hopes of finding his long lost father. In the process he finds his way back from a life of bitterness and despair. I can't wait for the sequel!"

DEBBIE LEWIS
Pastor's Wife
North Richland Hills, Texas

"*The Alabaster Cross* is a wonderful read! Richard Exley does a fantastic job of capturing Bryan Whittaker's inner conflict. Bryan questions God at every turn, and I was right there living the struggles with him. The dangers and difficulties of life in the Amazon Rain Forest were so real the jungle seemed to come right off the pages at me. I felt deeply satisfied when Bryan was finally able to resolve his issues with his father and with God! I look forward to reading the next Richard Exley novel."

SUSANNAH POGUE
Real Estate Associate
Tulsa, Oklahoma

"I didn't intend to read *The Alabaster Cross* in one nearly continuous setting, but I found myself unable to put it down. It is a beautiful book; a treasure. It has had a profound impact on my heart...one that I am still pondering. I love the depth, message, story, and heart of the book. I know God will bless this labor of love and will use it to touch many people!

ROBIN BOND
Businesswoman
Tulsa, Oklahoma

"Captivating from cover to cover. I couldn't put it down. The characters were so real I felt like I knew them, and the details about the Amazon Basin were fascinating. I can't wait for the sequel."

HILDEGARDE WALLACE
Tennessee Colony, Texas

"In *The Alabaster Cross*, Richard Exley has written a compelling and exciting story of mystery, adventure, and romance. A young man's passionate pursuit to discover the truth about his father's disappearance in the Amazon also leads him on a fascinating spiritual journey as he faces his own confusion, bitterness, and grief. This is a beautifully written story of faith, perseverance, forgiveness, and redemption. I was not only captivated by the adventure, I was also impacted in my own spiritual journey. Only a great book can accomplish both."

EDDY BREWER
Pastor
Grapevine, Texas

"I loved *The Alabaster Cross*! It's one of those books you can't put down and yet you don't want it to end. More please."

JEANIE KRUGER
Grand Junction, Colorado

"I usually don't read fiction, but I couldn't put *The Alabaster Cross* down. I didn't want it to end...not so soon anyway. The characters are so real they seem like old friends. I definitely see a sequel coming, and I hope it is very soon."

JULIA HINES
Athens, Georgia

"Although *The Alabaster Cross* is not a "missionary story" per se, as a career missionary I found Richard Exley's insights into the issues that missionaries deal with right on. The romantic relationship between Bryan and Diana is true to what often happens on the mission field, especially between those who feel isolated from their families and peers. And the anger that Bryan feels toward his missionary father and toward God is painfully real, dwarfed only by the healing he experiences. Combining adventure, romance, and real life issues, *The Alabaster Cross* will touch you in ways few books can."

KARLA WEIS
Missionary

"You cannot imagine my surprise when I began reading *The Alabaster Cross* and discovered that the places in the novel are places I have not only visited but also where I have ministered. Once I began reading, each chapter compelled me to continue—I could not put it down. Author Richard Exley, has masterfully crafted a novel of intrigue, mystery, passion, romance, and redemption. You may never have the opportunity to go to the remote places in this colorful novel, but Richard's writing style and thoroughly researched approach will transport you more quickly than any plane, boat, or canoe could ever do in real life."

JOHN MERRELL, Missionary/Director
International Media Ministries
Madrid, Spain

"*The Alabaster Cross* is an exceptional novel filled with captivating characters and a compelling story line. But more than that it is a beautiful picture of the depths our Heavenly Father is willing to go to show us how much He loves us. For those who have a past that has left them feeling like a failure and undeserving of God's love *The Alabaster Cross* is a powerful reminder that God will never give up on us and that there is no length to which He will not go to restore our lives."

SHERRY ECHOLS
Business Woman
Friendswood, Texas

THE ALABASTER CROSS

A NOVEL

RICHARD EXLEY

Emerald
Pointe
BOOKS

All Scripture quotations are taken from the *King James Version* of the Bible.

The glossary of Portuguese terms was adapted from *A Land of Ghosts* by
David G. Campbell (New York: Houghton Mifflin Company, 2005),
and is used with permission.

This novel is a work of fiction. Any references to historical events; to real people, living or dead;
or to real locales are intended only to give the fiction a setting in historical reality. Other names,
characters, places, and incidents either are the product of the author's imagination or are used
fictitiously, and their resemblance, if any, to real-life counterparts is entirely coincidental.

Published in association with Yates & Yates, LLP, Attorneys and Counselors,
Orange, California

10 9 8 7 6 5 4 3 2 1   10 09 08 07 06

The Alabaster Cross
A Novel
ISBN 0-97851-370-3
Copyright © 2006 by Richard Exley
P.O. Box 54744
Tulsa, Oklahoma 74155

Published by Emerald Pointe Books
P.O. Box 35327
Tulsa, Oklahoma 74153-0327

✝

To Brenda Starr Wallace Exley:

my wife,

my best friend,

and the love of my life.

All which I took from thee, I did but take,

Not for thy harms,

But just that thou might'st seek it in My arms.

All which thy child's mistake

Fancies as lost, I have stored for thee at home:

Rise, clasp My hand, and come!

Francis Thompson
The Hound of Heaven

✝

PROLOGUE
AMAZON BASIN, 1970

I WATCH AS THE old Indian makes his way across the open area toward me. He is naked except for a loincloth that is held in place by a leather string around his waist. A lifetime of exposure to the sun has made his dark skin coarse and his face a web of wrinkles. In his hands he carries a stained canvas satchel. The careful way in which he handles it makes me know that it is valuable to him.

As he approaches I stand to my feet. He stops before me and speaks solemnly in a language I do not understand. The first thing I notice is the dark stains on the canvas, and then my eyes are drawn to a leather patch that is stitched to the flap between the buckles. Although the leather is old and stained, there is no mistaking the initials carved into it.

In an instant, I am taken back to a night more than twenty years ago. It is raining, and the drumming of the rain on the corrugated tin roof of the mission house is all too familiar. The rainy season is just beginning, and the thought of being trapped inside for weeks on end is nearly more than I can bear. My sister Helen, who is four years older than I am, is reading a book by the light of a kerosene lamp. Unlike me, she is an easygoing child. Nothing seems to bother her.

I am more like my father, who is intense and sometimes impatient. As far as he is concerned, life is serious business and must be

11

lived with due sobriety. He comes from Puritan stock, and the generations that have separated him from his ancestors have done nothing to dilute their genes. Tonight, he is muttering under his breath as he hastily stuffs supplies into packs for his trip into the interior. Already there are two large bundles beside the front door, and a third one is nearly finished.

The table is covered with supplies—rice, beans, coffee, smoked meat, bandages, medicine, and other medical supplies. My mother is helping him pack by checking things off of a long list as he stows them away. On more than one occasion, this careful attention to detail has meant the difference between life and death. In the jungles of the Amazon Basin a person seldom gets a second chance.

Although Father likes to pretend that these forays into the interior are routine, they are not. Danger lurks everywhere. Travel is treacherous, especially during the rainy season. In addition, there is the ever-present threat of accident or illness, not to mention the hostility of the Amuacas.

So why does he insist on going? Why does he risk leaving his wife a widow and his children without a father? There are at least two reasons for every trip. One is foundational, and it never changes. My father is nearly consumed with a desire to take the gospel to those who have never heard it. As far as he is concerned, no risk is too great if he can but preach where no one has ever preached. The other reason varies with each trip, but it nearly always involves some kind of emergency.

Tomorrow's trip was occasioned when an Amuaca Indian stumbled into the mission compound more dead than alive. Using a combination of Portuguese and Indian dialects our indigenous workers were able to determine that his village had been stricken with a killing plague.

Knowing that penicillin often opens the door for the preaching of the gospel, my father immediately began making preparations.

I listen as he carefully outlines the route he intends to take. It makes little sense to me, but my mother seems to understand. She is very supportive, but even I can tell that she is more than a little concerned.

According to my father, the stricken village is located four or five days upriver in an area previously unreached by any missionary. In response to my mother's concern he acknowledges that the trip will be grueling. Battling against the current of a rain-swollen river will be exhausting and make for slow going, not to mention the very real possibility of a flash flood now that the rainy season has set in. Still, it is the only way. Trying to go through the jungle on foot would be impossible.

Having carefully closed the third pack, my father sets it beside the other two near the front door. Putting on his spectacles, he draws the kerosene lamp close and reaches for his Bible. Without being asked, we all cease what we are doing and give him our attention. Following a prepared reading schedule, he turns to today's passage, Isaiah 43:1-3, and reads aloud:

> "But now thus saith the LORD that created thee, O Jacob, and he that formed thee, O Israel, Fear not: for I have redeemed thee, I have called thee by thy name; thou art mine. When thou passest through the waters, I will be with thee; and through the rivers, they shall not overflow thee: when thou walkest through the fire, thou shalt not be burned; neither shall the flame kindle upon thee. For I am the LORD thy God, the Holy One of Israel, thy Saviour."

Although I am only seven years old and find much of the Bible incomprehensible, even I cannot miss the significance of this passage given the present circumstances. Tears are glistening in my mother's eyes, and even my father looks pleased. Taking her hand, he says, "The

Lord has spoken to us through His Word. No matter what dangers I may face, he will see me safely through."

After a brief prayer he bids my sister and me goodnight and sends us to bed. For some reason I cannot sleep, so I slip out of bed and make my way to the doorway that opens to the kitchen. A flimsy curtain serves as a door, and I pull it back the tiniest bit in order to peer out. My mother sits in a chair, her face in the shadows cast by the lamp. My father is moving about, gathering a few personal items for his trip. As I watch, I see him wrap his Bible and a leather-bound journal in an oilcloth and place them in his canvas satchel. Carefully he buckles the flap closed before reaching for my mother's hand...

CHAPTER
1

AWAKING EARLY, AFTER A fitful night in which I slept little, I make my way to the kitchen where I get the ancient percolator going. After pouring myself a mug of the steaming brew, I make my way to the porch overlooking the small backyard. It is not yet daylight, but to the east I can see the first hint of morning breaching the darkness. There is a chill in the air, but I know it won't last once the sun pushes its way into the sky. Here on the high plains of north-eastern Colorado the nights are cool, but during July and August the heat returns with a vengence each day. Taking a sip of coffee, I position myself on the porch rail and contemplate my uncertain future.

Although my mother and I were not close, her death has left me more than a little disoriented. I telephoned her infrequently and almost never came to see her; still, knowing she was here seemed to give me roots. Having lost my father at an early age, I now feel totally alone. Of course there's my sister Helen, but we have almost nothing in common. She's married to a local minister and to my way of thinking is something of a religious fanatic, while I haven't darkened a church door since I left home nearly ten years ago.

I am twenty-nine years old, and, although I would never admit outloud, my life is pretty much a mess. I dropped out of college after two years, and since then I have drifted from one dead-end job to another. Currently I'm a lineman for the power company, a good enough job as jobs go, but not something I want to do for the rest of my life. My divorce was final a few weeks ago, and I'm still reeling from the fallout. Thankfully there were no children, or things could have been worse.

My wife, or I should say ex-wife, said she loved me, but she could no longer bear to watch me destroy myself. Protesting, I said, "I don't drink or do drugs, at least nothing to excess. I go to work most days and come home when I am supposed to, so what are you talking about?"

"Bryan," she said, her eyes brimming with tears, "I love you, but you are so full of anger and bitterness you can't receive my love, and it's killing me."

I argued with her, professing not to know what she was talking about, but I knew all right. But knowing something and being able to do anything about it, or even wanting to do anything about it, are distinctly different things. Frustrated by my obstinacy she finally moved out and filed for divorce.

Thinking about it now, I realize I am tense with anger. Taking two or three deep breaths, I try to calm myself. Slowly my pulse rate returns to normal, and I find myself listening to the rumble of the big rigs out on the interstate at least a mile away. For a moment I envy the drivers' solitude and their freedom, but I know it is only an illusion. Like the rest of us they have deadlines to meet, and, though they may be hundreds of miles from home, they pack their troubles with them, of that I am sure.

Taking a sip of coffee, I realize it has grown cold, so I dump it into the flower bed at the base of the porch and retrace my steps into the kitchen. Rinsing out my cup, I place it in the rack to drain, noticing, maybe for the first time, that Mom never owned a dishwasher. Reluctantly I admit that her life wasn't easy; still, I cannot bring myself to feel much sympathy for her. Difficult though her life was, it was of her own making, at least in large part. She could have remarried. She didn't have to try to raise my sister and me by herself.

Wandering through the modest house in which I grew up, I realize that I can recall only a few good memories. Mostly, I remember my mother's sadness. She tried to be brave for Helen and me, but her grief tainted everything. Birthdays and holidays were strained affairs in which our forced gaiety inevitably succumbed to the omnipresent shadow of my absent father. Although I was too young to fully understand what had happened, I knew it was something terrible, a tragedy of such magnitude that our family might never recover.

The first few months were the worst. Many a night I would awaken and hear Mom sobbing, a sound so sad I thought my heart would break. Sometimes, I would slip from my bed and make my way on tiptoe, down the dark hallway, to sit on the floor before the closed door that shut her bedroom off from the rest of the house. One night, when her sobs seemed ceaseless, I dared to open her bedroom door, something that was strictly forbidden. When I did, so great was her grief that it seemed to suck me across the room and into her arms. For a moment she let her defenses down, and we clung to each other, mother and child, taking what comfort we could from one another.

Things might have been different if we could have built on that moment, but too soon she reverted to her rigidity and sent me back to my room—an act so grievous to me that I have never been able to forgive her. In my more magnanimous moments I am almost able to believe she thought she was protecting me, but she was wrong. By trying to shield me from her grief she left me to grieve alone, a burden no child should have to bear.

Looking back, I think that was when my grief turned into anger. For years it was just a wordless knot in the pit of my stomach, a smoldering resentment I could neither deny nor explain. I knew it was related to the tragedy that had befallen our family, but I couldn't explain how. My mother eventually worked through her grief, at least to some extent, but I have never been able to rid myself of this toxic rage. More than any other factor it defines who I am and charts my destiny, whatever that may be.

The ringing of the telephone jerks me from my troubling thoughts, and I hurry across the living room to answer it. Holding the phone on my shoulder, I manage a hello while fumbling through my pockets for my watch. It's my sister, and her condescending tone immediately grates on my already frayed nerves.

"Bryan, I just wanted to check in with you and see if there is anything we can do." When I don't respond, she continues. "Would you like for us to come by and pick you up on our way to the church? It's no trouble."

Forcing myself not to react, I reply, "Thank you, but I prefer to drive."

"Are you sure? It's no trouble."

"I'm sure."

"And Bryan, please don't be late."

Although I have a lifelong history of tardiness, I resent being mothered by her. Refusing to dignify her request with a response, I allow a sullen silence to hang between us. "One other thing," she ventures at last. "If you don't have anything to wear to the funeral, Rob would be more than happy to loan you a suit, or if you prefer, a sport coat."

"Helen," I reply, making no attempt to disguise my anger, "I'm quite capable of taking care of myself, so stop mothering me!"

Slamming down the phone, I pace the cramped living room as my anger subsides. At first glance her concern seems genuine, but I know better. What concerns her is not my well-being, but the family image. Rob is the senior pastor of a prestigious church, and she is afraid I will embarrass them in front of their congregation.

CHAPTER

2

THERE MUST BE AT least five hundred people here, I think, as I survey the nearly full sanctuary before spotting my sister and her family. Helen is seated on the second pew in the center section, directly in front of the pulpit, in an area that has been reserved for the family. The casket, an expensive stainless-steel model in mauve color with a lavish display of blood-red roses and deep purple orchids adorning it, is prominently displayed between the family and the pulpit. It looks ostentatious to me, but what do I know?

The soloist is finishing her number—a sickly sentimental hymn I vaguely remember from my childhood—as I slip down the aisle and into the pew beside Helen. She barely glances my way, but her disapproval is obvious. I'm not sure whether it's my golf shirt and blue jeans or the fact that I'm late, but she is clearly disgusted. Ignoring her, I focus on the pulpit where her pastor-husband is now firmly ensconced. Rob has a good voice, and with the aid of a first-class sound system its rich timber now fills the spacious sanctuary.

Looking around, I have to admit that it is a far cry from the cramped quarters we worshiped in when I was a kid. Rob has served as the senior pastor just over five years, and according to Helen church attendance has nearly tripled, now averaging almost six hundred worshipers each Sunday. Under Rob's leadership the congregation was able to purchase ten acres of prime property and build this handsome new facility. Although I would never admit it, I do admire what he has accomplished.

Turning my attention back to the service, I listen as Rob pays tribute to my mother. His homily is abundantly seasoned with anecdotes from her life; unfortunately, the woman he eulogizes is a stranger to me. I don't mean to suggest that he is being disingenuous, only that the portrait he paints is an unfamiliar one. The mother I remember was a somber woman consumed by a grief she could not escape. Of course, she may have changed in later years, but if she did it was too late to benefit me. Long before I reached adolescence I had succumbed to the anger that characterizes me to this day.

Almost before I realize it the service is over, and the funeral director opens the casket, while his aides move to facilitate the viewing of the body. Row by row the mourners pass by the casket, some pausing for just a moment to whisper a tearful good-bye. The faces filing by are familiar but different. The energetic adults of my childhood are gone, and in their place are these old people who have come today to mourn the passing of a dear friend, and on another level to contemplate their own mortality.

Finally, it is time for the family to say their good-byes, and I study them as they approach the open casket. Without question the years have taken their toll. My Uncle Vern is there, with Aunt Helen at his side, looking more vulnerable than I remember. His thinning hair is completely white now. Today there is pain in his face, and his shoulders are bowed with weariness and grief. Gone is my seemingly indestructible uncle, and in his place is this frail stranger, looking somehow small and uncertain before the relentless march of time. Aunt Helen stands beside him, clinging to his arm. Age has taken a cruel toll, and I hardly recognize her. She is wrinkled now and stoop-shouldered from osteoporosis.

Each silver hair, every wrinkle, the slowed steps, the quiet reminiscing, all testify to humanity's mortality and to mine, though I refuse to acknowledge it. Against my will, I find myself recalling a poem from my childhood, etched indelibly on my memory by the sound of my father's voice.

"Only one life, t'will soon be passed.

Only what's done for Jesus will last."

Though I was only a child, I still remember how my father would grip my narrow shoulders in his big hands. Looking me in the eye, he would say, "Bryan, when our days on Earth are done, when we look back on how we have lived our lives, what will be important to us then?"

With an effort I exorcise those unwelcome memories, discarding them as childish and irrelevant.

Now the funeral director is standing at my shoulder indicating that it is time for the immediate family to view the deceased. Standing, I step into the aisle and allow my sister and her two children to approach the casket first, where her husband joins them. She is sobbing softly, her cheek pressed against Rob's shoulder, while the children cling tightly to both of them. After a moment Helen turns to reach for me, but I have already started back up the aisle toward the exit. Even now, in the hour of grief, I feel like an outsider, maybe even an intruder.

†

It is early evening, the last of the guests have finally departed, and I am slouched in a leather recliner in the corner of the den at Rob and

Helen's new house. Helen is upstairs putting the children to bed, while Rob and I nurse yet another cup of coffee. Propriety requires that I say something complimentary about the service, but anger seals my lips. I'm not angry with Rob, I hardly know him; it's life that jerks my chain.

Having gotten the children settled for the night, Helen returns and joins her husband on the leather sofa across from me, the ghosts of our troubled past hovering all around us. We sit in silence for a minute or two while I study her face. She reminds me of my mother, the way she was after my father disappeared—putting up a brave front but unable to mask the sorrow in her eyes. Although Helen does not try to hide her grief, it is her strength I notice, her determination. Life will not get the best of her; of that I am sure.

Turning to Rob, she says, "After all these years Mom is finally at peace. No more wondering what happened to Dad, no more questions. It's kind of nice thinking of them being together again."

I should keep my mouth shut, but I can't seem to help myself. "Please," I mutter, not even trying to hide my sarcasm.

Helen glares at me, and something evil seems to raise its ugly head inside of me. "You don't get it, do you?" I fume. "Mom is dead. Dead with a capital D. When her heart stopped beating three days ago, she ceased to exist. If you want to believe some fairy tale about immortality, that's your business, but don't bring it up when I'm around. All that religious mumbo jumbo makes me sick!

"And let me tell you another thing; as far as I'm concerned, Mom died a long time ago, back in the Amazon Basin shortly after Dad disappeared. Sure, she went on breathing and taking up space, but as far as being a mother was concerned, she might as well have been dead!"

Helen looks shell-shocked, as if she cannot believe the depth of my anger or the blasphemy it has birthed. Ever the pastor, Rob speaks in a soothing tone, "Bryan, it sounds like you're really angry at God."

Before he can continue, I cut him off. "How could I be angry with God? I don't even believe in God! And if He does exist, He must be cruel or incompetent. How else can you explain the Holocaust or Hiroshima or even the madness in Vietnam? More to the point, what kind of a God would allow the children of devout parents to grow up without a father?"

Getting to my feet, I start toward the front door. Helen hurries after me, but I jerk my arm free of her grasp and fling the door open. "Please, Bryan…" she calls to me, but I do not look back.

CHAPTER
3

ARRIVING HOME FROM WORK, I deposit my lunch pail on the small counter before sitting down at the cluttered table where I begin sorting through the day's mail. I discard several pieces of junk mail before coming to an official-looking envelope. The return address is a title company, and I rip it open. Inside is a check for nearly ten thousand dollars. Mom's house has been sold, and this is my share of the proceeds. Holding the check in my hand, I can't help thinking how little she had at the time of her death—her house, an eleven-year-old car, a small life insurance policy, and less than five hundred dollars in the bank. Shaking my head, I mutter, "So much for the wealth of the wicked flowing into the house of the righteous."

Nearly nine months have passed since Mom's funeral, and I am feeling more disconnected by the day. Helen and I have spoken a number of times in order to work out the details of our mother's small estate. Our conversations have been polite to the point of stiffness. That her feelings are hurt is obvious, but I cannot bring myself to apologize. Now that the estate is settled, we will probably drift farther apart, each of us going our own way. Who knows, it's probably better that way.

Looking around the cramped kitchen, I cannot help but be disgusted. The place is a mess. The sink is overflowing with unwashed dishes, the table is littered with weeks of mail, and I can't remember the last time I took out the trash. Adjourning to the living room, I flop down on a beanbag—the only piece of furniture I have left after the divorce, not counting the thirteen-inch black-and-white TV. It's sitting on a cardboard box that I rescued from the Dumpster behind the apartment complex. A flat box with the remains of last night's pizza is on the floor next to the beanbag, as are a couple of empty beer cans.

I watch the evening news without really seeing it. In the background I hear an obviously distressed Walter Cronkite telling America that four students were killed when National Guardsmen opened fire during an anti-war protest at Kent State University, but it doesn't really register. For months, I have been slipping ever deeper into a black pit, leaving me mostly insensitive to anything other than my own despair.

First there was the divorce—a mercifully swift ending to more than three years of misery; still, it was a shock. I knew Carolyn was unhappy, but I had no idea she was considering divorce. I guess I should have paid more attention. In retrospect I can see the signs were all there. Maybe what hurts the most is how quickly she found someone else. In my darker moments, I can't help wondering if they had something going while we were still married. Not that it matters now, but it does eat on me.

The news program is showing pictures of the Kent State tragedy, and for a moment I stare at the TV in horror, but my outrage is short-lived. To my chagrin, I discover that I'm incapable of grieving for strangers, no matter how tragic their plight. Without consciously considering it, I conclude that my concussed emotions are simply maxed out. For all intents and purposes I'm suffering from sensory overload, and have been for a long time.

My mother's sudden death was just the final blow in a twenty-two-year saga of disappointment and death, a saga that began when my father disappeared while on a mission of mercy into the interior of the Amazon Basin. To this day I do not know what happened to him.

Was he killed by Indians? Did he drown in a flash flood? Was he bitten by a poisonous snake? Did he get lost in the jungle and starve to death? Only God knows, and He's not telling!

Pacing the cramped living room in deep agitation, I finally accept the fact that I cannot go on like this. My father's disappearance and all that it portends has haunted me my whole life. It has destroyed my faith, undermined my relationships, and left me a hollowed-out shell of a man. As a child, even as a boy growing up, I was helpless before the tide of my emotions. I did not understand what was happening to me, and I had no way of coping with it. Tragically, the only emotion I knew how to express was anger, and no matter how desperately I needed others, I always ended up driving them away.

Nothing has changed. My short life is littered with a string of broken relationships. Mom is dead, Carolyn has divorced me, and Helen tolerates me only because I'm her brother. If the truth be known, I cannot even stand myself.

Rob thinks I'm mad at God, and I guess I am. Why wouldn't I be? Who can trust a God who can't even take care of His most devout servants? Storming around the living room, I give the pizza box a hard kick, sending it crashing into the wall, scattering fragments of last night's dinner across the floor.

After a bit my anger gives way to a familiar despair. Hoping to drink myself into oblivion, I make my way to the refrigerator for a beer. As luck would have it, I downed the last two with my pizza last night. Too tired to go out, I decide to confront my melancholia without the aid of booze.

Although depression dogs my steps, I find myself thinking with unaccustomed clarity. To be free from these demons I now realize that I'm going to have to find some way to make peace with my past. The key is my father. If I knew what happened to him maybe I could move on with my life, but as long as his disappearance remains a mystery I'm a prisoner to my past. As far-fetched as it seems there's a part of me that wonders if he might still be alive. Maybe he was injured in an accident and is suffering from amnesia. Maybe he has been living all these years with the Indians deep in the interior.

Having finally given expression to the wordless hope I've carried in my heart since childhood, I find that my mind is racing. In 1948, when my father disappeared, much of the Amazon Basin was still as it was in the Stone Age. Some rubber plantations had been carved out of the jungle, and an oil company or two had established work stations deep in the interior, but for the most part life continued as it had for hundreds of years. An injured man, suffering from amnesia, could be nursed back to health by the Indians and adopted into their tribe. That being the case, he might never be heard from again. A far-fetched possibility to be sure, but it could happen.

Reason tells me that I'm thinking irrationally. The belief that my father is alive after all these years is just a pipe dream. More than likely he is dead. I'm not naive enough to believe otherwise. Still, I don't think I will be able to get on with my life until I know for sure. I'm still depressed, but for the first time in longer than I can remember I have a purpose, a reason for living. Rummaging through the stacks of mail cluttering the kitchen table, I finally locate a yellow legal pad. Grabbing a pen from the kitchen drawer, I sit down to draw up a list of things I'm going to need. I know that if this is going to work, I can't go off half-cocked. Normally money would be a huge problem, but with my half of the inheritance from Mom's estate I should be all right.

After a couple of hours I have filled nearly three pages with notes, and my plan is taking shape. In the morning I will call in sick and then I will hit several pawn shops and see if I can pick up some good camera equipment for a decent price. Maybe in the afternoon I will have time to go the library and do some research.

CHAPTER
4

AFTER POURING A SECOND cup of coffee for each of them, Helen sets the CorningWare coffeepot back on the stove before rejoining Rob at the dining room table. "It's been more than a month since we've heard a word from Bryan. I've left several messages on his answering machine with no response, and now his phone has been disconnected. This afternoon I tried to reach him at the power company, and they told me he no longer works there."

Her voice trails off, and Rob reaches across the table to comfort her. Squeezing her hand, he says, "I can understand your concern, but I'm sure it's simply more of Bryan's irresponsible behavior."

"You're probably right. Still, I can't seem to shake the feeling that there's more to it this time. Who knows, maybe I'm just feeling guilty for the way I treated him at Mother's funeral."

"Don't do that to yourself. If anyone should feel guilty about what happened at the funeral, it's Bryan. Given his uncouth behavior, I think you showed remarkable restraint."

"Be that as it may, I'm not going to be able to let this rest until we hear from him." She hesitates for a moment then asks tentatively, "If he hasn't called by the first of the week, do you think you could take a couple of days off and drive to Denver with me to check on him?"

"I could probably arrange that, but I don't really think it's necessary. Bryan's a grown man, and if he doesn't want to talk with us, there is no way we can force him."

"I know you're right, but I really want to reach out to him. I'm the only family he's got left, and he needs me whether he knows it or not." Wistfully she adds, "We need each other."

A wave of emotion threatens to engulf her, and she quickly pushes back from the table, spilling her coffee. Refusing to yield to her feelings, she stoically sets about clearing the table. At the kitchen sink she thoroughly rinses each plate before placing it in the dishwasher. It is probably unnecessary, but tonight it keeps her occupied, prolonging the inevitable moment when she will have to confront her feelings.

When the last dish has been rinsed and placed in the dishwasher, she wipes the counters and replaces the decorations on the dining room table, being careful to focus only on what she is doing lest her emotions overwhelm her. Finally she stands at the kitchen sink, rubbing lotion on her hands while watching her sons playing catch in the backyard.

The joy of her children offers no comfort this evening; in fact, it only seems to exacerbate the pain she feels when she thinks of Bryan and her own childhood. Seems her memories are divided into before and after categories. Before their father disappeared, her memories are carefree and fun-filled; the mission house a place of love and laughter. Located deep in the Amazon Basin, it was several days' travel from civilization; still, she had never felt deprived. How could she when her father brought her exotic birds and rare orchids when he returned from his trips into the rain forest? Sure, they had to make do with kerosene lamps for light and water from a cistern, but what is that to a child who knows she is safe within the circle of her parents' love?

After her father disappeared. She remembers the day he went away as if it were only yesterday. *It was raining, and what light filtered through the tall trees was weak, hardly light at all. The smell of coffee and the murmur of conversation had coaxed her awake, but she could not make herself leave the warmth of her bed. Then she heard the door shut and the sound of her father's boots on the porch. Flinging back the blanket, she had rushed to the window in time to see him cross the clearing as he made his way toward the river. He was carrying a heavy pack on his back and another on his arm. Rain dripped from the brim of his hat, and then the trees swallowed him up. She had thought nothing of it that morning, simply crawled back beneath the covers, never realizing that she had seen her father for the last time.*

Outside the kitchen window the day is nearly done, but Helen hardly notices, so engrossed is she in her thoughts. When Rob steps up behind her and slips his arms around her, she is startled. Pulling her against him, he puts his cheek next to hers and says, "A penny for your thoughts."

Turning toward him, she buries her face against his shoulder. "Hold me, Rob," she whispers urgently. "Hold me."

After a minute or two he takes her by the hand and leads her into the den. Once they are seated on the leather couch, he turns to her and says, "Helen, we need to talk. I know you are still grieving your mother's death, but there's something else, too…"

A tiny shudder shakes her shoulders, and she chokes back a sob. *How,* she wonders, *do I talk about something I've kept locked deep inside of me all these years? Will it help, or will it only make matters worse? Besides, it goes against everything I am. From a child I was taught to be a private person, keeping my own counsel and solving my own problems. Only the weak or the indiscreet made a public display of their feelings.*

Still, she cannot deny her need to talk, and her inner conflict is almost debilitating.

Taking a deep breath, she begins, hesitantly at first. "I've been revisiting my father's disappearance. It changed everything, you know. Our family never recovered. Mom did after a fashion, and I did too, but not Bryan. It's been more than twenty years, and it still defines our relationships. I just want to put it behind me and move on."

"Sometimes," Rob muses, "you have to deal with your past before you can embrace the future. Ignore it, and it is like a ball and chain that weighs you down."

Exasperated, Helen replies, "How do I deal with something that happened twenty-two years ago? I can't go back and change anything. I can't undo what's been done."

"The key is to make peace with your past, turn it into an ally instead of an enemy."

"How am I supposed to do that?"

"It's more of a process than an event. Why don't you start by telling me what you remember about that time?"

Helen closes her eyes and leans back against the couch. With almost no effort her thoughts return to the memories Rob interrupted a few minutes earlier. Picking up where she left off, she begins speaking in a voice that is hardly more than a whisper. "Several days passed, at least eight or ten, before a growing uneasiness settled upon the house. Even then we kept to our normal routine—lessons each morning, chores in the afternoon, Bible reading and prayers each evening, just the way Father had taught us. When two weeks passed without a word, the uneasiness turned into a knot of fear. We knew that Father had planned on being gone no more than eight or ten days. If he was careful he might make his provisions last for two weeks, not any longer. Even seven-year-old Bryan could do the math, and it added up to trouble, serious trouble. Mother tried to reassure us, carefully detailing any number of things that might have delayed Father's return, but she couldn't hide her concern. Worry became our daily bread, and a foul meal it was.

"In those days Mother aged before our eyes. It was obvious that she wasn't sleeping well, and her face grew pinched and gray, the light gone from her eyes. What made things even worse was our helplessness. There was simply nothing we could do. We had no way of communicating with the outside world, no way to go for help. After several weeks of rain, the jungle trails were impassable, and the rivers were raging torrents, too treacherous for all but most skilled boatman.

"No one suffered more than Bryan. He idolized Father and could not imagine life without him. His moods alternated between sullen withdrawal and a fearful clinging. For hours he would sit motionless before the window, staring into the surrounding jungle, willing Father to return. Hardly a night passed when he didn't cry out, tormented by fearful dreams. He wanted to sleep with Mother, or even me, but Mom would not hear of it. As a last resort he begged her to let him sleep with the lamp burning, but she would not. To her way of thinking, any departure from the established routine was a sign of weakness, and we couldn't have that, never mind that a little boy was dying on the inside, afraid and alone."

A hint of anger has seeped into the sorrow that colors her words, and she stumbles to a stop, feeling somehow disloyal to her mother. Unbidden tears slide down her cheeks, and she buries her face in her hands while silent sobs shake her shoulders. Putting his arms around her, Rob pulls her close, providing what comfort he can. After a while her sobs seem to exhaust themselves, and they sit in an intimate silence.

Finally Rob speaks. "Do you realize that we have been married almost thirteen years, and that's the first time you've ever talked about your father's disappearance?"

"I guess I've never thought about it. I do know it's something I've tried to forget. But Mom's passing seems to have opened all the old wounds. I know I will get through this. I've got the Lord and you and the boys. Bryan has no one. Once more he's that little boy alone in the dark."

CHAPTER

5

ALTHOUGH THE TRAFFIC IS light this Monday morning, allowing them to make good time, to Helen the journey from Sterling to Denver seems endless. Looking at the mostly gray countryside rushing past her window, she cannot help but think that "Colorful Colorado" is hardly colorful, except for the Rocky Mountains. More than half of the state is semiarid desert or irrigated farmland. Two interstate highways bisect it. Highway 70 runs east and west from the Kansas border through Denver, Vail, Glenwood Springs, and Grand Junction before entering Utah. Highway 25 cuts down through the state north to south. From the southern border of Wyoming it threads its way through Denver, Colorado Springs, Pueblo, and Trinidad before reaching the New Mexico state line.

Highway 70 provides the more scenic route, especially west of Denver as it enters the Front Range of the Rockies, climbing toward the Eisenhower Tunnel. Unfortunately, Rob and Helen's route follows Highway 76 and is hardly scenic. Being situated in the northeastern corner of the state, Sterling is separated from the state capital by a hundred and twenty-five miles of monotonous, semiarid, sagebrush-covered hills, giving way to bare prairie. Even in the spring the geography is virtually colorless, a blending of dismal gray and dusty brown. Fortunately, the speed limit is seventy miles per hour, reducing the stark countryside to a blur outside the car window.

For Helen, being unable to locate Bryan has been like reliving her father's disappearance twenty-two years ago—the same desperate hope giving way to a deepening dread, a growing certainty that something terrible has happened. Rob's calm assurances have produced only irritated frustration. How can he be so insensitive to her fears? Doesn't he realize what she is going through? Not even the mellow sound of the Bill Gaither Trio, emanating from the car's eight-track player, can take the edge off of her nerves.

She is rapidly running out of options, having already contacted the Colorado Highway Patrol, the Denver Police Department, and several hospitals, all to no avail. According to the highway patrol, Bryan had not been involved in an auto accident, nor was he a patient in any of the hospitals she called. Of course, the Denver police were no help at all. Given the facts—no evidence of a crime and Bryan's age—they wouldn't even file a missing persons report.

Finally, in the distance she can see the Denver skyline and behind it the Rocky Mountains' snow-covered peaks. Rummaging in the glove box, she finds a street map of the city and proceeds to give Rob directions. In short order they are pulling into the parking lot adjacent to the rental office for the London Square Apartments. Surveying the aging structure, Helen cannot help thinking that its shabby appearance makes a mockery of the elegant-sounding name.

Turning to Rob, she asks, "Can you believe Bryan would live in a place like this?"

Shrugging noncommittally, he turns off the ignition. "Why don't you go in and see what you can find out? I'll just wait here in the car."

Entering the rundown office, Helen is immediately assailed by an unpleasant odor combining the smell of fried food, stale cigarette smoke, and harsh disinfectant. There is an ashtray full of cigarette butts sitting on the corner of the scarred desk, but not much else.

Looking around, she concludes that the back half of the office must be the living quarters for the apartment manager; hence the repugnant odor. Impatiently she calls, "Anybody here?"

A young woman with stringy hair and an acne-scarred complexion enters the office without bothering to disguise her irritation. Her nametag identifies her as Mary. Impatiently she demands, "What can I do for you?" while a soap opera blares from the television in the apartment.

"I'm looking for my brother. He's one of your tenants; at least I think he is."

Taking a deep drag on her cigarette, the young woman flops in the chair behind the desk and pulls open a file drawer. "Name?"

"Helen. Helen Thompson."

"Your brother's name, please," she says with exaggerated patience, as if talking to a dimwitted child.

"Bryan Whittaker," Helen replies, hardly able to believe that this slovenly creature is making her feel so inept.

Slamming the file drawer closed, Mary makes a point of studying Helen. "So you're Bryan's sister? Your husband's a preacher, right?"

Ignoring her sarcasm, Helen tries a disarming smile. "I haven't heard from Bryan in nearly a month, and now his phone has been disconnected. Would you please give me his apartment number? I really need to talk with him."

Taking another drag on her cigarette, Mary inhales deeply, savors the moment, and then blows a cloud of fumes in Helen's direction. Finally she says, "Two-twelve South."

Hurrying toward the door, Helen calls a thank you over her shoulder.

"One other thing," Mary calls after her. "Bryan moved out last week, and before you ask, he didn't leave no forwarding address."

She is obviously enjoying herself, and Helen is sorely tempted to give her a piece of her mind but manages to restrain herself. Doing her best to remain calm, she returns to the desk and asks, "Do you have any idea where Bryan might have gone, what he was planning to do?"

"Nope. He made it a point not to tell me. Said you might come around looking for him, and it would be easier if I didn't know nothin'."

"Are you telling me Bryan doesn't want me to know where he's gone?"

"I ain't telling you nothin', 'cause I don't know nothin'."

Pushing back from the desk, Mary rises and starts for the apartment. As she turns to go, she says, "I think I hear my baby crying. I better see about her."

Helen remains at the desk trying to sort through her emotions. She's angry. Why would Bryan do something so cruel? Of all people he should know how devastating the disappearance of a loved one can be. Another part of her mind is grappling with Mary's behavior. What reason could she have for acting so rudely? That she was enjoying Helen's discomfort was obvious enough, but why?

Finally, she turns and makes her way toward the door. Rob is dozing as she approaches the car, and for a moment she resents his nonchalance. That he can be so unconcerned when she is obviously distraught is more than a little disconcerting. Jerking the car door open, she slumps in the seat, fighting tears of frustration.

Yawning, Rob asks, "Well, what did you find out?"

"It's worse than I thought," Helen says, struggling to control her emotions. "Bryan moved out sometime last week, and he didn't leave a forwarding address.

"That's not like Bryan. He can be a jerk, but he's never done anything like this. Even more puzzling is the fact that the apartment manager was obviously expecting me. She seemed to take a perverse pleasure in telling me that Bryan didn't want us to know where he had gone."

"That's weird," Rob concedes, "even for Bryan. He's done some strange things in the past, but nothing like this."

"You've got that right!"

"I know it must feel like his actions are directed at you, but I don't think that's the case. As you've pointed out on a number of occasions, he's never dealt with his feelings about your father's disappearance. That loss, combined with your mother's death, appears to have pushed him over the edge."

"You don't think he will harm himself, do you?"

"Not deliberately. But he could be pretty self-destructive if he doesn't get some help."

"What can we do?"

"Pray. Remember, God loves Bryan even more than you do, and He will take care of him."

"I want to believe that, but when I look back over the past twenty-two years, it doesn't seem like the Lord has done a very good job. Why should it be different now?"

"Sometimes we have to come to the end of ourselves before we allow the Lord to intervene. From the looks of things, Bryan is getting close to the breaking point."

CHAPTER

6

SITTING AT THE KITCHEN table, her head in her hands, Helen finds that she is weeping. Her Bible is open on the table before her—unread. Her journal is beside it—untouched—as is a cup of coffee, now grown cold. It feels like her life is spinning out of control, and she is powerless to stop it. The death of her mother, almost a year ago, was the tear that started the unraveling, but it didn't stop there. Now Bryan is gone, and against her will she finds herself reliving the tragedy of her childhood. Having looked into that black abyss, she now finds herself grappling with a grief that threatens to consume her.

At first Rob seemed to understand, but as her depression has deepened he has grown impatient. She can't really blame him. If the truth be known, she is disgusted with herself. *Look at me*, she thinks, *it is nearly noon, and I am still in my robe. The beds aren't made, and break-fast clutter covers the counter.* Being a perfectionist, she finds her slovenly behavior inexcusable, but try as she might she cannot escape the lethargy that renders her immobile.

Against her will her thoughts return to the previous night. *She had gone to bed early, leaving Rob to get the boys in bed, but she hadn't been able to sleep. When he came to bed around eleven o'clock he found her staring at the clock, her face a sorrowful mask. Slipping into bed beside her, he gently* rubbed her back. Touched by his tenderness, she turned toward him, burying her face against his shoulder. Apparently he mistook her need for comfort as an invitation to become intimate. When his desires became apparent, she tried to discourage him without rejecting his overtures outright, but to no avail. Finally, she was forced to turn her back to him and cling to her side of the bed.

For a few minutes neither of them spoke, although the silence between them seemed to crackle with anger. Never had she felt more betrayed, more misunderstood. How could he be so insensitive? Didn't he know what she was going through? How he could expect her to make love at a time like this was simply beyond her comprehension. Didn't he know she was grieving?

Squeezing her eyes closed, she refused to cry. No matter how unspeakable her anguish she would not give him the satisfaction of knowing that he had the power to reduce her to tears. She had always taken pride in her strength, and she determined to be strong now. Never mind that strength seemed to begat strength, pitting them against each other.

"Helen, you've got to get hold of yourself," he said, speaking calmly but without tenderness. "It's not like something happened to one of the boys. That I could understand. You're not even close to Bryan, and your father's been gone more than twenty years. I don't mean to be insensitive, but it's time you got over it. We need you around here."

Turning over, she glared at him. "I thought you were the one who told me I needed to deal with my grief. Now you're telling me to get over it. So, which is it—deal with it, or get over it?"

"Dealing with your grief doesn't mean making a shrine out of your sorrow."

"So that's what you think I'm doing—building a shrine?"

"That's what it looks like from here. All you seem to care about is that dysfunctional brother of yours and a father you can hardly remember."

"Rob," she pleads, "don't do this."

"Don't do what? Don't tell you the truth? Don't make you take an honest look at yourself and your family? Don't insist that you be a mother to your children? Don't expect you to be a wife to me?"

Tuning him out, she retreated behind a wall of silence. She could still hear him, but as if from a great distance. While he continued to rant she turned inward, seeking solace within herself, but it was no use. Try as she might she could not escape. His hurtful words pursued her, hunted her down, pounding her into submission, and finally making her willing to seek peace at any price.

Swallowing her pride, she had reached for him, "Let's not fight. Please."

He had turned away, feigning disinterest, but it was just a ploy. Already his anger was giving way to desire.

Surrendering to his desires, they made love, but for her it was mechanical, feeling more used than loved. Afterwards he turned over and fell into a deep sleep. Quietly Helen slipped out of bed and made her way into the bathroom. Stepping into the shower, she adjusted the spray while silent tears ran down her cheeks. She couldn't help thinking that the life she was now living bore only the slightest resemblance to the one she had known just months ago.

"What's happening to us?" she sobbed. It never used to be like this. Sure, we had our spats, but we didn't wound each other, at least not deliberately. Rob was never cruel or sarcastic, and I was never melancholy, never given to fits of weeping. Now depression dogs my days, and Rob has become a stranger.

"God help us," she prayed, "before we destroy each other."

Her painful introspection is interrupted by the doorbell. Realizing she is still in her robe, she decides to ignore it, but soon curiosity gets the best of her, and she slips into the guest room where she has a clear view of the front door. The woman standing on the front porch looks familiar, but she cannot place her. After ringing the doorbell a final time, the woman turns to go. When she does, Helen gasps. Although they have only met once, she would know her anywhere.

Hurrying to the bedroom window, she raps loudly. Once she has the woman's attention, she motions for her to wait and hurries toward the front door.

Opening the door, she says, "You're Carolyn, aren't you, Bryan's wife?"

"Actually I'm his ex-wife."

"Please come in." Noticing her hesitancy, Helen adds, "You'll have to excuse my appearance. I haven't been well, and I'm slow getting around today."

"I don't want to intrude. Perhaps another time would be better."

"Nonsense. Let me show you into the den. Once you're settled, I'll throw something on and join you."

Hurrying into her bathroom, Helen looks at herself in the mirror and groans. Opening her makeup bag, she grabs a bottle of base and quickly applies it. Once that is done, she reaches for her mascara and gives her eyelashes a quick brush. Finally she puts on a little lip gloss and runs a brush through her hair. Stepping out of her robe, she reaches for a silk blouse and a pair of jeans. Taking a final look in the mirror, she decides she looks passable. Grabbing her sandals, she hurries toward the family room.

What, she wonders, *could have brought Carolyn here? Maybe she knows something about Bryan.*

CHAPTER

7

PAUSING AT THE DOOR leading into the den, Helen observes Carolyn examining the family photos displayed on the mantle and in the bookcase adjoining the fireplace. After a moment she picks one up and studies it at length, a puzzled expression clouding her attractive features.

She's a striking woman, Helen muses, *with dark eyes and thick auburn hair. It's not hard to see why Bryan was attracted to her.*

Reflecting on her own disheveled appearance she feels somewhat intimidated; still, she's determined to be a gracious hostess. Smiling resolutely, she steps into the room. "I see you've found the rogues' gallery."

Glancing up, Carolyn flashes her a tentative smile. "I find family photos fascinating. They all have a story to tell."

Being a private person by nature, Helen cringes, sensing that her privacy is about to be breached, especially when she sees the photo Carolyn is holding. It's an old black-and-white snapshot of the family—all four of them—taken in front of the mission house. She is clutching a homemade doll while looking shyly into the camera. Bryan is glaring up at his father, who has a firm grip on his shoulder. Of course, both her mother and father look severe, an expression befitting missionaries serving in extreme circumstances. Behind the house the towering trees of the Amazon rain forest block out the sky.

Handing her the photo, Carolyn says, "Tell me about this picture. That's Bryan, isn't it?"

Hoping to appear nonchalant, Helen says, "Oh, that old thing. I don't even know who took it. I found it in some of Mother's things after she died. She passed away last August. I'm sure Bryan told you."

"I'm sorry. I didn't know. Bryan didn't tell me; not that he would have any reason to, since we were already divorced."

Grief now fills the silence that lies uncomfortably between them. Finally Carolyn says, "About the picture…"

Seeing she's not going to let it drop, Helen sighs before replying. "I believe it was taken in 1946. That means Bryan would have been four or five years old, depending on the month. He was already incorrigible, always has been. Probably always will be. See how Father is holding him in place."

Carolyn continues to study the photo pensively, and Helen finds herself talking nervously to fill the silence. "Our family spent several years as missionaries in the Amazon Basin. Father thrived on it, but it was more difficult for Mother. You can imagine what it was like for her with two young children, being so far from family and all, but I never heard her complain. Of course, everything changed when Father disappeared. Surely Bryan told you about that."

"As a matter of fact, Bryan told me almost nothing about his family. It wasn't something he was comfortable discussing. Anytime I brought it up, he would change the subject. If I pressed, he would get mad and storm out of the room or retreat behind a wall of sullen silence."

Shaking her head, Helen says, "That sounds like the Bryan I know."

"Do you have any more family pictures?" Seeing Helen hesitate, she hastens to add, "I don't mean to intrude, but it would mean a lot to me."

"Why this sudden interest in Bryan's family history?"

"It's not all that sudden. To tell you the truth, I was fascinated with Bryan the moment we met. Early on, his mysteriousness was part of the attraction, but after we were married I realized it was a shell, a way of keeping people at a distance. At first I thought it was just me, that maybe he didn't trust me, but in time I came to realize that it was himself he didn't trust, or maybe it was life."

Although she and Bryan have been divorced almost a year, Carolyn's emotions are still raw, and now she finds herself blinking back tears. Walking to the window, she stares out while struggling to regain her composure. Finally she asks, "What happened to him, Helen? Why is he so angry, so closed?"

Without speaking, Helen goes to a restored trunk sitting against the far wall. Opening the lid, she lifts out a box filled with old photos retrieved from her mother's house. Setting them on the coffee table, she motions for Carolyn to join her on the couch.

"It's a long story," she says, picking up a handful of pictures, "and not very pretty. Although Bryan was always an incorrigible child, he had a tender heart. He was only seven years old when our father disappeared, and it nearly killed him. Things might have turned out differently had Mother been more sensitive to what he was going through, but she wasn't. In her defense, she was grieving terribly and struggling to find her own way. Still, he was only a child, and he needed more than she was able to give him."

"When you say your father disappeared, what do you mean? What happened to him?"

"That's what made it so hard. We were never able to determine what happened. He went upriver to take some medicine to a village of Indians in the interior, and he never came back. After several weeks without a word, we were forced to conclude that he was dead—killed in an accident or by the Indians—but his body was never found.

"It was terrible for all of us, but no one suffered like Bryan. At first he refused to believe his daddy wasn't coming back. When anyone tried to explain things to him, he would cover his ears and run from the room crying. When mother tried to reason with him, he wouldn't listen. He just kept saying, 'God wouldn't let my daddy die! God wouldn't let my daddy die!'

"Of course, it was impossible for Mother to continue on the mission field with two small children, so those who make such decisions decided we should return to the States. Mother was relieved, I think, as I was, but Bryan was inconsolable. As far as he was concerned, we were abandoning Father.

"I don't think he's ever forgiven Mother; or me for that matter. More importantly, I don't think he's ever forgiven God. To this day he holds God responsible!"

While Helen has been talking, Carolyn has been looking through the pictures. Now she hands one to Helen, saying, "Bryan looks like his father, don't you think?"

Studying the photo, Helen is amazed at the resemblance. Looking at the picture of her father is like looking at Bryan—the same dark hair, thick and unruly; the same strong jaw and piercing eyes. Turning it over, she sees that it is dated in her mother's precise handwriting—*May 27, 1939.* Underneath the date her mother has written: *Ordination Service for Harold B. Whittaker. I gave him a beautiful alabaster cross on a gold chain as an ordination gift. He immediately put it on although he did not usually wear jewelry.*

Examining the photo once more, Helen can just make out the cross resting on her father's tie. Opening a drawer in the end table, she extracts a small magnifying glass and returns to the photo. Now the cross is clearly visible, and with it a host of memories flood back. In her mind, that cross is as much a part of her father as his eyeglasses. She never saw him without it, and now she understands why it was so special to him.

Puzzled, Carolyn asks, "What is it? What are you looking at?"

Handing her the magnifying glass, Helen says, "Look at the cross on my father's tie."

"I see it, but what's so special about it?"

"It's the only piece of jewelry, other than his wedding band, that my father ever wore. I never saw him without it. He wore it every day of my life. Now I understand why. It was a gift from my mother celebrating his ordination. Even as his wedding band symbolized his marriage to my mother, so that alabaster cross was a symbol of his covenant with the Lord."

Helen can tell that her explanation is incomprehensible to Carolyn, so she changes the subject. Scooping up the old pictures, she dumps them back in the box and heads for the kitchen, calling over her shoulder, "Come in here. Let's see what we can find to eat. You must be starved."

Once they are seated at the table enjoying sandwiches and a salad, Helen asks, "So what brings you to Sterling, and how did you find us?"

Thankful that her mouth is full, Carolyn makes a motion indicating that she will respond as soon as she swallows her food. *How,* she wonders, *can I say this without sounding like a neurotic female?*

"Finding you was the easy part. I still had the Christmas card you sent a couple of years ago, and it had your address on it."

"And?"

"I'm not sure how best to say this," Carolyn hedges, "so I'll just blurt it out. Filing for divorce was a terrible mistake. I realize that now. No matter how difficult living with Bryan was, it was better than living without him. I guess what I'm trying to say is that I'm still in love with him, and I want us to get back together."

"So what does that have to do with me? Are you hoping I will intercede for you with Bryan, or what?"

"Not exactly, but I would appreciate it if you would tell me how to contact him. He's apparently changed jobs and moved without leaving a forwarding address. If you don't feel comfortable giving me his address, I will understand, but at least give me his telephone number so I can call him."

The tears Helen has been fighting so hard to restrain now slip unbidden down her cheeks. "Oh, Carolyn, it seems we are in the same boat. I've been trying to contact Bryan for weeks without any luck. It seems he's just dropped off the face of the Earth. Rob tells me not to worry, that Bryan is a grown man and capable of taking care of himself, but I'm scared. When I recognized you at my door, I had a wild hope that you were bringing word from Bryan."

CHAPTER

8

IT IS LATE AFTERNOON, and I am drinking *cafezinho*—Brazilian coffee—at a sidewalk cafe in Cruzeiro do Sul, just off the Praça do Triunfo (the Plaza of Triumph). I've never tasted anything like it. It is so sweet and strong it makes my teeth ache. According to the waiter, the grounds are boiled in brown sugar and water. Whatever the case, I think I am addicted already. I may never be able to drink American coffee again.

Being a North American, I am something of a curiosity in this frontier outpost located on the banks of the Rio Juruá, near the Peruvian border. It is a raucous city made up mostly of Indians or Caboclos, a people of mixed heritage who, I am told, are masters at eking out a living along the rivers or in the forests. Walking the streets and along the riverfront, I have heard few Indian dialects. Almost everyone speaks Portuguese now, nearly all of the Indian dialects having been lost when they transitioned from the forest to the city.

Although I grew up speaking Portuguese, I had forgotten most of it after more than twenty years in the States. Still, it is coming back to me, and far quicker than I might have imagined. Of course, my accent is atrocious, but I'm having only a little trouble understanding what is being said. It's a good thing, for I haven't heard a word of English since I landed in Manaus more than a month ago.

The journey from Manaus to Cruzeiro was tedious and seemed to take a lifetime. For twenty-nine days the cargo barge on which I had secured passage plodded upstream. We began on the Rio Negro and drifted south fifteen kilometers into the Rio Solimoes, and from there we pushed against the current for five hundred kilometers to the mouth of the Juruá; then for three more weeks we negotiated its countless meanders, finally arriving in Cruzeiro late one afternoon a week ago.

Looking around, I can't help wondering what it must have been like for my parents when they arrived in 1941. The Japanese attack on Pearl Harbor was still months away, but much of the rest of the world was already at war. In Europe, Adolph Hitler's hordes were gobbling up one country after another, and England was under siege. Coming as missionaries to a foreign country under those uncertain conditions couldn't have been easy for my parents. In spite of myself, I cannot help admiring them. Whatever they lacked in wisdom, they more than made up for in courage.

While most evangelical and Pentecostal missionaries chose to work in the densely populated cities on Brazil's east coast, my parents felt "called" to the Indians and the unreached peoples of the far western Amazon River Valley, at one time the home of more than ninety-eight named tribes. By 1941, many of them had been forced into servitude on rubber plantations or enveloped by encroaching civilization. Nonetheless, there were still many indigenous tribes in the Brazilian Amazon that had not come into contact with outsiders. These were the people my parents longed to reach with the gospel, especially my father.

Passing myself off as a photojournalist on assignment from *National Geographic* has been easier than I expected. Unfortunately, securing the services of a reputable guide and the proper equipment is proving to be a considerable challenge. Both seem to be in short supply, and with my modest funds, hard to come by. Never a patient man, I have just about reached my limit. I know it would not be wise, but if I could find a decent boat, with a serviceable outboard motor, I might just strike out on my own.

Glancing at my watch, I toss a few *cruzéiros* on the table and prepare to leave when I catch sight of Eurico approaching across the plaza. Dressed in a dirty T-shirt, shorts, and sandals, he subsists by selling chewing gum and shining shoes, not to mention begging. He is an orphan, his parents having died in the most recent plague of cerebral malaria that struck Cruzeiro in 1967. Although he is only nine years old, he has lived on the streets for three years—a *peixote*, a street urchin—and he is savvy beyond his age.

"Hey, Bryan," he calls, "I think I've found a boat to take you upriver."

Motioning for him to sit down, I call to the waiter. "Bring this boy a plate of black beans and rice."

Turning his back to me, the waiter pretends he cannot understand my Portuguese, peixotes not being welcome in this establishment. In an instant I am on my feet, lunging after him. Grabbing him by the arm, I demand a plate of black beans and rice for Eurico. For a moment I think there might be trouble, then his courage seems to wilt before my size.

Although the cafe is mostly empty at this hour, the few patrons who are present watch in stunned disbelief. *Who*, they are probably wondering, *is this crazy foreigner who speaks such broken Portuguese?* A couple of them glare at me, but their anger is short lived when they realize I am not intimidated.

Without a word the waiter returns and grudgingly serves Eurico his black beans and rice. His displeasure is obvious, but I ignore him.

Instead, I turn my attention to Eurico who is hungrily attacking his food. Holding the spoon in his fist like a shovel, he proceeds to stuff his face, clearly relishing every mouthful. Watching him, I cannot help wondering whether it is the first time he has eaten today. Maybe it is the first time he has eaten in several days.

When he is finally finished, he wipes his mouth with the back of his hand and grins at me. "Are you ready to see the boat I've found?"

The day is nearly spent as we leave the cafe and cross the plaza toward the riverfront. To reach the tawny beach we must pass the *bairro flutuante*, a floating shantytown perched on spindly stilts or on huge pontoons of *assacu* logs. There are no sidewalks, only elevated planks leading from shanty to shanty. Beneath the elevated walkway there is a smelly accumulation of garbage and sewage, reminding me of Woodstock without the music. Noticing my disgust, Eurico assures me that when the rainy season comes with its floods, it will wash it away. Makes me thankful I am going upriver and not down.

The beach is better, but just barely. Instead of shanties there are canoes of every size imaginable and heaps of bounty from the river and forest. It reminds me of a cross between a AAA campground and a flea market, without the sanitary facilities, of course. We work our way through stacks of dried fish, *bolas* of raw rubber, coagulated slabs of *caucho* rubber, mounds of palm fruits, and piles of rough-hewn timber. Among all this bounty, Indians and traders camp around driftwood fires, while children run and play, oblivious to the adult world around them.

The water's edge is littered with more canoes than I can count. Most of them are relatively small, but there are several large ones that can only be described as broad-bellied houseboats. The one Eurico leads me to is painted a bright blue with *Flor de Maio* (Mayflower) in large white letters on its hull. It looks to be about ten meters long and is, according to its captain, as exquisitely adapted to its environment as any fish or otter. "*Flor* is broad-bellied," he explains, "with only a few centimeters of draft, enabling her to negotiate the river's tight meanders while sliding over sandbars and fallen logs." I cannot help noticing that the boat's roof is thatched, on top of which are a chicken coop and an herb garden planted in an old canoe.

Although the boat belongs to the captain, the man I must see is an American, a professor of biology, who has come to the far western Amazon River Valley to conduct ecological studies. He has chartered the boat for a four-month expedition, and, as fate would have it, his itinerary coincides with my own. Of course, I will leave him when we reach the mission station, which is located about ten days' journey up the Rio Moa after leaving the Juruá.

The captain has gone to fetch him, and I study the sky over the river as the day expires. As I do, I find myself recalling things I haven't thought of in years. Memories I thought were gone forever, washed away in a tidal wave of grief, now return with startling clarity. Above me the constellations materialize against the darkening sky: the Southern Cross, to its left Alpha and Beta Centauri, then Scorpio. For a moment it seems I can feel my father's hand upon my shoulder and his voice in my ear. "That's the Big Dipper," he says, pointing to a spot just above the northern horizon. "Looks like it's snagged on the limb of that *samaúma* tree, doesn't it?"

Chapter

9

MY NOSTALGIC REVERIE IS interrupted by the captain's gruff voice. Even in the gathering darkness I can tell that he has a face to match—sometime in the past his nose was broken, in a bar fight most likely, and it now sits a little crooked on his face. Still, his eyes are not unkind, and whatever violence once lurked there is now gone. Stopping directly in front of me, he gestures toward the man he has brought with him. "As I told you," he says, "the boat is mine, but Dr. Peterson here has chartered it. Any arrangements you wish to make will have to be worked out with him."

Extending my hand, I introduce myself, noting as I do that although Dr. Donald Peterson is a small man, no more than 5 feet, 6 inches tall, he has a commanding presence. Turning, he leads me to a wooden table near the prow, which is bathed in the lambent light of a kerosene lantern. Motioning for me to take the only chair, he positions a five-gallon can across from me and sits down on it. Putting his arms on the table, he demands, "So, why should I share my boat with you?"

Surprised by his directness, I hesitate before answering. "As I'm sure you know, it is nearly impossible to charter a boat, and harder still to find a reputable captain."

Interrupting, he says, "I would think that *National Geographic* magazine would have plenty of contacts. Why did they not make the arrangements for you?"

"Being a freelance photojournalist is not the same thing as being an employee of the magazine. I'm on my own out here. If I can deliver the story, they will buy it; but until then I've got to paddle my own boat, so to speak."

"Exactly what kind of article are you planning to write?"

All these questions are starting to make me uncomfortable, and I find myself unconsciously squirming. Instead of discussing arrangements and fares, he seems to want to interrogate me, and I cannot help wondering if he suspects that I am not what I purport to be.

Anger, always my first line of defense, now tempts me to blow him off, but I don't dare, this being my best chance to get upriver to the interior. Swallowing the heated words that are on the tip of my tongue, I force myself to reply carefully. "My research indicates that there are at least fifty indigenous tribes in the Brazilian Amazon that still have not come into contact with outsiders, maybe more. I'm here to do a photo essay on one of those tribes."

"An ambitious project to be sure, and a dangerous one," he muses, stroking his well-maintained beard. "Chances are you will never locate them. They are a nomadic people now, forced to move ever deeper into the forest to escape outsiders. As far as they are concerned, we are a dangerous enemy who must be avoided at all cost."

"Granted," I counter somewhat impatiently, "but if this were an easy project, someone else would have already done it."

Pursing his lips he poses yet another question. "If you do locate some of these indigenous people—not a likely scenario, mind you— how will you communicate with them?"

"I was hoping to secure the services of an Indian guide or a Caboclo, someone who speaks several Indian dialects."

"Do you have someone in mind?"

"No, I don't. Apparently they are in short supply and a lot harder to hire than I had anticipated."

Squatting on his haunches a few feet away, Eurico seems to be enjoying my discomfort. Although he can't understand a word we are saying, since we are speaking in English, he is quite capable of interpreting my body language, and Dr. Peterson is making me squirm. He is wearing an amused expression, which he makes no effort to disguise when I glance his way. I know he thinks I'm a soft touch, and maybe I am, but I can't help liking him. He's a born hustler, and it's a good thing too, or he couldn't survive on the streets. Having had his hand in my pocket since the day I met him, I imagine he is already calculating his finder's fee.

Turning my attention back to Peterson, I watch as he shakes his head and chuckles. "You're a bold man, to be sure. A bit naive, but I like your grit. You remind me of myself when I was your age. The first time I came to the Amazon Basin, I was as green as you are. I didn't know the first thing about botanical exploration beyond what I had learned in the classroom. Thankfully I was assisting an experienced botanist, so I was able to learn as we went."

He pauses for a moment, his eyes shining with pleasure in the soft glow of the kerosene lantern. "For a botanist, the Amazon Basin is paradise. There's no place like it on the face of the earth. For the past several years I have been studying an area consisting of a single hectare, approximately one hundred yards by one hundred yards—a mere speck in the vast Amazon Valley. Yet that tiny plot is home to more than twenty thousand individual trees comprising nearly two thousand species. To put that into perspective, let me remind you that in all of North America there are less than seven hundred species of trees."

My eyes must have glazed over, because he reins in his enthusiasm and returns to the subject at hand. "If we were to make room for you on our boat, how long would you be with us?"

"Not more than a couple of weeks, depending on your progress upriver. I've been told that there is a mission compound, what the Indians call an *aldeia*, located about ten days' journey up the Rio Moa. I plan to use it as my base camp, making forays into the jungle until I locate an indigenous tribe unspoiled by contact with outsiders. As I'm sure you know, that area was once the homeland of the Poyanara, Nokini, and Naua tribes. While my research indicates that nearly all of them have vanished through intermarriage with the Caboclos, I suspect that there may still be a handful hiding out in the more remote regions."

"If you do encounter any Indians, you'd better hope they aren't Nauas." Leaning toward me to emphasize his point, he adds, "Historically they have hated and distrusted all outsiders. It is reported that when João Augusto Correa, the newly appointed director of the Juruá Indian affairs, first encountered them in the 1850's—near the mouth of the Rio Moa, by the way—they spurned him. When he presented them with the usual gifts, they threw them into the river."

It is all I can do to keep from groaning out loud as he launches into yet another lecture about the Amazon Basin. *What is it about him,* I wonder, *that makes him feel he has to impress me with his vast knowledge?* Still, in spite of myself, I find that I am listening with increasing fascination as he drones on.

"There's another account involving a William Chandless; he was a British explorer commissioned by the Royal Geographical Society to chart the Juruá. According to the report, he and his party were attacked by Nauas in long, narrow canoes who were armed with large black shields and spears, as well as bows and arrows."

Feigning a confidence I do not feel, I wave off his concerns. "Your warning is duly noted, but I am sure we won't have any trouble. What you're talking about is ancient history. Those incidents happened more than a hundred years ago. Times have changed. Besides, it's not like we're rubber barons—how do you say it, *patrâos*—coming to enslave them."

Seeing I will not be dissuaded, he reluctantly returns to the business at hand, and we negotiate a price I can live with. In addition, he agrees to try to locate a reputable guide for me. According to him, I had better forget about buying a boat with an outboard motor. They are few and far between, and those who have them are not about to part with them, not even for hard cash. At my insistence, he agrees to see if he can locate a serviceable canoe that I can buy. We spend two more hours developing a list of the supplies I will need. When we finally finish, I am weary, but deeply satisfied. At last I am making progress. If all goes well, we will be on the river before the week is out.

CHAPTER

10

RETURNING TO MY ROOM, I undress in the dark and try to arrange my lanky frame on the small bed. Although I am exhausted, I find that I cannot sleep. Outside my window the street is alive with noise—music from the bar just below me, strident voices shrill with anger, the blaring of a horn, the roar of an unmuffled vehicle. Still, it is not the street noise that keeps me awake, but my hyperactive mind.

I try to still my anxious thoughts, but it is no use. The harder I try the more my thoughts jump around. They are just fragments, incomplete thoughts at best, disconnected like pieces of a jigsaw puzzle and elusive. Like slides projected on a screen they superimpose themselves one upon another, clear for a moment then dissolving to be replaced by a new image.

Without intending to, I find myself thinking of Carolyn, and for a moment I am transfixed. A rush of emotions are tugging at my heart, but with an effort I resist. Although the memories promise comfort, experience has taught me otherwise.

My resistance is short-lived, however, and now memories of Carolyn fill my mind. *The first time I saw her I was listening to a very forgettable band in a little club out on Colfax. I was nursing a beer at the end of the bar when she came in with a group of friends. She was dressed in*

black—black body suit and black hip-hugger pants with bell-bottoms. She had
a great laugh, and when she danced I couldn't take my eyes off of her. Finally
I worked up the nerve to ask her to dance, and we hit it off. As luck would
have it, I ended up escorting her home.

We were married six months later, in a high meadow just below Hahn's
Peak north of Steamboat Springs, Colorado. She wore ribbons in her hair
and carried a bouquet of wildflowers native to the Rocky Mountains. As long
as I live I will never forget how she looked as she walked across the meadow
to join me, the sunlight shimmering off her auburn hair. Nor will I ever
forget waking on our wedding night to find her weeping silently in the bed
beside me. She insisted it was nothing, just tears of joy, but when I pressed her
she admitted she was sad because none of her family had been present to share
her special day. That was my doing. I had insisted on a small wedding with
just a few friends and no family. It wasn't the first time I had hurt her, nor
would it be the last. It seemed I had a special talent for causing her pain, a
talent that would eventually convince her to divorce me.

Thinking of her has left a painful knot in my stomach, just as I
knew it would. Cursing myself, I get out of bed and make my way to
the small table in the corner of the room. Striking a match, I light the
kerosene lamp and wait for my eyes to adjust to the light. I could use
the bare light bulb hanging from the ceiling, but I prefer a softer
light. Eventually I locate my journal and something to write with.
After reviewing the notes from my earlier conversation with Dr.
Peterson, I try to calculate the supplies I will need for the next sixteen
weeks, but it is no use. My mind simply will not focus on how much
rice three people will need, let alone how much toilet paper.
Slamming the journal shut in disgust, I walk to the window and stare
down the dark street.

Unconsciously I note the eight-sided Cathedral of Nossa
Senhora de Glória, named for the city's patron saint, situated on the

far side of the plaza. Built of baked red bricks made from the Amazonian mud, it looks almost eerie in the dim moonlight, but it cannot hold my attention. Already my mind is conjuring up another memory. Although it is from an earlier time, it is no less vivid than my memories of Carolyn and is just as poignant.

It is the smell that lingers still—the sweet aroma of fresh sap emanating from rough-cut timbers. Mother has brought my father a dipper of water, and I watch as he greedily gulps it down, noting the golden specs of sawdust that cling to his sweaty forearms. Father is a jack-of-all-trades, equally at home with a hammer and saw as he is with the Bible. Today, as he has been for the past several weeks, he is building the mission house. Time is of the essence as the rainy season is not far off. From daylight to dark he hammers and saws with a determination few men can match.

Along with the water, my mother has brought a plate of food, and Father now sits on the unfinished stoop to eat his lunch. Mother sits beside him, and I find myself comparing them. He is all angles and sharp edges, lean muscles stretched over long bones, while she is, if not exactly pretty, at least attractive. She might be prettier if she didn't work so hard to appear stronger than she really is. She does this to please my father, or so it appears to me.

Having finished his lunch, he now hands his plate to Mother and gets to his feet. Seeming to notice me for the first time, he puts his big hand on my head and tousles my hair. His touch surprises me, for he is not a man given to displays of emotion. Being rare, I treasure the few times that he has been affectionate, relishing the sense of well-being his touch generates in me.

Outside my window, the street has grown quiet at last, and I catch myself yawning. Glancing at my wristwatch, I see that it is nearly 3 A.M. No wonder I'm getting sleepy. Turning to the table, I bend and blow out the kerosene lamp before making my way to the bed in the dark. Once more I try to fit myself on a cot not made for foreigners who stand more than six feet tall. By the time I work myself into a position approximating comfort, sleep has fled.

After more than a twenty-year absence, I have returned to the Amazon Basin to search for my missing father, and once more my thoughts gravitate to him. *In my mind I see him sitting at a rough-hewn table in the mission house. The rainy season has just begun, and the rain is gentle on the tin roof. Later it will come in torrents, making conversation nearly impossible, but for now it is pleasant, almost comforting. Father has pulled the kerosene lamp close so that the light spills generously across the pages of his open Bible. His brow is furrowed in concentration, and his lips move, mouthing the words as he reads. From time to time he marks a phrase or makes notes in the margin.*

Thinking about it now, I realize that education did not come easy for him. Still, whatever he lacked in intellect he more than made up for in determination. Among the other missionaries his self-discipline and devotion to duty was almost legendary. Unfortunately, he did not bring the same zeal to his relationship with his family.

The growing discomfort I now feel in my soul communicates itself to my body, and I thrash about on the small bed, seeking a comfortable position. I don't know why I bother. Even if I could get comfortable, it would do nothing to ease the hurt I have lived with for the past twenty-two years. A familiar depression now tempts me with thoughts of despair. Reluctantly, I acknowledge that the chances of finding my father alive after all these years are remote at best, more likely nonexistent. So why am I here? Why am I wasting my time? Why did I abandon my life in the States, such as it was, to come to this God-forsaken place?

Maybe what I'm really looking for isn't my father at all but something I lost when he disappeared. Overnight, I lost my orderly child's world with its comfort and security. The mission house became a fearful place. The sound of rain on the roof was no longer comforting, but tormenting, and the dim lamp left deep shadows in the corners of the room. Mother tried to be brave, tried to pretend everything was going to be all right, but sorrow leaked from every pore of her body, infecting everything she touched. Although we desperately needed each other, it seemed we were each lost in our own grief.

Thinking about it now, I experience a familiar rage. Life wasn't supposed to turn out like this. A boy isn't supposed to grow up without his father. A little boy's prayers are not supposed to go unanswered. God is not supposed to desert His people in the time of trouble. Love isn't supposed to be lost, and marriage isn't supposed to end in divorce.

A counselor I saw some years ago said I needed closure, that I needed to put the past behind me and get on with my life. He was wrong. What I need isn't closure, but revenge! One thing I know—I will never be able to put the past behind me until I know what happened to my father, until I make those who are responsible pay. And if there was some way to make God pay, I would make sure He got His too!

CHAPTER
11

"BRYAN! BRYAN, WAKE UP!"

As if from a great distance I hear someone calling my name. For a minute I don't remember where I am, and I look around the sparse room in confusion. Fighting to get awake, I manage to sit up on the side of the bed. Slowly things come into focus, and I make my way across the room to the window. Checking my watch, I see that it is barely 6 A.M. No wonder I feel like a zombie. I haven't been asleep much more than an hour.

Eurico is standing in the street just below my window, grinning from ear to ear. When he sees me, he calls, "Hurry, Bryan. I think I have located the perfect guide for you, but we must act quickly before someone else hires him."

His information jerks me awake, and I hurriedly pull on my jeans and a shirt, before splashing cold water on my face and running my fingers through my hair. In less than three minutes I am descending the stairs toward the street.

Without taking time to explain anything, he sets off across the plaza, and I fall in behind him. We pass the red brick cathedral and continue down the street toward the Ganso Azul (Blue Goose), one of the city's principal bordellos. A coffin maker's shop sits next door, and we slip between the two buildings and emerge in a small alley.

Proudly Eurico points to a drunk who has passed out in the alley behind the Blue Goose. He is snoring softly, his head resting in a small puddle of his own vomit. Glaring at Eurico, I say, "You woke me up for this?"

Without another word I turn on my heel and start back the way we came. I haven't taken more than a couple of steps before Eurico is tugging at my arm. "Wait," he says, "let me explain."

Shaking his hand off my arm, I continue down the alley. In an instant he has darted in front of me, blocking my path. I am about to step around him when he says, "Don't be a fool. You will not find another guide."

"That's not a guide," I hiss, indicating the prostrate figure. "That's nothing but a drunk."

"He's drunk now, but when he's sober you'll not find a better guide anywhere on the river. Ask anybody. They will tell you that Lako is the man you want."

"If he's so good, how come he's available?"

For the first time since I've known him, Eurico seems to hesitate. Finally he says, "Lako has a problem with *cachaça*."

Recognizing the word as the name of a cheap white wine, I question Eurico further. When I press him, he tells me Lako has just been fired for getting drunk and almost losing a boat.

Once more I turn to go, and Eurico hurries to keep up with my long strides. "Talk to Dr. Peterson," he pleads. "He will tell you about Lako. They have worked together many times."

Although I cannot imagine hiring a drunk for a guide, I change my course and head for the riverfront. Approaching the *Flor de Maio*, I spot Dr. Peterson checking things off a list as two men load supplies onto the boat. Catching sight of me, he hands his list to the captain and comes to greet me.

"Bryan," he says, smiling broadly, "what brings you to my boat so early in the morning?"

"I need a few minutes of your time if you can spare it."

"Of course."

Turning to Eurico he hands him some coins and says, "Perhaps you could bring us two cups of *cafezinho*, and get something for yourself as well."

Once Eurico is on his way, he turns to me. "Well, what is this about? I hope you haven't changed your mind about going upriver with us."

"Not a chance," I reply, "but there is a matter I would like to discuss with you." When he nods, I continue. "It concerns Lako. What can you tell me about him?"

Taking off his glasses, Dr. Peterson rubs the bridge of his nose before replying. "He's probably the most knowledgeable guide I've ever worked with. He is a *mateiro*, a woodsman, who can identify almost every plant in the rain forest. There aren't more than a handful of people in all of Amazonia who have his skill. He's a Caboclo, a descendent of the Amuacas on his mother's side. He learned about the river and the forest from her."

When he hesitates, I say, "There's a 'but,' isn't there?"

Clearing his throat, he says, "His wife and three children died about three years ago. That's when his serious drinking started. They fell prey to the most recent epidemic of malaria to strike Cruzeiro."

Unconsciously reverting to his scientific self, he explains. "It was a particularly virulent strain called cerebral falciparum malaria. It begins with a fever that induces coma a day or two after the first symptoms appear. It is almost always fatal. Most victims never wake up."

Warming to his subject, he continues. "It's particularly deadly for children and the elderly. Perhaps you've noticed the unusual demography that is characteristic of the Amazonian interior: a few elderly, a handful of children, and a shifting population of middle-aged people. Disease is what accounts for it, usually malaria. As beautiful as this land is, it can be deadly, especially for those who are most vulnerable."

When he pauses to take a sip of his *cafezinho*, I jump in. "That background information helps, but what I need to know is, should I hire him?"

"Bryan, I can't make that decision for you, but I will tell you that my inquiries about a guide for you have not been encouraging. If Lako is available, he may be your only choice. On the positive side, I happen to know that he owns a boat with a small outboard motor. If you do hire him, you could probably get the boat as well."

"What about his drinking? The last thing I need is to find myself deep in the interior with a drunk guide on my hands."

"Your concerns are legitimate, but I don't know what choice you have. We are heading upriver in two days, three at most. Unless you intend to go without a guide—not a wise thing to do—I suggest you see if you can get Lako on board."

I thank Dr. Peterson for his time and turn toward the plaza. In an instant Eurico is at my side, a smug look on his face. "Lako is a good man," he says, "you will see."

I grunt a reply, and he continues. "Do you want me to speak with him for you? I'm sure I could negotiate a deal you would be pleased with."

Shaking my head at his audaciousness, I give his shoulder a playful punch. "An introduction will do just fine. I'm quite capable of negotiating my own deals."

We walk in silence for a block or two, then I ask, "How would you like to make the trip upriver with me? I could use a 'Boy Friday,' and I think you would fit the bill."

Grinning at me, Eurico replies, "It's going to cost you—a lot. My services are not cheap."

CHAPTER

12

ONLY A DAY AND a half on the river, and already I'm growing impatient. Our progress seems minimal because of all the switchbacks. One moment the sun is in our faces, and the next it is burning the back of our necks as we maneuver the tight meanders. Despite our snail's pace I cannot help but admire the functionality of the *Flor de Maio*. It is perfectly adapted to the river, justifying everything the captain said about it.

Leaving Cruzeiro do Sul, the last visages of civilization quickly give way to the encroaching wilderness. For hours at a time we see nothing but the abundance of the rain forest with its never-ending variety of flora and fauna. Now and then, however, we pass a small clearing—a pioneer outpost I am told. They are all tragically similar. Each one has a dugout canoe hauled up on the riverbank. Nearby is an open-walled house on a platform of split *buriti* with a few posts from which to suspend hammocks and a thatched roof. Life is obviously difficult, and the inhabitants who stare back at us appear worn down by the ordeal. I am ashamed to admit it, but I am relieved when the *Flor de Maio* slides around the next bend, leaving them, and the sorrow their misery generates, in our wake.

Although the mouth of the Rio Moa is only ten kilometers from Cruzeiro, we are already in another world. I cannot help but wonder what could have possessed my parents to bring my sister and me to such an isolated and dangerous place. Even if they had no concern for their own safety, surely they weren't without feeling in regard to ours. Thinking about it now, I vacillate between conflicting emotions. A part of me admires their courage, while another part of me resents the risks they took. I cannot help thinking how different my life might be now if they had never come here.

They must have been made of sterner stuff than I am, for if the truth be told, every kilometer we journey upriver increases my anxiety. The deeper we venture into the interior, the more unforgiving it becomes. Danger lurks everywhere. It wears many faces. An accident, a snake bite, a violent storm, a crippling illness, even a simple miscalculation, can result in death. I suppose we are safe enough as long as we stay with Dr. Peterson's expedition, but once we leave this boat we will be on our own.

Glancing up, I see Eurico approaching, and once more I berate myself for bringing him along. What was I thinking? What business do I have taking a nine-year-old boy into the jungle? If I want to risk my own life, that is one thing, but I have no right to endanger his.

Grinning at me, he says, "Dr. Peterson has sent me to fetch you. He wants to talk."

Arising from a bag of rice upon which I have been reclining, I follow Eurico toward the shaded mid-deck where Dr. Peterson is sitting on an upturned five-gallon bucket. He motions for me to join him, and I do my best to make myself comfortable on a nearby bag of beans, noting as I do that nearly every inch of available space has been stacked with provisions, leaving almost no room to walk or sit. I never would have thought that it took so much stuff to supply twelve people for sixteen weeks.

Once I am situated, he asks, "How are things working out with Lako?"

"Okay, I guess. He's in a sour mood, but at least he's not drunk."

Glancing at the poop deck where the captain is busy at the helm, he says, "According to the captain, Lako was nearly beside himself when he discovered his stash of *cachaça* was missing. How did you manage that?"

Shrugging, I say, "It was no big deal. I had Eurico go through his things while I was talking with him."

"Good thinking," he says, raising his eyebrows in a gesture of admiration. "I probably wouldn't have thought of that myself."

"Me either," I reply, giving him a self-deprecating grin. "I've got my ex-wife to thank for that one."

"How so?"

"Her father was an alcoholic, and she told me a drunk never goes anywhere without a bottle. Growing up, it was her job to ferret out her father's stash. You wouldn't believe some of the ingenious places he hid his booze."

"I was married once myself," Peterson muses, changing the subject, "but it didn't last long. For some reason my wife didn't appreciate the fact that I spent months at a time trekking through the rain forest. She finally gave me an ultimatum. Told me I had to choose between her and the Amazon Basin. When she put it like that, I had no choice."

Spreading his arms wide to take in the territory on both sides of the river, he adds, "There's not a woman alive who can hold a candle to this."

I nod at him, but I have already tuned him out. While he rambles on about the wonders of the Amazon Basin I am slowly being sucked into a dark pool of regret. Why I allow myself to talk about Carolyn or even think about her is beyond me. Every memory is bittersweet. More bitter than sweet, if the truth be known. While we were married, I had eyes only for her faults—she was too needy, too clingy, too invasive. She was always saying we needed to talk. She wanted to meet my family. She wanted to know about my childhood. She always wanted more of me than I was able to give.

Now that we are divorced, all I can remember are the good times, but having thrown them away they too leave a bitter taste in my mouth. What could I have been thinking? How could I have allowed the pain of my past to ruin the best thing that every happened to me?

Experience having taught me that regret is an exercise in futility, I now force myself to focus on Dr. Peterson's words. They may be of little interest to me, but I am smart enough to realize that they are a needed diversion. I dare not give in to my bitter regret. I must not allow myself to succumb to the depression that has so debilitated me in the past. Too much is depending on this venture.

Now I hear him ask, "Perhaps you've heard of Harvard professor Richard Evans Schultes?"

When I shake my head, he says, "No matter. Let it suffice to say that he is the greatest Amazonian explorer of the twentieth century and an inspiration to an untold number of botanists like myself. In many ways he is a throwback to the great naturalists of the Victorian era. In 1941, he left Harvard for the Amazon, intending to be gone for only a semester. He didn't return for twelve years. During that time he lived among several previously unknown Indian tribes. He also collected some thirty thousand botanical specimens, including three hundred species new to science. In the process he endured unimaginable hardships, including beriberi and twenty-one bouts of malaria."

Intrigued in spite of myself, I ask, "What is beriberi?"

Ever the teacher, Dr. Peterson proceeds to give me a clinical definition. "Beriberi is a malady caused by a deficiency of vitamin B1 in the diet. Early symptoms include lassitude and numbness in the limbs and extremities. Gradually these give way to total degeneration of the nerves, resulting in muscular atrophy, a complete inability to move, and ultimately death."

"Is it always fatal?"

"The only treatment is massive doses of thiamine injected repeatedly over a period of weeks. A better solution is to get plenty of vitamin B1 in one's diet. An old adage says, 'An ounce of prevention is worth a pound of cure.'"

My mouth is suddenly dry, and I swallow before replying, only half in jest. "All this talk about malaria and beriberi is making me nervous."

Waving off my concerns, he says, "Take your quinine pills and eat plenty of rice and beans, and you'll be just fine."

"Quinine pills? What are you talking about?"

Looking at me in amazement, he asks, "Are you telling me that you're not taking quinine pills?"

"I didn't know I was supposed to," I protest. "No one told me I needed to."

"Didn't the *National Geographic* people give you any kind of orientation before sending you to the Amazon?"

"No."

"I find that hard to believe. That's not the way they normally operate. If anyone should know the risks involved out here, they should."

For just a moment I think I see a flicker of skepticism in his expression, and I move quickly to head it off. "Like I told you, I'm a freelance photojournalist. I submitted a proposal, and the editor liked the idea enough to give me a conditional assignment. What that means is that I take all the risks. I'm on my own out here until I deliver the article; then they will reimburse me for my expenses and pay me a healthy fee."

Being mostly ignorant of the inner workings of journalism, I'm just blowing smoke, but he seems to buy it. Hopefully I have alleviated his concerns.

Returning to the matter at hand, I say, "Obviously they should have been more helpful, but that's water under the bridge now. Is there any chance I can buy some quinine pills from you?"

"I wish I could help you, Bryan, but I can't. I'm responsible for every person on my team. The medication we're taking serves not only as a prophylactic, but also as treatment should any of us contact the disease. We must conserve our supply, holding it in reserve in case of an emergency. It could be the difference between life and death."

Although I'm disappointed by his response, to argue would be pointless. Feigning amiability I do not feel, I say, "That's understandable. I'm sure I'll be all right."

"I just had a thought," he says, his countenance brightening. "There's a clinic at the mission compound. You can probably get some pills from them."

Before I can respond, the captain calls from the poop deck. "I think we ought to make camp on that sandbar up ahead. It will be nearly dark by the time we get things set up."

"That sounds good to me," Dr. Peterson replies, getting to his feet. Eurico joins us, and we move to the prow in preparation for landing. Unconsciously I find myself slapping at mosquitoes, the risk of malaria now firmly fixed in my mind.

CHAPTER

13

DRYING HER HANDS ON the kitchen towel, Helen pours herself a cup of coffee and sits down at the table. Her Bible lies open before her, but she hasn't yet read a word. Between telephone calls and caring for a sick child, her morning has been a zoo. Mentally she berates herself. If she had gotten up when her alarm sounded, instead of hitting the snooze button, she could have finished her devotions before making breakfast. As a result, it is nearly eleven o'clock, and she still hasn't had her quiet time.

In recent weeks her self-discipline has deserted her. No matter how good her intentions, she simply can't seem to get motivated. Forcing herself to concentrate, she turns her attention to today's Scripture passage. She hasn't read more than a verse or two when Robbie calls from the bedroom. With an exaggerated sigh she shoves her chair back and gets to her feet. Pasting a pleasant look on her face, she heads for the bedroom to see what her younger child needs now.

"Mommy," he says, his blue eyes imploring her, "read me a book."

"Robbie, I don't have time to read you a book right now. I have a hundred things to do."

Ignoring his crestfallen countenance, she turns toward the kitchen. When she does, she is struck by the tone of her voice. To her consternation she realizes that she sounds just like her mother—

impatient and dismissive. She ought to say something to make it up to him, but she simply doesn't have the energy. Silent tears slide down her cheeks as she makes her way back to the kitchen table where she buries her face in her hands.

"Dear God," she prays, *"what's happening to me? I never used to be like this."*

After a time she blows her nose on a tissue and dabs at her eyes. The clock chimes, and she realizes it's time to prepare lunch. Closing her unread Bible, she puts it away along with her journal. Ignoring her guilty conscience, she tosses a salad and puts some potatoes on to boil. Once that is done, she takes a package of ground meat from the refrigerator and begins making patties.

The telephone rings, and she rinses her hands before answering it. Having been a pastor's wife for a number of years now, she manages a cheery hello in spite of the sorrow in her soul.

"It's me, honey," Rob says, without bothering to ask about her day or how Robbie is feeling. "Something has come up here at the office, and I won't be able to make it home for lunch. I hope you didn't go to any trouble."

Before she can say anything, he continues. "Well, I've got to run. I'll see you this evening."

Hanging up the phone, she yields to the tears she has been holding at bay. Not wanting Robbie to hear her cry, she retreats to her bedroom where she collapses on the bed. Burying her face in her pillow, she gives vent to the guilt and sorrow that have dogged her for weeks. Her fits of weeping are becoming more frequent, and she doesn't know how much longer she can maintain her facade. Pretending to be a perfect wife and mother has become nearly more than she can manage. Already her anxiety is affecting the boys. Jake has gotten in trouble at school, and Robbie is constantly complaining of a stomachache.

Determining to get hold of herself, she takes several deep breaths. Slowly her sobs subside. Hearing the bedroom door open, she tries to compose herself, but before she can dry her tears Robbie is on the bed beside her. "Mommy," he asks, his voice sounding small and frightened, "what's the matter? Why are you crying?"

Not trusting herself to speak, she simply enfolds him in her arms, burying his head against her chest. "I love you," she whispers, kissing his soft hair. "I love you so much."

Forty-five minutes later she has fed Robbie his lunch, read him a book, and given him his medicine. He was asleep when she tiptoed out of his room and returned to the kitchen table where she is now toying with half a sandwich while going through the day's mail. Suddenly she drops her sandwich and stares at the envelope she holds in her hand. It is one of those tissue-thin, light blue, aerogram envelopes favored by missionaries. It is addressed to her in a vaguely familiar scrawl, and she carefully slits it open with a paring knife. With trembling hands she unfolds it and begins to read.

August 23, 1970

Dear Helen:

    It is very late as I write this, and outside my window the city is as still as it is dark. Occasionally a dog barks, but other than that the only sound is the scratching of my pen as I write. I am sitting in a small room above a bar just off the plaza in Cruzeiro do Sul with only a kerosene lamp for light. Tomorrow, I will begin my journey up the Rio Juruá to where it is joined by the Rio Moa, and from there upriver to the mission compound where we once lived.

I will be traveling with Dr. Donald Peterson and his party. He is a botanist doing research in the rain forest. Our boat— really an exaggerated canoe—is about ten meters long with a broad belly. It is a kind of houseboat with a vegetable garden planted in a broken canoe atop the ragged thatched roof. I am told it is ideally suited for the river, so you need not concern yourself about my safety.

Once we reach the mission compound, I will be leaving Dr. Peterson, who will continue upriver to the Serra Divisor, near the border between Brazil and Peru. I hope to use the mission compound as a sort of base camp. From there I will make forays further into the interior in an attempt to make contact with some of the unreached Indian tribes. As you may have already deducted, my purpose in coming is to see if I can discover what happened to our father.

You must be thinking that I have lost my mind. What could I hope to learn after all these years? All I can tell you is that I have to try. I have reached a dead end. I can't go on with my life until I can make peace with my past. Much of the anger that controls me is rooted in these unresolved issues. Maybe I can find some answers here.

To assist me in my search, I have hired a guide named Lako. He is a half-breed, what the Brazilians call a Caboclo. His father was a Portuguese trader, and his mother was an Indian. He is a mateiro, a woodsman, who speaks several Indian dialects. Dr. Peterson has worked with him on a number of expeditions, and he assures me that Lako knows as much about the rain forest as any man in the Amazon Basin.

I don't need to tell you of the risks involved in a venture like this. You know them as well as I do. The Indians shouldn't be a threat, but you never know. A few weeks ago a missionary was found murdered near the Bolivian border here in Brazil. According to Dr. Peterson, he had been shot with four arrows, and both arms and one foot had been cut off. Be that as it may, I will not allow anything to keep me from doing what I have set out to do.

My purpose in writing is not to worry you, but to put your mind at ease regarding my whereabouts. I expect to be in the Amazon Basin several months, less if I find what I am looking for sooner than that. Not being familiar with the mail service, I don't know when I will be able to send another letter, so don't worry if you don't hear from me for several weeks. Of course, I do not expect you to write.

Give my love to your boys. They are the best.

Your brother,
Bryan

After reading the letter a second time, Helen carefully folds it and places it in her Bible. *"Thank You, Jesus,"* she whispers. *"Thank You, Jesus."*

Picking up the telephone, she dials Carolyn's number at work. When she answers, Helen blurts out, "I just received a letter from Bryan. He's in the Amazon Basin in Brazil. That's where my parents served as missionaries."

"That's wonderful," Carolyn says, speaking softly. "I can't talk right now. I have someone in my office, but I'll call you as soon as I get home, and you can give me all the details."

Replacing the telephone receiver, Helen takes a deep breath to steady herself. Although Bryan's letter has provided a momentary reprieve, her fragile emotions still leave her a little off balance.

Needing to share her good news, she considers calling Rob, but thinks better of it. He would probably just say, "See, I told you there was nothing to worry about."

CHAPTER

14

GLANCING UP, ROB WATCHES as his secretary makes her way across the office toward him. Placing several letters on his desk, she says, "If you would like to sign these, I will take them by the post office on my way home."

Checking his watch, he is surprised to see that it is nearly six o'clock. "You're working late, aren't you, Rita?"

"Doug is with his father, so there's no reason to hurry home."

Sadness colors her words, and he finds himself empathizing with her. Being a single mom with a fifteen-year-old son can't be easy, not to mention the pain of her divorce. Three years ago her husband left her for a younger woman with whom he now lives out of state.

Taking the side chair, she watches as he scrawls his name on the letters she has typed. Noting his weariness she thinks, *Something is troubling him, of that I am sure. He hasn't been his normal vivacious self in days, maybe not for a week or two.* She doesn't miss much, and to the best of her knowledge there is nothing unusual going on with the church, so what could be bothering him?

Replacing the pen in its holder, Rob pushes the letters across the desk toward her. In spite of himself he cannot help noticing her attractiveness. Although she is at least three or four years older than he is, no one would ever know it. Belatedly he realizes that she is studying him intently. "What is it?" he asks. "What's on your mind?"

"I'm concerned about you. You haven't been yourself lately."

Her concern touches a vulnerable place deep inside him, and without intending to he finds that he is comparing her sensitivity to what he perceives as Helen's all-consuming self-absorption. The comparison is disconcerting, and, too late, he makes a futile effort to redirect his thoughts. Unfortunately, they seem to have a will of their own, and he finds himself thinking that going home used to be fun, but now he never knows what to expect. On the best of days there is little joy and no spontaneity. Even when Helen makes an effort to be attentive to him and the boys, there is always an underlying sadness. No matter what their needs, she seems preoccupied, overwhelmed with concern for her dysfunctional brother.

Rita's comment hangs in the silence between them, and he finds himself listening to the clock ticking, the sound of traffic drifting in from the street, and the heavy beating of his own heart. The office area is unusually quiet, and belatedly he realizes that they are alone. Apparently everyone else has already gone for the day. They should leave now; he knows that, but he cannot bring himself to spend another evening dealing with Helen's moods. If he works late enough, she may already be in bed when he finally arrives home.

Sensing his reticence, Rita says, "Let me make you a cup of coffee, and then we can talk about it if you like."

When she goes to the coffee bar in the workroom, Rob moves to the large window that overlooks an open field. For a moment he thinks of his two boys, feeling guilty that he is going to miss dinner yet again. He hasn't spent much time with them in the last few weeks; still, it's not really his fault. Helen's instability has upset the emotional equilibrium in their family, throwing all of their relationships out of kilter. He has tried to reason with her, but to no avail. She seems lost in a world of her own, a place where she cares only about the dead or the missing.

Immersed in his thoughts, he doesn't hear Rita return, and he is startled when she places her hand on his shoulder. Turning, he sees that she has placed two cups of coffee on the end table between the couch and the love seat. He glances a question in her direction, and she says, "Since it's after hours I thought it would be less formal this way, more like friends instead of secretary and boss. Besides we'll be more comfortable."

Studying her face as he takes a seat on the couch, he is surprised to see nothing but friendly concern in her eyes. Chiding himself for suspecting her motives, he takes a sip of his coffee. Replacing the mug on the coaster, he tells himself to be careful. No matter how innocent her motives, he is playing with fire, and he knows it. A man in his emotional state should not be alone with a woman, other than his wife, under any circumstances.

Placing her hand on his arm, Rita says, "So, are you going to tell me what's troubling you?"

When he hesitates, she adds, "Remember, you're the one who is always encouraging us to lean on each other, to trust each other with our hurts."

Her hand is scorching his sleeve, and he reaches for his coffee cup, forcing her to remove it. Taking a sip of coffee, he says, "Using a man's own words against him is hardly fair, you know."

Smiling, she says, "I thought anything was fair in love and war."

Startled, he replies, "I didn't realize this was either love or war."

"It's not. I have a bad habit of saying the first thing that pops into my mind, and that just slipped out."

"Well, that's good to know. Love would be futile since I am already married, and you are far too beautiful to be my enemy."

"My, my, my," she says with a mischievous look in her eye. "There is a man behind that clerical collar after all." When he rolls his eyes toward the ceiling, she adds, "Are we going to continue our verbal sparring all evening, or are you going to tell me what's bothering you?"

Before he can reply, the telephone on his desk rings, and he moves across the room to answer it. "It's probably Helen," he says over his shoulder. "I forgot to tell her that I would be working late."

"Hello. This is Pastor Thompson."

"Daddy, when are you going to come home?" Jake asks, his words piercing Rob's heart.

"It won't be long, son. As soon as I finish a few things here at the office I will be on my way."

"I thought you said you were going to come home early so you could teach me how to throw a football. Now it's dark, and you still aren't home."

Before Rob can reply, the phone clicks in his ear. Replacing the receiver in its cradle, he turns toward the couch where Rita is collecting their coffee cups in preparation for leaving. "It sounds like you'd better head for home. Your family is waiting."

"There's no need to rush off. Let's finish our coffee. A few more minutes won't matter."

"It's better this way," she replies, exiting his office.

Returning to the window, he stares into the dark until he sees her car turn onto the street. As the car's taillights fade in the distance he makes his way to his desk where he turns on the banker's lamp with its green shade. The room is now dark except for the pool of light falling on his leather desk pad, a darkness matching his mood.

Burying his face in his hands, he prays, *"Dear God, what's wrong with me? Why can I be a caring pastor to everyone except my own wife?"*

CHAPTER
15

I AM SQUATTING NEAR the fire, which is now mostly coals, glowing in the deepening darkness. There is really no need for it, the temperatures being mild, but it does provide a gathering place before we disburse to our hammocks and mosquito nets for the night. Several of the crew have already turned in, and Eurico keeps nodding off. Nearby, Dr. Peterson and Lako are involved in an animated discussion about the Jivaro Indians—the famed headhunters of the Amazon Basin.

Slapping at a mosquito, I try to push the risk of malaria from my mind. I simply can't believe I could have been so stupid. How I could have overlooked antimalaria medicine in all my preparations is beyond me. What a cruel trick of fate it would be to come this far only to die in the jungle. With an effort I force myself to think of other things, being careful where I let my thoughts take me. Experience has taught me that my memories are a minefield that must be traversed with utmost care.

Taking a drink of coffee, I discover it has grown cold. Throwing it out, I reach for the coffeepot nestled in the coals. Using my shirttail as a pot holder, I splash hot coffee in my cup and move to the other side of the fire. Squatting near Lako, I listen as Dr. Peterson explains why the Jivaros shrink the heads of their vanquished enemies into a gruesome tsantsa about the size of a baseball.

"The practice seems unspeakably grotesque to us," he says, speaking softly so he won't disturb those who are trying to sleep, "but once you understand their culture, it makes perfect sense. According to their customs, the head of their enemy was the only proof that they had fulfilled their obligation to take blood revenge. Most Jivaros would consider any victory incomplete if they were unable to return with one or more trophies."

"Say what you will," I counter, interrupting their discussion, "it's a barbaric practice if you ask me."

"No more so than what some of our soldiers are doing in Vietnam."

"What are you talking about?"

"Surely you've heard the reports of GIs cutting off the ears of dead Vietcong for souvenirs, haven't you?"

"That's different, and you know it."

Before the argument can get out of hand, Lako interrupts. "According to my mother, the Jivaros believe that the tsantsa itself possesses magical power." Turning toward Dr. Peterson, he asks, "What do you know about that?"

I'm still fuming as Peterson launches into another lengthy explanation. As far as I'm concerned, comparing the barbaric practice of head-hunting to the atrocities committed by a few rogue GIs is just plain stupid. The military doesn't condone that kind of behavior, let alone encourage it. In fact, they condemn it! If I'm honest though, I'd have to admit that what's really bothering me is the possibility that my father's head might be hanging from some Indian's belt.

Pushing that gruesome thought from my mind, I turn my attention to Dr. Peterson once more. "According to my studies," he says, "the Jivaros believed that possessing the tsantsa itself would assure the warrior good luck. He could expect the spirits of his dead relatives to bestow abundant crops and good fortune on him in the future. Of course, he could anticipate corresponding misfortune if he did not avenge their murders properly. A powerful two-pronged motive, if you see what I mean."

Still not satisfied, Lako asks, "Isn't there more to it than that? I seem to remember my mother saying something about taking the soul captive."

"You're right," Dr. Peterson concurs. "One of the main reasons the Jivaros prepared the tsantsa was to paralyze the soul of their dead enemy. This not only kept his spirit from escaping and taking revenge upon the murderer himself, it also prevented his soul from continuing into the afterlife where it could harm the murderer's dead ancestors."

My attention wanders as they banter back and forth for a few minutes more. Finally, Lako yawns and gets to his feet. "I guess I'll see if I can find my hammock. I think I've had all the head-hunting I can take for one night."

I wait until he has slipped into the darkness, then I nod at Eurico who follows him, moving as silent as a shadow. Giving me a questioning look, Peterson asks, "What's that all about?"

"Just a precaution," I explain. "Alcoholics are resourceful, and I want to make sure Lako stays sober."

"You're a cagy one, aren't you?"

"The way I figure it, there's no sense taking chances."

"Well, I guess I'll call it a night," he says, getting to his feet.

Reaching for his arm, I say, "Before you go, I'd like to ask you a couple of questions about those headhunters. That is, if you don't mind."

Sitting back down, he nods in my direction. Clearing my throat, I try to disguise my nervousness. "What chance is there that I might run into some Jivaros in the course of my work? I wouldn't want anything to happen to Eurico."

Laughing, he gives me a punch on the shoulder. "Worried about your head, are you?"

When I grin sheepishly, he continues. "You've got nothing to worry about. The Jivaros live along the Ecuadorian Coast. To my knowledge they've never been in this part of the Amazon Basin."

Relieved, I poke at the fire, coaxing a small flame from the dying embers. "How do they do it? How do they shrink a human head to the size of a man's fist without totally destroying it?"

"No one knows for sure; that is, no one except the Jivaros. Scientists are still trying to figure it out."

Disappointed, I start to rise. "Well, I guess I'll turn in."

"Not so fast," he says. "Although we have no scientific evidence of how it is done, I once read an account written by an explorer who claimed to have witnessed an actual head-shrinking ceremony sometime near the end of the last century. I think his name was Up De Graff or something like that."

As he begins to describe the grisly process I simply shake my head in amazement. Is there no end to his knowledge of the Amazon Basin? My curiosity piqued, I lean in close so as not to miss a word, and with the magic of a born storyteller he weaves a tale that holds me spellbound.

"Following a raid on a neighboring Indian tribe, in which the Jivaros took nine heads, they retreated to a sandbar where they proceeded to peel the heads. Once this was done, the incision from the crown of head to the base of the neck was sewn together using a bamboo needle and palm leaf fiber. Pressing the lips tightly closed, they inserted bamboo splinters to keep them together. The eyelids were held closed and the eyebrows were kept from falling by small bamboo pegs set vertically between the upper rim of the eyelashes and the shoulders of the corresponding eyebrows. The nasal passages and ear holes were temporarily plugged.

"Each 'head' was then filled with hot sand, allowing it to expand to its normal proportions while retaining its distinct features. Next, the boneless heads were placed in a special pot filled with cold water. Within half an hour the water had been brought to a boiling point, and the heads were removed. Up De Graff said it is critical to remove the heads just before the water actually boils. This prevents the softening of the flesh and keeps the hair from falling out. When the heads were removed, they had shrunk to about one-third their original size.

"By now the Indians had prepared a large quantity of hot sand, which they proceeded to pour into the heads at the neck opening. The heads were then ironed with hot stones taken from the fire. This process was repeated for the next forty-eight hours until the skin was as smooth and as tough as tanned leather. In the process the heads gradually shrunk to the size of an orange. When done right, I am told that the shrunken heads are exact miniatures of their former selves. Every feature, hair, and scar is retained intact.

"Over the next year the Jivaros will celebrate a series of three tsantsa feasts commemorating their victory. The main reason for the ceremonies is to show their departed relatives that they have fulfilled their obligations of blood revenge. During the feasts the Jivaro warriors smear themselves with blood and dance with the shrunken heads to dramatize the killing and increase their own prestige. And as strange as it may seem, considering the care and diligence that goes into the preparation of the heads, they are often discarded immediately following the final celebration."

We sit in silence for several minutes, each of us lost in his own thoughts. Finally, Dr. Peterson gets to his feet and stretches. "We've got a long day ahead of us tomorrow. We had better get some sleep."

I watch as he makes his way through the darkness toward his hammock. Poking at the coals, I coax one last flicker of flame from the dying fire. I'm tired, but I doubt if I can sleep. My mind is racing, and I struggle to keep a host of disconcerting memories at bay. Forcing myself to concentrate, I turn my attention to the coming day. If things go as planned, we should reach the mission compound sometime in the afternoon or early evening. What happens after that is anybody's guess. Having no real experience in the Amazonian Rain Forest, I have only the vaguest idea of how to proceed. Hopefully, I can draw on Lako's expertise.

CHAPTER

16

MY HEART IS BEATING slow and heavy in my chest as the *Flor de Maio* glides around one final bend in the Rio Moa and nudges up against a heap of sun-whitened sand. Leaping from the boat, several of the crew move quickly to secure it with long ropes to some of the more sturdy trees. Eurico is tugging at my arm, anxious to look around before dark, and Lako wants to know where to off-load our supplies. Ignoring them, I continue to stare at the place I once called home.

Along the river's edge, the munguba trees are bright with white flowers as big as soccer balls. On the upper reaches of the riverbank the first cecropias appear, and behind them are stands of *jauarí* palms. Finally, in the distance where the *várzea* (floodplain) grades into the permanent forest, the pale-trunked ucuuba and the *samaúma* trees come into view. Of course, Dr. Peterson is quick to point out these details to me. I pretend to be interested, but in reality I have eyes only for the mission compound beyond.

Much of it is just the way I remember it—the towering trees shutting out the sky, the sound of the river, the calling of the birds. Little by little things begin to come back to me. The swing Father put up for us in the *samaúma* tree in front of the house, the path leading down to the river where the canoe was beached, and the time he killed a deadly *pico da jaca* snake with his machete. It was lying in the grass near the mission house, a place where we often played. Afterwards he gave us a stern lecture, telling us to always be on the lookout for snakes.

To reinforce his warning he related a harrowing tale about an Indian who had been bitten on the tip of his finger by a *pico da jaca* hardly bigger than a large worm. "A baby *pico da jaca*," he said, "may appear harmless, but it has the same anticoagulant venom as an adult snake. This one must have hit an artery, because the Indian hemorrhaged to death within two hours, blood pouring from his mouth, eyes, nose, and gums."

I was scared stiff and wouldn't leave the house for the rest of the day. That night I was tormented with dreams in which my bed was filled with snakes of all sizes. Terrified, I awoke crying and ran into my parents' bedroom. Father threatened to spank me if I did not return to my bed, but for once Mother defied him. Picking me up in her arms, she carried me into the small living room where she rocked me until I finally fell back to sleep.

Dr. Peterson, calling to me from the edge of the trees, returns me to the present. Grabbing my camera, I leap to the beach and make my way toward him. "Lako will see that your supplies are unloaded and stored. Let's walk up to the compound, and I'll introduce you. I know most of the missionaries, at least those who have been here for any length of time."

Surveying the compound as we walk, I am amazed to see not one house, but three. In addition there is a medical clinic and what appears to be a small schoolhouse or maybe a chapel. All three houses are of modest size and simple construction, but the one Father built is the smallest. I cannot help thinking that the house that loomed so large in my memory is hardly more than a shack.

In the stream that runs along the edge of the compound, someone has rigged up a waterwheel to generate electricity. Having been a lineman for the electrical company back in Colorado, I find the ingenuity fascinating. Unfortunately, the generator has a limited capacity, and it appears the clinic is the only building with electrical power. Apparently the rest of the compound still uses kerosene, what my mother used to call "coal oil."

Approaching the clinic, we find ourselves surrounded by a number of Indians who are seeking treatment for themselves or for their children. A few are dressed as we are, but most of them are attired in their native garb. The revulsion I feel is immediate and nearly overpowering. A saner part of me knows my reaction is irrational, but I seem powerless to do anything about it. These, or at least their kind, are to blame for everything that is wrong with my life. Were it not for their kind, my parents would have never come to this place, and my father would not have disappeared.

Out of the corner of my eye I see Dr. Peterson watching me with a puzzled look on his face. Belatedly, I realize my disgust must be obvious. Quickly focusing my Nikon, I begin shooting pictures, hoping to disguise my feelings. The misery I see through my viewfinder is heartbreaking, but I am unmoved. I take a few more shots, and when I have my emotions under control I risk a look at Dr. Peterson. He is still studying me, but his earlier skepticism seems to be gone. I am relieved when I catch his eye, and he motions for me to join him. Working my way through the Indians, I am careful to keep my expression neutral.

Inside the clinic, I am amazed to see an attractive blond-haired woman examining a feverish Indian baby. Her hair is pulled back, but a few strands have worked loose, and she has to keep brushing them out of her eyes. Her movements are economical, and she is completely focused as she works; still, nothing can disguise her natural gracefulness.

"Who's that?" I mouth to Dr. Peterson.

Grinning at me, he says, "That's Diana Rhoades. She's a medical missionary from Minnesota."

What she is, is a sight for sore eyes, and after weeks on the river I am finding it nearly impossible to take my eyes off her. She's wearing a white lab coat over blue jeans and some kind of pullover shirt. Although the lab coat is loose fitting, it cannot hide the pleasing contours of her body.

After giving the listless baby an injection of penicillin, she wipes her hands on a towel and comes to greet us. "Hello, Don," she says, extending her hand toward Dr. Peterson. Glancing toward me, she asks, "And who might this be?"

Without waiting for Dr. Peterson to introduce us, I thrust out my hand, "I'm Bryan Whittaker, a freelance photojournalist on assignment from *National Geographic* magazine."

Attempting to regain control of the conversation, Dr. Peterson interjects, "Bryan is hoping to do a photo-essay on some of the indigenous people groups who haven't yet had contact with the outside world. I suggested that he might be able to use the mission station as his base camp. Do you think that's a possibility?"

Shrugging noncommittally, she says, "That shouldn't be a problem, but it's not my decision to make. You'll have to talk with Gordon Arnold. He's the senior missionary and in charge of the compound."

Not wanting to appear subservient to Dr. Peterson, I quickly ask, "Where can I find this Arnold fellow?"

"He went upriver earlier today, but he should be back before dark. Why don't you and Don join us for dinner, and we can talk about it then."

Before I can reply, Dr. Peterson says, "That sounds great. We'll come up to your house just after dark."

"I'm afraid my place is too small. Besides, I'm supposed to have dinner with the Arnolds tonight, so why don't you meet me there. I'll let Eleanor know that she'll have two more guests for dinner." Turning back to her patients, Diana says, "Well, if you will excuse me, I have work to do."

CHAPTER

17

IT IS FULLY DARK as Dr. Peterson and I prepare to make our way toward the mission compound to join Diana Rhoades and the other missionaries for dinner. Wanting to make the best impression possible, I have bathed in the river and trimmed my hair. I am wearing my best pair of jeans and a clean chambray shirt. In memory of my father, I have applied a liberal amount of Old Spice cologne; at least that is what I tell myself, not yet willing to admit that it is Diana I want to impress. Out of the corner of my eye I note that Dr. Peterson has taken pains with his appearance as well, and I can't help wondering if Diana has this effect on all men.

The full moon reflecting off the white sand made the riverbank nearly as bright as day, but here on the trail, under a canopy of towering trees, it is uncomfortably dark. With a flashlight to guide him, Dr. Peterson is walking briskly, and I have to hurry to match his pace. As we near the compound I hear the rumble of a small diesel engine, and through the trees I see the glow of lights. Belatedly I realize that at least one of the mission houses has a diesel-powered generator to provide electricity. Quite an improvement, I muse, over the kerosene lamps I remember from my childhood, even if the noise is distracting.

The windows are open, and as we approach the house I can hear voices although I cannot make out any words. Stepping onto the porch, Dr. Peterson raps loudly on the door. It is opened almost immediately by a huge bear of a man. I stand nearly three inches over six feet, but he towers over me. I cannot help thinking that he must seem like a giant to the Indians who are for the most part a people of small stature.

"Dr. Peterson," he bellows in a voice to match his physique. Stepping aside, he ushers us into his home. A matronly woman—Eleanor, I presume—appears from the back of the house smiling with genuine warmth. She is clad in a simple housedress and is wiping her hands on a towel as she gives her cheek to Dr. Peterson in greeting. I watch in amusement as he presents her with a bottle of wine. Although she accepts it with surprising grace, I can't help thinking that he doesn't understand the missionary culture very well or he would have brought another gift.

As they chat, catching up on what has been happening in their lives, I study the mission house. It is somewhat larger than the one my father built, but it is basically the same construction. The roof is made of corrugated tin nailed directly to rafters made from rough-cut lumber. The walls are covered with wood planks of various widths that have been neither painted nor stained, giving the house a lingering aroma of raw wood. Stained planks of random widths make up the flooring. I cannot help noticing that they are pulling apart in places, and I can only conclude that they must have been put down before they were completely seasoned.

Eleanor Arnold obviously has a gift for homemaking, for although the furnishings are plain the room is warm and inviting. The dark floors are covered with brightly colored rugs—what we used to call braided rag rugs when I was a boy. On a small coffee table there is a vase filled with fresh orchids of exquisite color and beside it a worn Bible. Against the far wall there is a bookcase partially filled with books. The remaining shelves house a collection of family photos. Not being a reader, I ignore the books as I make my way across the room to study the smiling faces looking back at me from their small frames.

That the Arnolds are a happy family is immediately apparent. Whether the pictures are posed or candid, they radiate a carefree exuberance. The contrast with my own childhood is painfully obvious, kindling a familiar anger. Once more I find myself resenting those who have what I was denied, and I am tempted to storm out of the house in disgust. Only the knowledge that I desperately need their cooperation if I am to accomplish my task keeps my anger in check.

Turning from the photos, I make my way to the window where I stare into the dark, trying to cleanse my mind of the painful memories that haunt me. Conversation swirls around me, and laughter flows from across the room, but I am mostly oblivious to them. The voices I hear are inside my head, and try as I might I cannot still them. Lost in my thoughts, I do not hear Diana approach, and I am startled when she calls my name.

"Bryan, isn't it?" she asks with a smile.

"Dr. Rhoades," I reply, forcing myself to be cordial although my earlier enthusiasm has waned.

"Diana will be fine," she says, "unless you would like for me to think of you as a patient."

"Diana it is."

Before I can say more, Eleanor calls us to dinner. Since there is no dining room, we file into a country kitchen where we are seated around a plank table covered with a checkered oilcloth. Dr. Peterson manages to maneuver himself into the chair beside Diana, and I find myself seated beside Eleanor. Glancing around the kitchen is like revisiting my early childhood. There are open shelves instead of cupboards, and in the corner sits a kerosene refrigerator much like the one I remember. Calico curtains enclose the shelves below the counter, and on one end there is a hand-cranked coffee grinder. Eleanor has lit two kerosene lamps, and Gordon steps outside to shut off the generator before joining us at the table.

"Thank you, dear," she says before turning to me. "I appreciate electric lights, I surely do, but I find the noise nearly intolerable, especially during dinner."

Nodding my agreement, I savor the moment. Like her I welcome the quiet, and in the stillness I can hear the night sounds from the jungle although I can't differentiate the individual voices in this vast chorus of insects and frogs.

At the end of the table Gordon bows his head to say grace, and I am nearly overcome with nostalgia. In my mind it is my father's voice I hear returning thanks, not Gordon's. Across the table from me sits ten-year-old Helen, a thin wisp of a girl, and it is my mother who sits beside me. Gordon's hearty "amen" jerks me back to the present, and we begin passing heaping platters of delicious-smelling food.

Between bites Dr. Peterson keeps up a steady monologue, regaling us with sundry bits of information about the rain forest and its diverse inhabitants. Now he's talking about a bird called a japiim, which will only build its nest in a colony—often several dozen nests in a single grouping. Somewhere near each colony there is always a nest of predatory wasps. "Why," he asks rhetorically, "do these birds, which could build their colony of nests on any tree in the forest, choose to raise their babies next to hundreds of voracious, meat-eating wasps?"

I nearly snort in disgust. Who cares why some dumb bird builds its nest next to a colony of predatory wasps? Apparently Diana does, for she is hanging on Dr. Peterson's every word. Jealousy now feeds the anger that is ever a part of me, tempting me to vent my disdain for the pompous Dr. Peterson. With an effort I choke back my sarcastic response lest I offend her, although why I should care what she thinks is beyond me.

When no one ventures an answer, Dr. Peterson continues in his officious way. "The wasps protect the japiim from botfly maggots. Without the wasps, the japiim population would soon be extinct. Nothing in nature is faster than a botfly. In the blink of an eye, a female botfly can dart into a japiim nest, lay her microscopic egg on a chick, and escape before the parent notices anything. Soon the egg hatches into a ravenous maggot that will burrow into the chick and eat it alive from the inside out."

Finally, Eleanor speaks up. "Don, I hardly think that is appropriate dinner conversation."

"Don't be silly, Eleanor," Diana says, coming to his defense. "We all know what life is like in the Amazon Basin. Personally, I find the discussion fascinating."

Encouraged, Dr. Peterson says, "The wasps attack the flies in midflight, paralyzing and feeding them to their own hungry larvae." Smugly he concludes, "To the wasps the japiims are slow-moving lures that attract the botflies. To the japiims the wasps are near-supersonic rapiers that guard their babies from enemies as invisible as the air itself."

Without a word Eleanor gets up and begins to clear the table, her displeasure obvious. Once the dishes are stacked in the sink, she moves to the coffee grinder where she grinds the beans. Oblivious to her efforts, Diana remains at the table engrossed in conversation with the men. While waiting for the coffee to perk, Eleanor dishes up dessert. Glancing at Diana, as she works, she gives her a disapproving look.

After serving the coffee, she rejoins us at the table. Interrupting Diana in mid-sentence, she turns to me, saying, "Tell us about yourself, young man. What brings you to this part of the world?"

As quickly as I can I relate my cover story and then turn to Gordon. "I was hoping to use the mission station as my base camp; with your permission, of course."

"That shouldn't be a problem as long as you understand that this is a mission compound. You and your party would have to abide by our rules. We don't allow liquor, and, of course, any kind of promiscuous behavior is absolutely forbidden."

Darting a look in Dr. Peterson's direction, I am pleased to see him squirming as he realizes the inappropriateness of his earlier gift. Returning my attention to Gordon, I reply, "I understand, sir. We would expect to abide by the rules of the compound. Of course, I would plan to make a contribution to your cause as a gesture of good faith."

"Perhaps he could use Whittaker House," Diana interjects. "The Fergusons won't return from their furlough for six or seven months."

Pretending ignorance, I ask, "What is Whittaker House?"

"It's the first house you passed as you came up from the river," Gordon explains. "It was named in honor of the man who built it. Harold B. Whittaker was the first missionary in this part of the Amazon Basin. He lost his life while ministering to the Indians in 1948, leaving a wife and two young children. Most of us consider him a martyr."

Out of the corner of my eye I notice Dr. Peterson studying me with a thoughtful expression on his face. Realizing I have aroused his curiosity, I curse my stupidity. He has a quick mind, and no doubt he suspects it is more than a coincidence that the martyred missionary and I have the same last name.

Getting to my feet, I thank Eleanor for a lovely dinner before turning to Gordon once more. "Thank you for considering my request. If you decide to allow us the use of Whittaker House, that would be splendid, but it's not necessary. I'll check with you sometime tomorrow to see what you've decided."

Dr. Peterson is unusually quiet as we walk back to the river where our boat is beached, and I can't help wondering what he is thinking. No doubt he is pondering the scientific probability that the martyred missionary and I just happen to have the same last name. Given the fact that Whittaker is a rather uncommon name, the chance that it is a mere coincidence is slight. Once more I curse myself for my stupidity. Had I not drawn attention to the name with my questions, he might have never even noticed they were the same, especially given his preoccupation with Diana.

In an attempt to keep my growing paranoia in check, I try to objectively assess the situation. Even if he suspects the truth, there's not much he can do. It may be unethical to pretend to be a freelance photojournalist, but it is not criminal. My duplicity may well taint our relationship, but he's going to be leaving in a day or two anyway, so that's no big deal. Probably the most damaging thing he could do would be to share his concerns with Gordon Arnold or Diana Rhoades. If they were to decide that I can't be trusted, it would seriously undermine our relationship, not to mention complicate my mission.

Hoping to divert his attention, I ask, "If you were me, where would you start? You know this part of the Amazon Basin far better than I do, and any help you can give me would be greatly appreciated."

Stopping near the boat, he turns to face me. "It's late, Bryan, and I'm tired. Why don't we talk about this in the morning?"

I watch as he makes his way to his hammock and climbs in. Seeing that he is in no mood for conversation, I follow suit. Arranging my mosquito net, I try to settle down for the night. In the distance a jaguar screams, causing me an involuntary chill. After a bit I realize that I am unconsciously scratching a mosquito bite, awaking my dormant fear of malaria. For all I know I may already be infected. Tomorrow I will speak with Diana and see if she can spare some quinine pills.

Chapter

18

THE SUN IS BARELY up when Eurico brings me a scalding cup of coffee, black and sweet with brown sugar. Rolling out of my hammock, I move to the riverbank where I splash water on my face, ridding myself of the last of my grogginess. Reaching for my coffee, I watch as the emerging sun moves across the river, chasing the last of the darkness away. Upriver the rain forest is draped in swirling bands of early morning mist, and I find myself marveling at its beauty. Across the river two scarlet macaws are splotches of red against the green canopy.

Moving back to the fire, I fill a tin plate with black beans and rice before situating myself on the ground with a large log for a backrest. Several of the crew are present, but Dr. Peterson is nowhere to be seen. Lako sits apart from the rest, a fierce scowl clouding his dark features. He is obviously not a happy man, and I bless whatever powers may be for having the foresight to remove the spark plugs from his outboard engine. Otherwise, I'm convinced he would have taken his boat and slipped away, drink having a fierce hold on him. I hope I have not made a mistake in hiring him, but what choice did I have?

Squatting on the ground beside me, Eurico is shoveling rice and beans into his mouth at a furious pace. Shaking my head, I marvel at his capacity. I am a big man with an appetite to match, but I cannot keep up with him. He eats as if he fears each meal may be his last. Thinking about his life as a *peixote*, I can see why. Equally amazing is his attitude. Although he is an orphan and has been on his own since he was six years old, he embraces life with an exuberance I both envy and fear.

Wiping his mouth on the back of his hand, he says, "So when do we go into the jungle?" excitement dancing in his eyes.

"In good time," I reply. "In good time. By the way, where is Dr. Peterson? I haven't seen him this morning."

"He's having breakfast with the missionary doctor."

My stomach knots, and I can feel the color rising in my cheeks. Grinning mischievously, Eurico says, "She's beautiful, no?"

Leaning back against the log, I take a sip of my coffee in an attempt to appear nonchalant. Behind what I hope is a calm exterior my emotions are raging. A part of me is jealous, although there is no logical reason for me to be. I only met Diana yesterday, and we haven't exchanged more than a few words. She has obviously been friends with Dr. Peterson for some time, so why shouldn't they have breakfast together? Unfortunately, my emotions are immune to reason.

A more legitimate concern is what they might be discussing over breakfast. As tired as I am of his pontificating, I can only hope that he is regaling her with useless trivia about red howler monkeys or Morpho butterflies, whose wings are stained-glass blue. On the other hand, if he is discussing his suspicions regarding my true identity, it could complicate everything.

Getting to my feet, I call to Eurico. "Let's go see what the beautiful doctor is up to."

I deliberately choose a circuitous route, one that will allow us to approach Dr. Rhoades' house from the rear. If possible I would like to eavesdrop on their conversation. Eurico quickly perceives what I am doing, and he gives me a knowing smile. As far as he is concerned, I am a jealous suitor doing the kind of thing jealous suitors do. I should be embarrassed, but I shamelessly allow him his misperception, his presence providing good cover should I be discovered.

Fortunately, they are taking breakfast on the small porch, and their voices carry clearly in the still air. As I hoped, they are speaking English rather than Portuguese, so I need not concern myself with what Eurico might hear. And as I feared Dr. Peterson is discussing his concerns about me.

Taking a bite of toast, he chews slowly, then he asks, "Don't you find it the least bit curious that Bryan has the same name as the missionary who founded this mission station? I mean, what are the chances of that? They must be related. Bryan may even be his son."

"So what if he is?" Diana replies with more than a hint of amusement. "I think you're making something out of nothing. There's nothing sinister about being the son of a martyred missionary." Teasingly she adds, "In fact, I find it rather fascinating."

Frustrated, Dr. Peterson says, "That's not what's troubling me, and you know it. If he is the son of Harold Whittaker, and I'm inclined to believe he is, then why is he being so secretive about it?"

"I'm sure he has his reasons. Maybe he doesn't want the baggage that comes with being the son of a missionary legend."

"I still don't like it. And to my way of thinking the fact that you refuse to take my concerns seriously borders on disrespect."

"I'm sorry, Don," Diana replies in a conciliatory tone. "I certainly don't mean to be disrespectful. Perhaps it would be helpful if you could help me understand why you're so concerned."

"What can I tell you that I haven't already told you? I don't think he is who he claims to be, and if he's not then he must be up to something no good."

"Do you mean you don't believe he's Bryan Whittaker, or you don't believe he's a photojournalist on assignment from *National Geographic?*"

"Oh, he's Bryan Whittaker all right, but he's no photojournalist. The *National Geographic* people would never send anyone down here so unprepared. Would you believe he's not even taking antimalaria medicine? He claims no one told him he needed it."

For the first time Dr. Rhoades' eyes register concern. "You can't be serious."

"Oh, I'm serious all right. When I told him that no one goes into the jungle without it, he nearly begged me to let him have some of our supply."

"Don, this is serious. We've been hearing reports of an outbreak of malaria upriver for several weeks. When Gordon returned last night, he confirmed it. Without medication, Bryan is at great risk. He could die."

"I suggested that he might get some from your clinic."

Dr. Rhoades frowns before replying. "That could be a problem. Our stock has been depleted by the recent outbreak, and if it should turn into a full-blown epidemic, we will need everything we have and more."

Draining his coffee cup, Dr. Peterson stands to leave. "One last thing. What happened to Harold Whittaker? How did he die?"

"No one knows. At least that's the story I get. Apparently he went into the jungle to take medicine to a remote tribe and never returned. He may have gotten lost or died in an accident, but most likely the Indians killed him. Probably the Amuacas."

Motioning for Eurico to follow me, I quickly retrace my steps. Once I am safely in the trees, I stop to ponder what I have learned. As I suspected, Dr. Peterson is onto me. Not that it seems to matter, at least not to Diana. Apparently she doesn't care whether I am Harold Whittaker's son or not. That being the case, I will continue my ruse. Pretending to be a photojournalist provides good cover for my true mission.

Of greater concern is the very real threat of a malaria epidemic. If I don't get some quinine pills, I could die. Depending on how many I can get from Dr. Rhoades, I may have to send Eurico to plunder Dr. Peterson's supply. I hope it doesn't come to that, but I can't let anyone or anything stop me from doing what I have come to do.

CHAPTER

19

HAVING ARRIVED AT THE Village Inn restaurant a few minutes early, Helen is seated in a booth by the window toying with her Dr. Pepper while waiting for Carolyn to get there. Last night she told Rob she was driving to Denver for a day of shopping, a topic that would have normally prompted further discussion, perhaps even an offer to join her, but not this time. In fact, he didn't even ask what time she expected to be home. Probably no big thing in many marriages, but it definitely signaled a none-too-subtle shift in theirs. Like his newly acquired habit of working late at the church, it indicated a disturbing disinterest. *What*, she wonders, *has conspired to drive Rob and me so far apart? More important, will we ever find each other again?*

For a moment tears swim in her eyes, and she wills herself not to cry. Concentrating, she hears the murmur of conversation around her and the clatter of dishes and silverware as a bus boy clears the table across the aisle. Turning toward the window, she stares with unseeing eyes at the rush-hour traffic clogging both Federal Boulevard and Interstate 70. To the west, the Front Range shoulders its way above the urban sprawl, dusty brown after a long, dry summer. In her mind, she cannot help contrasting it with the towering rain forests of the far western Amazon Basin where Bryan searches for their missing father.

Thinking about it, she decides that the thing with Rob started with her mother's death and then Bryan's disappearance. At first he was supportive, but as her depression deepened he grew impatient. His insensitivity complicated things, causing her to withdraw, to turn inward. For the first time in thirteen years of marriage she began keeping things from him. Just her feelings at first, and then things that happened, like the first time Carolyn came to the house. She still hasn't told him of their developing friendship or the letter Bryan sent from the Amazon. Keeping secrets hadn't been a conscious decision, just something that sort of evolved. She had planned to tell him, but she just couldn't seem to find the right time. If she told him at this late date, how would she explain her earlier secrecy? "Oh, what a tangled web we weave when at first we practice to deceive!" or as her mother would say, "What a fine kettle of fish this is."

Lost in her thoughts, Helen doesn't notice Carolyn's arrival and is surprised when she slips into the booth across from her. Smiling, she says, "Sorry I'm late. The traffic was terrible."

A waitress arrives to take Carolyn's drink order and deliver menus. After she leaves, Helen asks, "Would you like to order now, or should we chat for a few minutes before we eat?"

"If you don't mind, I'd like to order. I skipped lunch, and I'm famished."

Picking up the menu, Helen studies it without really seeing it, her thoughts focused on Carolyn. She is an enigma. Poised and articulate, she is obviously a very capable person, yet beneath her confident exterior there is an insecurity she can't completely disguise—a neediness Helen recognizes, not unlike her own. Helen's is rooted in her father's disappearance, but she has no idea what trauma gave birth to Carolyn's—her divorce from Bryan perhaps, or something lacking in her childhood. *We're all wounded human beings*, she thinks, *in one way or another. No one goes through life unscathed.*

The waitress returns, and Helen orders something without really noticing what—a spinach salad she thinks. She and Carolyn make small talk until their food arrives, exchanging information without saying anything of substance. With a twinge of sadness, Helen realizes that is the way she and Rob now relate. When their food is served, Carolyn eats with an appetite and seems to genuinely enjoy her Monte Cristo sandwich, while Helen picks at her salad.

Once the table has been cleared, Carolyn orders a cup of coffee. After the waitress brings it, Helen reaches into her purse and extracts Bryan's letter. Sliding it across the table, she says, "This is the letter I called you about. The one Bryan sent from Brazil. You already know what it says, but I thought you might like to read it for yourself."

Picking up the tissue-thin, light blue, aerogram envelope, Carolyn studies the address in Bryan's familiar scrawl. "I would recognize his handwriting anywhere," she says wistfully. "I've never seen anyone else make their *T*s or their *R*s the way he does."

Unfolding the letter, she reads it quickly, then she reads it a second time, slower, paying attention to every detail. When she finishes, her eyes glisten with tears. Reaching across the table, she squeezes Helen's hand. "Thank you for sharing Bryan's letter. It means a lot to me."

Placing the letter on the table between them, she turns toward the window and blinks back her tears. *How much of this is my doing?* she wonders. *Bryan has his own issues, to be sure, but maybe what I did pushed him over the edge. If anything happens to him, I will never forgive myself.*

"What is it, Carolyn?" Helen asks, noticing her sudden pensiveness.

Deeply touched by Helen's concern, Carolyn momentarily considers confiding in her. The need to tell someone, anyone, is nearly overwhelming, but the fear of rejection leaves her tongue-tied. No matter how heavy her burden, she cannot risk losing Helen's friendship. Tenuous though it is, it's the only link she has with Bryan.

Retrieving the letter from the table between them, she asks, "What do you think Bryan means when he writes, 'I have reached a dead end. I can't go on with my life until I can make peace with my past. Much of the anger that controls me is rooted in these unresolved issues. Maybe I can find some answers here'?"

Helen carefully considers her words before replying. "Bryan is still angry about Father's disappearance twenty-two years ago, and it's destroying him. Not what happened to our father, but the way he responded to it."

Frowning, Carolyn says, "I don't think I understand."

"When bad things happen, it seems to me that we have three choices. We can curse life and look for some way to express our grief and rage. Or we can grit our teeth and endure it. Or we can accept it. Bryan chose the first alternative, and it's proved to be terribly self-destructive, as you well know."

"I can see that," Carolyn says thoughtfully. "What about you? How did you deal with it?"

"That's a good question, and one I hadn't given much thought to until recently. I think Mother's death has forced me to look at some things I've tried to ignore."

"How so?"

"Thinking about it now, it seems Mother and I chose to grit our teeth and endure it. It's better than cursing life, I guess, but just barely.

What's really sad is it left us with no way to help Bryan when he needed us most."

"What's going to happen to Bryan?" Carolyn asks, concern clouding her dark eyes. "If he does discover what happened to his father, will it make any difference?"

"I don't think so. Knowing 'how' or 'what' or 'why' doesn't change anything. Nothing Bryan learns can undo what happened twenty-two years ago."

"You make it sound so final, so hopeless."

"Think about it, Carolyn," she says, leaning across the table. "Nothing can change the past. Not even God. But with God's help we can change how we look at it and even how we feel about it! What happened to Dad isn't what's destroying Bryan; it's what he's doing to himself because of it."

"So…are you saying it was a waste for Bryan to go to the Amazon?"

"Not necessarily, but the truth he seeks won't be found in the past. There's only one thing that will heal his troubled heart—not answers, or even understanding, but only unconditional trust in the wisdom and sovereignty of God."

"How will Bryan find that 'unconditional trust'?"

"He doesn't have to. God puts it inside each of us; it's part of our nature. Sometimes, as in Bryan's case, it gets buried beneath years of hurt and anger, but it's still there."

To the west a late summer thunderstorm is building up over the foothills, and jagged flashes of lightning illuminate the undersides of the towering thunderheads. As the storm approaches, the early evening turns dark, causing Helen to look at her watch. It is almost eight o'clock, and she really should be starting for home seeing as she has a two-hour drive ahead of her, longer if the storm hits.

As she begins to gather her things, Carolyn asks, "What can we do? How can we help Bryan?"

"At this point I think all we can do is pray."

Without considering what Helen might think, Carolyn blurts out, "I don't know how to pray."

"Just talk to God out of your heart. Don't worry about saying 'right' things; say 'real' things—whatever enters your mind. Tell God what you're feeling, share your concerns about Bryan, and ask Him to protect Bryan and bring him home safely."

"That's all there is to it?" Carolyn asks in amazement. "I don't have to learn any special techniques or anything?"

Laughing, Helen tells her, "Praying is like riding a bike. It's something you learn by doing."

It is starting to rain as they exit the restaurant. Exchanging a quick hug, they promise to stay in touch before hurrying through the rain to their cars.

CHAPTER

20

ACCORDING TO THE CLOCK on the dashboard of Helen's 1968 Oldsmobile Cutlass, it is 10:43 P.M. as she exits the interstate and turns west toward Sterling. She crosses the three bridges spanning the South Platte River, wrinkling her nose in disgust as she catches the first whiff of the feedlots. Following Highway 14 through town, she passes Pioneer Park before turning north on Decker Drive toward home. The lights are still on in the den as she pulls into the driveway, a sign, she hopes, that Rob is waiting up for her. They need to talk. They cannot afford to let their relationship continue to slide.

"I'm home," she calls out, setting her purse on the kitchen counter before heading into the den. The television is on, and a plate and glass sit on the end table next to Rob's favorite chair, but he is nowhere to be found. Moving down the hallway toward the master bedroom, Helen notices that a light is shining under the door to Rob's study. Pausing, she hears the murmur of his voice, but she can't make out what he is saying. Resolutely, she turns the door handle and steps into the room just as he is replacing the telephone receiver in its cradle. Belatedly, he turns toward her, a sheepish look on his face. For a moment neither of them speaks, then he says, "So how was your trip to Denver? Did you have a good time?"

"Who were you talking too?"

Her words are hard, demanding, and he immediately becomes defensive. "What concern is it of yours who I talk to? Don't you trust me?"

Ignoring his questions, she presses. "Why the secrecy, Rob? Do you have something to hide?"

"Don't talk to me about secrecy. I'm not the one running up long-distance charges calling Denver four and five times a week." Turning to his desk, he picks up the telephone bill. "Before you accuse me of having something to hide, maybe you ought to explain these charges."

Thrusting the telephone bill toward her, he says, "And while you're at it, why don't you tell me about Bryan's letter."

"Bryan's letter, what are you talking about?"

"Helen, please," Rob says, his voice suddenly weary, "your duplicity is so transparent. We both know what letter I'm talking about."

How did it come to this? Helen asks herself, disappointment nearly overwhelming her. Is it possible that just an hour ago she was driving home in anticipation of telling Rob everything? Why then, is she now so determined to keep her own counsel, and at what price? Reason tells her to come clean with Rob, to tell him everything, but hurt and anger render her mute. On another level, she's shocked to think that he might be involved with someone else, even though she has to admit the signs are all there. Over the past few weeks he has grown emotionally distant, started "working" late, and stopped making love with her. Equally disconcerting is the fact that he dare suggest she might be involved with someone else. After thirteen years of marriage he should know her better than that.

She is suddenly tired, more tired than she has ever been, and without another word she turns to go. Before she can leave the study,

Rob steps between her and the door, blocking her path. "You're not leaving until you tell me who he is." When she doesn't respond, he grips her by both shoulders and demands, "Who did you go to Denver to see? What's his name?"

"Rob, please," she sobs softly, trying to push past him.

"Who is he?" Rob insists. "Tell me his name!"

"Don't be ridiculous, Rob," she lashes out angrily. "I went to Denver to shop."

"If shopping was all you had in mind, why didn't you ask me to come along like you usually do? I would have enjoyed spending the day with you."

Their angry voices must have awakened Robbie, for he is standing in the hallway just outside the door, a frightened look on his face. Jerking free of Rob's grasp, Helen goes to him. Kneeling down, she enfolds him in her arms. "It's okay, honey," she says softly, moving her mouth against the top of his head. "Would you like a graham cracker and a glass of milk before I put you back to bed?"

"No thank you," he says, trying hard not to cry. "Mommy, would you sleep with me? I'm scared."

"No, she will not," Rob says sternly, before Helen can reply. "You are too big to sleep with your mother."

Ignoring him, she takes Robbie by the hand and leads him to his bedroom. "Come on, honey. Mommy will stay with you until you fall asleep."

Rob watches them until Helen closes the door to Robbie's bedroom, then he turns toward the master bedroom, torn between anger and grief. In the walk-in closet he finds a blanket and a pillow and makes his way back to the den. Taking off his shoes and his shirt, he tries to get comfortable on the couch, but to no avail. Try as he might he cannot imagine who Helen is seeing. Where could she have met him? Nothing about her life lends itself to adultery, certainly not with someone who lives in Denver. Caring for two children and a home makes it nearly impossible for her to develop any kind of extracurricular relationship. Maybe he is wrong. Maybe there isn't anyone else, but then how does he explain all those phone calls to Denver?

He is still awake, wrestling with his tormenting thoughts, when he hears Helen slip down the hallway into their bedroom. He listens to her close the door and then lock it, making no effort to disguise what she is doing. *Sending me a message no doubt*, he thinks. As angry as he is, he still loves her no matter what she has done. Tempting though it is, he refuses to define their entire relationship by what's happening now. The current situation notwithstanding, they have had a wonderful marriage these past thirteen years, and God has blessed them with two beautiful boys. With God's help they will get through this. He doesn't know how, but he knows they will. They have to.

CHAPTER
21

RETURNING TO THE RIVER, after meeting with Gordon Arnold, I discover that Dr. Peterson and the bright blue *Flor de Maio* are gone. When I realize what he has done, I curse him soundly. He has played me for a fool, and with his departure I have lost whatever chance I may have had of confiscating some of his quinine pills. Now my only hope rests with Dr. Rhoades, and based on her conversation with Peterson it doesn't look good. "Stupid," I mutter. "Stupid, stupid, stupid."

Eurico and Lako watch in amusement as I storm about the beach, giving vent to my anger. Eventually it exhausts itself, and I make my way toward them, flopping down on the beach beside Eurico. A few meters away, Lako is leaning against a bag of rice, glowering in my direction. Having suffered at my hand for the better part of two weeks, he seems to take a perverse pleasure in seeing the tables turned on me. He doesn't say anything, but neither does he try to disguise his satisfaction. It's clear to me that Dr. Peterson's action meets with his approval.

After stewing a few minutes longer, I get to my feet, saying, "Let's get these supplies moved up to Whittaker House. We're going to use it as our home base for the next few weeks." Shouldering a hundred-pound bag of rice, I set off up the trail with Lako following suit. Eurico brings up the rear carrying our hammocks and mosquito netting.

I am perspiring heavily, and my lungs are on fire by the time we reach the mission house, but Lako seems none the worse for wear. Dumping my bag of rice on the porch, I lean on the rail, gasping for breath. Grinning at me, Eurico says, "Maybe you'd better carry the hammocks next time." I take a playful swipe at him, and he dances out of reach, merriment lighting his dark features. Once more I am astounded by his high spirits, and I simply shake my head in wonder. Considering what he has suffered in his young life, his resilience is truly amazing.

After Lako and Eurico head back to the beach for another load, I unlock the door and step into the house where I spent the first seven years of my life. I am not a sentimental man, anger being about the only feeling I allow myself, yet I am nearly undone by the rush of emotion that now seizes me. The house is smaller than I recall and of cruder construction; other than that it is just as I remember it. Moving to the windows, I open the shutters, letting in the late afternoon sunlight. In the far corner I hear a small creature scurrying to escape the light, but I pay it no mind.

The table my father built out of rough planks still sits where it always did. It is worn smooth in places and dark with age, but other than that it looks the same as I remember it. *How many meals*, I wonder, *did the four of us share at this very table; how many lessons did Helen and I do; how many nights did we listen as Father read from the Bible, the kerosene lamp drawn close to illuminate the page?* The memories are poignant, and my throat is tight with feeling as I run my fingers along the edge of the table.

Moving to the head of the table, I place my hands on the back of the chair in which my father was sitting the last time I saw him. In an instant it all comes back to me—*the relentless drumming of the rain on the corrugated tin roof, the pungent smell emanating from the kerosene lamp, the steam rising from the cup of coffee Mother places on the table at my father's elbow. He is not a man given to displays of affection, but on this night he responds to her caresses. His back is to me, so I cannot see his face, but Mother's is clearly visible over his shoulder, being illuminated by the glow of the lamp. There is joy in her face this night, but it is tainted with concern, and tears glisten in her dark eyes. After a moment Father releases her, and she returns to her chair, but she continues to stare at him.*

My room is just off the kitchen, and a flimsy curtain serves as a door. I have pulled it back the tiniest bit, just enough to allow me to peer out, and as I watch I see Father carefully wrap his Bible in oilcloth before putting it in his canvas satchel. Picking up his journal, he repeats the process, being careful to make sure no corner is left exposed. After placing it with his Bible, he buckles the leather straps, securely closing the satchel. As he sets it on the table, I cannot help noticing the leather patch that is stitched to the flap between the brass buckles. Even in the dim light I can clearly see my father's initials which have been carefully carved into it.

While Father has been finishing his packing, my mother has loosed her hair, and now it falls around her shoulders. She is slowly brushing it, and I marvel at the way it catches the light from the lamp. Getting up, my father moves to her chair where he reaches for her hand. Taking his hand, Mother allows him to lead her to their bedroom. Although I am too young to understand what is happening, even I know that it is special. I cannot remember ever seeing my father's face so full of feeling or my mother's so beautiful.

Hearing Lako and Eurico on the porch, I hastily compose myself and go to join them. Seeing they have filled nearly half of the small porch with our supplies, I ask, "Is this all of it?" Without bothering to answer Lako turns and starts back down the trail toward the river.

Before hurrying after him Eurico says, "A couple more trips, and we should be done."

I watch them disappear down the same trail that my father followed the morning he left, never to return. Thinking about it now, I am tempted with a familiar despair, but I refuse to dwell on it. This time I will turn my bitterness into action. No more self-pity for me. I will learn what happened to my father, or die trying.

I consider going back inside, but think better of it, not being in the mood for any more memories. Instead, I find myself wandering under the towering *samaúma* trees where I once played as a boy. Someone has replaced the rope swing my father made for Helen and me with a porch-type swing, fastened with thick ropes to a large branch overhead. Suddenly tired, from the inside out, I plop in it and begin to slowly swing, letting my mind wander.

A half-dozen thoughts tug at me, but I resist them. I do not have the energy for thinking just now. After a while, I glance up to see Diana approaching with two tall glasses. Joining me on the swing, she hands one to me, saying, "Sweet tea. There's nothing better."

Taking a sip, I nod. "Not bad. Not bad at all."

"It's better ice cold, but there's no ice in the Amazon, so we will have to make do."

We swing in silence for a minute or two, sipping our tea. It's been a long time since I have been close to a woman, and I find her nearness pleasant but somewhat disconcerting. Without intending to, I find myself comparing her with Carolyn, the only woman I have ever loved. At first glance they don't appear to be alike at all. Carolyn is petite with thick auburn hair and coffee-colored eyes, while Diana is blonde and at least 5 feet, 6 inches tall, but at their core I sense they are much the same—kind and caring.

"I didn't think they drank iced tea in Minnesota," I finally venture.

"They don't, not much anyway. In fact, I never heard of sweet tea until I went to med school in Florida, but I was hooked after the first glass. It's the official state drink, you know," she says, only half kidding.

Taking a swallow of her tea, she turns serious. "So what about you, Bryan, where are you from?"

Her question makes me uncomfortable, and I try to decide whether she is just making conversation, or if she is following up on Dr. Peterson's suspicions. As casually as I can I say, "I grew up in northeastern Colorado. Since then I've knocked around quite a bit. What about you? How did you end up in the Amazon? It hardly seems the place for a woman like you."

"A woman like me," she asks in mock seriousness. "What is that supposed to mean?"

Responding in kind, I say, "You're young, you're beautiful, and you're single, so why would you want to come to the Amazon?"

Growing serious, she replies, "I was seventeen years old in 1956, when Jim Elliot and those other missionaries were killed by the Auca Indians in Ecuador. I'm sure you remember it. It was all over the news, and *Life* magazine ran a huge story about it."

I don't recall anything about it, but I don't want to appear uninformed, so I mumble, "Just vaguely."

"It was the turning point in my life," she continues, emotion coloring her words. "Until then I had planned to follow in my father's footsteps and become a surgeon, but from that time forward all I could think about was becoming a medical missionary. When I surrendered my life to God's call to become a missionary, I told Him that I was not only willing to live for Him but also to die for Him if that would further His cause."

She's studying me, trying to gauge my reaction, and I concentrate on not letting my face give anything away, but on the inside I'm in turmoil. Her words have a familiar ring. I heard my father say the same sort of thing more times than I can remember. It didn't make any sense then, and it certainly doesn't make any sense now. Why someone like Diana Rhoades would be willing to risk her life in order to provide medical care for illiterate Indians in the Amazon is beyond me.

It would probably be wise for me to keep my mouth shut, but I can't; this whole subject is a sore point with me. Still, I don't want to offend her if I can help it, so I do my best to appear nonchalant. Casually I say, "As much as I respect your feelings, it's hard for me to understand how the murder of some missionaries could inspire you to become a missionary yourself. I mean, how can you trust a God who can't take care of His own?"

"Bryan, you're looking at this all wrong. Those missionaries didn't die because God failed to protect them. He didn't let them down. But you can be sure that what happened at Palm Beach will be turned around for good."

"Wait a minute. Are you telling me that God planned their murder? If that's true, then God is even worse than I thought! That would make Him a murderer, or at least an accomplice."

Grimacing, Diana says, "You know that's not what I'm saying. I'm a medical doctor, not a theologian, so I probably can't explain things to your satisfaction, but I'll try. My understanding of what happened at Palm Beach is not based on the events of that day, but in what has happened since. Five missionaries died, and when the news of their deaths reached America, hundreds of young people, just like me, committed their lives to missions. We pledged ourselves to take their place. Where once there were five missionaries, now there are hundreds. God brought good out of an evil situation.

"Did He cause the Aucas to kill those missionaries so He could bring good out of an evil situation? I don't think so. Did He allow it? Maybe. For certain He has redeemed it—He is using that tragedy to further His Kingdom."

"That's easy enough for you to say," I blurt out, without considering my words. "You would probably feel differently if one of those men had been your father."

Instantly, I realize I have said too much, for Diana is studying me intently. Before she can say anything, I change the subject. "This is a little embarrassing, but I need to ask a favor of you." When she nods, I continue. "I know you will probably find this hard to believe, but no one told me I needed to take antimalaria medicine, and I ended up coming here without any. When Dr. Peterson learned of my predicament, he suggested that I might be able to get some quinine pills from you."

Frowning, she takes a minute before replying. "I would like to help you, Bryan, but I'm not sure I can." When I raise my eyebrows in question, she continues. "There are at least two problems. As you may have already heard, there's been an outbreak of malaria in some of the villages upriver. If it becomes a full-blown epidemic, we will need all the medicine we have."

Her reasoning infuriates me, but I try not to let my feelings show. How she could consider the needs of illiterate Indians more important than the needs of her own kind escapes me. Isn't my life more valuable than theirs? Apparently it's not, at least to her way of thinking.

"Perhaps of even greater concern," she says, "is the possibility that you may already be infected. You really should have started taking the pills weeks ago. Of course, if you come down with malaria, we will treat you, but otherwise I really don't think there is anything I can do."

Never good at controlling my temper, I have exhausted my patience. Getting to my feet, I throw out the rest of my tea and thrust my glass at her. Without a word I turn on my heel and stomp off. "Bryan, wait," she calls after me, but I ignore her. With or without her help I am going to find out what happened to my father. And when I do, I will take whatever action is necessary, regardless of the consequences!

CHAPTER
22

IT IS STILL DARK when we make our way to the river, a thick layer of low-hanging clouds threatening rain. After pushing Lako's boat off the sandbar, we quickly load our supplies, being careful to distribute them evenly. By the time the three of us have arranged ourselves among the provisions, even I can tell the small boat is seriously overloaded. Once more Lako tries to convince me to lighten our load, but I adamantly refuse. Shaking his head, he mutters something under his breath, but I ignore him.

After shoving off, we drift with the current while Lako fiddles with the engine. He tugs at the pull cord several times, but the engine refuses to start. *Great*, I think, *just what we need—an engine that won't run.* By now huge drops of rain are pitting the dark river, causing me to reach for my poncho. Wrapping it around me, I hunker down, shivering even though the temperature is mild.

Ignoring the approaching storm, Lako continues to fiddle with the engine. Adjusting the choke yet again, he tugs at the pull cord. The engine sputters and coughs, spewing an oily cloud of exhaust. Cursing, he jerks on the pull cord repeatedly until the engine finally fires. Quickly adjusting the throttle, he coaxes it to run. After a few seconds it settles into a steady rhythm; he turns the boat into the current, and we move upriver.

We are leaving a day earlier than I had originally planned, but given the scene with Diana, I thought it best to be on our way. Besides, there was nothing further to be gained by delaying our departure. I would have liked to ask Gordon what he knew about my father's disappearance, but I didn't dare risk arousing any further suspicion. In retrospect, it might have been better to have been up front about everything from the beginning. Be that as it may, it's too late now. For better or worse I am committed to being a quasi photojournalist.

In my more rational moments, I cannot help thinking that what I am doing is utterly insane. There's not a chance in the world that my father's still alive after twenty-two years, nor do I have much hope of discovering what happened to him. Sometimes I think I must have a death wish. God knows I've thought of killing myself enough times; I've just never had the courage to do it. Is that what this little adventure is all about—a subconscious desire to die? Maybe I'm looking for a way to end my life without having to do it myself, kind of like those people who force the police to kill them. Suicide by police I think is what they call it. In my case it would be suicide by Indians, suicide by snakebite, or maybe suicide by malaria. There are a lot of ways a person can die in the Amazon jungle.

Last night, over a meal of corned beef and black beans, I told Lako I wanted to locate some Amuacas unspoiled by contact with the outside world. For a moment he just looked at me, slowly chewing a mouthful of corned beef. Finally, he said, "What you are suggesting is dangerous. The Amuacas are fierce warriors who have been known to kill outsiders on sight."

Not to be deterred, I pressed him for an explanation. "Why do they hate outsiders so?"

Contempt flavoring his words, he said, "Because you are systematically destroying their way of life." When I started to protest, he silenced me with a wave of his hand. "Not you personally, but your kind—rubber barons, oil companies, and missionaries."

Visibly upset, he pushed back from the table and began pacing around the cramped room, anger loosing his tongue. "My mother was an Amuaca, and her people suffered horribly at the hands of the *patrãos*. Unlike many tribes, the Amuacas refused to submit to the rubber barons who had stolen their lands, often attacking and laying siege to the rubber estates. In turn, the rubber barons employed squadrons of professional killers to hunt them down and kill them. These hunting parties often waited until the Indians had a religious festival before attacking. Once the Indians were drunk on fermented manioc or stoned on *caapil*, they would sneak into the camp, cut the strings on the Indians' bows, and throw their arrows into the fire. The hunters then slipped back into the forest and gunned down the disoriented and unarmed Indians with their Winchesters, killing the men and older women. The young women and children were spared to be used as slaves."

Lako glares at me, anger contorting his rugged features, daring me to dispute his account. Eurico has fallen silent, watching this exchange warily. When I don't say anything, Lako continues, his anger ebbing a little. "These things I know because my mother told them to me. She was just a young girl when this happened, and the hired killers carried her back to the rubber estate where she was turned over to the boss of the estate. Later, she escaped to Cruzeiro do Sul by hiding on a boat going downriver. My father, a Portuguese trader, married her and saved her from life on the streets."

The memories have taken their toll, turning his anger into despair, and the need for a drink is heavy upon him. Sitting back down at the table, he buries his face in his hands. After a while he wearily lifts his head. "I have heard other things too, worse maybe in their own way. A Witoto child was given fifty lashes for stealing a loaf of bread. Another time a trader wrapped an Indian woman in a kerosene-soaked Brazilian flag and set it on fire because she refused to sleep with one of his men." His voice trails off, but the sadness lingers.

His words troubled me last night, and they trouble me still. Although I feel nothing but contempt for the Indians—holding them responsible for the tragedy that defines my life—my sense of justice is outraged. I try to make some sense of Lako's account, using economic arguments and what little I can remember about "manifest destiny" from my high school history class, but it is no use. No matter how I frame it, there is something terribly wrong. What the European immigrants have done to the Indians in the Americas is simply abhorrent. Try as I might there is no way I can justify it in my own mind.

Here in the Amazon, those Indians who tried to cooperate with the Europeans have fared hardly better than those who fought to maintain their way of life. Eurasian and African diseases—smallpox, yellow fever, measles, and malaria—decimated their population. According to Dr. Peterson, half of the native population of the state of Acre died in the peak years of the rubber boom from 1900 to 1913. Those who survived exist in a netherworld of indentured servitude to the *mateiro* (surrogate manager for the rubber baron).

According to all accounts, rubber tapping is a brutal endeavor, consuming most of the day and night. During the night the *seringueiro* (rubber tapper) must score the trees and attach the cup to catch the sap. A few hours later he must return to collect the latex. During the day he must slowly dribble the latex over a smoky rotisserie so that it coagulates into a *bola*. Of course, no single human can sustain such a pace for very long, forcing the *seringueiro* to take a wife who will perform the daytime chores while he sleeps.

In exchange for the privilege of tapping the rubber trees, the *seringueiros* are indentured by debt to the *mateiro* who manages the rubber estate for the landlord who lives in Cruzeiro do Sul. The *mateiro* is the absolute ruler, both boss and banker. He sells each *seringueiro* an *aviacáo:* a grubstake of coffee, salt, sugar, gunpowder, a vial of penicillin, a bottle or two of *cachaça*, a kilo of lead shot, batteries, and the two hundred or so tin cups in which to collect latex. In return, the tappers are contractually obliged to sell their rubber to the *mateiro* in exchange for the essentials of life on the frontier. It is a demeaning life, and death is the only way out. It is little wonder that those Indians who refuse to be domesticated have a fierce hatred for outsiders.

What I can't understand is why they lump us all together. Missionaries and rubber barons have absolutely nothing in common except the color of their skin. As far as I can tell, my father felt nothing but compassion for the Indians, being willing to risk his life to bring the gospel to them. So why should they consider him and his kind their enemy? A nagging voice in the back of my mind tells me I'm doing the same thing in regard to the way I think of the Indians, but I pay it no mind.

I must have dozed off, for when I awaken the rain is easing a little, and the sun is low in the sky. Lako is still hunkered down in the rear of the boat, one hand on the throttle of the outboard engine. From time to time he turns it just a little to keep us centered as we follow the river's meandering course ever deeper into the wilderness. I turn sideways in the boat so I can watch him, studying his dark face. He is a Caboclo, a half-breed—part Amuaca, part Portuguese—yet not really fitting in with either. I can only hope he is as competent as Dr. Peterson believes, and trustworthy, for where we are going, he is our best hope.

Facing forward, I begin searching for a place to camp. It is raining again, as it has been for most of the day, and already the weak light is fading. There's at least an inch of water in the bottom of the boat, and my feet are wet. It's not really cold, but I feel chilled to the bone and feverish, my damp clothes clinging uncomfortably to my aching body. All I want to do is find a place to get out of this rain and crawl into my hammock.

CHAPTER
23

THE DAY HAS BEEN grueling, but it is finally over, and Diana is straightening the clinic's one examining room when she hears the door open. Turning, she sees Gordon enter the room, and she gives him a tired smile. "What brings you to the clinic?"

"I thought maybe we could talk, if you have a few minutes."

"Sure, just let me finish up here." Almost as an afterthought she adds, "There's some sweet tea in the refrigerator. Why don't you pour us a couple of glasses and take them to the porch. I'll join you there as soon as I'm done in here."

By the time she finally makes it to the porch, Gordon has nearly finished his tea. Sitting down in a bamboo chair, she sighs wearily and reaches for her glass. It is still raining, as it has been for most of the day, but she hardly notices. Having been in the Amazon through three rainy seasons, she is used to it. Staring across the mission compound in the gathering darkness, she sees the yellow glow of the kitchen window at the Arnold house. In her mind she pictures Eleanor bustling about the kitchen preparing dinner. For just a moment she envies her. Not the domestic duties as such, but her family. More and more of late Diana has found herself yearning for a husband and children of her own. It can never be, she knows that, but it doesn't stop the yearning.

Turning to Gordon, she says, "So what's on your mind?"

Clearing his throat, he replies, "I've spent a lot of time thinking about Bryan Whittaker, and I'd like to get your take on him."

"What are you looking for?"

"Nothing in particular, just your impressions."

Diana takes a sip of her tea, allowing her a moment to organize her thoughts. "He seems like a nice enough guy, but he's wired awfully tight. He's pretty closed too, real private. Why do you ask?"

"Some things Dr. Peterson said before he left are raising some questions. I was showing Bryan the Whittaker House when Peterson came by our place, so I missed him, but he spoke with Eleanor. Apparently he no longer believes Bryan is who he claims to be."

"What does Eleanor think? She's usually a pretty good judge of people."

Smiling warily, he replies, "She thinks Dr. Peterson is just jealous because you took a shine to Bryan."

Diana can feel herself blushing, and she is thankful for the deepening dusk. *Surely I'm not that transparent*, she thinks. Taking another drink of tea, she finally says, "I've hardly 'taken a shine to Bryan'—as Eleanor so charmingly put it—seeing I just met him, but it's obvious something is bothering Dr. Peterson. He mentioned his suspicions to me as well."

"So what do you think?" Gordon presses. "Is Bryan on the up-and-up, or is he trying to pull a fast one on us?"

Thoughtfully, Diana says, "Dr. Peterson is convinced that it is more than a coincidence that Bryan's last name is Whittaker. He even went so far as to suggest that Bryan might be related to Harold Whittaker, maybe his son."

"I know. He said the same thing to Eleanor."

"Is that possible, Gordon? What do you know about Harold Whittaker's family? Did he have a son who would be Bryan's age?"

"I'm checking into that, but it may be weeks before we know anything. It's not like we can pick up the telephone and call the Division of Foreign Missions."

They sit quietly for a minute or two, each engrossed in their own thoughts. "If Bryan is not on assignment for *National Geographic*," Diana muses, thinking out loud, "what possible reason could he have for coming here? And if he is Harold Whittaker's son, why would he pretend otherwise?" Shaking her head, she says, "For my part, Gordon, it seems more logical to think he's who he claims to be. Nothing else makes much sense."

"That's what Eleanor says, but I've got a funny feeling about this whole thing."

Getting to his feet, he hands Diana his glass and turns to go. Placing her hand on his arm, she says, "Before you go, would you tell me what you know about Harold Whittaker? All this speculation has aroused my curiosity."

Sitting back down, Gordon clears his throat. "This could take a few minutes. I didn't know Harold well, having only seen him once or twice, so most of what I'm going to tell you is hearsay. By all accounts he was a hard man—not mean, mind you, just hard. Stubborn might be a better word. Once he made up his mind, there was no give in him. That wasn't necessarily a bad thing, especially in his day. A lesser man probably could not have done what he did.

"In 1941, when he brought Velma and their little girl to Acre, there was not another missionary within five hundred miles. The mission board wanted Harold to work out of Cruzeiro do Sul, but he refused. He remained in Cruzeiro only long enough for Velma to give birth to their second child. Once she was back on her feet, he loaded his family on a boat, and they made their way up the Rio Juruá. He brought some building materials with them, but much of what he needed he made himself. With the help of a few Indians he cleared this area, built the first mission house, and started learning Indian dialects. He must have had a gift for languages, for he compiled extensive notes and vocabulary lists. When Velma returned to the States after Harold's death, she donated his notebooks to the mission board, and they are still being used to teach Indian dialects to new missionaries.

"Theirs was a hard life. They were isolated, and the conditions were primitive. Once or twice a year Harold would take a canoe downriver to Cruzeiro do Sul for supplies, but Velma and the children never went with him. It was too dangerous; besides, there would have been no room for supplies, and that was the whole reason for going.

"By all accounts he was a tireless worker and absolutely fearless when it came to taking the gospel to those who had never heard. Unfortunately, he was nearly impossible to work with. In 1946, the mission board sent another missionary couple upriver to help the Whittakers, but that didn't last long. Whether the conditions were too primitive, or Harold was too dictatorial, no one seems to know. Probably it was a little of both. It was too bad really, because Harold had made inroads with several groups of Indians, and he had established a small school at the mission compound, and they needed the help.

"Say what you will, no one could fault his commitment or his courage. Once he made a daring trip down the Rio Juruá at the height of the rainy season when the river was several feet higher than normal. It was teeming with logs, uprooted trees, and other debris, making canoe travel treacherous, but that didn't stop him. An Indian boy had fallen somehow and ripped his belly open. He was in shock, and his intestines were hanging out when the boy's father brought him to the mission compound. Whittaker carefully pushed them back in and wrapped the boy's belly in several layers of bandages to keep them from falling out again. He knew that without proper medical care the boy didn't have a chance, so he decided to try to get him to the hospital in Cruzeiro. After wrapping him in blankets, he laid him in a dugout canoe and set off down the river. For the next three days he battled the flooded river, hunger, and exhaustion, but he did not stop, not even to snatch a few hours of sleep. When he finally reached Cruzeiro do Sul, he was out on his feet, but the boy was still alive."

"Did the boy make it?" Diana inquires anxiously. "Were they able to save his life?"

"Unfortunately, no; but that in no way diminishes what Whittaker did." Gordon pauses for a moment before continuing. "That's what makes his disappearance in 1948 so puzzling. By that time he was a skilled woodsman, a *mateiro*. If anyone could take care of himself in the jungle, it was Harold. He was competent and resourceful."

Impatiently Diana asks, "So what do you think happened?"

"No one knows. He may have drowned or been bitten by a poisonous snake, but more likely he was killed. Probably by the Amuacas, but it could have been the *batedores*. The rubber barons hate missionaries almost as much as they hate the Indians."

Getting to his feet, Gordon stretches before turning to go. "Oh, one other thing. It appears Bryan and his crew slipped away before daylight this morning or shortly thereafter. Eleanor was sure disappointed when she found out. She was planning on fixing supper for him this evening."

Stepping off the porch, he pulls his hat low against the rain and turns toward home. Diana watches him disappear into the dark before going inside the clinic in search of her poncho. Reluctantly, she replaces the quinine pills in the cupboard, mentally berating herself for not giving them to Bryan last night. What could she have been thinking?

CHAPTER

24

IT IS NEARLY DARK as Lako maneuvers our small boat into the mouth of the Rio Azul and heads upriver. He's alert now, straining to see in the gathering gloom as night closes in around us. The steady rain that has been falling most of the day is heavier now, further reducing his visibility and slowing our progress. Feverish though I am, I cannot help noticing that the Rio Azul is considerably narrower than the Rio Moa, and full of snags, causing Lako to be especially careful lest he hit something and damage the prop.

Suddenly he cuts the power, slowing our forward movement almost to a standstill. Although my head is throbbing painfully, I force myself to pay attention. Above the steady drone of the outboard engine I hear the sound of barking, coming from the far bank among a tangle of fallen tree trunks. Switching on a powerful flashlight, Lako plays the light over the snarled shoreline. A dozen pairs of tiny ruby red eyes look back at us, causing Lako to curse, and I hear him mutter, "Hatchlings," under his breath.

Now he plays the light along the shore, probing the tangled vegetation. "What is it?" I ask. "What are you looking for?" Ignoring me, he continues scanning the jumbled mass of tree trunks and broken branches that choke the far bank. Not finding what he's looking for, he turns the light on the river. Almost immediately he spots a large pair of eyes, as bright as burning coals. As he plays the light over the water, I suddenly realize that I am looking at a crocodile, a huge crocodile. Her head must be nearly a meter long, and her back looks as broad as our boat. She is between us and the far bank, about four or five meters away.

Even in my feverish condition I am beginning to put things together. Somehow we have come between a mother crocodile and her babies, and she is furious. The look on Lako's face tells me everything I need to know. "Get the gun," he hisses. "Be quick." My hands are shaking as I fumble with the pack, and before I can secure the pistol the crocodile is upon us. Slamming the side of the boat with her broad tail, she drives us sideways, nearly capsizing us. Lako guns the outboard engine, and the boat lunges forward, nearly turning over before he can get it straightened out. In our wake we hear the crocodile smack the river with her tail and bellow, causing my blood to run cold.

Once we have put a safe distance between the crocodile and us, Lako slows the boat, and we take stock of our situation. Amazingly, the boat appears to be relatively undamaged, and none of us is any worse for the wear.

"I knew we were in a dicey situation," Lako tells me, "as soon as I saw those tiny ruby red eyes. It wouldn't have been so bad if it had been spectacled caimans or even a smooth-fronted caiman, but I knew that wasn't the case."

"How so?" I ask.

"Spectacled caiman have reddish yellow eyes, while the smallest and most aggressive of the caimans—the smooth-fronted caiman—have dull yellow eyes. The black caiman, the largest of the species, are the only ones with red eyes, and coming between a mother crocodile and her babies can be deadly."

Although I find Lako's narrative fascinating, I'm having trouble staying focused. Now that the adrenaline rush is wearing off, I realize that my head is throbbing painfully, and I'm nearly too weak to sit up. Lying back against a stack of provisions, I find myself wondering if this is how my father died. Did some enraged crocodile rip him asunder? Remembering my own sick fear just moments ago, I hope not. If he really is dead, I pray he had a better death than that.

It is fully dark when we finally find a suitable place to make camp. Pulling the boat up on the sandbar, we make it secure for the night. I try to help set up camp, but I find that I'm too weak to do much. Slumped against a pack, I watch as Lako moves with practiced skill. In a matter of minutes he has stretched a tarp between four trees, making an effective shelter from the rain. Beneath it he hangs our hammocks and arranges our mosquito nets. While he is doing so, Eurico builds a fire and cooks fried plantains, a slab of bacon, and some beans.

Not waiting to eat, I stumble to my hammock and manage to roll myself into it, gasping for breath. I can't remember ever being so weak. Every muscle and joint in my body hurts, I have a blinding headache, and I am shaking with fever. Eurico tries to get me to drink something, but I cannot force it down my raw throat.

Sometime later, through a feverish haze, I hear Eurico badgering Lako with questions. It is still raining, and they have retreated to their hammocks under the tarp. In such close proximity the drone of their voices grates on me like a dentist's drill. I try to shut them out, but it is no use.

"I thought we might be in trouble," Lako says, "when I heard the caimans barking." Glancing in Eurico's direction, he does his best caiman imitation—a nasal *unkh! unkh! unkh!* "Anyway, that's when I stopped the boat and got my flashlight. As soon as I saw those ruby red eyes I thought, *Uh oh! Where's mama?*"

"How did you know she would be around?" Eurico asks.

"The time of the year for one thing. The start of the rainy season—just about now—is when the caimans hatch. Their mothers are fiercely protective and guard their babies for several months after they hatch, making this a dangerous time to be on the river."

He pauses before adding almost wistfully, "It's not as dangerous as it used to be, for there are not nearly as many black caimans as there once was. Their hides are valuable, and they have been hunted nearly to extinction. A single two-meter hide will bring ninety thousand *cruzéiros* if sold in Cruzeiro do Sul or Tabatinga. That's the equivalent of a month's labor on a rubber estate. I've known hunters to take as many as eighteen or twenty caiman a night, making it a lucrative but dangerous business."

Exhausted, I sleep fitfully for a short while, and when I awake they are still talking. The fire is smoky now, just smoldering in the steady downpour. Occasionally the wind shifts, bringing the smoke under the tarp, causing Lako to curse, but Eurico only laughs. I alternate between violent chills and night sweats, thrashing about in my hammock, praying for morning.

Sleep overtakes me once more, and Diana comes to me in my feverish dreams, a yellow-haired angel whose touch is as soft as air. I reach for her, but she drifts away like fog carried by the wind. She returns sometime later to cool my parched throat with spoonfuls of sweet tea. Her breath is warm on my face, and her words bring me comfort although I can't understand what she is saying.

Sometime later a splitting headache pulls me awake, and I reach for Diana only to discover that it is not her but Eurico who is placing cool cloths on my scorched forehead. My thirst is like a thing alive, but I can only manage a swallow or two before the nausea overwhelms me. Closing my eyes, I search for sleep and for whatever relief can be found in my feverish dreams, longing for the comfort of a woman's touch.

Chapter 25

LIFTING MY HEAD, I try to take in my surroundings, but the room spins out of focus, forcing me to close my eyes and lie back. Just raising my head required a Herculean effort, leaving me weak with exhaustion. Night sweats have soaked the sheets, and the smell of my illness nearly gags me. Turning my head ever so slowly, I try to keep the room in focus. In the far corner there is a small table with a kerosene lamp sitting on it. It is turned low, making the circle of yellow light small and dim; still, it hurts my eyes, spreading needles of pain deep inside my head.

Closing my eyes against the light, I try to figure out where I am and how I got here. My head feels heavy, my thoughts slow and cumbersome. Vaguely I recall Lako holding me as Eurico forced a bitter concoction down my throat, but the details are lost in a thick haze of pain. Later, I remember lying in the bottom of the boat nearly convulsing with chills, the relentless rain striking me in the face, a punishment nearly as cruel as death. The movement of the river beneath the boat was torturous, fever having made my skin as sensitive as an exposed nerve. I tried to cry out, to beg for mercy, but my throat was swollen nearly closed, and my tongue was as stiff as a stick. Falling back, I remember praying to die, so how did I get here?

Sleep slowly reclaims me, and when I awake again, the first hint of daylight is seeping into the room. From another part of the house comes the mummer of voices and the aroma of coffee brewing. Once more I try to lift my head, pausing as a wave of dizziness causes the room to tilt and spin. When it passes, I allow my eyes to sweep the room without moving my head. The lamp has been blown out, and in the rocking chair next to the table someone sleeps beneath a blanket.

The room looks vaguely familiar, and as the darkness recedes I realize that I am back in the house my father built. While I am still trying to get my bearings, the bedroom door opens just a crack. When he sees that I am awake, Eurico steps into the room, smiling broadly. He has brought a cup of coffee and a piece of toast for Diana. He places them on the small table next to the lamp before touching her on the shoulder. She is instantly awake, reaching one slim arm out from beneath the blanket to tousle Eurico's dark hair. He steps away, pretending indifference, but his pleasure is obvious even to me.

Realizing I am awake, Diana steps across the room to lay her hand upon my brow. "Hmm," she says, "it looks like your fever has finally broken." To be sure she thrusts a thermometer under my tongue. While waiting for it to register, she takes my pulse and listens to my lungs. Her touch is purely professional; still, I take pleasure in it. Although I am thankful for her expertise, I am having trouble thinking of her as a doctor.

The sour odor of my illness hangs in the closed air of the bedroom, and I am embarrassed to have her see me this way. I motion for Eurico to open the window, allowing some fresh air into the room. Studying the thermometer, Diana says, "You still have a slight temperature, but I think the worst is behind you." Turning to Eurico, she says, "Go fetch Mrs. Arnold. We're going to give Bryan a bath."

"That won't be necessary," I say, pushing myself up in the bed. In an instant the room begins to spin, and I feel like I am going to faint. Seeing my sudden pallor, she helps me lie back down. "You've had a rough go of it, Bryan, and it's going to take some time for you to get back on your feet."

After the dizziness has subsided a little, I ask, "How long have I been sick? My days and nights all seemed to have run together."

"Five days. Six if you count today."

Returning to the rocking chair, she sits down and takes a sip of her coffee, grimacing when she discovers that it has grown cold. Turning her attention back to me, she says, "You're lucky to be alive. If it hadn't have been for Lako, you probably wouldn't have made it. He brewed a potion from the bark of the cinchona tree and forced you to drink it. That's probably what saved your life."

"He used the bark from what kind of tree?" I ask, amazed by Lako's resourcefulness.

"The cinchona tree; that's where we get quinine."

I hear Eurico return, and in short order he enters the bedroom bringing a cup of coffee and a piece of toast for me. Although I haven't eaten in days, I only take a bite or two of my toast and just a swallow of coffee. The effort leaves me exhausted, and I am thankful when Eurico takes the coffee from me, allowing me to lie back. I am drifting toward sleep when I hear him telling Diana about the crocodile that nearly capsized our boat.

When Eleanor arrives, she and Diana help me out of bed and into the rocking chair. Although they are gentle, I have to grit my teeth to keep from groaning out loud. My joints ache, and my skin is sore to the touch. Once I am settled, Eleanor strips my bed, turns the mattress, and remakes it. While she is doing that, Diana bathes me.

The soapy water is warm, and her touch is gentle. I close my eyes, luxuriating in the moment, the fresh smell of soap replacing the rancid odor of my sickness. She is the consummate medical professional, giving me a sponge bath with practiced skill; still, I find her touch comforting in ways that would be difficult to explain.

Far too soon she is finished, and they help me back into bed. Eleanor fusses over me, fluffing my pillow, adjusting the shutters on the window to redirect the light without limiting the breeze, holding my head up so I can take a sip of water. From across the room Diana watches, faintly amused. I try to hold her with my eyes, but I am too tired. As if from a great distance I hear her bid Eurico good-bye, telling him she will check on me this evening. For the first time in days I am free from fever, and my sleep is untroubled.

Chapter

26

DIANA AND I ARE sitting on the porch, a pitcher of sweet tea on the table between us. It has stopped raining for the first time in days, and above the towering *samaúma* trees the wind is scrubbing the last of the clouds from the sky. Bright bars of late afternoon sunlight filter through the leaves, causing the rain-wet grass to glisten. I've never been a man much given to nature, but the seductive beauty of the Amazonian Rain Forest is working its magic on me.

Before Diana came, I put a close-focusing telephoto lens on my Nikon and roamed around the compound taking close-ups of the colorful flowers. Most of them were unfamiliar to me, but I did recognize some orchids. Viewed through my close-focusing zoom lens, the detail was amazing. Tiny veins stood out in sharp relief against the lighter shades of the petals. By using a wide-open aperture, a fast shutter speed, and a long focal length, I was able to blur the background while the colorful petals, decorated with sparkling beads of water, were in sharp focus. The blending of light and color was truly amazing.

Looking at Diana, I decide that I would like to photograph her, but I don't ask. Instead I compose pictures in my mind as she talks. She is relating some antic Eurico pulled, and her face is full of feeling. I like the way her eyes sparkle when she laughs and the way the setting sun backlights her blonde hair, causing it to shimmer with a dozen different shades. Now she turns serious, a pensive look replacing her early gaiety. She was pretty in the first picture, laughing gaily, but now she is beautiful. I am so absorbed in my imaginary photography that I miss her question.

"I'm sorry," I mumble. "What were you saying?"

Giving me a playful poke, she says, "Pay attention, bud. I was asking you who Carolyn is."

"Carolyn?" I manage, raising my eyebrows questioningly.

"Yes, Carolyn," she says. "When you were delirious with fever, you kept calling for her."

Being careful to keep the feeling out of my voice, I reply, "She's a girl I once knew a long time ago."

Diana looks at me, waiting for me to go on, but when I offer nothing more she turns away.

Her question has spoiled the moment, and now the memory of Carolyn crowds all else from my mind.

We have only been married a week, and I am content in a way I can never remember being. Carolyn is sitting cross-legged on the floor of our one-bedroom apartment, reading to me from a book of poems by Rod McKuen, her voice rising and falling in lyrical cadence. Although I'm not much of one for poetry, I like the sound of her voice and the way she makes me feel when she reads to me. Mostly, I just like being close to her.

Putting the book down, she looks at me, her neediness naked in her eyes. "Bryan," she says, emotion filling her face, "promise me that you will love me forever."

I know what I should say, but she has caught me by surprise, and for the life of me I cannot get the words out. Finally I mumble, "Forever is a long time."

It takes a moment for my words to register, and then she seems to shrink before my eyes. Too late I realize what I have done. In my need to be totally honest I have confirmed her worst fears. I reach to comfort her, but she turns away. Later that night we make love, fiercely, desperately, but for all our passion we cannot undo the damage my words have done. Carolyn clings to me desperately even in sleep, and my shoulder is damp with her tears.

Although I am unable to sleep, I force myself to lie perfectly still lest I wake her. Staring at the ceiling, I can't help thinking how unlike each other we are. I'm an absolute pragmatist. She's a hopeless romantic. I'm stoic. She's sentimental. I haven't shed a tear in twenty years. She cries over anything—weddings, movies, even poems. In a way that is still wordless and unacknowledged, I know that our marriage is doomed. It is not our differences that will do us in, but our hurts. Hers have made her needy; mine have made me indifferent. She tries too hard, while I hardly try at all. She is clingy, while I am emotionally distant—hardly the stuff of which healthy relationships are made.

With an effort, I push Carolyn from my mind and focus on the present. Having turned away a moment ago, Diana is now staring across the mission compound, a faraway look in her eyes. Hoping to recapture our earlier camaraderie, I reach for the pitcher of tea and refill our glasses. Extending her glass toward her, I say, "Sweet tea for a sweet lady." She gives me a tremulous smile before reaching for her glass. When I hand it to her, our fingers touch, giving me an unexpected pleasure. She must have felt it also, for there is a spot of color in her cheeks as she takes a sip of her tea.

Studying her, I think, *It's been a long time since I have felt this way about a woman, and it scares me. Even if Diana feels the same way—and I have no reason to think she does—there's no future for us. She's a missionary, and I don't even know if I believe in God anymore, not to mention the fact that I'm divorced.*

Smiling at me over her glass, she says, "A penny for your thoughts."

"Don't throw your money away," I reply, grinning sheepishly. "They're not worth it."

"Why don't you let me be the judge of that?"

Hoping to turn her attention away from me, I get to my feet, saying, "Let's walk to the river. Having been incapacitated for the past few days, I'm starting to feel restless."

"Are you sure you're up to it?" she asks, her concern evident.

"I think so. Besides, if I get tired, we can always come back."

"Okay. Just let me step inside and get a flashlight. As you've probably noticed, night comes quickly in the Amazon."

Once we are out of sight of the mission houses, I take her hand, enjoying the warmth of her skin next to mine. We walk slowly, for I am not nearly as strong as I thought I was. When we reach the river at last, it is nearly dark, a sliver of moon hanging just above the water. Slipping my arm around her waist, I pull her close to me. Nestling against my side, she rests her head against my shoulder.

As much as I am enjoying the moment, I suddenly feel faint. Taking my arm, Diana guides me to an uprooted tree that has been deposited high on the sandbar by an earlier flood. Easing me to the ground, she says, "Lean back against the tree; you'll feel better in a few minutes." I lay my head back and close my eyes. She places her hand on my forehead, checking for fever. "Malaria," she explains, "is a dangerous disease. Its effects linger long after the initial fever has passed."

After a moment she grows quiet, and we sit in silence, the murmur of the river and the calling of night birds are the only sounds. Thinking about it, I realize that this is one of the things I like most about her. She's as comfortable with silence as I am.

Although I would simply like to enjoy the moment, I cannot still my anxious thoughts. I can't help thinking that I'm being unfair to her, that I'm taking advantage of her somehow. She's lonely and vulnerable living in this remote place, and I'm probably the first man her age that she's seen in months, maybe a year or two. I can't help wondering if she would be interested in me if we had met under different circumstances. More important, what interest would she have in me if she knew that I had been married before?

I don't want to hurt her, and though it pains me to admit it, I know I'm a troubled man, not fit company for any woman. If we don't end this relationship now, someone is going to get hurt, and hurt bad; probably both of us. God only knows what possessed me to let my feelings get so far out of hand. It won't be easy, but after tonight I'm determined to go back to just being friends. I feel bad for her, but it's for the best. Who knows, she's probably thinking the same thing herself.

Pulling her close, I kiss the top of her head. "I suppose we ought to be getting back. It's late, and I'm terribly tired."

We make our way, hand in hand, up the trail toward the mission compound. Knowing this will undoubtedly be the last time we ever do anything like this, I savor every moment. Just before we step out from under the trees, Diana turns to me. "Thank you, Bryan, for a wonderful evening." Standing on her tiptoes, she brushes my lips with a kiss, and then she is gone. I watch until she unlocks her door and steps inside. Then I turn toward Whittaker House, a heavy sadness making my throat ache.

Chapter

27

IT'S LATE SATURDAY AFTERNOON, and Rob's desk is covered with books, commentaries, and several translations of the Bible, but his sermon notes are in shambles. He usually has his sermon finished by Thursday afternoon, but not this week. Try as he might he simply hasn't been able to pull anything together. Tossing his pen on the desk, he puts his head in his hands.

It's been four days since Helen returned from Denver, and he is no longer sleeping on the couch, but he might as well be. There have been no outbursts of anger since that first night, just an unnatural politeness. Household duties are carried out by rote, family obligations fulfilled, daily tasks completed, but it is like they are sleepwalking. And the hurt never goes away.

They are speaking to each other again, but carefully lest they inflict some new hurt, and in some ways their guardedness is more painful than anything they might say. They make small talk, try to pretend everything is as it should be, but there is a deadness in their voices, a tragic reminder of what is happening—a thing from which their marriage may never recover. Jake and Robbie are bewildered. They creep through the house on tiptoe hardly ever raising their voices above a whisper.

Opening his desk drawer, Rob extracts the infamous telephone bill and studies it for the hundredth time, trying to divine something from the now familiar list of numbers. If Helen won't tell him whom she's been calling, maybe he should just contact the telephone company and see what he can learn. Or better yet, why not just call the number in Denver himself and see who answers. But he cannot bring himself to do that, so he drops the bill back in the drawer.

Restless, he gets to his feet and walks across the office to stare out the window. In the park across the street a group of boys are playing football, but he hardly sees them. In his mind he is reviewing thirteen years of marriage.

It's not the special moments he remembers, not the anniversary dinners or the foreign vacation, but the mundane details. Little things, which at first glance hardly seem worth mentioning, yet as the years have gone by they have become daily rituals, little gestures of love that set his heart to singing. He remembers the simple pleasure of coming home to familiar sounds—the hum of the vacuum cleaner, bathwater running, and conversation from the other room. And he remembers the smells—skin cream and shampoo, clothes fresh from the dryer, furniture polish, and coffee brewing.

It's not that these things have ceased to exist, but without love they are no longer special. Now sounds are just sounds, and smells are just smells, nothing holy or sacred about them at all. Bathwater running is just that, nothing more, and furniture polish smells sterile, antiseptic, not like love at all. "Oh, Helen," he whispers, "what have we done? What have we done?"

Hearing someone rummaging around in the outer office, he goes to see who it is. "Rita, what are you doing here on a Saturday afternoon?"

Giving him a warm smile, she replies, "I might ask you the same question. Aren't you supposed to be cooking out in the backyard or playing football with the boys or something like that?"

"Helen took the boys to the school carnival, so I thought I would try to finish my sermon."

"Don't you usually do your sermons on Thursday?"

Grimacing, he replies, "It's been a rough week. I haven't been able to get my thoughts together."

"Is there anything I can do to help? Can I make you a cup of coffee or go out and get you a sandwich?"

"No, I don't think so. I'm not hungry, and I've already had way too much coffee."

Putting her hand on his arm, Rita asks, "What is it, Rob?"

Taking a seat on the corner of her desk, Rob stares into space. Finally he says in a tired voice, "Things aren't going very well at home."

"Oh," she murmurs, "I'm really sorry to hear that. The ministry can be so hard on a marriage."

"I'm afraid it's more than that..." his voice trails off.

"What do you mean?"

Without replying, Rob walks back into his office. Rita hesitates just a moment before following him. "Please shut the door, Rita. I don't think anyone will be coming in on a Saturday, but I don't want to take a chance of anyone overhearing us."

Taking the phone bill from his drawer, he hands it to her. She quickly examines it and then looks at Rob questioningly. "Is there something in particular I'm supposed to see?"

His embarrassment evident, he points out the almost daily calls to the same number in Denver. "Oh," Rita says again, flashing back to her experience with her unfaithful husband and his duplicity. "Does this mean what I think it means?"

"All I know for sure is that Helen has been making regular calls to that number in Denver for the past few weeks. When I confronted her, she got angry and refused to discuss it. I fear the worst, but I don't want to believe it." He turns away and walks to the window, not wanting Rita to see the tears now clouding his vision.

"Do you know whose number this is?"

"No. I haven't been able to bring myself to do any investigating. Just the thought of it seems like a betrayal of Helen...even our marriage."

"Why don't you call the phone company and contest the charges. That way they will have to tell you the name of the person she's been calling."

"You know I can't do that. This is a small town, and I'm a prominent pastor. If word of this got out, it would cause a scandal."

Sighing, she says, "You're right. I hadn't thought of that." As an afterthought she asks, "Have you thought about calling the number to see who answers the phone?"

"What good would that do? Unless I'm willing to identify myself and explain why I'm calling, it seems like a waste of time to me."

"I guess you're right. So what are you going to do?"

"I don't know, what I can do except hang in there and hope Helen comes to her senses."

Overwhelmed with grief, Rob stumbles to the couch. As he buries his face in his hand, his shoulders shake with silent sobs. Sitting down beside him, Rita puts her hand on his shoulder. "It will be all right, Rob, believe me I know. Right now it feels like the end of the world, but it's not. It's not."

Chapter

28

PLACING HER STEAMING CUP of Earl Grey tea on a coaster, Helen sits down in her favorite chair. Curling her feet under her, she sighs with exhaustion. Being a wife and mother is demanding enough, but it's the emotional stress that is wearing her out. For the first time since she married Rob thirteen years ago, she feels completely alone. She needs a friend, someone she can talk to, someone she can confide in, but she has no one. There are several ladies in the church whom she considers friends, but she wouldn't dare confide in them. Even as angry as she is, she would never do anything that might hurt Rob's ministry.

Silent tears stain her cheeks as she sips her tea. The children are in bed, and she is alone again. Rob probably won't be home until ten o'clock, maybe later, depending on how the board meeting goes. Not that it matters. Even when he's home he's not really here. She probably should talk to him about that stupid phone bill, but every time she thinks about it she gets mad. How dare he question her faithfulness? If she is honest with herself, she has to admit that her stubborn silence is only making things worse. Even knowing that, she still can't bring herself to make the first move. Whittaker pride, she supposes, the curse of her genes.

There's really only one person she can talk to, only one person with whom she feels safe—Carolyn. But calling her probably isn't wise. Who knows what Rob might do when he discovers she's been calling Denver again. On the other hand, what does it matter? He doesn't trust her anyway.

Picking up the phone, she carries it back to her favorite chair, grateful that the phone has a twenty-foot cord. Nervously she dials the number and listens impatiently as it rings—four times, five times, six times. She is just about to hang up when Carolyn answers with a breathless hello.

"It's me, Helen. Are you busy, or can we talk for a few minutes?"

"We can talk. Just give me a minute to catch my breath. I was just finishing my exercises."

In the background Helen can hear the canned laughter of a television sit-com, and she pictures Carolyn in leotards with a towel around her neck. Considering her own lanky frame, she experiences a moment of envy as she remembers Carolyn's petite figure. *Oh well*, she thinks, *there's nothing I can do about it. Being lanky is as much a part of my Whittaker genes as my temperament.*

Gulping a diet drink, Carolyn says, "You haven't received another letter from Bryan, have you?"

"No, I haven't heard from him. Not that I expected to."

Now that she has Carolyn on the phone, she doesn't know where to start. How does she tell a virtual stranger the most intimate details of her life? Yet if she doesn't tell someone, she doesn't think she can go on. Taking a deep breath, she begins. "Carolyn, there's something I need to talk about, and I don't have anyone else. Do you mind?"

"Of course not. What's troubling you?"

"It's Rob," she says, emotion choking her. "He thinks I'm having an affair."

"What? Are you kidding me?"

"I only wish I were."

"So help me here. Why does Rob think you're cheating on him?"

"Who knows? There's probably a number of things. I've been battling depression, and Rob doesn't know how to cope with it. One thing has led to another, and we have just seemed to drift apart." Her voice fades, leaving her thoughts unfinished.

Finally Carolyn says, "It still doesn't make much sense. Is there something you're not telling me?"

Sobbing softly, Helen tells her about the telephone bill and Bryan's letter. She concludes by telling her that Rob knows nothing about their friendship.

For two or three minutes neither of them speaks, and then Carolyn asks, "Why don't you explain things to Rob? Just tell him that you've been calling me. I'll vouch for you."

"I can't! It would be like admitting I've done something wrong, and I haven't."

"That's silly, Helen. You don't want to let this go on. These things have a way of getting out of hand; they seem to take on a life of their own, and before you know it you're no longer in control of your life."

"There's nothing I can do—"

"Helen, get hold of yourself. This isn't just about you. You have two boys to think about."

At the mention of the boys, Helen wavers. Their well-being is more important to her than her own, and she cannot deny that they are suffering. Robbie, always a sound sleeper, now wakes up crying almost every night. And Jake is constantly getting in trouble at school, mostly for fighting.

"It's not that easy, Carolyn. And I haven't even told you the worst part."

"There's more?"

"Rob may be involved with someone else."

"Why in the world would you think that?"

"He has started working late, and we never make love anymore."

Thoughtfully Carolyn replies, "Obviously things could be better between you and Rob, but that doesn't mean he's having an affair. He's a minister, for heaven's sake!"

"I overheard him talking with someone on the phone, and when I asked him about it, he refused to discuss it."

"Did he say something incriminating?"

"No, I mean I don't know. The door was closed, so I couldn't make out what he was saying. But I can tell you, he sure got a funny look on his face when I walked in."

"That's all you've got?" Carolyn asks incredulously. "And you conclude he's having an affair?"

Slightly annoyed, Helen demands, "What else do I need?"

"Listen to yourself, Helen. You're doing the very thing Rob did; you're jumping to conclusions. He could have been talking to anyone—his mother, a member of the congregation, anyone."

"Whose side are you on?"

"Yours, of course, but that doesn't mean I'm supposed to let you do something foolish in the heat of emotion." When Helen doesn't respond, she continues. "When things got rough for Bryan and me, I began interpreting everything he did in the worst possible light.

Before long I had convinced myself that divorce was the only answer and that it was entirely Bryan's fault. Too late, I now realize that divorce didn't solve anything."

"I'm not considering divorce," Helen replies defensively. "It's not an option when you're in the ministry, unless you want to lose everything you have—your reputation, your ministry, your income."

"So what are you going to do?"

"I'm not sure. Maybe things will get better on their own. Maybe Rob will come to his senses and apologize—"

Frustrated, Carolyn says, "I'm hardly qualified to give you advice, considering the mess I've made of my own life." Pausing, an idea occurs to her, and she asks, "Helen, you're a minister's wife. What kind of counsel would you give someone in your situation?"

Talking with Carolyn has helped, and for the first time in days Helen is able to sort through her feelings without being overwhelmed. Pondering Carolyn's question, she tries to think rationally, objectively. Musing, she says, "That puts it in a different light, doesn't it? What would I advise someone in my situation? Hmm…

"I think I would tell her that you can't punish your husband without destroying yourself, and that if you insist on holding onto your hurts you will wreck your marriage. I'd tell her that refusing to forgive your husband in order to make him suffer is crazy. It's like drinking poison and expecting your husband to die. With God's help you need to forgive him and move on. If you can't do it for your husband, or even for yourself, you should do it for your marriage and for your children. Bottom line, I would tell her to let it go and get on with her life."

Lifting her eyebrows questioningly, Carolyn says, "So…"

CHAPTER
29

EURICO AND I ARE on the porch packing supplies when I see an Indian enter the mission compound and jog to the clinic where Diana is treating patients. Slipping off the porch, I walk to a vantage point outside her window where I can watch him. Pushing his way into the examining room, he gestures for her to come with him. Using a combination of Portuguese and a Kachinawa dialect, he explains that his wife has been in labor two days, but still hasn't been able to give birth. Concern clouds Diana's features as she realizes that both the mother and baby could be in danger. Moving quickly, she puts together a medical kit. It is already early afternoon, and if she is going to reach the village before dark there is no time to waste.

Rejoining Eurico, I can't help thinking that this emergency could not have come at a more inopportune time. Gordon Arnold has gone to Cruzeiro for supplies, and Lako is upriver trying to locate some sign of the Amuacas, leaving no one available to go with Diana. She has likely made similar trips alone, but it doesn't seem like a very good idea to me.

Glancing up, I see her approaching. "Bryan," she calls, hurrying toward Eurico and me. "May I have a word with you?"

Stepping off the porch, I go to meet her. "What's on your mind?"

"There's a medical emergency in the Kachinawa village about three hours from here. I was wondering if you could spare Eurico to go with me. As late as it is, we probably won't be back until sometime tomorrow."

On an impulse I say, "How about if Eurico and I both go? Now that I'm feeling stronger, I'm starting to get cabin fever hanging around here."

I can see that my offer both surprises and pleases her. Since our river walk I have been avoiding her, and on those occasions when circumstances have thrown us together, I have been painfully polite. It is obvious that she would like to take me up on my offer, but she cannot in good conscience allow me to come along. I have not yet fully recovered from my recent bout with malaria, and better than anyone she knows how grueling the trip will be. Shaking her head, she says, "Thank you for the offer, but I can't let you do that. Medically speaking, it wouldn't be a good idea. You could have a setback."

Before she can finish, I interrupt her. "Well, if I do have a setback, expert medical attention will be readily available. Give us fifteen minutes, and Eurico and I will be ready to go." She starts to protest, but I have already turned back toward Whittaker House.

It is raining lightly as we enter the forest a few minutes later, packs on our backs. We are walking single file behind the Kachinawan, and I am bringing up the rear. He is naked except for a loincloth. In his left hand he carries a sharp machete, which he wields with a casual expertise, clearing the crooked trail for us. Although it is steep and muddy, he moves at a rapid clip. Neither Eurico nor Diana seems to have any trouble keeping up, but my lungs are already on fire, and I feel light-headed. Gritting my teeth, I force myself to keep pace.

The first fifteen or twenty minutes are torturous for me, but after a while I seem to fall into a mind-numbing rhythm. Putting one foot in front of the other, I plod on, the steady rain dripping off the brim of my hat. Up ahead, Eurico and Diana carry on a running conversation. I cannot make out what they are saying, but from time to time Eurico's high-spirited laughter drifts back to me. Shaking my head in amazement, I think, *Is there no end to his optimism? Would to God I had just a measure of his spirit.*

We have been walking for the better part of two hours when I realize it is growing dark. Glancing at my wristwatch, I note that it is too early for nightfall. Belatedly, I realize that the steady rain is giving way to a full-fledged storm. Overhead, thunder claps, and lightning streaks across the sky. Soon we have to lean into the wind to keep from losing our footing, and the driving rain stings like pellets. Our ponchos offer some protection, but not much, and I desperately search the rugged terrain for some kind of shelter.

The trail ahead of me is dark, making it impossible to get more than a glimpse of either Diana or Eurico, except in the sudden glare of lightning. Once or twice I see Diana look back to check on me in the flare of light. I'm grateful for her concern, for the heavy rain has turned the muddy trail slick, making for treacherous footing. More than once I have had to hang onto the vines and branches bordering the trail to keep from going down. Surely we will have to stop soon. No one can keep going in a storm like this.

But keep going we do, for another hour and a half, and the storm never lets up. I take a nasty fall when we start down the far side of the ridge, cutting my hand on something sharp. Probably a thorn or a rock, but it's too dark to tell. By now I am tired and past the point of caring. Blindly, I put one foot in front of the other, cursing the day I decided to come to this wretched place. When I am sure I cannot take another step, we enter a clearing where there is a *maloca*, a native longhouse.

Motioning Diana to the door at the near end of the *maloca*, the Kachinawan leads Eurico and me to another door at the opposite end. He is trying to tell us something, but I cannot hear him above the roar of the wind and the pounding of the rain. Finally, he takes me by the arm and shoves me into the *maloca* where I collapse on the floor in exhaustion. Squatting beside me, Eurico looks around, his eyes bright with interest. Reaching into his pack, he extracts a chunk of dried fish and begins eating. Hunger gnaws at my belly, but I cannot summon the energy to eat.

As my eyes adjust to the dim light, I realize that we are in a large room open to the steeply slanting roof. Although I am not good at estimating distance, I would guess that it is nearly twenty-five meters in length and about fifteen meters in width. As best I can tell, it is a sort of communal house shared by a number of families. Several Indians stare at us with unabashed curiosity, and once again I try to imagine why my father would be willing to risk his life for these illerate Indians who live as if it is still the Stone Age.

After motioning for us to stay put, the Kachinawan hurries to the far end of the longhouse where Diana waits. He says something to her and then turns, and she follows him to a room-like compartment located against the back wall where an obviously pregnant young woman is writhing in pain. The compartment is situated fairly close to the door where we entered, and from our vantage point we have a clear view of what is happening.

Working with practiced efficiency, Diana examines the woman, all the while talking to herself in English. "This doesn't look good. I can see the baby's bottom in the birth canal, and if I am not mistaken his legs are crossed Indian-style." The mother is on her hands and knees, pushing with each contraction, but to no avail. It appears the baby is simply too large to be born breech.

Placing her stethoscope on the mother's belly, Diana checks the baby's heartbeat. Grimacing, she hastily extracts a scalpel from her kit and quickly performs an episiotomy in a desperate attempt to enlarge the birth opening. The Indian woman screams in pain and lashes out at Diana, catching her in the face with the back of her hand. Rubbing her cheek, Diana places herself directly behind the mother and tries to manipulate the baby. It's a desperate move, but with the baby's heart beating erratically she doesn't have much choice. There's little or no chance of success, but she must do something; after two days of hard labor, both mother and child are in grave danger.

I have no idea how long Diana continues her desperate vigil, for sleep overtakes me. I try to stay awake to provide what moral support I can, but it is no use. Exhausted, I slump against the wall and fall into a troubled sleep. Sometime later I am jerked awake by the mournful wail of Indians singing the death chant, a wail so excruciatingly painful that listening to it is like looking into the abyss. Apparently both the mother and her baby have died.

Diana is sitting off to one side, alone, her face a suffering mask in the flickering light. Never have I seen anyone look so desolate, and my heart goes out to her. She is crying, silent sobs shaking her hunched shoulders. I move to comfort her, but she turns away, a prisoner of her grief. Exhaustion finally overcomes her, and I lay her head in my lap and cover her with my poncho. She sleeps fitfully, troubled by dreams that cause her to whimper and cry out. "I'm sorry," she says over and over again. "Mommy is so sorry."

CHAPTER
30

MORNING IS JUST A smear of light on the rim of the sky when we slip out of the longhouse and turn toward the mission compound. Although the rain has ceased, the ground is totally saturated, and wisps of low-lying fog float among the trees, giving the rain forest a surreal appearance. Eurico and I munch on pieces of smoked fish as we start up the steep trail, but Diana refuses to eat. We climb slowly, weariness weighing us down as much as the heavy mud that collects on our hiking boots. Directly in front of me is Diana, and although she does not slow us down, it is obvious that last night's failure weighs heavy upon her. Why anyone should care so much about an unknown Indian baby and his illiterate mother escapes me, but it is obvious that she does. Not even Eurico can coax a smile out of her.

Blindly, she forces herself to put one foot in front of the other, oblivious to her surroundings. As she climbs the muddy trail, she is lost in her thoughts, in memories she believed she had forever put behind her when she came to the Amazon. Now she cannot exorcise them no matter how hard she tries. Against her will, she finds herself reliving the past...

Opening the door on the passenger's side of the station wagon, the large woman motions for Diana to get in. After closing the door firmly, she walks around to the driver's side of the car and slides under the steering wheel. Out of the corner of her eye Diana sees another person in the back seat, but she can't tell whether it is a man or a woman. She wants to turn around and look, but she is afraid of appearing too curious.

Without warning, the unidentified person leans forward and places a thick black patch over each of Diana's eyes and quickly ties a cloth strip around her head to hold them in place. "I wish we didn't have to do this," a female voice says, "but we can't take any chances."

Fear makes Diana's heart pound, and her breath comes in ragged little gasps. This can't be happening to me, she thinks, it can't. As if from a great distance, she hears the engine starting. She senses the motion of the car as they turn onto the street, and she can't help wondering where they are taking her, not that it really matters. Desperately she tries to empty her mind, tries to expel the malignant thoughts that feed her fears, but she is powerless against her abused imagination. With cruel persistence it gives birth to a host of unwelcome questions. What if the abortionist isn't really a doctor, just a hack? She doesn't really have any way of knowing. She doesn't even know his name. Gary managed to get a telephone number from a friend he worked with, but beyond his recommendation they know nothing. What if he injures her, makes it impossible for her to bear children?

Fear enflames her imagination, and she suddenly has a vision of herself, a petrified, shivering creature, lying on an examining table in an emergency room. She is bleeding profusely and moaning softly. With a desperate determination she forces the image from her mind only to find it replaced by an equally sinister one. Now she is pinched-faced, prematurely old, and childless. Her friends are talking about her, whispering behind their hands. "Poor thing," they say, "she can't have children. Something happened when she was just a young woman. Who knows…"

When Diana is sure she cannot bear the suffocating blindness a moment more, the car finally turns into a driveway and comes to a stop. Quickly the two women help her from the car and up the back steps. Although the eye patches prevent her from seeing anything, she has the distinct impression she is not in a doctor's office or a medical clinic. Rather than the antiseptic odor so common to hospitals and clinics, she smells food cooking, and faintly, from another room, she hears what sounds like a television playing.

Leading her into a small room, the large woman brusquely tells her to undress from the waist down. After she has done so, the large woman helps her onto a cold table and unceremoniously places her feet in a pair of metal stirrups before scooting her hips almost off the end of the table. A wave of embarrassment washes over Diana, and her face feels flushed. Never has she felt so exposed, so vulnerable.

Finally, the doctor comes in and takes her medical history. Without any attempt to put her at ease he shoots his questions at her rapid fire. Is this her first abortion? Has she been pregnant before? When was her last period? Is she allergic to any drugs? Although his manner is not unkind, it isn't caring either. She is left feeling more like a customer than a patient, a non-person really.

The ever-present black patches prevent her from seeing anything; still, she senses what is happening around her. The large woman is behind her, ready to hold her on the table should the pain become unbearable. The unidentified woman from the back seat is assisting the doctor. Diana hears him ask for dilators and experiences severe cramping as he begins enlarging her cervix. Once that is done he calls for a curette and she feels him cutting and scraping inside her uterus. The pain is nearly unbearable, and she grips the table, biting her lip to keep from crying out.

As if in a dream she hears the doctor ask, "Have we got it all?" And after a moment a woman's voice answers, "I don't think so. I can only find one arm."

The doctor curses softly as he goes back to work with a cruel urgency. The pain is so great Diana thinks she is going to pass out. It feels like she is being *ripped apart as he scrapes and probes in search of the offending member. Finally she hears him mutter, "Here it is. I've got it."*

After the doctor leaves, she is given a single sanitary napkin to absorb the bleeding. The large woman helps her get dressed before leading her to a back room where she lies on a cot. Never has she felt so alone or so ashamed. In the darkness she sobs softly, but finds no relief. With haunting repetition the woman's words echo in her mind: "I can only find one arm...I can only find one arm..."

When the big woman finally returns, she is aghast to discover that Diana's clothing and the cot on which she is lying are soaked with blood. Cursing, she hurries out of the room, returning momentarily with the other woman in tow. Quickly they help Diana change sanitary napkins, in an effort to absorb the bleeding, all the while arguing in angry whispers.

"We've got to get her out of here, and quick."

"Yeah, but where are we going to take her? We can't take her back to her boyfriend like this. It's too dangerous."

"If we don't get her to a hospital immediately..." the big woman doesn't finish.

"Let's get her into the car," the other woman replies, "and then we'll decide what to do."

As if from a great distance Diana hears them arguing, but she can't relate it to herself. She seems swathed in great bands of gauze that give everything a certain surrealism. Everything feels like it is filtered through layers and layers of insulation. It is like a dream, a terrifying dream, in which she can only move in slow motion.

Helping her to her feet, the two women support her as they make their way down the back steps and toward the car. Once they have her settled on the back seat, the unidentified woman takes command. "Find a public telephone, and we'll call for a taxi. The cab driver can take her to the hospital."

In a kind of detached way Diana realizes that her life is ebbing away with each drop of blood she loses. Yet, she isn't afraid, not really. She almost welcomes death, the same way she now embraces her searing pain. It is her just due, a kind of penance for what she has done. An abortion shouldn't be painless, *she thinks.* I should suffer the same way my baby suffered. *And again the haunting words,* "I can only find one arm...I can only find one arm..."

Death looms before her, a wide dark chasm, and, on the far shore, a beautiful little girl is calling to her. She is perfect in every way, except that she has only one arm. Golden curls surround a cherubic face set off with bright turquoise blue eyes, her impish mouth is spread wide in a beautiful smile, and with her one arm she reaches for Diana. "Mommy," *she cries.* "Mommy!"

Diana must have passed out, because the next thing she remembers is hearing voices arguing in the shadowy light of a distant streetlamp. "All you have to do is take her to the hospital," *the unidentified woman says.* "No one will hold you responsible for anything."

"And what if she dies in my cab?" *a man's voice demands.* "What then?"

The woman's voice, impatient now. "She's not going to die in your cab!"

"You can't guarantee that," *he replies, growing angry.* "Look, there's blood all over your seat."

"We can't stand here arguing all night. I'll pay you a hundred dollars to take her to the emergency room. All you have to do is take her and leave."

"Not on your life, lady. I'm not getting involved in this. Not for a measly hundred dollars. Not for five hundred dollars."

With that he returns to his cab, guns his engine, and is gone. Returning to the station wagon, the unidentified woman is confronted by the driver who demands, "What are we going to do now?"

On the back seat Diana drifts in and out of consciousness. She isn't really afraid, not anymore. Death is no longer an enemy to be feared, but a welcome friend. In death she will be free from this awful pain. In death she will be reunited with her baby. She will explain to her what really happened. "Mommy really wanted you, sweetheart, but there were circumstances beyond her control. And Mommy never knew they were going to hurt you. Please believe me. I would never let anyone hurt you."

The voices rise again, tense, arguing.

"If we don't do something soon, she's going to die."

"Don't you think I know that?"

"Let's just go to a cheap motel and check in using a false name. We can put her in bed and leave. No one will ever be the wiser."

"Don't you care what happens to her?"

"Of course I care. But I'm a realist. It's too late for her. Even if we get her to a hospital, she won't live."

"The motel's out! I won't leave her to die. That could be my daughter back there."

"So what are we going to do?"

"We're going to drive her to the nearest hospital and leave her at the emergency room entrance."

"Are you crazy? What if someone sees us?"

"Don't argue with me. Just drive."

The motion of the car initiates a fresh spasm of pain, and Diana moans in agony. She tries to pray, but can't. After years of religious conditioning she feels she has been cut off from the mercies of God. She has committed a mortal sin. She killed she feels she has been baby. God will not hear her prayer. Death is no longer a welcome escape, but simply a prelude to eternal damnation. She must not die, not now, not yet.

With a desperate determination she fights to remain conscious while the station wagon speeds through the dark streets. Pain is her ally now, and she *clings to it the way a frightened child clings to her mother's hand. As long as she writhes in pain, she is still conscious, still alive. She must hang on until they reach the hospital.*

At last they turn a corner and slow to a stop, half a block from the emergency room entrance. "This is as close as we dare to get," says the driver. "Any closer, and there's a good chance someone will see us."

The unidentified woman quickly takes the bulb from the car's dome light and shoves it into her coat pocket. "There's no sense in taking a chance on someone getting a good look at our faces," she reasons. Opening the rear door of the station wagon, she bends down and grasps Diana by the shoulders. "Can you hear me?" she whispers urgently. When Diana groans an acknowledgement, she continues. "You're in serious trouble. If you don't see a doctor immediately, you will bleed to death. Do you understand me?"

Diana manages a hoarse, "Yes."

"You are less than half a block from the hospital's emergency room entrance. We can't get you any closer without taking a chance on being seen. We're going to help you out of the car, then you're on your own. Give us thirty seconds before you remove the blindfold."

Without giving her a chance to reply, they clumsily drag her out of the car. The movement causes her excruciating pain, and a wave of darkness threatens to engulf her. The concrete is cold and hard against her back, in sharp contrast to the warmth of her life's blood that soaks her slacks. Vaguely she hears a car driving away, and she reaches up to remove the blindfold. For the first time in several hours she can see, but it is hard to focus.

She feels light-headed, and it takes her a minute to become acclimated to her surroundings. With an effort she forces herself to think, to remember. She is bleeding a lot, that much she does know, and if she doesn't get help immediately, she will die. The pool of yellow light spilling across the concrete some distance away must be the emergency room entrance, *she thinks.* I've got to make it that far.

Taking a deep breath, she pushes herself to her knees where she pauses, swaying dizzily for several seconds, while she waits for her head to clear. Eventually, she is able to make it to her feet. Desperately she focuses on the distant pool of light. If I can just make it that far, *she thinks,* they will save me.

After a half-dozen stumbling steps she feels herself falling. The cold sidewalk comes rushing up to meet her, and she lets out a painful whimper as she hits the concrete. Nearly soundless sobs shake her limp body as she lies there in the dark. Like a person who is freezing to death, she is tempted to just lie there, to simply give in to the beckoning black oblivion. It would be so easy. All her troubles would be over. With an effort she pushes the seducing darkness away. She must not die, not now, not yet.

Once more she fights through her painful weakness and staggers to her feet. A wave of nausea washes over her, and she thinks she is going to pass out. With a desperation born of fear she clings to consciousness and somehow manages to keep from falling. Weakly she puts one foot in front of the other. "Concentrate," *she tells herself.* "One step at a time. You can do it."

The pale, hunched-over creature, who now struggles toward the distant pool of light, in no way resembles the vivacious young woman she was just hours ago. Now she trails dark drops of her life's blood on the sidewalk behind her and fights to still the accusing voices inside her head.

Every four or five steps, she is forced to stop in order to regain her strength. "Please, God," *she prays,* "don't let me die like this. Send someone to help me." *But no one comes, and once more she wills herself to push one foot in front of the other. Just fifteen more feet, she thinks, stumbling. Just eight more feet... But her strength is gone, and she feels herself falling.*

We are descending an unusually steep portion of the trail when Diana stumbles and falls. Before I can get to her, she begins to slide down the mountain toward the rain-swollen stream a hundred feet below. Picking up speed, she bounces off trees and brush as she continues her downward plunge. Desperate to save her, I leap down the mountain after her. My frantic rush soon causes me to lose my balance on the steep and uneven terrain, and I find myself tumbling down the mountainside. After plunging about fifty feet, I manage to stop myself when I hit a particularly tangled mass of vegetation. Clearing my head, I look around and spot Diana lying in a heap about fifteen or twenty feet below me, unmoving. Already Eurico is carefully working his way down the mountain toward us. Although I am badly bruised, I don't think anything is broken. Pushing myself up, I free myself from the tangle of vines and make my way toward Diana, fearing the worst.

Chapter

31

ALTHOUGH EVERY PART OF my body is hurting, I pay it no mind. My only concern is for the yellow-haired woman who lies in a twisted heap, just above a sheer drop-off, about twenty feet down the mountain from me. Glancing up toward the trail, I see Eurico carefully working his way toward us. The mud is slick, making the footing treacherous, and he has to descend on all fours. I am using the same technique to work my way across the mountain and down to where Diana lies in a tangle of vines and undergrowth. The thought that she might be seriously injured, perhaps fatally, causes my heart to race, and I am nearly sick with fear.

Kneeling beside her, I am relieved to see that she is breathing. A gash on the side of her head is bleeding profusely, and her leg is bent at a grotesque angle. Carefully I ease myself into position just above her. Bracing my feet against some roots that are protruding from the mountainside, I put my hands under her arms and pull her toward me. She groans painfully as I ease her into a better position, and I am thankful that she is still unconscious or the pain would be excruciating.

Easing down beside me, Eurico stares at Diana's blood-soaked hair and her pasty white face, his eyes wide with concern. "Will she be all right?" he asks, his voice sounding small and frightened.

I try to reassure him, but I don't have the strength. Now that the adrenaline rush is subsiding, I feel faint. My head is ringing, and there is a roaring in my ears. Lying back against the mountain, I rest my head on the muddy ground and try to stop the sky above the towering trees from tilting and spinning. A wave of nausea knots my belly, forcing me to swallow several times to keep from vomiting. As if from a great distance I hear Eurico's voice, frantic with concern. "Bryan. Bryan…"

I must have passed out, at least momentarily, for when I come to, Eurico is bathing my face with a piece of cloth torn from his shirt. *How*, I wonder, *did he get it wet? Surely he didn't risk his life to climb down to the storm-swollen stream.* Before I can think to ask him, my thoughts begin to drift, and try as I might I cannot focus. Vaguely I recall that Diana is injured, and I force myself to sit up. The mountain tips dangerously, forcing me to grab for Eurico. He steadies me until the worst of the dizziness passes.

A blinding headache causes me to squint against the weak light that filters through the canopy of leaves overhead. Not surprisingly, it has started to rain again, making a miserable situation even more difficult. Diana is still unconscious, and Eurico is looking toward me for guidance. I must have suffered a concussion, for I'm having trouble thinking clearly. Concentrating, I manage to tell Eurico to gather two or three handfuls of moss. While he is doing that, I rip my T-shirt into strips. We place the moss on Diana's head wound to staunch the bleeding and hold it in place by wrapping her head in the strips of cloth from my T-shirt.

We are going to have to have help. On the best of days I would have trouble getting Diana back to the trail, but given my own condition it is impossible. Not only am I weak from my recent bout with malaria, I am also badly bruised from my tumble down the mountain.

One knee is throbbing painfully, and I can hardly bend it. If the truth be known, I may need help getting back to the mission compound myself. I wish I could remember when Lako planned to return. Without his help we are going to be in real trouble.

"Eurico," I ask, trying not to let my anxiety show, "do you think you can find your way back to the mission compound?" He nods vigorously, trying to reassure himself as much as me. "Bring Lako back with you, Gordon Arnold also if he has returned from Cruzeiro. We will need a stretcher for Diana and a crutch or some kind of walking stick for me. I think Diana has a broken leg, so we will need a splint or something we can use to fashion a splint. Can you remember all of that?"

He nods, but I insist that he repeat it back to me. "Bring Lako and Gordon back with me and a stretcher to carry Diana. A splint for her broken leg and a walking stick for you."

"That's good. Now before you go, look around and see if you can find my rifle. I think I dropped it on the trail. This is jaguar country, and I don't want to spend the night unarmed. While you're at it, see if you can locate Diana's medical kit."

Without a word he begins to work his way up the mountain toward the trail, being careful not to lose his footing. Diana is still unconscious, but it looks like her bleeding has stopped. I wish there was something else I could do for her, but I don't know what it would be. Cursing my ineptitude, I lie back and close my eyes, resting my head against the muddy ground. I still have a blinding headache, but at least I seem to be thinking more clearly now.

"Bryan," Eurico calls. "Bryan, I found it. I found Diana's pack with the medical kit in it."

"Great! Now see if you can find my rifle."

Closing my eyes, I try to create some kind of timeline. At a fast pace it is a good three-hour walk from the Kachinawa village to the mission compound. We had been walking about forty-five minutes when Diana fell; that means Eurico still has a good two or two and a half hours of walking before he reaches the compound. Rubbing the mud off the cracked crystal of my wristwatch, I see it has stopped running. Well, at least I know what time it was when the accident occurred: 7:47. With the rain it is impossible for me to even approximate what time it is now. Still, we surely haven't been here much more than an hour, making it about nine o'clock. If Eurico can make it to the compound by noon, it's possible that help could be here by three or four o'clock this afternoon. That is, if Lako is there, and if there are no unforeseen problems.

Eurico is back, and he has brought Diana's pack and my rifle. In his face I see a mixture of fear and determination. He's so independent and optimistic that I usually have a hard time remembering that he is just a nine-year-old boy. Not today. Soaking wet and covered with mud, his dark eyes bright with tears he is determined not to shed, he looks his age. Gripping his shoulders, I say, "You can do this, Eurico, you can do this. Diana is depending on you."

Suddenly he throws himself into my arms and begins to sob uncontrollably. For just a moment I don't know what to do. In that instant I am my mother, and I think I understand her for the first time. It wasn't cruelty, or even insensitivity, that caused her to let me grieve alone. It was confusion. She didn't know how to respond; she never realized that her comfort would make me strong, not weak. After the briefest hesitation I wrap Eurico in my arms and crush him to my chest. Now I am sobbing, shedding the tears I have kept locked inside of me for a lifetime.

Our weeping lasts only a few seconds, a minute at most, but something monumental has happened inside of me, and inside of Eurico too, I am sure. Rubbing his eyes with the heels of his hands, he says with fierce determination, "I will return with Lako. We will save Diana, never fear."

Without another word he begins the climb up the mountain toward the trail. It is raining harder now, and about halfway up the slippery mud gives way and he loses his footing. In an instant he is sliding down the mountain on his belly, frantically grabbing for something to stop his downward plunge. He probably doesn't slide more than fifteen or twenty feet, but in those few seconds my heart refuses to beat. Sitting up, he gives me a wave to let me know that he is all right. "Be careful," I call as he resumes his climb, angling across the mountain this time rather than climbing straight up. Reaching the trail, he pauses for a moment to catch his breath. Giving me a final wave, he disappears into the thickening rain.

Without thinking, I glance at my wristwatch to check the time, cursing under my breath when I remember it's broken. With no way to tell time, the day drags on interminably. After checking my rifle to make sure it is in working order, I lay it over a root to keep the action out of the mud. Next I go through Diana's medical kit looking for anything that might be helpful, without much luck. She does have some aspirin, and I swallow four of them in an attempt to dull the pain of my injured knee as well as my headache. I find some smelling salts and consider trying to rouse her, but I think better of it. The fact that she has not regained consciousness may be a blessing in disguise. As badly as her leg is broken, the pain would surely be unbearable, and that may not be the worst of her injuries.

It is raining harder all the time, causing the already saturated ground to shed water in sheets. The steep mountainside is like one huge waterfall with rivulets of water cascading all around us. I have covered Diana with my poncho, but there is no way to keep her dry. Although the temperature is moderate, the wind has come up, chilling me to the bone. My teeth are chattering so hard it hurts, and I know Diana must be faring even worse. Every few minutes I check her pulse, but other than that I don't know what to do. She is growing more restless, so she may not be unconscious much longer.

In a desperate attempt to keep my mind occupied I try to picture the trail and imagine where Eurico and the rescue party might be. It is no use. Not only is the trail unfamiliar to me, but yesterday's storm made it impossible to identify any landmarks. I can only pray that Eurico does not lose his way. If he does, it may be too late for Diana.

I must have fallen asleep, for when I awaken the rain has almost stopped, but it is considerably darker. Realizing the rescue party should have arrived by now, I fear for Eurico. If anything has happened to that boy I will never forgive myself. Diana is thrashing about and moaning with pain. Leaning close, I take her hand in mine and try to assure her that everything is going to be all right. Trying to rise, she says, "Where's my baby? I must find my baby." Gasping in pain, she falls back, whimpering in agony, her grief so raw I turn away, unable to bear it.

Thus begins the longest night of my life. It is full dark now, and in the distance I hear a jaguar scream. Working the bolt action on my rifle, I jack a cartridge into the chamber and put the safety on. I stare into the night with unseeing eyes and pray for the morning.

CHAPTER

32

CAROLYN IS SUDDENLY WIDE awake, her heart pounding, every sense hyper-alert. Fear is a bitter taste in her mouth, like the metallic taste of the copper pennies she sucked as a child, but she doesn't know why she's afraid. Not daring to move, she strains to hear what might have awakened her. Not the traffic in the street, for that is always there, nor the ticking of the grandfather clock in the small living room, nor the furnace that has cycled on. These are all familiar sounds, hardly noticed, and they would not have awakened her. So why is she wide awake, hyper-alert, pumped up on adrenaline?

Bryan. She's afraid for Bryan. Bryan's in danger.

What she heard wasn't the breaking of a window or the groan of a door being forced open. The sound that awakened her was inside her head or maybe deep in her subconscious. It was Bryan's voice, full of fear, calling for help.

Taking a deep breath, she tries to relax. It was probably just a dream, or so she tells herself, although she cannot recall dreaming. All she can remember is Bryan's voice, desperate in its urgency, insistent in its pleading. "Help me! Help me! Will somebody please help me?"

For fifteen tormenting minutes, she watches the luminous numbers on her bedside alarm, trying to will herself to relax, but it is no use. Her anxiety has not dissipated; if anything, her concern for

Bryan has intensified. *What does this mean? I need to talk with someone, but who can I call? Who would understand my fears? Helen! But I can't call Helen; it's the middle of the night, for heaven's sake.* Flinging back the bed covers in frustration, she tugs on her robe and makes her way to the kitchen where she brews herself a cup of tea.

While it is steeping she tries to imagine what kind of danger Bryan might be in. The Amazon Basin, according to Helen, is an extremely dangerous place, and all those who go there do so at their peril. In the rain forest danger comes in many forms—deadly diseases, poisonous snakes, hostile Indians, natural disasters, not to mention the ever-present risk of getting lost in that trackless wilderness. Maybe Bryan is deathly ill, or perhaps he is lost, or maybe he has broken his leg while exploring in some remote place and has no way of getting back to civilization. Her fear-infected imagination conjures up any number of dreadful possibilities.

Sitting down at the kitchen table, she reaches for the Bible that Helen gave her and begins leafing through it while waiting for her tea to cool enough to drink—anything, she thinks, to take her mind off of Bryan. It falls open to a page where she had placed a black-and-white photo of five-year-old Bryan standing in front of the mission house. It is one Helen gave her the first and only time she went to the Thompson home in Sterling. As she looks at it now, her anxiety ratchets up another notch or two. Bryan is in trouble, of that she is sure. Regardless of how irrational her fears may seem, she knows her concerns are real, no matter that she cannot explain them.

Sipping her tea in the predawn darkness, she vacillates between fear and guilt—fear for Bryan and guilt for her part in this tragic dilemma. She has replayed the scene at least a hundred times in her mind, without being able to make it come out any differently. What seemed so right at the time seems insanely stupid in retrospect. Bryan is not a man who can be manipulated. She knew that, so why did she try? How could she have been so selfish, so foolish? To have expected Bryan to react in any other way makes no sense at all. If only she could undo what she did. If only she could bring Bryan back, she would love him as no woman has ever loved a man, his melancholy moods and brooding anger notwithstanding. *If something happens to him, I will never forgive myself, never!*

The clock in the living room chimes the hour, and belatedly she realizes it has been nearly two hours since fear first awakened her. Her nerves are still as taut as a bowstring, but she decides she had better try to get a couple hours of sleep. She has a demanding job, and her schedule for tomorrow is heavy. Studying the old black-and-white photo one final time, she hugs it to her breast before returning it to its place in the Bible. As she is replacing it, her eyes are drawn to the Scriptures. Although she has never read the Bible, the words of Psalm 91 seem to leap off the page and seize her mind.

> *"I will say of the LORD, He is my refuge and my fortress: my God; in him will I trust. Surely he shall deliver thee from the snare of the fowler, and from the noisome pestilence....**Thou shalt not be afraid for the terror by night;** nor for the arrow that flieth by day; nor for the pestilence that walketh in darkness; nor for the destruction that wasteth at noonday. A thousand shall fall at thy side, and ten thousand at thy right hand; but it shall not come nigh thee....Because thou hast made the LORD, which is my refuge, even the most High, thy habitation; **there shall no evil befall thee, neither shall any plague come nigh thy dwelling.** For he shall give his angels charge over thee, to keep thee in all thy ways. They shall bear thee up in their hands, lest thou dash thy foot against a stone....Because he hath set his love upon me, therefore will I deliver him: I will set him on high, because he hath known my name. He shall call upon me, and I will answer him: **I will be***

with him in trouble; I will deliver him, and honour him.
With long life will I satisfy him, and shew him my salvation."

0The language is archaic, making the words seem awkward and clumsy, but there is no mistaking their meaning. Bryan may be in trouble, even in grave danger, but according to this passage, God promises to protect him: *"I will be with him in trouble; I will deliver him....With long life will I satisfy him."*

For the first time in hours Carolyn's fear begins to ease just a little. Nothing has changed—it's still dark, she's still alone, she's received no word from Bryan—but everything is different. Nothing like this has ever happened to her, and she is at a loss to explain it, yet it is too real to be denied. Once more the words of the ancient Scriptures fill her thoughts: *"Thou shalt not be afraid for the terror by night....Because thou hast made the Lord...even the most High, thy habitation."*

Now she has an almost overwhelming need to pray, to communicate her deepest feelings to the One who is communicating with her. But what does she know about praying? For that matter, what right does she have to pray? She is not a religious person. Her Catholic friends were forever talking about "Hail Marys" and "Our Fathers," but she has no idea what that means. What was it Helen said about praying the last time they were together? That there are no special techniques to learn. That she should just talk to God out of her heart, the way she would talk to a trusted friend.

Clasping the Bible to her chest, she bows her head. The tears of a lifetime swim in her tightly closed eyes and spill down her cheeks. The apartment is empty except for her, yet she has a nearly overwhelming sense that she is not alone. The Presence is comfortably close, but not intrusive, and so real she opens her eyes to see if someone is sitting across the table from her. Of course no one is there, but the sense of the nearness is not diminished.

Almost without realizing what she is doing, she begins to pour out her thoughts and feelings, the words tumbling out of her without conscious effort. Listening to herself, she realizes, maybe for the first time, just how much pain and guilt she has stuffed down inside her heart over the course of her short life. Much of what she has repressed is ugly, shameful, and she can hardly bear to speak of it. Yet she senses no disgust, no rejection from the One whose presence is now nearer to her than the breath she breathes and more real than life itself. How long this holy catharsis continues she does not know; but wave after wave of release flows out of her, purging her soul of its deepest hurts, leaving her feeling as pure as a newborn child.

When at last the purging ceases, she sits at the table emotionally wrung out but at peace in a way she has never been. Now she hears herself repeating the name of Jesus over and over again. "Jesus," she whispers, "Jesus, Jesus, Jesus…" as she senses His unconditional love enveloping her.

The blaring of the radio alarm from her bedroom jerks her from her reverie. Pushing back from the kitchen table, she hurries to shut it off, all the while trying to put her night's experience into a context she can understand. In the shower she shampoos her hair and then steps out and blows it dry. She puts on makeup and dresses for work. Quickly she makes her bed and tidies the room, just as if nothing extraordinary has happened. Yet she is different, although she would be hard pressed to explain in what way. At peace with herself maybe, or more optimistic about the future. Checking the time, she decides to give Helen a call. Perhaps she can explain what all of this means.

CHAPTER

33

ENTERING THE KITCHEN, ROB is pleasantly surprised to see that Helen has prepared a real breakfast for a change. As things became strained between them she seemed to lose interest in the little things that he had come to take for granted. Instead of bacon and eggs for breakfast he started getting cold cereal, and even then she made him feel like she was doing him a favor. This morning she gives him a cheerful smile before going to the counter to pour his coffee. Pleased, he turns toward the table, but before he can sit down the phone rings. Reaching for it, he says, "Hello, this is Pastor Thompson."

Having expected Helen to answer the phone, Carolyn is momentarily at a loss for words. Belatedly she stammers, "Uh...could I speak with Helen please?"

"May I tell her who's calling?"

"Carolyn. Carolyn Whittaker." Almost as an afterthought, she adds, "Carolyn Whittaker from Denver," with the emphasis on Denver.

Puzzled, Rob hands the phone to Helen while mouthing "Carolyn Whittaker."

Putting her hand over the mouthpiece, Helen says, "Go ahead and eat. This might take a while."

When she returns a few minutes later, Rob and the boys are just finishing breakfast. Checking the time, she realizes the boys are going to have to hurry or they will miss the school bus. Hustling them into their coats, she hands them their lunches and brushes their foreheads with a kiss before pushing them out the door. Returning to the kitchen, she pours herself a cup of coffee and joins Rob at the table in the breakfast nook.

He watches her put strawberry preserves on a slice of toast while munching on a piece of bacon. When it becomes apparent that she has no intention of discussing the telephone call from Carolyn Whittaker, he clears his throat and asks, "Is Carolyn Bryan's ex-wife?"

"Yes she is."

"And does she still live in Denver?"

"As a matter of fact, she does."

It's obvious that Helen is not going to make this easy for him, but then why should she? He's done everything but come right out and accuse her of having an affair. He supposes she does have a right to feel indignant, all things considered. Without meeting her eye he says, "I suppose that explains the phone bill?"

"I suppose it does."

"So why didn't you tell me? I've been living in agony thinking…" Not daring to put his suspicions into words, he lets his voice trail off.

"Go ahead and say it, Rob. You can't hurt me any more than you already have."

"What do you mean, hurt you?" He demands, suddenly defensive. "Do you have any idea what you've put me through?"

When she doesn't respond, he continues. "What did you expect me to think? You haven't been yourself in weeks, months really. And then we get a phone bill with repeated calls to an unknown number in Denver—"

Her earlier joy has been replaced by a weary resignation, and she cuts him off saying, "Rob, I don't have the time or energy for this, so if you don't mind, let me finish my coffee in peace."

Taking a deep breath, he tries to calm himself. Choosing his words carefully, he says, "Helen, what I'm trying to say is that I'm sorry. I misjudged you, and I hope you can find it in your heart to forgive me."

Tears glisten in her eyes, and she dabs at them with her napkin before responding. "I want to forgive you. I want things to be the way they used to be, before any of this happened, but I don't know if that's possible. I'm afraid that what I thought we had wasn't real, that it was just something I made up, something I imagined, because I wanted it to be like that."

"What are you talking about? Of course it was real." When she doesn't respond, he continues. "We can get past this, you'll see. We just have to forgive each other, put this behind us, and move on."

"Exactly what do we need to forgive, Rob?"

"You need to forgive me for doubting you, and I need to forgive you for keeping things from me."

"Oh Rob, I wish that's all there was to it."

"What do you mean? What else is there?" Uncertainty clouding his features, he asks, "Is there something you haven't told me?"

Wearily Helen grimaces. "No, there's nothing I haven't told you, but the fact that you find it necessary to ask that question proves my point. Something at the core of our relationship has shifted, and I don't know if it can be fixed."

"Helen, you're scaring me," Rob says, looking at her intently. "Granted, we're going through a rough time right now, but it's nothing we can't work out with God's help. You believe that, don't you?"

Shrugging, she asks, "Does it matter what I believe?"

"Of course it matters! What we believe determines our destiny. You know that."

"Well then, I'll tell you what I believe, or at least I'll tell you what I don't believe. I don't believe you're the man I once thought you were. That's what's breaking my heart. And that's what I can't forgive. I can't forgive you for not being who I thought you were."

"What in the world are you talking about? You're not making any sense."

"I don't know how to make it any clearer than that."

"Look. I've been under a lot of pressure, we all have, but I will make it up to you."

"If that's supposed to reassure me, it doesn't. What happens the next time you're under a lot of pressure, or we go through a rough spell? Will you be there for me or—"

"Helen. Listen to me. I haven't been myself lately. That's what I'm trying to tell you. Can't you understand that?"

Shaking her head, Helen says, "I hate to quote your own sermons back to you, but you're the one who said, 'Pressure doesn't make us into something we are not. It simply reveals what we are.'"

"Don't do this. Please don't do this."

"Don't do what? Don't tell you how I really feel? Don't force you to take a hard look at yourself? Rob, if we're going to get past this, we're going to have to be honest with ourselves and each other."

"Why are you making this so hard?" Rob pleads. "Why can't you just forgive me and let us get on with our life?"

Realizing Rob is never going to understand, Helen is tempted to bang her head on the table in frustration. Exhausted, she finally concedes. "Okay, you're right. I forgive you."

Her insincerity feels so transparent she expects Rob to see right through her, but apparently he doesn't, or maybe he just doesn't want to. Pushing his chair back from the table, he moves behind her and begins to massage her knotted shoulders. "I'll make it up to you, Helen, you'll see. Maybe we can get away for a few days, just the two of us."

Getting to her feet, she gives him a perfunctory hug before taking him by the arm and walking him to the door. Kissing him good-bye, she says, "You had better hurry or you'll be late for staff meeting."

After watching him drive off, she returns to the table where she collapses into her chair and buries her face in her hands, weeping. *Oh Rob, what's happened to you? What happened to the man I married, the man who was so understanding and caring, the one who seemed to know what I was feeling even before I did? How can I trust you with my heart if you don't even know me or care about the things that are most important to me? You never asked about Bryan, not even after you found the letter he wrote from the Amazon. You're obsessed with the phone bill, ready to believe the worst about me, but when you learn the truth, you don't even ask me about my relationship with Carolyn.*

Getting up from the table, Helen dries her tears and begins clearing the breakfast clutter. Drawing on the fortitude that has served her in good stead through the years, she squares her shoulders and determines to make the best of things. *I can do this. I can be a loyal and faithful wife, even if my husband never understands how he has hurt me. With God's help I will love him, but I don't know that I will ever be able to trust him with my heart again.*

CHAPTER

34

I MAY HAVE FALLEN asleep, but I don't see how, given the fact that I'm lying in the mud on the side of a steep mountain. I'm wet and cold, and every part of my body hurts. Anyway, I'm wide awake now and fully alert. Something is moving about in the darkness, but I don't know what it is. Straining to see, I stare into the night until my eyes water, wishing I had night vision like almost every other creature in the forest. Nature has endowed them with a tapetum—a reflective layer at the back of the eyeball that bounces light through the sensory rods and cones of the retina a second time—enabling them to turn night into day. Unfortunately, God did not see fit to equip us human beings the same way, and try as I might I cannot penetrate the darkness.

Be that as it may, whatever is out there is getting closer. Reaching for my rifle, I ease myself into a sitting position and slide the safety off. The wind shifts slightly, and I smell the pungent odor of urine. That can mean only one thing—a jaguar is prowling in the brush not far away, scent-marking his territory. He probably smells blood, Diana's blood, and is moving in for the kill.

Wiping my sweaty palms on my jeans, I try to keep my hands from shaking. Steadying my rifle, I desperately search the shadows for even a hint of movement, for something to shoot at, but I can't see anything. Maybe I should fire a round or two in hopes of scaring him off. Then again that may not be a very good idea. If he lunged out of the darkness just as I fired my rifle, he would be upon us before I could chamber another round. Still, I've got to do something, but what? I'll never be able to maintain this kind of vigilance all night. Already the muscles in my arms are cramping, and my eyes feel gritty, like they're full of sand.

Holding my rifle in my right hand, I feel around in the darkness for something to throw, a stick or a stone. Locating a rock about the size of a man's hand, I hurl it into the brush and let out a blood-curdling scream. As the echoes of my scream die in the distance, I hear the rock clattering down the face of the mountain. In the silence that follows I strain to hear the slightest sound. Nothing. Now all I hear is the noise of my own breathing loud in my ears, and the smell of my sweaty fear is strong in my nostrils.

Sensing something behind me, I ease myself around so I can see up the mountain. Two yellow eyes glow in the dark, and my blood runs cold. I have just time enough to raise my rifle before the jaguar launches himself at me. I don't remember firing, but I see the muzzle flash a split second before the big cat crashes into me, throwing me backward down the mountain. I land on my back, hard, knocking the wind out of me, but I manage to hang onto my rifle. The jaguar lands on top of me, his weight pinning me down. Desperately I try to free my rifle for another shot even as we are sliding down the steep slope. Abruptly we crash into a tangle of brush and undergrowth not unlike the one that stopped Diana's downward plunge yesterday. Heaving with both arms, I try to throw the jag off of me before he crushes my head in his powerful jaws. I manage to get partially free before becoming entangled in the brush. Frantically I kick my legs, struggling to free myself even as I am trying to work the bolt on my rifle.

In my haste I lose my grip, and the gun slips out of my hands. Frantically I feel for it, my desperation fueled by a fear for Diana as well as for my own life, but I cannot locate it. Without the rifle I have no chance, but I am not going to die without a fight. Somehow I manage to get a death grip on the jag's throat. Gritting my teeth, I squeeze with all my might, praying that he doesn't use his rear claws to disembowel me. Belatedly, I realize he's not moving. He's dead!

In an instant all the strength drains out of me, and I fall back as limp as an old rag. The aftermath of the adrenaline rush leaves me exhausted, every muscle in my body trembling. The big cat's weight is heavy upon me, but I don't have the strength to push him off. Lying there, gasping for breath, I hear Diana calling. "Bryan, are you all right?"

"I'll be fine," I croak. "I just had the wind knocked out of me. Give me a minute to catch my breath."

When I can finally breathe again, I free myself from the tangle of vines and underbrush, gritting my teeth against a spasm of pain that threatens to incapacitate me. Feeling around in the darkness, I finally locate my rifle in a tangle of vines. Chambering a fresh round, I put the safety on and sling it over my shoulder. Carefully I work my way back up the mountain to Diana, where I position myself among the roots to keep from sliding down the slope again. Thankfully, it is no longer raining, but now we have to contend with the mosquitoes, and they have returned with a vengeance, drawn by the smell of our blood and sweat.

For the first time since her fall yesterday morning, Diana seems fully conscious. Even though she is in excruciating pain, she appears to be thinking clearly. After checking her own pulse, she concludes that she is not in shock and reasons that after this much time she doesn't expect that to be a problem. A badly broken leg appears to be the worst of her injuries, but it shouldn't be life threatening if we can get her back to the mission compound without aggravating anything. After locating my water bottle, I help her drink, noting as I do that she is burning with fever. Since she doesn't appear to have any internal injuries, I find four aspirin in her medical kit and give them to her. They probably won't do much for the pain, but they should help with the fever.

Once I have quenched my thirst, she hammers me with questions regarding our situation. I tell her what I know, downplaying the possibility that something may have happened to Eurico. "Lako was supposed to return sometime yesterday, but he probably didn't get back until just before dark, making it impossible for them to set out before morning. I'm sure they will head out at first light. They'll probably be here between nine and ten o'clock."

Diana is too experienced in the ways of the Amazon Basin to be conned, and I can tell she is considering not only what I've told her, but what I didn't say as well. Without both Gordon and Lako it will be next to impossible to get her up the mountain to the trail, and that's just the beginning. Getting her back to the mission compound will be grueling, both for her and those carrying her.

After a while she sleeps, or at least she pretends to, moaning softly from time to time as a spasm of pain causes her body to jerk. I doze off now and then, exhaustion overcoming our miserable accommodations, but for the most part I wrestle with my demons. After weeks in the Amazon I am no nearer to finding out what happened to my father than when I first got here. Sometimes I wonder what difference it will make whether I learn anything or not. Nothing I do will ever give me back the years I've lost. Even, if by some miracle, I was to find Dad alive, we couldn't go back and relive the past twenty-two years. So, what am I doing out here? Why am I risking my life?

Around and around go my thoughts, but I can never seem to find a resolution. As I am nearing sleep, an ancient proverb floats to the surface of my mind: "The foolishness of man subverts his way, and his heart rages against the Lord." *Is that what I'm doing?* I wonder. *Am I destroying my life and blaming God?*

CHAPTER
35

IT HAS BEEN NEARLY twenty-four hours since Diana lost her footing and plunged headlong down this steep mountain, but it seems much longer, pain and fear having the power to expand time. Although we are not far from the equator, we have spent a miserable night, wet and chilled to the bone. The rain forest acts like a huge swamp cooler, covering millions of square miles. The incredible evaporation of moisture from the wet jungle floor continues after the sun has set, sucking heat out of the muggy air. Given our wet clothes and exposed position, hypothermia is a real danger.

Overhead, the sky brightens with the first hint of day, and I sigh with relief, hungering for the sun's warmth. Pushing myself up into a sitting position, I roll my shoulders in an attempt to ease my knotted muscles. My injured knee is throbbing painfully, and try as I might I cannot find a position where it doesn't hurt. The air around me is thick with insects, and I wave my hand in a futile attempt to shoo them away. The ground is crawling with them as well, reminding me that the Amazon Basin has more insects per square meter than any place on the face of the earth. If we make it back safely, I will never again take the simple comforts of home for granted.

From my vantage point, I watch the sun push above the horizon, slowly revealing the splendor of steep ridges towering above deep gorges shrouded in the early morning mist. As stunning as the view is, I hardly notice it. Given our precarious situation, all I can think about is rescue. Although I know that if the rescuers left at daybreak they can't be here for another two hours, I still find myself straining for the slightest sound signaling their approach.

Hunger knots my stomach, but I try to ignore it. The piece of smoked fish I ate on the trail yesterday morning is long gone. Spotting Diana's pack where Eurico left it, I pull it to me. Rummaging through it, I find a couple of biscuits, a small chunk of cheese, and some smoked fish. Greedily, I devour one of the biscuits and half of the cheese. My water bottle is empty, so I take a long drink from Diana's.

She is still asleep, howbeit restless with pain. I wish there was something I could do for her, but I don't know what it would be. Seeing her shiver, I take off what's left of my shirt and wrap it around her. It's not much, but I don't have anything else. I hope Lako or Gordon thinks to bring some dry clothes, as well as some medical supplies. There are only four or five aspirins left in Diana's medical kit, and not much else. She must have left most of the supplies she brought with the Indians; a compassionate gesture, but not very wise in retrospect.

Glancing down the mountain, I spot the dead jaguar in the tangle of brush that stopped our downward plunge. Protruding from his left hindquarter is what appears to be the end of a spear that has been broken off just behind the point. That being the case, it would explain why I was able to get a shot off before he was upon me. A crippled hind leg would slow his pounce appreciably. That may also explain why I was able to hear him moving about in the brush. Although he poses no threat now, the memory of last night's desperate struggle causes my heart to race.

A breeze has come up, scattering the mosquitoes, for which I am thankful, but it also chills me to the bone. Wrapping my bare arms around myself, I try to hoard the warmth of the sun, but it is too low in the sky to provide more than a hint of the warmth to come. Diana is awake now and shivering violently from the cold.

"Bryan," she croaks through cracked lips, "try to warm me with your body. I'm freezing, and I'm afraid I might have hypothermia."

Carefully I position myself against her and wrap my arms around her in a desperate attempt to share some of my meager body warmth. It's excruciatingly painful, given her badly broken leg and who knows what other injuries, but we have no choice. Laying my face next to hers, I jerk back in surprise. She is burning with fever, and given her parched skin and dry lips, I fear she is becoming dehydrated. I start to release her so I can retrieve her water bottle, but she clings to me desperately.

Placing my mouth next to her ear, I say, "Diana, you're burning up with fever. Let me get you some aspirin and a drink of water."

"In a minute," she mumbles. "Hold me, Bryan. I'm cold, so cold."

Pressing my body close to hers, I try not to think what will happen if we don't get help soon. After several minutes, her chills ease a little, and I am able to disengage myself and retrieve her medical kit, along with her water bottle. Lifting her head, I help her drink, noting how weak she is when I do. After she has quenched her thirst, I give her three of the five aspirin, saving the last two for later. I try to get her to eat something, but she refuses. Exhausted, she lays her head back, but she does not release my hand. Scooting closer, I try to warm her as best I can.

She sleeps, if I can call it that, and when she wakes the aspirin have taken effect, bringing her fever down, but doing almost nothing for her pain. Her broken leg has swollen to at least twice its normal size, and at her insistence I get a scalpel from her medical kit and slit the seam on the leg of her jeans. Hopefully, that will relieve some of the pain by reducing the pressure on her broken leg. As I work, I cannot help but see the discolored flesh of her upper leg with the bone protruding against it. The pain must be awful, and when we try to move her it will be horrendous. Hopefully, Gordon will think to bring some morphine; otherwise, I don't know how we will ever get her back to the mission station.

As the sun climbs higher in the sky, the temperature rises accordingly. Its warmth works its way into my bones, and I tell myself that I will never complain about the heat again. It seems to revive Diana a little, and she eats a bit of biscuit and a couple of bites of smoked fish. Mostly she craves water, and with less than half a bottle left I fear the worst. If Lako and Eurico don't get here soon, dehydration will become a problem for her.

Taking my hand, she says, "Bryan, there's something I need to tell you." Puzzled, I replace the cap on the water bottle and give her my undivided attention. "I guess what I really mean is, there is something I need to confess."

Holding up my hand, I stop her. "Diana, I'm hardly qualified to hear anyone's confession, and certainly not yours. This isn't really a good time either."

Before I can continue, she interrupts. "What do you mean?"

Choosing my words carefully, I reply. "Under normal circumstances you probably wouldn't even consider telling me what you're about to confess. So why don't you wait until you get back on your feet, in your own environment, and then if you still feel the same way we can talk about it."

For just a moment disappointment flickers in her eyes, then it is replaced by the fierce determination for which she is known. "I've thought about it most of the night," she says, "and I've made up my mind. This can't wait."

I don't want her to do this, and I desperately search for a way to stop her. If she confesses some dark secret, it may well be the end of our friendship. Not that I will judge her or hold whatever she tells me against her. Rather, once things get back to normal, she will likely regret having told me, and then she will begin avoiding me.

"Listen to me, Bryan," she presses. "I'm a doctor, and I know what condition I'm in. If help doesn't arrive soon, I may not make it out of here. I don't want to die with this on my conscience."

There's nothing I can say to that, so reluctantly I acquiesce.

Now that I've agreed to hear her confession, she seems hesitant to begin. Finally, she takes a deep breath and forces herself to look me in the eye. In a voice I have to strain to hear she says, "Do you remember asking me why I came to the Amazon Basin, why I would choose to spend my life alone, serving as a medical missionary?"

When I nod, she continues. "What I told you was the truth, but not the whole truth. As a seventeen-year-old girl I was called to missions, but I never imagined serving alone. I was sure I would marry a man who shared my passion and that we would spend our lives ministering together. Unfortunately, I made a terrible mistake when I was twenty-one years old, and I've been paying for it ever since."

Regret chokes her, and she looks away, humiliated. We sit in silence for several minutes as she tries to regain her composure. I listen to the sound of the wind in the trees, the roar of the river below, and the chattering of monkeys overhead. Finally she speaks again, shame coloring her words. "He was the class president, a pre-med mission major just like me, and we were engaged. One night we went too far, and although I told myself I would never let it happen again, I did. Once we crossed that line, it seemed impossible to go back to the way we were before it happened. Of course, we didn't use anything. That would have made it seem premeditated, and neither of us was willing to acknowledge that. I was scared out of my mind, but I told myself if anything happened, we would just get married."

As she spells out the painful details, I force myself to maintain eye contact, but that is all I can do. I have no words of wisdom for her, and I'm certainly not qualified to give her absolution. What am I going to say: "It's okay. We all make mistakes"? I don't think so.

Reining in my thoughts, I turn my attention back to Diana, forcing myself to listen as she continues her tragic confession. "Gary panicked when he learned I was pregnant. He was angry and seemed to think it was all my fault. He said we couldn't marry under those conditions, that when the baby was born early everyone would know what we had done, and it would ruin our plans for ministry."

Stumbling to a stop, she bites her bottom lip and tries to keep from crying while silent tears make wet streaks down her scratched and bruised cheeks. It hurts me to see her like this, and it is all I can do not to turn away. Instead, I squeeze her hand to reassure her. Seeming to draw strength from my gesture, she takes a deep breath and says, "Against my better judgment, I allowed Gary to convince me to have an abortion. He said it wouldn't change anything. We would still get married after graduation, just like we had planned, and we could always have more children."

She is sobbing now, uncontrollably, the memories of that tragic experience overwhelming her, regret making her tears bitter. Leaning close, I cradle her head with my arm, comforting her as best I can. There's more she wants to tell me, I'm sure, but right now it is impossible for her to continue. She is undone by the memory of the tragic mistake she made as a young woman, and the intervening years of penance have done nothing to relieve her torment.

Before she can compose herself and resume her confession, I hear Eurico's shrill voice calling our names. Twisting around so I can look up the mountain, I see him standing on the trail waving at us. As I watch, he is joined by Lako and Gordon, and a minute later by Eleanor. With a pack slung over his shoulder he scrambles down the steep slope toward us. Taking the water bottle he thrusts at me, I drink greedily while he keeps saying, "I told you I could do it, Bryan. I told you I could do it."

CHAPTER

36

JUDGING BY THE SUN, it is nearly noon, meaning we don't have a minute to waste if we are going to make it back to the mission compound by dark. Already Lako and Gordon are laying out equipment in preparation for bringing Diana up the mountain. It looks like they have brought some kind of rappeling gear, although it is hard to tell from here. I'm not sure how they plan to use it, but it is obvious that they will need something to help them get Diana back to the trail. Considering how steep the mountain is where we are, it would be virtually impossible for them to carry her without assistance of some kind.

Eleanor is making her way down the slope toward us, angling across the mountain rather than trying to come straight down. She is short of breath and perspiring profusely when she finally reaches us. After a cursory examination of Diana and me, she sets to work. Handing me a pack, she says, "Eat. We may not have time later." From a second pack she extracts a bottle of morphine and a hypodermic needle. Turning to Diana, she asks, "How much should I give you?"

Reaching for the syringe, Diana carefully fills it and injects herself. As soon as the morphine hits her she begins to relax, the worst of the pain loosing its grip. I try to get her to eat, but she simply shakes her head and closes her eyes. Once the morphine has taken effect,

Eleanor gives Diana's leg a thorough examination while I wolf down several pieces of smoked fish and some kind of fruit I don't recognize. I've eaten tastier meals, but never one I enjoyed more. Although I am still weak, the food has renewed my energy.

Lako and Gordon have wrapped their rappeling ropes around a couple of trees on the far side of the trail, and they are rappeling down the mountain toward us. They have brought a makeshift stretcher and some rough-hewn slats and leather straps for making a splint. Moving out of the way, I let them go to work. Without asking, Lako examines Diana's leg, causing her to grimace in pain in spite of the morphine. Motioning for Gordon to hold her by the shoulders, he positions himself at her heels and begins exerting pressure with his left hand on the broken femur while at the same time pulling her heel toward him with his right hand. Diana screams in pain before passing out. Lako continues to exert pressure until the bone appears to be lined up, then he moves quickly to put the splint on her leg, fastening it with the leather straps. Once that is done, they carefully place her on the stretcher, securing her with some strips of cloth.

Now comes the hard part. The trail is at least thirty meters up the mountain, and the intervening terrain is extremely steep. Again Lako takes charge, showing Eleanor and me how to use the rappeling ropes to help him and Gordon get Diana up the mountain. It's not the way rappeling equipment was designed to be used, but it should work. As per his instructions, Eleanor and I brace our feet against some protruding roots and take up the slack in the ropes.

Lako positions himself at the uphill end of the stretcher, squats, and grasps a stretcher pole in each hand. Once Gordon is in position, he nods, and they lift the stretcher bearing Diana. Although she probably doesn't weigh more that 120 pounds, both Gordon and Lako are straining. Eleanor and I lean back against the ropes to help them keep their balance on the steep slope, taking up the slack as they make their torturously slow ascent. One misstep and they could drop the stretcher, sending Diana plunging down the mountain, probably to her death. Seeing Eleanor nearing the limits of her strength, Eurico hurries to help her.

After Lako and Gordon have gone about ten meters, they stop to rest, easing the stretcher down. I am thankful for the momentary reprieve. The muscles in my arms and upper back are cramping with exhaustion, and my injured knee feels like someone has stuck an ice pick in the joint. Diana has regained consciousness and is groaning softly. I can't even imagine the kind of pain she must be in. Lako and Gordon are both drenched with sweat as they lean against the mountain to catch their breath. To my left, Eleanor is wrapping the rope around her waist in case she loses her grip. It provides a margin of safety for Lako, but it's risky for her. I consider doing the same thing, but decide against it.

The sun is directly overhead, turning the rain forest into a giant sauna, making it hard for me to remember that Diana and I were fighting hypothermia just a few hours ago. Sweat is streaming down my face and burning my eyes. With my free hand I swat at the mosquitoes and sweat bees, but it does little good. They are impervious to my most determined efforts and return with a vengeance the instant I stop swatting at them.

Far too soon, Lako signals that they are ready to resume their torturous ascent. Gritting my teeth against the pain in my knee, I lean back against the rope, taking up the slack. Eleanor and Eurico are doing the same. Suddenly Gordon's foot slips, and we all gasp as the stretcher tips dangerously before he regains his footing. The sudden lurch sends a jolt of pain ripping through Diana's injured leg, causing her to scream in agony. Only the tension on the rappeling rope fastened to his waist keeps Gordon from going down. Turning to Eleanor and Eurico, I mutter between clinched teeth, "I don't know whether the rappeling gear was Gordon's idea or Lako's, but whoever thought of it was a genius."

Once more Lako and Gordon stop to rest, and not a minute too soon either. My hands are cramping, and I feel like I am about to faint. I'm embarrassed by my weakness, but there's nothing I can do about it. My recent bout with malaria has simply left me far weaker than I could have imagined, not to mention the toll the last thirty-six hours have taken on me. Now I wrap the rope around my waist, not trusting my strength any longer. It puts me at greater risk, but I can't take a chance with Diana's life. If something happened to her because of my weakness, I would never forgive myself.

While we rest, I find myself thinking about my father. As a boy I just assumed he had been killed by the Indians, but now I don't know. Having come to the Amazon seeking revenge, I now wonder if I am not wasting my time. In light of recent events, it seems likely he died of less sinister causes—an accident or illness most likely. Without help, something as common as a broken leg can mean death in the jungle. Given what I've learned in recent weeks, I should probably turn around and head for home; that is, once we have gotten Diana back to the mission compound. It's not likely I'm going to learn my father's fate or avenge his death. Still, I can't imagine living the rest of my life without coming to some kind of resolution.

Lako jerks on the rope, signaling that it is time to begin the final leg of the ascent. Although I feel faint from exhaustion, I force myself to lean against the rope, clinching my jaws against the pain that seems to seek out every muscle and joint in my battered body. Already my fingers are cramping, and my knee feels like it's on fire. I can only imagine what it must be like for Gordon and Lako straining to carry

Diana up this steep grade. Drawing on every bit of strength I have left, I lean against the rope, willing them up the final three or four meters. When, at last, Diana is safely on the trail, I collapse against the mountain, gasping for breath.

I hardly have time to catch my breath before Lako is thrusting a water bottle at me and telling me to drink. Hurriedly, he helps Eurico and Eleanor gather the packs. Once they start up the mountain, he slings my rifle over his shoulder and tries to help me to my feet. Gritting my teeth against the pain, I try to stand, but it is no use. My injured knee will not support my weight. Waving off his help, I flop down on my backside and begin scooting up the mountain backward, propelling myself with my one good leg and both arms. It is slow going, but I don't know what else to do. When I finally reach the trail, the palms of both hands are bleeding, and I'm completely spent. Only God knows how I'm going to make it to the mission compound.

I want to check on Diana, but I'm simply too tired to move. Belatedly, I realize that I can hear Eurico talking to her, so she must be all right. Eleanor wraps my injured knee with an elastic bandage for support. I doubt if it will help much, but I am grateful for the thought. The kindness she has shown me is what I've hungered for my whole life.

Glancing up, I see Gordon approaching with my walking stick. Squatting beside me, he says, "We can't delay any longer, or we'll never make it to the mission station before dark. Diana is a strong woman, but she has suffered a serious injury, and I don't want her to spend another night in the jungle if I can help it. If you can't keep up with us, we'll have to go on ahead. We'll come back for you, but right now Diana is our first priority." With that, he helps me to my feet and returns to the stretcher.

Leaning on my walking stick, I venture a tentative step, then another, grimacing in pain as I do. "Eleanor," I call. "Is there anything you can give me to help me with this pain; maybe a shot of morphine? Without something I don't think I can do this."

Picking up a pack, she hurries to Diana. Kneeling beside her stretcher, they talk in hushed tones. Finally, Eleanor rummages around in the pack and finds something. After showing it to Diana, who nods, she hurries toward me. "Take these. They won't kill the pain, but maybe they will help. It's the best I can do."

I'm replacing the cap on my water bottle when Lako and Gordon pick up Diana's stretcher and head out. Eleanor falls in behind them, while Eurico drops back to join me. Although the pace is moderate, it is too fast for me, and we soon lose sight of them. I encourage Eurico to catch up with Lako and Diana, but he refuses to leave my side. If the truth be told, I'm grateful for his company.

With each step it feels as if someone is twisting the ice pick in my knee, and it takes all the strength I have just to put one foot in front of the other. As difficult as climbing is, it is much easier than descending. Going uphill I can lean on my walking stick and pull myself upward. There's no corresponding technique when I am going downhill. When the trail is especially steep, I am forced to sit on my backside and slide down. As the day wears on I find myself falling with increasing frequency. Each time I do, it is harder to get up. If Eurico were not with me, I don't think I could force myself to keep going.

The sun is low in the sky when I escape to a place deep inside myself in an attempt to distance myself from the ever-present pain. It is a technique I mastered as a boy. In this inner sanctum my father is not dead, nor does my mother lose herself in grief. Here God can be trusted to protect those who serve Him. He does not turn a blind eye to the dangers evil has brought into the world nor a deaf ear to the prayers of His children. Here my nights are not filled with a fearful dread, nor is my sleep fitful. Here there is no grief, no self-loathing, no self-blame. Here there is...

It's no use. The pain transcends all else, numbing my mind, and I blindly force myself to put one foot in front of the other. Day is gone, swallowed up by a night so black it is impossible to see my hand in front of my face. Eurico has a flashlight to illuminate the trail directly in front of us, but it does nothing about the darkness that now smothers us. Although I've never been claustrophobic, it now feels like the darkness and the jungle are closing in on me, and I fight a rising panic.

Thankfully, it is not raining, but in the distance I hear the low rumble of thunder, and I wonder how much longer it will hold off. If this trail were any muddier, I don't know how I would make it, seeing I'm already having trouble with my footing. Each time I fall, I am tempted to give up, but somehow I keep going hour after hour; stumbling, falling, and rising again in a marathon of misery. When we finally stagger into the mission compound sometime after midnight, I am nearly incoherent with pain and exhaustion. Eurico helps me out of my filthy clothes, and I collapse on the bed in more pain than I have ever known.

CHAPTER
37

TWO FULL DAYS HAVE passed since the dramatic rescue of Diana, and I'm finally starting to feel human again. My knee remains badly swollen and painfully sore. With the aid of a cane Lako made for me, I am able to get around, but not very well. This morning I have limped out to the porch where I'm soaking up the sun. I'm restless, but I don't have the stamina to do much. Hours of uninterrupted thinking have aggravated my normal restiveness while doing almost nothing to resolve my inner conflict. I'm as unsettled as I've always been, maybe more so. Be that as it may, I am determined to press ahead. What choice do I have?

Lako has located some Amuacas deep in the rain forest, but he couldn't tell whether they have had any contact with the outside world or not. If they have, he says, it's minimal. Either way, he thinks it's a good place for us to start. From the river, where we will have to leave our boat, it is a hard day's walk to their longhouses, with several steep ridges to cross in order to get there. That means we can't even think about going until my knee heals, probably another ten days or two weeks at least. At my insistence, he is planning another excursion into the jungle. Hopefully, he will be able to locate another group or two. It's hard not to be part of these expeditions, as impatient as I am to learn whatever I can about my father's disappearance. Still, I have to admit that we're really not losing much time. Lako is simply saving me a lot of unnecessary legwork. Once he has located their longhouses, we can go directly there rather than wandering around in the rain forest trying to locate them.

Across the way, I see Eleanor heading for Diana's house with a tray of food. On an impulse I limp down the porch steps and head that way. At the door, I hesitate for just a moment before rapping softly. Almost immediately Eleanor answers my tentative knock. When she sees me, her face lights up with a warm smile. "Come in, Bryan. You're just in time to join us for a cup of tea."

Inside the door, I pause to survey the cramped living room while she heads for the kitchen to prepare my tea. Although the type of construction and the building materials used are comparable to the other mission houses that's where the similarities end. Gordon and Eleanor's home radiates personality, even Whittaker House has a certain ambiance, but Diana's house is stark in its austerity. If I didn't know better, I would never believe that she has lived here for more than three years. There are no rugs on the floor, no family photos, not even a hint of a personal touch anywhere. It looks as if she just moved in and hasn't had time to decorate. *What*, I wonder, *does this say about her?*

Before I can formulate any conclusions, Eleanor returns with my tea, and I follow her into the small bedroom where Diana is propped up in bed. Although she looks considerably better than she did the last time I saw her, it's apparent she has been through a rough ordeal. Her face is bruised and swollen, and her eyes are dull with pain; still, when she sees me she manages a smile. "Bryan," she says, reaching for my hand, "it's so good to see you."

The warmth of her greeting releases a tightness in my chest that I didn't realize was there until it was gone. This is our first encounter since the night we spent together on the mountain, and I've been afraid she wouldn't be comfortable around me, considering the things she disclosed. Apparently, my fears were ungrounded, or maybe she doesn't remember a thing. Whatever the case, I'm relieved. Bending down, I brush her forehead with a kiss. Out of the corner of my eye I see Eleanor smile knowingly. Like most women she is a matchmaker at heart. Handing me my cup of tea, she says, "I'll just leave you two young people to visit while I prepare something for lunch."

Taking a seat in the chair that Eleanor has pulled close to the bed, I study my tea while trying to think of something to say. Conversation does not come easy to me, and it's harder still when I feel deeply as I do now. Given my troubled past, I had decided that the only decent thing for me to do was to distance myself from Diana. Unfortunately, my feelings are immune to reason, and I find myself longing for her more with each passing day. I realize we have almost nothing in common and that making a life together will be next to impossible; still, I cannot deny what I feel. The fact that Diana has some issues of her own only makes her more desirable to me. If anyone can understand the pain I have lived with, I think she can. Not that I have any intention of dumping it on her.

After a sip of tea, I ask, "How's your leg?"

Grimacing, she replies. "It hurts all the time, but that's to be expected. I think Lako got the bone set. Given the severity of the break, that was no small feat. Of course, it's impossible to tell without an X-ray, and that's out of the question seeing that the nearest hospital is in Cruzeiro. Obviously, I'm in no shape for a trip down the river."

"Are you going to put a cast on it?"

"Probably not. We're not really equipped to do that, and this splint seems to be working fine. Of course, it limits my mobility. I really shouldn't try to get up for at least a couple of weeks. By then the bones should have started to knit together, and if I'm careful I can probably get around on crutches."

Talking seems to have tired her, and she closes her eyes. My knee is hurting, and I shift my weight trying to find a comfortable position. Instantly her eyes open, and she says, "You're not leaving, are you?"

"No. I'm just changing my position."

"Good. I like having you here even if I can't stay awake. It's the pain medication, I think."

As she drifts toward sleep, I find myself unconsciously comparing her to Carolyn. Although they each have their own issues, they appear to have handled them differently. Having grown up with an alcoholic father, Carolyn is terribly insecure and in need of constant reassurance. When we married, I think she was looking for the father she never had rather than a husband, at least in some ways. In time, her neediness scared me, and I withdrew, afraid that if I got too close it would consume me. Of course, I could not have articulated that thought then. I just knew I had to have some space or I was going to die. This only exacerbated her insecurities, setting in motion a deadly dance that ultimately destroyed our marriage.

Thinking about her has released a montage of bittersweet memories that now plays in my mind. Some of them are so tenderly poignant that I ache with desire, while others are so painfully sad it is all I can do not to cry. One clip plays repeatedly...

We are watching a movie about a couple of guys, and one of them is mentally handicapped. He is a big man who doesn't know his own strength. His friend tries to look out for him, but he is always messing things up. He's not mean; in fact, he seems to be tender-hearted in a simple sort of way. Unfortunately, he kills everything he loves—little puppies, baby rabbits, and ultimately a girl. He doesn't mean to kill them, but not knowing his own strength, he squeezes them too tight. And even after they are dead, he goes right on petting them.

As we are driving home after the movie, I turn to Carolyn and say, "You're like that guy, the big one. You always hold things too tight."

"What are you talking about?" she asks, fear pinching her words. "You're not making any sense."

"You're killing me," I say, "just squeezing the life out of me, and you don't even know it."

For a block or two she doesn't say anything, and the only sound in the car is the hum of the tires on the street and the rush of the wind past the windows. Finally, she speaks in a voice so sad I think her heart will break, "If you're asking me to love you less, I can't do that." When I don't say anything, she continues, her voice cracking. "It's kind of sad, isn't it? You want me to love you less, and I want you to love me more."

"Bryan." Diana's voice calls me back from the past. "Hold my hand."

Moving my chair closer to her bed, I take her soft hand in mine. When I do, she seems to relax, giving herself to sleep. Studying her profile against the pillow, I decide if I ever marry again my wife will have to be a woman like Diana—strong and independent, a woman who loves me but doesn't need me. If I learned anything from my first marriage, it was that love cannot survive where need is too great.

CHAPTER
38

WHEN I AWAKE FROM my nap, it is late afternoon, and the sun is low in the sky above the river. Leaning on my cane, I limp into the kitchen where I brew a pot of coffee. When it is ready, I pour a cup and hobble out to the porch. Making myself comfortable, I settle down to await Eurico's return. He has gone to the river to catch our supper, and he should be getting back anytime now. Having positioned myself where I have a clear view of the trail, I sip my coffee, savoring its scalding sweetness.

"Bryan," Gordon calls as he makes his way across the compound toward me, "you've got some mail. I picked it up in town when I went in for supplies, but with everything that was going on when I got back I forgot to give it to you."

"Thanks," I reply, as he hands me a small package about the size of a book. "I just made some coffee. Why don't you get a cup and join me."

"I think I will," he says, heading toward the kitchen.

I'm sure the package is from Helen, and a quick glance at the return address confirms this. It was a no brainer, given the fact that she is the only person who knows where I am, not to mention the only one with any reason to write to me. Opening the package, I quickly skim the letter before stuffing it back in the envelope when I hear Gordon returning.

He's too polite to ask about the package, but he does nothing to mask his curiosity. "A note from a friend," I say nonchalantly, "and a book." He seems satisfied with that explanation, and we make small talk as the light fades. It is all I can do to mask the impatience Helen's letter has birthed in me. I can't wait for him to leave so I can read it carefully, noting not only what she has written but what's between the lines as well. Often, what she doesn't say is as important as what she does say.

Unfortunately, Gordon is in a talkative mood, and it is nearly dark before he finally decides to head for home. Lako has returned from a day of scouting, and he is coming up the trail with Eurico who has a nice stringer of fish. We will eat well tonight, although that is of little interest to me now. I hobble into the house while Lako builds a fire and prepares to grill our fish. Striking a match, I savor the sulfurous odor it produces, so reminiscent of my childhood spent in this very house. As the match burns down, I quickly light the kerosene lamp. Pulling it close, I open Helen's letter, the yellow light spilling across the page.

Dear Bryan:

I cannot tell you how much I have suffered these past few weeks or how much strain your "disappearance" put on our family. As you can probably appreciate, I am sorely tempted to chew you out, but I won't. Suffice it to say that your thoughtlessness opened a lot of old wounds. It was like reliving Father's disappearance all over again.

Having gotten that off my chest, let me thank you for your letter! It was a Godsend. At least I know you are alive.

My purpose in writing is twofold: (1) While going through Mother's things I found one of Father's early journals, which I am enclosing. Hopefully, it will contain information that will help you in your search. (2) Carolyn and I have become friends. When she couldn't locate you, she came to me seeking information. I have found her to be a wonderful person and a dear friend when I sorely needed one. She's still very much in love with you and deeply regrets the divorce.

The boys send their love. Write when you can.

Your sister,
Helen

P.S. I'm praying for you.

After reading the letter for the third time, I carefully fold it and return it to its envelope. I find Helen's tone more than a little puzzling. She doesn't sound like herself. Something is going on, but I have no idea what it might be. And the part about becoming friends with Carolyn is really weird. Knowing both of them, I can't imagine that they have anything in common. Her letter has raised a host of questions that now ricochet inside my head clamoring for answers, but I have none.

Laying the letter aside, I reach for the journal. It is leather-bound with brass corners, not unlike the one I saw my father wrap in oilcloth and place in his satchel that fateful night so long ago. *How many evenings,* I wonder, *did I look up from my lessons to see him writing in this journal, or one like it, while sitting at this very table?* Holding it in my hands, I find I am strangely reluctant to open it. It's more than just words on a page; it's a piece of my father. It's the story of his life, or at least part of it. What right do I have to read words he intended for his eyes only? Still, if it will help me make peace with my past, I'm sure he wouldn't mind.

Taking a deep breath, I open it and prepare myself to see life through his eyes. The pages are yellow with age, and in places the ink has faded, but there is no mistaking my father's handwriting. The entries are dated, and I quickly scan several pages. Most of them are nondescript—random thoughts, a prayer list, ministry goals, things like that—but occasionally my father bares his soul in a way I could never imagine. Putting the scattered entries together, an image emerges of a deeply devout man who was painfully aware of his own shortcomings.

February 2, 1939

Hitler's hordes are marching across Europe. England and France are preparing to defend Poland in case of German attack, and the world is in an uproar. While Hitler's war machine poses a threat to free men everywhere, an even greater threat lurks within. In truth, our most deadly enemies are within ourselves— unholy thoughts, vain ambitions, bitterness, anger, and lust, not to mention fear and greed.

It's not weakness that causes me to fail, but willfulness. I am tempted to rationalize rather than repent, but I must not succumb. Rationalization is deadly and must be avoided at all costs. Only true repentance produces life.

I take hope because God is greater than the evil within. Through the blood of Jesus I can defeat these unChristlike attitudes and desires. My part is to honestly face them, call them what they are, and refuse to compromise or make excuses for myself. If I do that, God will deliver me.

May 9, 1940

I'm not very good at prayer—truthfully it hasn't been a high priority. I'm a doer, and prayer "feels" like a waste. I'm ashamed to admit that, for I know it's not a waste, but it feels that way. It's frustrating; it's so easy to miss the connection between prayer and the answer. I'm not trying to justify my inconsistency, just confess it. I know I will only learn to pray by praying, so help me, O Lord, to pray more faithfully.

Pausing, I put my finger between the pages and contemplate what I have read. I'm not sure what I was expecting when I opened my father's journal, but nothing in my experience could have prepared me for what I have found. When I was a boy, he loomed larger than life, and he could do no wrong in my eyes. An imposing figure, he was stern and exacting, intimidating really. The man revealed in his journal is far more human, no less committed but certainly more approachable. Without question he loved God, but he struggled too. He made mistakes, failed to live up to his high ideals, yet he pressed on with a single-minded devotion that I both envy and fear.

Everything I have read so far was written before I was born, so I flip through the pages looking for the day of my birth—January 30, 1941. *What*, I wonder, *was he thinking? Was he thankful for a son? Did he have great dreams for me? Did he want me to become a missionary and follow in his steps?* These and a hundred other questions haunt me as I search for his journal entry on the day I was born.

Bryan Scott Whittaker—8 lbs. 13 ozs.

The hospital here in Cruzeiro do Sul is primitive, and the conditions are deplorable, but Velma and the baby are fine. The Lord has given us a son to carry on the family name and hopefully to follow in my footsteps, the Lord willing.

As I write these words Velma is sleeping, our newborn son cradled in her arm. Looking at him, I realize I am embarking on the most important assignment of my life. And that if I fail as a father, all my other achievements will be diminished.

My relationship with him will shape his relationship with his Heavenly Father. Unconsciously, he will attribute to God the Father the strengths and weaknesses he sees in me, his Earthly father. My words will shape his self-image, giving him the confidence to follow his dreams or locking him in a prison of inferiority.

Help me, O God, to love him unconditionally, to discipline him consistently, and to rear him in the nurture and admonition of the Lord.

Though I am not a man given to tears, I am overcome with emotion. Stumbling into the bedroom, I fling myself across the bed and stuff the corner of a pillow in my mouth to stifle my sobs. The loss I feel is as great now as it was twenty-two years ago, maybe even more so. As a seven-year-old boy I grieved for my father, for the imposing figure who ruled our world. Tonight I'm grieving, not just the loss of my father—both the man I knew and the one I've caught a glimpse of on the pages of his journal—but also the man I might have been. For twenty-two years I have been raging at life and shaking my fist in the face of the Almighty, and where has it gotten me? Nowhere! If the truth be told, I'm just a scared little boy living inside a grown man's body.

I want to believe in God, I need to believe in God, but I can't. I have no faith, no confidence. When my father disappeared, my faith died. I prayed and I believed, but nothing came of it, so how can I trust God now? How can I trust a God who turns a deaf ear to a small boy's desperate prayer? How can I trust a God who can't take care of His own? Yet for all my hurt and anger, I need God. I need a Heavenly Father! But I can't bring myself to pray. I think I'm afraid to pray, afraid that He won't be there; then I will be absolutely desolate and without hope. As long as I don't pray, I can hang onto the possibility that God might be there. But if I pray, and He doesn't answer, I will have nothing—and I can't risk that final disillusionment, not yet anyhow.

The door slams, and I hear voices in the kitchen. Quickly I dry my tears and hide Helen's letter and the journal beneath the mattress. I don't know why I bother; neither Lako nor Eurico can read English; still, I feel better having put it away. At the wash basin I splash cold water on my face and run my fingers through my hair. Glancing in the tiny mirror, I'm relieved to see that I've washed away every trace of my tears. Unfortunately, I can do nothing about the sorrow lodged in my chest.

When I sit down at the table, Lako and Eurico are already eating, a whole smoked fish on each of our plates. Although I have no appetite, I force myself to eat. Peeling back a flap of dry skin, I use my fingers to pull the tasty meat off the bone. Having no napkins, we lick our fingers repeatedly. It's not something I would do back in Denver, but it's kosher out here, at least when there are no ladies around. Both Lako and Eurico are sucking on the head, which I am told is the tastiest part of the fish. Although I have tried to adapt to the local culture as much as possible, I can't bring myself to suck on a fish head, no matter how tasty it is. Seeing I'm not going to indulge, Eurico makes short work of mine.

It's not late, but I'm completely worn out. The lingering effects of the malaria, combined with everything else, have totally depleted whatever energy reserves I might have had. Leaving the two of them to clean up the kitchen, I make my way back to the bedroom. I would like to read more in my father's journal, but I don't have the strength. Instead I crawl into bed, fighting to keep my grief at bay until sleep overtakes me.

CHAPTER
39

A LITTLE MORE THAN two weeks have passed since Diana's ill-fated visit to the Kachinawa village, and she is finally able to get out of bed. Maneuvering carefully on her crutches, she makes her way to the small living room where Eleanor has prepared an improvised chaise lounge. She would like to sit on the porch in the sun, but it is raining again, so she settles for the living room. By the time Eleanor has arranged the pillows around her and gotten her leg situated, she is light-headed with weakness. "Wow," she says, "I never would have believed that lying in bed for a couple of weeks could turn me into such a pansy."

Patting her on the shoulder, Eleanor asks, "Is there anything I can get you before I go?"

"A large glass of sweet tea, please."

Leaning her head back, Diana closes her eyes and lets her mind wander. As has often been the case of late, she finds herself thinking of Bryan and the unusual turn of events that brought them together. *What if he hadn't gotten malaria and been forced to return to the mission station? What if Gordon and Lako hadn't both been gone when I had to go to the Kachinawa village to try and help that poor woman give birth? What if Bryan and I hadn't been injured and forced to spend the night together on the mountain? What if both of us hadn't had to spend the better part of the last three weeks recovering? Had things happened any other way, we might have been like ships passing in the night, never getting to know one another.*

Around and around her thoughts go, but no matter how she looks at it she comes to the same conclusion—their relationship is part of God's plan. There are simply too many "coincidences"—"God incidences," as her mother would say. The Amazon Basin is a huge place. It encompasses over two million square miles of tropical rain forest. That's a little more than half the size of the United States. Bryan might have gone anywhere in that vast area in search of subjects for his *National Geographic* article, but he didn't. He came here, to this tiny mission compound. The chances of that happening by accident are simply astronomical. As far as she is concerned, it is God's doing; it couldn't be otherwise.

Hearing the front door open, Diana looks up, expecting Bryan, but it's only Gordon. Hiding her disappointment, she murmurs a greeting as he sits down in the chair next to her. Hearing her husband's voice, Eleanor calls from the kitchen, "Would you like a glass of sweet tea?" When he answers in the affirmative, she brings a pitcher and two glasses. Setting them on a wooden crate that serves as a table, she fills their glasses and then excuses herself.

After taking a drink of tea, Gordon clears his throat. "Diana, there's something I need to discuss with you."

When he hesitates, she says, "Sure. What's on your mind?"

Now he shifts uncomfortably in his chair while studying the floor between his feet. Once or twice he clears his throat, but he still can't seem to find the right words. Finally, Diana takes pity on him, saying, "Out with it, Gordon. What did I do this time? Did I mess up my monthly report again?"

Thankful for the opening, he replies, "I wish it were something that simple..." Again he pauses, searching for the right words, and as the silence lingers Diana finds herself growing concerned. Frantically she searches her memory for something she might have done, some breach of etiquette or even an unintended violation of missionary protocol. For the life of her she can't think of a thing.

Setting his glass of tea down, Gordon forces himself to look her in the eye. "Surely you know how Eleanor and I feel about you. You're like one of our children, and anything that affects you concerns us. That's why I feel like I have to say something even if it's awkward. If anything was to happen, and I hadn't spoken with you regarding my concerns, I would never forgive myself."

To Diana his words sound stilted; still, she does not question his sincerity. He is a good friend and a wonderful missionary. When he hesitates yet again, she says, "Just spit it out, Gordon. All this hemming and hawing around is making me nervous."

"It's about Bryan," he blurts out, letting his unfinished statement hang in the air between them.

"What is it?" she asks, concern coloring her words. "Have you learned something about Bryan that I should know?"

Shifting uncomfortably in his chair, Gordon replies. "No, I still haven't heard anything from the missions department."

"So what is it?" Diana demands impatiently. "What has Bryan done that I should know about?"

Forcing himself to look her in the eye, he says, "You may not realize it yet, but you and Bryan have feelings for each other; anyone can see that. Look how much time the two of you have been spending together. That's understandable given the circumstances, but it's hardly wise. Who knows where this could lead?"

Sighing, Diana says, "Gordon, I appreciate your concern, but I can assure you that it's unnecessary. In a few days, Bryan will be heading into the interior to complete his assignment. After that, he will be returning to the States, and I will probably never see him again. Besides, we're just friends."

"Diana, you're one of the most competent people I know, a fine missionary and a wonderful doctor, but I think you're underestimating the power of your emotions."

When she starts to protest, he holds up his hands. "Please hear me out, and then you can respond. What do you really know about Bryan? Is he a believer? Do you know anything about his family, his background? Have you considered what would happen if the two of you were to fall in love and marry? Would you give up your missionary appointment and return to the States? Would Bryan be willing to live here as the husband of a missionary doctor? Would the mission board even allow it? These are just some of the things that concern me. I'm sure if you stop to think about it you will agree these are issues that can't be ignored."

Although she doesn't want to admit it, his concerns echo her own. For days she has refused to acknowledge them, but they haven't gone away. No matter how she justifies her relationship with Bryan, she cannot deny that there will be complications. She's just not ready to deal with them, and by forcing her to do just that Gordon is making her defensive. On a more objective level she realizes that she is overreacting, but she cannot seem to help herself. Fuming, she thinks, *What right does he have to interfere in my private life? My relationship with Bryan is no concern of his. I'm a grown woman, for Heaven's sake, and a doctor.*

With an effort she forces herself to speak calmly. "Gordon, I'm thirty-three years old. I'm not a teenybopper. I think I'm quite capable of managing my own relationships. I have no intention of becoming romantically involved with Bryan, or any other man for that matter, but if I were it should be no concern of yours."

Gordon starts to speak and then thinks better of it. What can he say that he hasn't already said? Diana's blasé response simply confirms his worst fears. It's obvious that her emotions have already blinded her to the risks involved in any relationship with Bryan. No matter what he might say, she would simply dismiss him as a meddling old man. Putting on his hat, he steps onto the porch where he pauses for just a moment before turning toward home.

After he is gone, an unbidden tear slips down Diana's cheek, and she quickly wipes it away, determined not to cry. It's obvious her response has hurt Gordon, and she regrets that, but it couldn't be helped. No matter how good his intentions were, he had no business interfering in her private life. At least that's what she tells herself.

His questions have unsettled her; she can't deny that. She doesn't want to consider the future; she just wants to savor the moment. Given her situation, she knows there is little or no chance for marriage; still, of late she has found herself wondering what it would be like to spend the rest of her life with Bryan. It will never happen, but she has thought about it. She keeps telling herself that all she wants is to enjoy a few days of innocent romance before Bryan leaves, but in her heart of hearts she knows better.

So what does she really know about Bryan? Almost nothing, she has to admit, beyond the fact that he is a freelance photojournalist, and she has only his word for that. Although they have spent the better part of every day together for the past two weeks, he has hardly been transparent. He could be married for all she knows, but she doesn't think so. At least he's not wearing a wedding band. She checked that out right up front. Of course, it doesn't mean anything. A lot of men don't wear jewelry, especially here in the jungle.

Thinking back over the conversations they have had, she realizes that Bryan has been especially adept at avoiding self-disclosure. Using charm and finesse, he always seems to redirect the conversation without appearing to do so. Two or three instances come readily to mind, like the time she asked him his age.

Studying his profile, she can't help but notice how young his skin looks. On an impulse she asks, "Bryan, how old are you?"

Giving her a lazy grin, he says, "Why is a woman's age off limits but not a man's?"

Caught up in his playfulness, she replies, "Because a woman is only as old as she feels."

"So this is what young feels like," he murmers, his fingers feather soft upon her cheek.

Somehow they never got back to the question of his age. Another time she asked about his childhood.

He is sitting in the chair beside her bed, the late afternoon sun shining through the shutters, laying horizontal bars of light across the foot of her bed. "Tell me about yourself," she said. "I want to know everything—where you lived, what you were like as a little boy, your first day of school, who your first girlfriend was…everything."

"My first girlfriend," he muses, a hint of playfulness in his tone, "let me see. She was a beautiful blonde from Minnesota. Not your typical blonde, no sir! She was no airhead, not this girl. She was a doctor, and not just any kind of doctor either. A missionary doctor, that's what she was. The first time I laid eyes on her I knew she was in love with me."

Slapping him playfully, she says, "Come on, Bryan, you don't really expect me to believe I'm your first girlfriend, do you?"

"There may have been others before you," he concedes, "but they have been erased from my memory. Once I saw you, everyone else was forgotten."

Thinking about it now, she realizes that's how talking with Bryan went anytime she tried to get personal. He had an uncanny way of deflecting attention without ever appearing to be defensive. Maybe he's just unusually modest, one of those rare individuals who are truly interested in others. That's what she would like to believe, but now she wonders if she is just being naive. Gordon's intrusive questions have opened Pandora's box, and try as she might she can't get it closed again. Without a doubt she will have to have a heart-to-heart talk with Bryan, if that's possible.

CHAPTER

40

SUPPLIES ARE STREWN ALL over the kitchen and living room of Whittaker House—rice, beans, coffee, smoked meat, bandages, medicine, and other medical supplies. I am marking things off my list as Lako and Eurico pack containers in preparation for a thirty-day expedition into the jungle. Lako, who is an experienced *mateiro*, helped me prepare the list to ensure we have everything we will need. In spite of our careful attention to detail, I have no illusions. Experience has taught me that the Amazon Basin is a perilous place. Disaster and disease can, and often do, strike without warning. We had to abandon our first expedition after only two days when I was stricken with a severe bout of malaria. The lingering effects still plague me, and I never know when I will succumb to fever or night sweats; nor have I fully regained my strength. Be that as it may, I am determined to see this expedition through.

It is early evening by the time we get the last of our provisions packed and ready to be carried to the river. Thankfully, Lako and Eurico will take care of that chore. My knee is still giving me trouble, so I don't want to push my luck. Once they have moved the supplies to the boat, they will spend the night on the beach in order to guard them. Our provisions would probably be safe enough, but there is no sense in taking any chances.

Following them to the river, I strip down to my underwear and plunge in. The water is surprisingly cool, and though I would like to linger in order to watch the sun set over the mountains, I waste no time bathing. Back at Whittaker House I pull on a clean pair of jeans and my only chambray shirt. After combing my hair, I apply a liberal amount of Old Spice cologne and check my appearance in the small mirror above the wash basin. Realizing I still have almost thirty minutes before I am supposed to meet Diana for dinner at the Arnolds', I reach under the mattress and retrieve my father's journal. Pulling the kerosene lamp close, I prepare to revisit the past.

Nothing in my life has prepared me for what I am discovering about my father. He's not at all like the man I remember as a child, or perhaps I should say he is far more complex than the one-dimensional man I knew. In our home he was a man of few words, at least with Helen and me, but on the pages of his journal he is profound in his insights and on occasion even eloquent. His strict adherence to discipline caused me to think him stern, even rigid, but his writings reveal another side. It was his love, his passion for God, that drove him.

My throat is thick with feelings, and my eyes blur when I realize how little I know of this man who was my father and how badly I have misjudged him. In many ways I have his temperament. Although I feel things deeply, it has been nearly impossible for me to express my feelings, except anger, of course. I always thought I was this way because of what happened, but now I suspect it is as much temperament as circumstances. Apparently he was the same way. Around us the only time he displayed his emotions was when he got mad. But in the privacy of his writings his words are full of feeling.

I leaf through his journal, reading portions at random, and now my eyes alight on an entry made on October 10, 1944.

"He that loveth father or mother more than me is not worthy of me: and he that loveth son or daughter more than me is not worthy of me."—Matthew 10:37

My parents are committed Christians who taught me from an early age to love God with all my heart, mind, soul, and strength. Hence loving God more than my parents was never a struggle for me. Where Helen and Bryan are concerned, it's a different matter. Sometimes I fear I love them to the point of idolatry—that is, more than I love my Savior. I want to provide for them and protect them from the difficulties of life. I always want to be there for them, to counsel, to love, and to guide. Sometimes, I love them so much I hesitate to take the risks I know the Lord is requiring of me. What would happen to Velma and the children if I were to lose my life in service for Christ? Who would provide for them?

Many of the unreached Indians are notorious killers, and taking the gospel to them involves the ultimate risk. Were it not for my family, laying down my life in order to bring them to the Savior would be the highest honor I could ever desire. No one knows the conflict my love for my children creates for me, not even Velma. O Lord, give me wisdom and grace that I might live worthy of You. Help me to understand that I can be the kind of husband and father my family needs only if I am fully committed to You, even if that means losing my life for Your sake.

His words pierce my heart, cutting me to the quick. How many times have I railed at him in my mind, accusing him of selfishly putting his ministry before his family, of giving no thought to the jeopardy in which he was placing us, never realizing the depth of his love? I still don't understand why God would allow me to lose my father at such an early age, but for the first time ever I am confident of my father's love. He loved me! He really loved me!

Reading his journal is like having a conversation with him, only better. In person I doubt if he could have been this transparent. Checking my watch, I see that I have just time enough to read one more entry. The next one is dated October 23, 1944, nearly two weeks later. He must have still been wrestling with the same issues, for on this occasion he wrote:

> *Ministry must always be a balance between vision and relationship, a balance between the Great Commandment (loving God) and the Great Commission (taking the gospel to the entire world). Vision enlarges and energizes us, while relationship refreshes and nurtures us. Vision focuses on doing God's work, while relationship focuses on being with God. Vision without relationship exposes us to unholy ambition. Relationship without vision tempts us to become narcissistic. Help me, O God, to balance my vision with relationships lest I become consumed with the ministry and lose my relationship with You and with my family.*

Tossing the journal on the bed, I head for the door. I'm still mulling over his words when I step off the porch and head toward the Arnolds'. It's the rainy season, and to the west the sky over the Serra Divisor is boiling with thunderheads. Nearer, the night is electric with lightning, the air smelling of fresh ozone. Downdrafts, cold and heavy with moisture, trouble the towering treetops. Hurrying through the darkness, I make it to the Arnolds' porch just as the storm hits, the rain rattling off the tin roof with a deafening roar. For a moment I feel sorry for Lako and Eurico, huddled under a tarp in this rain, but my concerns are short-lived when I hear the sound of Diana's laughter.

The house is as I remember it, warm and inviting. In the kitchen, Diana is sitting on a chair keeping Eleanor company while she cooks. I would love to join them, but I feel constrained to remain with Gordon, and he has returned to his chair in the living room, so I take a seat on the couch across from him. Apparently he has been reading, for an open book rests on the table beside his chair, and the kerosene lamp has been pulled close. We make small talk, but he is not his normal jovial self. Instead, he seems pensive, even preoccupied, as if he has something on his mind.

Finally, he clears his throat and says, "I understand you're going upriver tomorrow." When I nod, he continues. "You're heading into some pretty rough country, and if anything happens, you're on your own. There won't be anyone to come to your aid."

Shrugging, I reply, "Calculated risks are part of the job."

Getting up, he walks to the bookcase and returns with four or five copies of *National Geographic*. Holding them up so I can see what he has, he says, "I've been a longtime subscriber to this magazine, and for the life of me I haven't been able to locate any of your articles." Without giving me a chance to reply, he opens one of the magazines and makes a show of perusing the credits page. Casually he asks, "Who did you say assigned you your article?"

"Bill Snyder," I say, picking a name out of the air. "He's one of the assistant editors."

"Hum, I don't see him listed here."

My mind is racing. Given the mail service in the Amazon Basin, or lack thereof, I can't image that he has the latest edition, so I reply, "If you don't have the 1970 spring or summer edition, it's not likely he would be listed. He was promoted to assistant editor at the end of last year."

I feel like a bug under a microscope, but I try not to let my anxiety show. Why this sudden interest in my cover story? I can't imagine that Gordon would have gone to the trouble of contacting the *National Geographic* office to check up on me, but I guess that's possible. Maybe he telegraphed them from Cruzeiro when he went in for supplies. Be that as it may, I'll just try to bluff my way through.

"Diana tells me that Lako has located a group of Amuacas up near the Serra Divisor."

He throws this out while replacing the magazines in the bookcase, and I'm momentarily confused by his sudden change in direction. If he's hoping to keep me off balance in order to trip me up, he's doing a good job.

"That's right," I reply, determined to keep my responses as short as possible until I can figure out where he is going with this conversation.

Returning to his chair, he removes his glasses and rubs the bridge of his nose. "No missionary has ever been able to reach the Amuacas. They have a fierce hatred for all outsiders. Most of the missionaries in our organization think they probably killed Harold Whittaker."

At the mention of my father I'm thrown off stride again. As casually as I can I ask, "Is he the missionary who founded this station?"

Before he can respond, Eleanor calls us to dinner. As we are making our way to the kitchen, he drapes an arm over my shoulders. "Interesting coincidence, isn't it, that you both have the same last name? Whittaker—that's not a very common name, now is it?"

CHAPTER

41

AS ALWAYS, ELEANOR HAS prepared a feast. Her culinary genius lies in her ability to make the ordinary special. We use the same staples at Whittaker House, but the finished product is unlike anything she prepares. Like the first time I shared dinner here, the food is delicious, the kitchen cozy with its checkered tablecloth and kerosene lamp; unfortunately, that is where the similarity ends. Tonight there is a tension in the air that is almost palpable. Diana and Gordon have hardly said a word to each other, and although Eleanor is doing her best to stimulate conversation, the rest of us remain uncomfortably quiet. What should have been an enjoyable dinner has turned into a miserable meal, the click of silverware against glass plates sounding unnaturally loud in the suffocating silence.

When we are finally finished with dinner, I offer to help Eleanor clear the table and do the dishes, but she refuses my aid. Leaning close, she flashes her eyes at Gordon who is retreating to the living room, then whispers, "Pay him no mind. He means well, but he has a habit of meddling in things that don't concern him."

Getting up from the table, she retrieves Diana's crutches and brings them to her. At the door she kisses Diana on the cheek before giving me a hug. "You two run along and enjoy your evening. It will be a while before you see each other again, so don't waste what little time you have with us old folk." Gordon glares at her, but she ignores him and heads toward the kitchen to clean up.

Opening Diana's umbrella, we step off the porch and turn toward her house. The crutches make things awkward, but I manage to keep the rain off without tripping her. We have almost reached her house before either of us speaks. I finally break the silence. "What was going on back there? I've never seen Gordon like that."

"He was being a stinker, wasn't he?"

"You could say that," I reply as I help her up the step and onto the porch. Closing the umbrella, I lean it against the door jam to dry. Inside the house it is pitch black, and Diana waits by the door while I feel my way toward the table where the kerosene lamp sits. I should have brought a flashlight, but I keep forgetting how dark it is out here in the jungle. Bumping into the table, I locate a box of matches and strike one. Across the room, Diana makes a show of clapping her hands. "Don't mock me," I say threateningly, "or I'll blow out this match and leave you stranded in the dark."

"Please don't," she begs. "I might break my other leg."

Her laughter is like music to my ears, especially after the ordeal at the Arnolds'. Removing the globe, I light the lamp and adjust the wick. The lambent light fills the room with a soft yellow glow, making even the primitive furnishings somehow inviting. Pushing the door closed, Diana crosses the small room to the makeshift chaise lounge. Easing herself down, she uses her hands to position her injured leg. Sighing softly, she leans her head back and smiles.

Sitting on the floor beside her chair, I lean back and rest my head against her leg. She runs her fingers through my hair, and I can't help imagining what it would be like to spend the rest of my life with her. Just as quickly I realize that I'm not thinking clearly. Even if Diana feels the same way I do, there's no future for us. Once she learns my real reason for coming to the Amazon, she will despise me. In an instant I am tempted with despair, but with an effort I resist such melancholy thoughts, determining to live only for the moment.

"Bryan," Diana says, her voice thick with feeling, "look at me."

I reposition myself so I am sitting on my knees facing her. Taking my face in her hands, she looks deep into my eyes. "Bryan Scott Whittaker, do you know that I love you?"

Her words stun me, and for a minute I am speechless. Finally, I stammer, "I love you too, Diana Rhoades, but I'm afraid to say it. There's no future for us, no—"

Putting her finger on my lips, she hushes me. "Not now, Bryan. Not tonight. Just hold me."

I hesitate for just a moment before, I take her in my arms, cradling her head against my chest, the smell of her hair as clean and fresh as rainwater. I want this moment to last forever. No past. No future. Just this moment. Just us.

My heart is so full of feeling I think it will burst. Without realizing what I am doing, I find myself kissing her hair, her eyes, the tip of her nose, and finally her lips. Her arms are around my neck, her fingers in my hair. Her joy, it seems, is as great as my own. Her mouth is against my ear. "Where have you been all my life," she whispers, "where have you been?"

Finally, the pain in my bum knee becomes unbearable, and I have to get off of it. Sitting on the floor beside her chair once more, I rest my head against her leg and lose myself in her eyes. She traces the contours of my face with her finger, talking softly all the while. "I think I've always loved you, Bryan Whittaker, I just didn't know it. When I was just a little girl in pigtails, I loved you. At my high school prom, I loved you. Every night in my dreams, I have loved you, and when I am old I will still love you, and it will be your face I remember when my life is drawing to a close."

I don't know what to say, so I hold her hand to my lips and kiss it. Her eyes are shiny with tears, and my heart hurts. "Are you sad?" I ask.

Pursing her lips, she nods. "Yes, I'm sad, but it's okay because I'm happy too. I'm happy for tonight, for us. If this is all we ever have, just this one kiss, this one night, I'll treasure it forever."

For a time we sit in silence, each of us lost in our own thoughts. I'm remembering the way she looked the first time I saw her, and how gentle was her touch when she cared for me while I had malaria, and the terror I felt when she plunged down the mountain. In my mind I see her sitting in the swing beneath the towering *samaúma* tree; her eyes are sparkling, and her face is full of laughter, the afternoon sun backlighting her blonde hair. I fix these images in my mind, carefully noting each detail. Somehow I know it will be important later, years from now, when all I will have are my memories.

The earlier fury of the storm has passed, and now a gentle rain pings against the metal roof, creating what will always be in my mind a kind of music. And in the future when I look back on my days in the Amazon, this is what I will remember—the soft glow of a kerosene lamp, the murmur of rain on the roof, and Diana's fingers in my hair. And no matter where my travels take me, the drumming of rain on a tin roof will always sound like love to me—Diana's love.

It has grown late, and although I have no desire to go, propriety demands that I bid her goodnight and return to Whittaker House. When I rise to go, she clings to my hand. After a moment I hand her crutches to her, and she walks me to the door. Taking her in my arms, I hold her against my chest, a roaring in my ears. "I love you, Diana Rhoades," I say hoarsely, emotion squeezing my throat. Her crutches clatter to the floor as she hugs my neck, covering my face with kisses. In the dark my lips find hers, and for a moment time is suspended. When at last I break away, my cheeks are damp with her tears. Bending down, I pick up her crutches and hand them to her. Turning, I hurry down the steps, never looking back.

"God go with you, Bryan Whittaker," she calls into the night, as I plunge through the dark toward Whittaker House. As I open my door the wind shifts, bringing me the sound of her sobs. My eyes blur, but I steel myself against any emotion that might deter me from the task ahead. Even though I love her, there can be no future for us, and the sooner I distance myself from these emotions the better it will be for both of us.

CHAPTER
42

THE LATE OCTOBER SUN is high in the Colorado sky, causing the stained-glass windows to drench the sanctuary in a rich tapestry of softly diffused light. To Helen the effect is mesmerizing, and, without intending to, she allows her mind to wander as Rob is nearing the end of his sermon. Should anyone glance her way she looks attentive, having long ago perfected the ability to appear engrossed in Rob's sermon even when her mind is someplace else. Today, she finds herself reviewing the past few weeks. Thankfully, she has come to terms with her situation. Her marriage may not be what she once thought it was, but then whose marriage is? On the bright side, Rob is a good man, a faithful husband, and an attentive father. That he appears incapable of understanding her is a continuing source of pain, but it is something she will just have to learn to live with. Maybe in time he will become less self-absorbed and more sensitive to the things nearest to her heart. Be that as it may, she is determined to make the best of things.

As the congregation rises for the closing hymn, she returns her focus to the service and her responsibilities as the pastor's wife. Following the benediction, she quickly makes her way to the foyer where she chats with members of the congregation as they are leaving. Although she is not naturally gregarious, she still looks forward to the few minutes of personal interaction each week. Today she tousles a small boy's hair, while listening to his mother talk about a book she read. "You really should get it, Helen. It will open your eyes to things about prayer you've never even considered." Catching herself, she hastily adds, "Well, at least I had never considered them."

Smiling graciously, Helen says, "Thank you. I'll look for it."

A young couple approaches, hardly able to contain their joy. "What a beautiful baby," Helen gushes, causing them to smile with pleasure.

"We were wondering if we could have our baby dedicated the Sunday following Thanksgiving. Our parents will be in town, and it would be the perfect time for us."

"I'm sure you can, but you will need to call the church office and set it up. Ask for Rita. She's the pastor's secretary, and she schedules all the baby dedications."

Helen excuses herself when the volunteer children's ministry coordinator approaches, a determined look on her face. Turning to her, she smiles a greeting. "What is it, Gloria?"

"Would you please remind Pastor that children's church ends promptly at twelve o'clock. When he goes over, it makes it really difficult for us. I've talked to him about it on at least two occasions, but it doesn't seem to do any good. I thought maybe a word from you would help."

Giving Gloria's hand a squeeze, Helen says, "We appreciate everything you do for the children. You are truly a Godsend. I'll speak to Rob, but I can't promise you it will do any good. You know how these preachers are."

Placated, at least momentarily, Gloria thanks her and turns to go. As she is leaving, Rita walks up. She is a striking woman with a knack for coordinating her outfits to achieve maximum effect. In her company Helen inevitably feels gangly, her outfits poorly fitting and dowdy. They're not, but she feels that way just the same. Forcing a smile, she says, "Hello, Rita. You look lovely as always."

They chat for a moment, exchanging information without really saying anything. Helen is searching for a way to extricate herself from the conversation when Rita leans in and pats her on the arm, saying confidentially, "I'm so glad things are better now for you and Rob. I know the past few weeks have been really hard on both of you."

In an instant Helen feels the blood rush to her head. Although she continues the conversation, her smile firmly pasted on, it is all she can do to hold herself together. Had she discovered that Rob was having an affair with Rita she could not have felt more betrayed. How dare he share the intimate details of their marriage with another woman, any woman, but especially with this woman. What was he thinking? By confiding in Rita, he has broken faith with her, betrayed the sacred trust at the heart of their marriage. She feels like she is suffocating, as if all the air has been sucked out of the room. She has to get away from this woman; she cannot stomach her pseudosweetness a minute more, but she cannot let Rita see that she has sorely wounded her either.

Over Helen's shoulder Rita sees Rob approaching and quickly turns toward him. Taking his hand, she says, "Wonderful sermon, Pastor, wonderful. It really spoke to me."

Her fawning manner is so transparent it makes Helen want to gag, but Rob seems taken in by it. Ignoring Helen, Rita continues. "Since you won't be in the office tomorrow, there's a couple of scheduling things I need to go over with you, if you have a minute."

Glancing at Helen, Rob suggests, "Why don't you take the boys and go on home and get dinner on the table. Rita can drop me off at the house on her way home."

Without waiting for her reply, he turns toward the church offices. Inside Helen is boiling, but she will not give Rita the satisfaction of seeing how upset she is. After a moment she calls after Rob, "Don't be long. You know how hungry the boys are."

Driving home, Helen hardly notices the giant elm trees and cottonwoods even though they are arrayed in autumn splendor. Nor is she aware of the towering blue sky or the bite of October air or even the slightly acrid odor of burning leaves. In her mind she is still in the church foyer, watching Rob allow himself to be expertly manipulated by Rita. The smugly superior smile Rita gave her before turning to follow Rob into his office burns like a brand in her memory. With an effort she maintains a calm facade for the boys' sake, but on the inside the acid of anger is burning a hole in the lining of her stomach.

Pulling into the driveway, she sees a vaguely familiar car parked in front of the house. *Who can that be?* she wonders, while unlocking the front door. Sending the boys inside, she calls after them, "Change your clothes before you go outside."

Turning back to the street, she sees Carolyn getting out of her car. *Oh no*, she thinks, *not company, not today.* Forcing herself to be gracious, she calls, "Carolyn! How nice to see you. Come in. You're just in time for Sunday dinner."

Once inside the house, Helen moves by rote, putting her purse and car keys on the table in the entryway before hanging her coat in the hall closet. In the kitchen she puts on an apron over her Sunday best before taking a package of frozen corn from the freezer. From the refrigerator she gets fresh vegetables for a salad, placing them on the drain board by the sink.

She makes conversation with Carolyn without really thinking about it while her mind conjures up images of Rob and Rita. He is standing behind her, leaning over her shoulder, his body brushing up against hers while studying the calendar on her desk. Rita laughs at something he says, and the pleasure he takes in her laughter is plain in his face.

Determinedly, Helen thrusts the images from her mind. Turning to Carolyn, she says, "There's another apron in the bottom drawer if you would like to help me get dinner on the table."

"Sure," Carolyn says, rummaging in the drawer. "What would you like me to do?"

"Why don't you prepare the salad while I get the roast out of the oven and make gravy. Once that's done, we'll need to set the table in the dining room."

As she is slicing the roast, Helen hears a car turn into the driveway. Laying the knife on the counter, she moves to the kitchen window, being careful to stay far enough back so she can't be seen. She watches as Rob gets out of the car and turns toward the house. When he is about halfway up the walk, Rita rolls down her window and calls to him. Returning to the car, he bends down and leans toward the open window.

Once more Helen feels the blood rush to her head. Although she cannot hear what they are saying, the fact that they are flirting is obvious enough. She wills herself to look away, but she cannot tear herself away from the window, no matter how painful the scene before her. Finally, Rob glances at his watch and steps away from the car. Mouthing a sultry "good-bye," Rita backs out of the driveway while he remains rooted to the spot, staring after her until she disappears around the corner at the end of the block. He lingers a moment more before straightening his tie and heading toward the door.

Turning back to the kitchen, Helen realizes that Carolyn has been watching the drama in the driveway over her shoulder. Now she asks, "What was that all about?"

Feigning a nonchalance she doesn't feel, Helen replies. "The usual church business. Rita is Rob's secretary, and since he's not in the office on Mondays there are often things that have to be taken care of on Sunday, especially if he doesn't want to be bothered on his day off."

"I don't mean to presume," Carolyn ventures, a look of concern clouding her features, "but that hardly looked like church business out there. Besides, what was that woman doing bringing Rob home?"

How do I answer that question? Helen wonders, searching for the right response. Finally she says, "Normally, I would have remained at the church office with Rob, but I didn't want the roast to burn; besides, Rita comes right by here on her way home."

Her explanation is a bit disingenuous, but she's in no condition to discuss the matter now. Turning back to the roast, she arranges the slices of beef on a serving platter along with the potatoes and carrots. As she stirs the gravy she can feel Carolyn's questioning stare burning a hole in her back. She hasn't fooled her, of that she is sure, but what can she say? Now is not the time to get into this; besides, she is hanging onto her composure by her fingernails. Any discussion of the matter, and she is sure to fall apart. That must not happen; the boys would never understand.

Pouring the gravy into a gravy boat, she turns to Carolyn. "Why don't you put the food on the table while I round up Rob and the boys. I'm sure they're starving."

Fixing a smile firmly in place, she goes in search of her family, determined to pretend that Rob's latest indiscretion is of no consequence. It will require a Herculean effort, for the discovery of the emotional bond he shares with Rita has left her reeling, her inner world completely out of kilter.

CHAPTER

43

TAKING A SIP OF her coffee, Helen rubs the back of her neck and tries to relax. Sunday dinner was torturous, the strain of maintaining her cheerful facade taking a fearful toll on her frayed nerves. Interacting with Rob, while pretending she wasn't dying on the inside, was nearly more than she could bear. Of course, he was oblivious, or so it seemed, but she caught Carolyn watching her intently as the meal progressed. Now Carolyn reaches across the table and takes her hand. "Are you all right, Helen?" she asks.

Instantly, all the pain Helen has been keeping at bay rushes back, flooding her eyes with tears. Refusing to cry, she maintains her fragile composure, but not without a determined effort. Taking a ragged breath, she says, "Please, I can't talk about it right now." Her voice is pinched with pain, foreign sounding even to her own ears.

For a moment Carolyn studies her distraught friend; then she gives her hand a gentle squeeze before withdrawing her own. She wants to say something—a comforting word—but the rawness of Helen's emotions has rendered her mute. From the backyard she hears the children's voices, gleeful with excitement as Rob throws the football with them. In the distance a car horn blares, and there is the screeching of tires skidding on pavement. Across the table Helen's ragged breathing slowly quiets itself. Like a frightened child backing away from a dangerous precipice, she carefully steps back from the grief that threatens to overwhelm her. Finally, she speaks with a forced calmness, "So what brings you to Sterling?"

What indeed? Carolyn thinks, as she struggles to refocus her thoughts. Hastily she composes a reply. "A couple of things, I guess. You're the only link I have with Bryan. I don't suppose you've heard from him…Of course not, or you would have called."

With a shake of her head Helen confirms Carolyn's assumption and adds, "I've written to him. Some weeks ago now, and I sent him one of Father's early journals. I found it when I was going through some of Mother's things."

"Journal?"

"It's like a dairy, only it focuses on spiritual issues. I like to think of it as a way of charting my spiritual progress."

While Helen continues to talk, Carolyn's thoughts go to the spiral notebook in her purse. Maybe she has been journaling and didn't even know it. She'll have to ask Helen about that. Tuning back in to the conversation, she hears Helen say, "I told Bryan that we had become friends." She pauses for a moment, carefully considering her words. "I also told him that you're still very much in love with him and deeply regret the divorce."

Reaching across the table, she touches Carolyn on the shoulder. "You don't mind, do you?"

"I guess not," Carolyn muses. "I just don't want to appear needy. Bryan hates that."

Pushing her chair back, she crosses to the sofa where she retrieves her purse. Returning to the table, she extracts the spiral notebook and hands it to Helen. "What's this?" Helen asks before opening it.

Nervously tugging at a strand of hair, Carolyn replies, "Just some stuff I felt like writing down—scriptures mostly, plus some thoughts and feelings, stuff like that."

Quickly perusing the first few pages, Helen immediately notices the predominance of scriptures. Carolyn has filled page after page with verses written in her precise handwriting, highlighting certain words and phrases. Occasionally she has jotted a comment or a question, but for the most part it is just scriptures. After scanning several verses, Helen realizes most of them deal with forgiveness.

"Remember not the sins of my youth, nor my transgressions."

Psalm 25:7

"Blessed is he whose transgression is forgiven, whose sin is covered."

Psalm 32:1

"For I will forgive their iniquity, and **I will remember their sin no more."**

Jeremiah 31:34

Forgetting her own anguish for the moment, she turns to Carolyn. "Thank you for sharing your journal with me. Your trust means a lot to me."

"I have no one else," Carolyn replies, moved nearly to tears by Helen's kindness. "You're the only person who would understand. Besides, you gave me the Bible."

"So I did, didn't I?"

"Helen, may I ask you a question?"

"Certainly."

"What's happening to me? Ever since the night I heard Bryan calling for help, things have been so different."

"Different? In what way?"

"This is probably going to sound strange, but I don't feel so alone anymore. Don't get me wrong—I still get lonely, especially in the evenings or when it's time to go to bed. But even then I don't feel alone, not like I used to."

"That's because you're not alone. Jesus is with you, now and always. He will never leave you. The 'sense' of His presence will vary in intensity, but He's always there no matter how you may feel. Sometimes His presence will be so real you could swear someone was in the room with you. Like the night you heard Bryan calling for help. Then there will be times you don't 'feel' His presence at all, but He's still there."

Excusing herself, Helen goes to get her Bible from another part of the house. While she is gone, Carolyn makes her way into the living room. The windows face the backyard, and she can't help noticing that the sun is already far down in the sky, casting long shadows across the lawn. Rob is throwing the football to the boys who take turns running pass patterns. The scene is idyllic, like something out of a Norman Rockwell painting, but it's deceiving. At its core this family is struggling, hurt and misunderstanding pushing it to the brink. The clock chimes, startling her, sounding unnaturally loud in the still house. She really should get on the road. It's a two-hour drive to Denver, and she has a full week ahead of her. Still she hesitates, reluctant to leave without confiding in Helen, the burden of her secret being nearly more than she can bear.

In her mind Carolyn reviews the week ahead, not because she needs to, but as a way of avoiding the unpleasant task before her. *What will Helen think? Will she lose all respect for her once she learns the truth?*

Will she have anything more to do with her? Maybe she will pretend nothing has changed even while she finds plausible reasons for avoiding her. These and a hundred other thoughts tumble through her mind while she waits for Helen to return.

At last Helen re-enters the room and takes a seat on the couch before opening her Bible. She switches on a lamp to supplement the fading light and motions for Carolyn to join her. Carolyn pretends interest as Helen points out various scriptures, but in her mind she is reliving her act of betrayal and the subsequent guilt. That, more than anything Bryan did, is what finally pushed her over the edge. It has tormented her ever since, and no amount of rationalization or penance can long still the accusing voices within.

Glancing up, she sees that Helen has stopped speaking and is looking at her. "I'm sorry," she stammers, belatedly realizing that a response is required of her. "My mind must have wandered. Please forgive me."

"Of course, I was simply saying that since you don't have a church home in Denver, you might want to spend weekends here and go to church with us. We have a comfortable guest room, and you could come down on Saturday and go home after Sunday dinner."

"That's awfully kind of you, but I couldn't put you out."

"It's no trouble. If the truth be known, I could use a little feminine company around here."

"I would love that, I really would. But before we make a decision about that, there's something I must tell you."

Before she can say anything else, Rob and the boys troop in from the backyard. Their faces are ruddy from the cold, and the boys are talking a mile a minute. "Mom," Jake says, bursting with enthusiasm,

"Dad says I have great hands. I'll probably be a pro football player when I grow up."

Not wanting to be left out, six-year-old Robbie pulls on his mommy's sleeve. "I have great hands too."

"You sure do," Helen replies, kissing the palms of both his hands, causing him to giggle with delight.

"Could we have some of that chocolate sheet cake with a scoop of vanilla ice cream?" Rob asks. "The boys and I have worked up quite an appetite."

Giving Carolyn an apologetic smile, Helen closes her Bible and heads toward the kitchen. The moment is gone, and Carolyn doesn't know when she will have another chance to confide in Helen. A part of her is relieved, but on another level she is terribly disappointed. The burden of her secret has become nearly too heavy to bear. Sighing wearily, she follows Helen into the kitchen to see if she can help get the cake and ice cream on the table.

CHAPTER

44

AWAKING SUDDENLY FROM A sound sleep, Rob lies perfectly still, trying to recall what awakened him. The house is quiet and dark, just as it should be. No one has turned on a light; no one has flushed a toilet or closed a door; still, something woke him. He strains to hear the boys, but he hears nothing—no thrashing about in their beds, no crying out in the throes of a troubling dream, no coughing. Slipping out of bed as quietly as he can to keep from waking Helen, he moves silently down the hallway to their room. They are sleeping peacefully, and he lingers for a moment, savoring the miracle of their presence. What a gift they are—the joy of his life.

Satisfied that all is well, he tiptoes out of their room and turns toward the hall bathroom where he relieves himself without turning on the light. After flushing the toilet, he waits until it has refilled before opening the door. Making his way back to the master bedroom, he slips into bed, being careful not to disturb Helen. After thirteen years of marriage, her presence in bed beside him is a continuing source of comfort. Now he turns toward her side of the bed, reaching out with his foot to touch her leg before giving himself to sleep.

But he touches nothing. Where Helen should be curled up in sleep the bed is empty, the sheets cool to his searching foot. His eyes flash to the bedside clock: 1:39. What is Helen doing out of bed?

Blindly he reaches for the lamp on the nightstand. After fumbling in the dark he finally manages to turn it on. Helen is gone! The covers on her side of the bed are turned back. Although he tells himself there is nothing to be concerned about, his heart is beating slow and heavy in his chest.

Pulling on his robe against the chill, he heads downstairs in search of her. There's not a glimmer of light anywhere, and he experiences a growing dread as he makes his way through the den and into the kitchen. The guest bedroom is empty, the bed undisturbed. His study is dark, the door open. Finally, he turns toward the formal living room, desperation giving birth to a gnawing fear.

Glimpsing her profile in silhouette against the picture window, he says, "There you are," relief making his words come out in a rush. Stepping into the living room, he notes that she is sitting in a corner of the sofa, her knees pulled up against her chest, staring out the window into the dark.

"Are you sick?" he asks. "Can I get you something?"

She doesn't answer, and he moves across the room to sit beside her. The diffused light from the streetlamp halfway down the block glistens off her tear-damp cheeks. Reaching for a tissue, he moves to dry her tears. When he touches her, she turns away as if his touch is repulsive to her. "What is it?" he asks. "What have I done?"

"How could you?" she hisses. "How could you?"

"How could I do what?" he pleads, genuinely puzzled.

"Don't play dumb with me," she counters, glaring at him.

"What are you talking about?" he beseeches her, taken aback by her vehemence.

Lunging to her feet, she towers over him. Anger makes her face hot and her eyes flash. "How could you confide in that woman? How dare you make her privy to the difficulties in our marriage?"

In an instant Rob flashes back to yesterday. He sees it again but with new perception. *Stepping into the foyer following the service, he sees Rita with her hand on Helen's arm. She is leaning in, speaking confidentially. In an instant Helen's face turns a sickly grey, and then she pastes her pastor's wife smile on and pretends all is well.* Yesterday it hardly registered, but now he sees it for what it was. Rita has betrayed his trust, without realizing what she was doing most likely, but still the damage is done.

Now his mind is racing as he tries to decide how to respond. Should he play dumb and act as if he has no idea what Helen is talking about? That's probably not a good idea given her state of mind. Maybe he could pretend that he doesn't understand what all the fuss is about. After all, he did nothing more than confide in a mutual friend. Where's the harm in that?

Instead he counters, "Don't try to tell me you haven't confided in Carolyn. That's what all those phone calls were about, isn't it?"

"That's different."

"Hardly."

"Rob, Carolyn is not a mutual friend or a member of our congregation, nor is she a man."

"So?"

"How would you feel if I confided in one of your board members? What if I told him that you were acting strange—working late, skipping dinner, not making love with me? What if I told him I suspected that you were involved with another woman?"

"Helen, I can explain—"

"No! I'm sick of your explanations. This time you're going to listen to me. I don't know if you're just too naive to see what's happening, or if you simply like playing with fire."

Interrupting, Rob demands, "What are you talking about?"

"I'm talking about you and Rita! It's obvious she has a thing for you, and anyone can see that you enjoy it. That little scene in the driveway yesterday was so transparent."

"What were you doing spying on me? Don't you trust me?"

"Spying?"

"That's what I said, spying!"

"Rob, you and Rita were mooning all over each other just outside the kitchen window. I could hardly miss it. To make matters worse, Carolyn saw it all. I've never been more humiliated."

Her anger spent, Helen moves to the far end of the sofa and collapses in a heap, burying her face in her hands. Rob simply stares out the window into the darkness, his body tense with emotion. Finally Helen speaks, weariness making her voice flat. "What are you going to do about Rita?"

"Do? What are you talking about?"

"Rob, things can't continue the way they are. I simply won't stand for it."

"Help me here. I don't think I understand what you're getting at."

"Do I have to draw you a picture?" Helen demands impatiently. "You're going to have to replace Rita."

"Are you out of your mind? Rita needs this job; besides, what would I tell the board?"

"You should have thought of that before you let things get out of hand."

"Things are hardly out of hand," Rob fumes, getting to his feet. "Rita is a good person and a loyal friend. I couldn't do that to her."

"You can, and you will," Helen says, her voice hard with determination, "or I will take matters into my own hands."

"Don't threaten me!"

"I'm just telling you how it is. I've been up most of the night, and I've given this a lot of thought. Rita has to go. If you don't get rid of her, I will go to the board."

"Are you out of your mind? What are you trying to do, destroy me?"

"Destroy you? You know better than that! I'm trying to save you from that woman and from yourself."

Getting to her feet, Helen turns toward the door. "Wait a minute," Rob says, reaching for her arm. "Let's talk about this."

"I'm through talking," Helen says wearily. When he tries to restrain her, she jerks her arm free of his hand and makes her way toward the guest bedroom.

CHAPTER

45

AFTER TOSSING FITFULLY FOR the better part of two hours, I finally drag myself out of bed, cursing the storm and my hyperactive mind. It's like a jackrabbit—jumping all over the place. My body aches with weariness, and dawn is no more than a couple of hours away, but I can't fight the bed any longer. Given the treacherous journey ahead of us, I desperately need the rest, but thinking about it only seems to aggravate my insomnia. Anyway, if the weather doesn't let up, we won't be going anywhere.

The storm is roaring in my ears as I feel my way in the dark to the kitchen table where I strike a match and light the kerosene lamp. With a second match, I light a burner on the cook stove and put some coffee on to boil. The storm has returned with a vengeance, and the pounding rain sounds like handfuls of rocks hitting the tin roof. In the distance, I hear trees breaking and crashing. Moving to the shuttered window, I try to peer out, but I can see nothing. Suddenly a bolt of lightning streaks across the sky, and in the flash of light I glimpse the damage already done. The compound is littered with broken branches and other debris. A giant *samaúma*, at least sixty meters (two hundred feet) tall, has crashed across the path leading to the river. Just as suddenly the light is gone, and darkness envelops the compound once more, amplifying the roar of the wind-driven rain.

A gust of wind shakes the house, and in the dim light of the kerosene lamp I see several places where the tin roof is leaking. I fear for Eurico and Lako, exposed as they are, but there is nothing I can do. As far as that goes, I'm hardly safer here. If that *samaúma* tree had fallen on Whittaker House, it would have squashed me like a bug. Be that as it may, the storm is beyond my control; there is absolutely nothing I can do. Either I will survive, or I won't. With that grim thought in mind, I return to the stove and pour myself a cup of coffee.

Sitting down at the table, I put pen to paper and write:

Dear Helen:

It's the middle of the night, and I cannot sleep. Outside a fierce storm is raging, but inside Whittaker House I am warm and dry. I'm almost fully recovered from a bout of malaria that laid me low, and later this morning we are scheduled to head upriver to the Serra Divisor— a range of low mountains on the border between Brazil and Peru. Lako, my guide, has located a group of Amuacas in the area who have had little or no contact with outsiders. I'm eager to interact with them, and a little fearful, as most of the missionaries here seem to think it was probably Amuacas who killed our father. But who knows? Anyway, I'm hopeful they will have information that will help me discover what happened to him.

Speaking of our father, did you read any in his journal before sending it to me? If you didn't, you should have. It's interesting stuff. It's a hodgepodge really—a lot of day-to-day trivia interspersed with some deeply personal material. I had no idea our father was such a complex man—but then how could I have known, seeing I was only seven years old when he disappeared? Being four years older than me, you may remember him differently; but, be that as it may, I still think you would find his journal a fascinating read.

Let me give you an example of what I'm talking about. In this entry, dated November 7, 1936 (that would have been before they came to the mission field, wouldn't it?), he writes about his haunting loneliness. Can you imagine that? Lonely, our self-reliant father? Who would have ever thought such a thing? Anyway, here's what he wrote:

"Have you ever felt totally alone, as if there were no one who really knew you, no one with whom you could truly share your heart, your soul? In No Man Is an Island *Thomas Merton writes, 'No one is more lonely than a priest (minister) who has a vast ministry. He is isolated in a terrible desert by the secrets of his fellow men.'*

"Loneliness can be nearly debilitating, but it should not be viewed as a weakness or character defect. Just as the body expresses its need for food through hunger, so the soul expresses its need for relationships through loneliness. In realiy, it is a positive force in our lives. That's not to say that it is painless, but only that it is the primary factor in moving us out of isolation and into community.

"Maybe the secret is to stop fighting our loneliness and embrace it. Perhaps we should make peace with our pain, make it an ally instead of an enemy. When we do that, existential loneliness becomes solitude—a holy aloneness in which we discover intimacy with God. Emotional loneliness—so much a part of modern life—then becomes the basis for relationship, moving us out of isolation into a shared intimacy. And as improbable as it seems, we, the walking wounded, can experience community—that is, fellowship with both God and man."

Can you believe that? I mean who would have ever imagined that our father struggled with loneliness? Not me! From my perspective he was the original "The Lone Ranger." Maybe I'm more his son than I ever realized. On the outside I'm prickly—like a porcupine—but on the inside I'm desperately lonely.

Laying down my pen, I rub my eyes. Lack of sleep has made them feel dry and gritty, not to mention the strain of writing in such low light. The wind no longer shakes the house, so maybe the storm is letting up, but it's hard to tell since the rain continues to hammer the roof with a malevolent fury. There's a knot in my stomach and a tension between my shoulders at the base of my neck. Belatedly, I realize that thinking about my father has stirred up all the old feelings—loss, fear, inadequacy, and anger, mostly anger. I had hoped writing about him would help me recapture some of the good feelings I experienced when I first read his journal. But it hasn't worked. All I feel is the same old anger—anger at him for heading off into the jungle and putting us at risk. I'm angry with God too, for lots of reasons, but mostly for not looking after my father. And I'm angry with my mother for not looking after me, for letting me grieve alone and grow up bent.

And there's a new dimension to my anger as well. I hate it that my father never allowed us to see his softer side, his loneliness, his fears, and his humanity. Why did he always have to pretend to be so strong? Did he think we would love him less if we saw him cry, or if he talked about the things that bothered him on the inside? Would it have been so hard for him to wrestle with me on the floor, or kiss me goodnight, or tell me that he loved me? Reading about his feelings in his journal provokes mixed emotions in me. A part of me is comforted by the knowledge that he experienced those feelings, but on another level I'm deeply grieved because he never expressed them to us. His anger is all he ever let us see, anger and the back of his hand.

A nagging voice, far back in my mind, keeps asking me the same questions: *If I feel so strongly about the way my father repressed his emotions, why am I doing the same thing? Why is anger the only emotion I will allow myself to express? Why do I keep pushing people away when I'm so desperately lonely on the inside?* Now it's Carolyn's voice I hear inside my head. *"Bryan,"* she says, her voice thick with feeling, *"I love you, but you are so full of anger and bitterness you can't receive my love, and it's killing me. I can't bear to watch you destroying yourself."*

Enough of this, I think, pushing my chair back from the table. Getting up, I make my way to the shuttered window and try to look out. The rain is still falling in sheets, but a weak light is pushing the darkness back, suggesting that the night is finally coming to an end. I try to locate Diana's house through the driving rain, but it is impossible to see more than a few feet. Fear for her safety tempts me, but I push it down. It returns with a vengeance, conjuring up images of her body crushed and broken beneath the wreckage of her house. Telling myself that she is fine, that I would have heard the crash if a tree had fallen on her house, helps clear my mind. The gruesome images fade, but a cold knot of fear still lies like a rock in the pit of my stomach.

Turning from the window, I go to the stove and pour another cup of coffee. It is scalding hot and bitter, hardly fit to drink; still, I take a big swallow. Sitting down at the table, I pick up my pen, determined to finish Helen's letter before heading out.

> *It's scary to realize how much I'm like our father. Like him, I've never been able to share my feelings with anyone—not you, not Mom, not Carolyn, not anyone. Yet, put a pen in my hand, and I gush like Old Faithful. That's what I'm doing now—gushing, just letting it all flow out. A stream of consciousness, I think someone called it.*

> *I feel like a soldier on the eve of battle. Having gone upriver once already, I know the dangers that await me; sickness and death are everywhere. I could die, but I don't think I will. Still, just in case I don't make it back, there are some things I need to say.*

> *Since you and Carolyn have become friends—something I still find hard to believe since to my way of thinking you and she have*

almost nothing in common—there are some things I would like you to tell her for me.

Please tell her that I forgive her—she will know what I'm talking about. It has taken me a while, but I now realize that the failure of our marriage was largely my fault. Tell her that I am sorry I hurt her, more sorry than she will ever know.

Tell Rob he did a great job at Mom's funeral. I should have told him myself, but I was too full of hurt and anger.

Tell the boys I love them, and if I make it back from the Amazon, I will bring them an authentic shrunken head. Just kidding!

I know I've acted like a donkey most of my life, especially toward you and Mom. Please forgive me. It had almost nothing to do with you. It was all about me and the pain I've lived with since our father disappeared. I guess anger was my way of grieving—a terribly destructive way, for it destroys everything it touches. I can't imagine the pain I've caused you, but if it's anything like the pain I've inflicted on myself it must be unspeakable. Please forgive me. If I make it back, I'll try to make it up to you.

I wish I could tell you that I'm whole—free of pain and anger—but I can't. I'm making progress, or I could never have written this letter, but I've got a long way to go. Hopefully, I will find the answers I seek, maybe among the Amuacas or some other isolated tribe—maybe in Father's journal or maybe even inside myself.

Anyway, thanks for sending Father's journal and for your letter.

> Bryan Whittaker
> Whittaker House
> Amazon Basin
> October 29, 1970

I read the letter one final time before folding it carefully. After addressing it to Mrs. Helen Thompson, I place it in a larger envelope along with a note asking Gordon to mail it the next time he goes to Cruzeiro for supplies. The storm is finally over, and I carry the coffeepot to the back porch where I scatter the grounds and throw out what remains of the coffee. After rinsing out the pot I set it back on the stove. I'm tempted to check on Diana, but I don't think I'm up to another emotional good-bye. Instead, I wrap father's journal in oilcloth and place it in my backpack. After blowing out the lamp, I head toward the river, noting as I do that Diana's house is still standing and looks none the worse for the storm's violence.

CHAPTER

46

SLASHING THROUGH ONE FINAL tangle of
vines and underbrush, I finally reach the trail leading to the river.
Though the temperature is mild, I am sweating profusely and gasping
for breath. With the *samaúma* tree blocking the head of the trail, I was
forced to cut my own path. No big deal, or so I thought. Put a machete
in the hands of an experienced *mateiro*, and wielding it appears almost
effortless, but it proved to be a lot harder than it looked.

Evidence of the storm's fury is everywhere—trees are down,
broken branches and debris litter the ground. It was obviously worse
than I imagined, and concern for the well-being of Lako and Eurico
pushes me forward in spite of the shortness of my breath. Rounding
one final bend in the trail, I see the river before me—the current is
strong, and the water is dirty, the color of milk chocolate. It has risen
several feet during the night, overrunning the beach where our
supplies where stacked. Someone has pulled the boat to higher
ground, but neither Lako nor Eurico are in sight. With a sick feeling
in the pit of my stomach I continue toward the river, hoping against
hope that nothing has happened to either one of them.

To my left I spot a scrap of colored cloth caught in some underbrush. Working my way closer, I see a shallow gully washed out by an
earlier flood. A canvas tarp has been staked down on one end and

stretched across the gully where it is tied to some trees on the other side, forming a makeshift shelter. Hearing me approach, Lako crawls out from under the tarp. His clothes are wet and filthy, and his face is grey with exhaustion. "Where's Eurico?" I ask anxiously, while sliding down the muddy embankment.

With a motion of his head he indicates the shelter, and I bend down to peer under the tarp. As my eyes adjust to the half-light, I spot Eurico curled up into a ball against the muddy bank, a bloody rag tied around his head. My heart catches in my throat until I see his small chest rising and falling with the rhythm of his breathing. Straightening up, I turn to Lako. "What happened to him?"

"He got hit by a falling branch. He's got a nasty gash, but other than that he seems to be all right."

Looking around in amazement, I ask, "How did you end up here?"

"When the storm got really bad I knew we had to find shelter below ground. Having spotted this gully a few days ago, I knew it offered the best chance for protection. Of course, by the time we made it here we were soaked, and the gully was a muddy mess."

Eurico crawls out from under the tarp, having been awakened by our voices. When he sees me, he gives me a lopsided grin while rubbing his wounded head. "How are you doing, big guy?" I ask, giving his shoulder a playful punch. He grimaces in pain, and I drop to my knees to get a better look at him. When I do, he passes out. Thankfully I am able to catch him before he hits the ground.

He is unnaturally pale, and his breathing is shallow and rapid. Getting to my feet, I scramble out of the gully and head for the mission compound with Eurico in my arms. Over my shoulder I call to Lako. "I've got to get Eurico to Dr. Rhoades. My backpack and camera equipment are beside the boat. Get them and come up to the house."

Guilt assails me as I rush toward the mission clinic, attacking with a cruel vengeance. I can't help thinking that if I hadn't been so preoccupied with Diana I would have insisted that Eurico stay at Whittaker House rather than sending him to the river with Lako. I can't believe I could have been so irresponsible. From the size of that gash on his head, he must have taken quite a blow. No doubt he has a concussion; I just hope his skull isn't fractured. If he dies, I will never forgive myself.

I don't think I even believe in God anymore, yet as I hurry across the mission compound I find myself praying, begging God to spare Eurico's life. At the last second I veer toward Diana's house, realizing it's too early for her to be at the clinic.

Rushing up the steps, I give the door a couple of sound kicks. "Diana, come quick. Eurico's been injured."

"Get him inside," she says, after opening the door. Moving out of the way so I can get through, she calls after me. "Lay him on the kitchen table so I can examine him."

He is gagging as I lay him down, and before I can get a pan he vomits all over the floor. Ignoring the mess Diana moves to the other side of the table and begins examining him. After taking his pulse, she checks his eyes and places a blood pressure cuff on his skinny arm. Glancing in my direction, she says, "He has obviously suffered a brain concussion, but I don't think his skull is fractured. Without an X-ray it is impossible to be sure, but I feel reasonably certain."

"Put some water on to boil so we can get him cleaned up," she commands, every inch the doctor. "While you're at it, would you wipe up that vomit? I would hate to slip in it and break my other leg."

While I'm working on the floor Eleanor arrives and immediately takes charge, ordering Diana to rest her broken leg until she can get Eurico cleaned up. With a wash cloth and a basin of warm, soapy water she sets to work on Eurico. He groans softly as she strips off his muddy clothes and begins bathing him. At Diana's direction I hurry to the clinic for a local anesthetic and sutures, plus some antibiotic cream.

Eurico is still unconscious when Eleanor finishes bathing him. He doesn't even flinch when Diana injects the Novocain and sets to work stitching up the gash in his head. It's a ragged wound requiring eleven stitches. While she's doing that, I bring a cot from the clinic and set it up beside the bed in her room. With practiced skill Eleanor prepares a bed for Eurico.

When Diana is finished, I gently lift him from the table, stunned at how little he weighs. Never would I have imagined he was so slight. Being full of life, he seemed larger than he actually is, but now I realize just how small he is, frail even. After laying him on the bed, I look at Diana anxiously. "He's going to be all right, isn't he?" I ask, fear making my voice tight.

"He should be fine, but the fact that he hasn't regained consciousness concerns me." She pauses before continuing, choosing her words carefully. "Vomiting is not a good sign either; but his vital signs are stable, and that's good. We will just have to wait and see how he does. The next twelve to twenty-four hours will be critical."

Her words panic me, and I lunge from the room, hardly able to believe the sudden turn of events. Just yesterday Eurico was full of life, joyous in his anticipation of going upriver into the jungle, and now he's hanging between life and death. Diana calls to me from the bedroom, but I do not stop. I can't. I feel like I'm smothering, and I have to get out of the house. Rushing across the compound, I turn toward the river, searching for a place where I can be alone.

A familiar anger seizes me, and I scream at the Almighty, shaking my fist at the impassive sky. "Don't do this to me," I shout; tears of grief and rage blinding me. "How dare You punish an innocent child to get back at me? Kill me if You must, but spare Eurico."

My anger exhausts itself as quickly as it came, leaving me empty and afraid. Falling face down on the muddy ground, I beg God to spare Eurico's life. I bargain with the Almighty, making promises I know I will never be able to keep, promising anything that might turn the tide in Eurico's favor. I feel like I'm seven years old again and praying for my father to return. It was futile then, and it feels futile now.

Gnashing my teeth, I pound my fists against the ground and scream, but nothing I do seems to make any difference. Now I'm weeping, great gasping sobs wracking my body, but still I find no relief. Slowly my sobs subside, finally giving way to a sorrowful whimpering, leaving me limp with grief. "He can't die, he can't!" I whisper over and over again through clinched teeth.

After a time, I feel a heavy hand upon my shoulder, and when I turn I see Gordon Arnold kneeling beside me. Not willing for anyone to see me in this condition, I lunge to my feet, shoving his hand away. Before I can flee he grabs me and crushes me to his chest in an enormous bear hug. Nearly mad with grief and rage, I pound his chest with my fists, trying my best to break away, but I cannot. No matter what I do, he will not let me go.

Overwhelmed by the strength of his presence, I finally give myself to his embrace, sobbing like a fatherless child. Now he holds my head against his chest, comforting me until at last I grow quiet. "What is it, Bryan," he asks. "What is it?"

"It's Eurico," I manage, my words coming out in a strangled sob.

"Eurico's part of it, I know, but there's more. What is it, Son?"

I want to tell him everything, but I can't. Instead I ask, "If there's a God, how can He let something like this happen?"

Shrugging his shoulders, he looks at me with sorrowful eyes and says, "I don't know, Bryan. I wish I did, but I don't."

Taking me by the arm, he leads me to an uprooted tree that has been deposited high on the bank by an earlier flood. Sitting down on it, we watch the muddy river in silence. At last he speaks, "Many years ago, long before Eleanor and I became missionaries, we were serving as pastors of a congregation in the Midwest. Within our congregation there was a young couple expecting their first child. They prayed for a healthy baby with a gentle disposition and a spiritual aptitude, but they were given a colicky child who cried incessantly.

"In desperation they made an appointment to see me. 'Why,' they pleaded, 'did God not answer our prayers? We prayed in faith. We did everything we were taught to do, so why didn't it work?'"

Nodding my head, I think, *The very question I've asked a thousand times.*

"I had no answer," Gordon continues, "and my heart hurt for them. A few weeks later the doctor discovered that their baby had a painful hernia, and surgery was scheduled. The appointed day arrived, and I went to the hospital to be with them. Long before I located them I could hear their baby wailing. Her anguished cries echoed forlornly down the long hospital corridors. Turning a final corner, I saw that young mother nervously pacing the hallway trying to comfort her baby, while her husband looked on helplessly.

"Approaching her, I asked, 'What seems to be the problem?'

"'She's hungry,' the distraught mother replied. 'The doctor told us not to feed her after ten o'clock last night.'

"'Surely you're not going to let that stop you?' I asked with a straight face. 'Your baby is obviously starving, and not to feed her is terribly cruel.'

"She looked at me like I had lost my mind. Finally she said, 'It's dangerous to have surgery on a full stomach, especially for a baby. Surely you know that—'

"Without giving her a chance to finish I interrupted. 'Well, at least explain things to her. She must think you're a sadist. You carry her in your arms next to your breast, but you won't feed her. As young as she is, she knows you could feed her if you wanted to, if you really cared.'

"'Don't be silly,' she said, struggling to control her irritation, 'you can't explain something like that to a three-month-old baby.'

"Gently I said, 'I know what you're doing is an act of love. I know you have your baby's best interest at heart. But she doesn't understand that, and there's no way you can explain it to her.'

"At last understanding began to brighten her tense features, so I continued. 'That's the way it is with God. He is too wise to ever make a mistake, and too loving to ever cause one of His children a needless pain. Still, He must sometimes risk our misunderstanding in order to do what's best for us. And we're simply too 'young,' too finite, to comprehend His infinite wisdom.'"

Gordon is a kind man, and I don't want to hurt his feelings so I simply nod, pretending to understand. It's a good enough story, but it does little or nothing to help me resolve my issues. Eurico is unconscious. My father is still missing, and I am just as full of grief and anger as I have been all my life. Finally Gordon claps me on the back and says, "Let's go check on Eurico. He may have regained consciousness by now."

CHAPTER

47

STEPPING TO THE DOORWAY of Diana's bedroom, I see her bending over Eurico's twisted torso while Eleanor struggles to pin his thrashing legs to the bed with her ample body. "What's happening?" I scream, but neither woman seems to hear me. Pushing past me, Gordon lends his strength to the struggle while I stand frozen with fear. Eurico's small frame jerks in one final convulsion and then grows still. For a moment I think he is dead, and then I hear him gasp for breath.

Once the crisis has passed, Gordon and Eleanor slip out of the bedroom, and I kneel beside Eurico's bed, taking hold of his hand. He is moaning softly and squirming as if in pain, his hand unnaturally dry and hot to my touch. Lifting his T-shirt, Diana examines him carefully, biting her lip in despair when she notices a spreading rash. Finishing her examination, she tenderly straightens his T-shirt and covers him with a sheet. She moves to the other side of the room, motioning for me to join her.

"What is it?" I demand in a hoarse whisper. "What's happening to Eurico?"

Diana's eyes glisten with tears, and when she speaks I have to lean forward to hear her. "He undoubtedly has a brain concussion, but that's not what I'm concerned about. It wouldn't produce the symptoms he's exhibiting—irregular fever, hypersensitivity, rapid pulse and respiration, not to mention convulsions." After pausing for a moment to reflect, she continues in a self-deprecating tone. "The injury to his head distracted me, or I would have paid more attention to his other symptoms—not that it would have made any difference, seeing I have no way to treat him. The final piece of the puzzle was the rash—a petechial rash to be exact."

My heart is pounding, and there is a roaring in my ears. "Diana," I croak, "you're scaring me. Tell me he's going to be all right. Tell me he's not going to die."

She's rambling now, repeating herself. "I was distracted by his head wound, but it's probably a nonfactor, having nothing to do with what's going on now."

Taking her by the shoulders, I shake her gently, trying to get her attention. "What are you talking about? Tell me what's wrong with Eurico!"

"He has meningitis," she answers in a hollow voice, "probably caused by a parasite he picked up somewhere."

"It's treatable, isn't it?" I press. "Surely you've got medicine, haven't you?"

"Bryan," she says, irritation giving her voice a sharp edge, "this isn't Denver, Colorado. We're in the farthest regions of the western Amazon..." Her voice trails off, but there's no need for her to say more, her message is clear. Letting go of her shoulders, I stumble across the room and fall on my knees beside Eurico's cot. Through tear-blurred eyes, I study his youthful countenance, cringing each time he grimaces with pain. I want to caress him, hold him on my lap, and cover his face with kisses, but I dare not. Even the slightest touch causes him to recoil in pain.

Diana takes a seat on the foot of bed beside me, and I turn to her. Her face is full of grief and heavy with hopelessness. It's obvious to me that she has given up, so I decide to take matters into my own hands. Getting to my feet, I announce, "I'm taking Eurico downriver to Cruzeiro. Surely the hospital there will have medicine to treat him."

"I can't let you do that, Bryan," she says, shaking her head sadly. "The trip would kill him. He would never make it to the hospital. Even if he did, there's no guarantee they would have the medicine he needs."

"Well, I can't just sit here and watch him die," I fume, fear feeding my anger. "I love that little guy, and he's counting on me. I have to do something."

"We can pray," Diana suggests, but I cut her off before she can say more.

"Pray? Are you crazy? Prayer is like spitting in the wind. It's a total waste!"

She looks at me aghast, the force of my anger taking her aback. Without a word, she collects her crutches and leaves the room. I didn't mean to be so blunt, and I certainly didn't mean to hurt her, but I couldn't help myself. The whole idea of prayer is repugnant to me. All it does is raise false hope. If there were anything to it, I wouldn't have grown up without my father.

Going to the window, I stare across the compound, oblivious to the destruction left in the storm's wake. My anger slowly dissipates to be replaced by a black despair. Eurico is deathly ill. He's going to die, and there's not a thing I can do to prevent it. Never have I felt so helpless, so alone; unless it was when my father disappeared. Then I was just a child, but now I'm a man. There ought to be something I can do to help Eurico, some way I can save his life. But there's not...

What will I do without Eurico? I've come to depend on his impish grin and infectious laughter to keep my black moods at bay. He's like a son to me. I feel closer to him than I've ever felt to my own flesh and blood. It's not fair. In his nine years, he has already suffered more than most people do in their entire life, and he has overcome so much it is almost unbelievable. What kind of God would treat an innocent child this way? It's so unfair, so senseless, so cruel.

He groans painfully, and I turn from the window. He's trying to say something, but his words come out garbled and unintelligible. Moving to his cot, I notice that his head is drawn back, causing his neck and back to bow slightly. I try to reposition him, being ever so gentle, but he cries out in pain. "Diana," I call, "come quickly. Something's happening to Eurico."

Limping into the room on her crutches, she casts them aside and bends to examine him. Noting the characteristic bow of his spine, she bites her lip and wipes at her eyes with her sleeve. "What is it?" I ask. "What's happening?"

"Nothing I didn't expect, but it's progressing more rapidly than I anticipated," she explains, her words heavy with her own grief. "In the next forty-eight to seventy-two hours Eurico's condition is going to deteriorate even more dramatically. Already the bacteria in his bloodstream has migrated to his meninges where it is localized, creating enormous pressure on his brain. If he doesn't already have a blinding headache, he soon will due to the increased pressure of the cerebrospinal fluid. It's quite likely he will suffer more convulsions, and as his bodily functions shut down he may also experience vomiting, constipation, urine retention, and ever-increasing stiffness of the neck muscles."

By the time she finishes she is weeping, and I put my arms around her, pulling her to my chest. "There's no reason why he has to die," she sobs, gasping for breath. "With sulfadiazine he would be as good as new in a few days, but we don't have any. I'm sick to death of watching children die just because there's no money for medicine!"

There's nothing I can say, so I simply hold her, providing what comfort I can. On another level I am tormented by the images her words have produced. The thought of Eurico writhing in pain, his body twisted and misshapen, is nearly more than I can bear. The death of a child, any child, is obscene, but what Diana has described is ghoulish. No one should have to die that way, and certainly not Eurico.

Releasing Diana, I pace the cramped room, cursing under my breath. After a moment, she places a hand on my arm to calm me, but I turn away and resume my pacing. Once more, fear and helplessness are feeding my anger, pushing me dangerously close to the point of no return. In my rage, I'm on the verge of losing control, and it's all I can do not to kick the furniture or hurl things. Diana watches me closely, but she doesn't say anything, and after a while I begin to calm down, rage giving way to despair.

We pass an endless afternoon sitting in the bedroom near Eurico, mute with grief. His pain is unrelenting, and he stirs restlessly, crying out from time to time, but he never acknowledges our presence. Others come and go—Eleanor bringing food for which we have no appetite, and Lako who quickly turns away, sickened by the memories evoked by Eurico's suffering. Late in the afternoon, Gordon comes to sit with us. He hardly utters a word, but Diana seems strengthened somehow by his presence, although from time to time silent tears slide down her ghostly white cheeks. The day is nearly done when he finally excuses himself, leaving the three of us to face the night alone. I hear him close the door, and in the gathering gloom the ominous shadow of death seems to fill the room.

CHAPTER
48

MOONLIGHT IS STREAMING THROUGH the bedroom window when Diana awakens, but she hardly notices it. Groggy with sleep, she fights to free herself from the remnants of a dream that has left her sick with fear. Only it's not just a dream but a memory, and against her will she finds herself reliving it again.

With vivid clarity she hears the unidentified woman say, "If you don't see a doctor immediately, you will bleed to death." Then she remembers falling, struggling to reach the light, then nothing.

In her semiconscious state she mistakes the lamp in the corner of her hospital room for the light illuminating the emergency room entrance and struggles mightily to reach it. The pain is unbearable, but she has to reach the light; it is her only hope. Gritting her teeth, she hurls herself against the railing on her bed, tearing out her IV in the process. Somehow she manages to get out of bed, only to collapse on the cold floor.

Rushing into the room, the night nurse sees Diana dragging herself toward the pool of light emanating from the lamp in the far corner of the room. Her arm is bleeding where she has torn out the IV, little drops of bright red blood glistening in stark relief against her pale skin. Exhaustion weighs her down, and she is tempted to yield to the seducing black oblivion, to give into the tempting darkness. Yet, something inside her clings to life with a fierce tenacity. She must not die. She will not die!

The combination of pain and drugs has left her disoriented, and when the nurses try to help her back into bed she fights them with a terrible desperation. In her confused state she mistakes them for the big woman and her unidentified companion. They are trying to put her on the bed so they can abort her baby. They want to kill her baby!

Although she is weak from pain and loss of blood, fear gives her a desperate strength, and it takes several nurses to subdue her. "Please," she begs, as they restrain her, "don't kill my baby."

For a moment she lies on the cold floor, restrained by their heavy hands, her breath coming in ragged little gasps, her abused body trembling from exhaustion. By now the pain is excruciating, and her hospital gown is soaked with blood where she has torn the stitches from her incision. What have they done to me? she wonders, as she struggles to remain conscious.

Dimly, as if from a great distance, the memory of her abortion returns. Once more she sees herself on the examining table, shamefully exposed, her feet in metal stirrups. As if in a dream she hears the doctor ask, "Have we got it all?" And after a moment a woman's voice, "I don't think so. I can only find one arm."

Turning her head, she closes her eyes in a vain attempt to escape the memory. It is no use. No matter where she turns, the awful voice follows her, haunts her: "I can only find one arm..."

In desperation she now embraces the medication that one of the nurses has injected. For a moment she seems to be floating. The pain is receding. Once more she is escaping into the sanctuary of a drug-induced sleep. But this time it is different. In the nether world, between consciousness and unconsciousness, she finds herself face to face with a tragically beautiful little girl who has only one arm. "No!" Diana screams. And in the nether world she tries to run, tries to escape the ever-present child with her single arm and enormously sad eyes, but it is no use. Everywhere Diana turns, the child is there, staring at her, always staring.

"Who are you?" Diana cries. "Why are you following me?"

In response the little one-armed girl utters a single word: "Mommy."

Now Diana fights to escape the seducing power of the pain medication. The darkness it induces is no longer warm and friendly, but terrifying. Like a black pool of water it closes over her, and she feels as if she is drowning. In desperation she fights to swim to the surface, but her legs seem weighted. Glancing down, through the murky darkness, she sees that the child has wrapped her one arm around her legs and is clinging to her with a death-like grip.

Once more she struggles to free herself, but it is no use. Her strength is gone, and the child will not let her go. Now she is falling, sinking deeper into the black pool. And out of the darkness she hears a voice, terrifyingly familiar, "I can only find one arm." And then the darkness closes over her.

Sick with fear, Diana forces herself to sit up on the edge of the bed, her broken leg stretched out before her. Rubbing the sleep from her eyes, she struggles to orient herself. *This is the mission house,* she thinks, *and I am in my own bedroom, so why do I have this sick feeling in my stomach? The abortion was a long time ago, and while it has left me with a permanent grief, the pain I am experiencing now is too raw, too fresh, to be related to that experience.*

Slowly her eyes scan the room, noting the details—the crutches leaning against the wall by the head of her bed, the smudge of light cast by the kerosene lamp sitting on a wooden crate next to the chair in the far corner, the partially opened shutters. Satisfied, she reaches for her crutches and makes her way into the kitchen for a drink of water. Reluctantly, she forces herself to recall the events of yesterday and last night; when she does, she is nearly overwhelmed with a fresh spasm of grief.

Returning to the bedroom, she goes immediately to the cot where Eurico is groaning in his sleep. The characteristic bow of his neck and spine is slightly more pronounced, and from time to time he mumbles incoherently. Even in the dim light cast by the lamp, she can see that his rash is spreading. Laying her hand gently against his cheek, she notes that his fever has returned. Biting her lip, she can't help thinking that in spite of her medical expertise, she is helpless before the rising tide of his illness. Prayer is the only weapon she has left. Taking his hand in her own, she tries to pray, but before she can form the words her concussed emotions give birth to another malignant memory.

As if from a great distance, Diana hears voices, and she feels someone examining her abdomen. Forcing her eyes open, she sees a doctor's white coat and experiences a momentary fear, mistaking him for the abortionist. But that couldn't be, she realizes, for she was blindfolded the entire time.

"Where am I?" she asks, her voice sounding frightened, almost childlike.

"You are in the Lutheran Medical Center," the tall man in the white coat replies, "and I am Dr. Collins."

"But how did I get here?" she asks, puzzled. "What am I doing here?"

"Apparently someone left you at the emergency room entrance last night. You had passed out from shock and loss of blood. You were in pretty bad shape by the time we found you."

As he continues to speak, filling in the particulars, Diana's memory begins to return. It is fragmented at first, but by concentrating she is able to recall the events, at least in part. She remembers the blindfold and the drive across town. Although she knows she has had an abortion, she cannot bring herself to remember the details.

Her painful effort to reconstruct the events of the last twenty-four hours is stopped short when she hears the word "hysterectomy."

"What did you say?" she demands.

Patiently Dr. Collins explains. "Although we had to remove the uterus, in order to stop the hemorrhaging, we were able to save the ovaries..."

He continues his explanation, but Diana hears no more. Her worst fears have been realized. She will never bear children. She feels violated, raped. Yet, it is worse than rape, for she has lost something more precious than her innocence. They have robbed her of her womanhood, left her a permanently disfigured creature. In an instant she has become—a barren woman.

Silent tears spill down her cheeks, and she closes her eyes tightly against the pain. Never has she felt so desolate, so utterly alone. A great emptiness fills her soul along with a hopelessness as bleak as the lunar landscape. Involuntarily she hugs herself, but finds no comfort in the emptiness of her arms. A soft whimper escapes her lips, something akin to the cry of a wounded animal. Like Rachel of old weeping for her slain children, Diana cannot be comforted.

Mercifully Dr. Collins' voice calls her back from the abyss. "You had a very close call," he says, "but it appears that the worst of it is behind you now. If you don't try any more stunts like the one you pulled this morning, we should have you out of here in about a week, maybe ten days. Tomorrow the nurse will help you get up, but until then I want you to stay in bed and give that incision a chance to heal." Giving her hand a gentle squeeze, he leaves the room to continue his rounds.

As soon as he is gone a host of malevolent thoughts set upon her. Wearily she tries to sort them out but soon finds that she doesn't have the strength. Once more she seeks escape in sleep's warm womb. In sleep she can keep her pain at arm's distance. In sleep she can escape the terrifying reality of what has befallen her, at least for a time. In sleep she is not sterile, she is not a victim of those who used and abused her. In sleep...

But sleep will not come, and finally Diana turns her face toward the wall and embraces her grief. She is grieving all she has lost. Not only her aborted baby, but all the babies she will never be able to bear. Now she is *weeping uncontrollably, hysterically, her anguished cries spilling out of the room, echoing down the nearly deserted hospital corridors, bringing a pair of nurses on the run. Entering the room, they see Diana cradling a pillow, rocking slightly as she continues to wail.*

With a sweep of her arm the first nurse closes the curtain, separating Diana from the wide-eyed woman in the other bed. Gently the nurse begins to stroke her hair the way a mother might comfort a distraught child. "It's going to be all right," she says softly, while trying to determine if Diana is having a reaction to the medication, or if she has simply lost control of her emotions. "Go ahead and cry," she says. "You've been through a lot. You have every reason to be upset."

"They killed my baby," Diana wails, as the nurse continues stroking her hair. "They killed my baby."

A second nurse injects a sedative, after consulting with Dr. Collins by phone. Slowly Diana's anguished sobs begin to subside as the powerful medication takes effect. As she drifts toward the drug-induced oblivion she begins to hum softly, filling the semidark room with a haunting melody from her childhood.

"Hush, little baby, don't you cry.

Momma's so sorry she let you die…"

It has been years since Diana has had a flashback, and now she has had two in the past hour. Eurico's impending death must have triggered them. In the short time she has known him he has become like a son to her, and losing him is like losing a child of her own. Giving his fingers a soft kiss, she notes that it is nearly morning, dawn having stitched a border of light around the shutters. Turning toward the chair in the corner where Bryan was sitting the last time she checked Eurico, she sees a folded sheet of paper with her name on it. With trembling hands she unfolds it and reads:

Dear Diana:

> *I can't do this!*
>
> *Please forgive me for abandoning you,*
>
> *but I can't bear to sit here and watch Eurico die.*
>
> *Lako and I have gone upriver to find the Amuacas.*

Love,

Bryan

Grabbing her crutches, Diana launches herself toward the front door. Flinging it open, she hurries outside to stand on the edge of her porch looking toward Whittaker House. It is dark, without a sign of life, and in her heart she knows it is too late. Bryan is gone.

"Bryan Whittaker," she screams, loud enough to wake the dead, "don't you dare leave me." Stumbling to the steps, she sits down, letting her crutches clatter to the porch behind her. Burying her face in her hands, she sobs uncontrollably. "Please Bryan," she sobs. "Please don't do this to me."

CHAPTER

49

IT IS STILL DARK as I follow Lako down the trail toward the river, morning not yet a hint on the horizon. The air is deadly still, heavy with humidity. An undulating layer of mist is suspended over the trail about eye level, herded by the heat of our bodies into little eddies that taper into the forest. Lako has warned me to keep a sharp eye out for pit vipers—they hunt at night, identifying their prey through the heat-detecting sensors embedded around their lips—but I am walking blindly, having eyes only for what I see in my mind.

Fortunately, we encounter no snakes, and when the trail opens onto a high sandbar overlooking the river, we pause to catch our breath. Although the temperature is moderate, the humidity has pasted my shirt to my back. In this moment, I despise the Amazon Basin and everything about it. I hate the heat and the humidity along with the disease-carrying insects and parasites that flourish here. I hate the isolation and the primitive living conditions and the Indians with their ignorance and Stone Age lifestyle. Most of all I hate the disease that is slowly sucking the life out of Eurico. And I despise my helplessness, the fact that I am powerless to do anything to save him.

Pushing those troubling thoughts from my mind, I turn my attention to the tasks at hand. It is still too dark to see the river, but we can hear it a few meters away. The lazy, meandering body of water we followed from Cruzeiro to the mission compound is gone. The rainy season, with the help of the storm two nights ago, has transformed it into a swollen torrent, strong and sullen. Although I'm impatient to be on our way, we dare not leave before daylight. The Rio Moa is now dangerous, thick with debris—trash from the river margin, the remains of decomposing animals, trees that have toppled from its flood-ravaged banks, and huge logs drafted by the rising water. Any of the larger things could capsize our small boat should we hit it in the dark.

Already Lako is hauling what's left of our supplies from the makeshift shelter where he and Eurico weathered the storm. He is piling them near the boat to be loaded as soon as it is light. Even in the dark I can tell that we have a limited supply, some of our foodstuff having been washed away in the rising water two nights ago. He assures me that we can supplement our rations by hunting, but his assurances have done little to ease my mind, experience having taught me that the Amazon is an unforgiving place.

With the first hint of light we shove the boat partway into the river, being careful to keep it firmly grounded lest the current snatch it away before we can load it. Once the supplies have been stowed, Lako climbs in and starts the motor. He lets it run for a couple of minutes until it settles into a steady rhythm. Given the strength of the current, we dare not launch the boat until we are sure the motor is going to perform. Finally he nods, and I shove the boat the rest of the way into the river and climb aboard. Gunning the engine, Lako deftly guides us into the channel, being careful to avoid all manner of debris carried by the current.

I must have dozed off for a few minutes, for the sun is now pushing its way above the treetops lining the riverbanks. In the shaded areas, under the trees on the far bank, the early morning fog still hugs the water. As I watch, the encroaching sun slowly burns it away without doing any damage to the humidity. Now the heat wraps itself around me like a wet towel, and the morning slowly works its way toward noon. From time to time I glance at Lako to see how he is faring, but he seems immune to the heat and discomfort that torment me.

After two nights with little or no rest, I am nearly exhausted, so I make myself as comfortable as possible and try to sleep, but it is no use. Against my will, my thoughts return to the mission compound. By now Diana has surely found the note I left, and she must know what a jerk I am. I hate myself for what I did, but there was no way I could bear to watch Eurico die. Abandoning Diana at a time like this was an act of cruelty so cold I don't think I will ever be able to forgive myself. I know she won't forgive me, nor do I expect her to.

I try to tell myself that it is better this way, that there was no future for us, but I cannot escape the utter despair that threatens to consume me. Trying to convince myself that my feelings for Diana weren't real doesn't help either. I love her, and there is no way I can pretend otherwise. The thought of losing her and Eurico both is nearly more than I can bear, a loss from which I may never recover.

As we round a sharp bend in the river, my torturous ruminating is cut short by a shout from Lako. Looking up, I see a huge log bearing down upon us. He tries to maneuver the boat to escape the log, but the current slides us sideways, and we careen into it, nearly capsizing. In an instant we are entangled in its root ball, and the current is shoving us downstream. At any moment we could be crushed against the bank or slammed into another log. Grabbing a machete, I begin hacking at the vines and roots that have ensnared our boat, while Lako works the throttle in an attempt to free us before the big brown muscles of water smash us into something else.

Suddenly we break free, and the boat lurches forward, nearly throwing me overboard. Before Lako can get it under control we have careened into the flooded forest, bashing into a stand of trees. Cutting the engine, he tosses me a rope, and I tie the boat to a nearby tree.

"That was close," I say, relief making me feel almost giddy. Lako just grunts before reaching for his backpack. After guzzling a long drink of water, he rummages around and finds a piece of smoked fish, which he devours in three or four huge bites. Although I have no appetite I follow suit, knowing it is important to keep my strength up. Before I can finish my fish, he has closed his eyes and is asleep. Occasionally, he interrupts his snoring to slap at the *pium* flies nibbling at his ankles.

Wiping my greasy fingers on my jeans, I give him a mock salute for a job well done. I can't help feeling grateful to Eurico for insisting that I hire Lako. When I first saw him lying in the alley, in his own vomit, I was sure he was just another alcoholic. Now I'm having second thoughts. Recent events have caused me to reevaluate my opinion. Given the gut-wrenching pain I feel when I consider Eurico's impending death, I can only imagine what Lako must have suffered losing both his wife and his children. That kind of pain, I am now ready to concede, could drive the strongest man to drink. If the truth be known, I would give almost anything for a bottle of Lako's cheap white rum; anything to help me block out the image of Eurico writhing in pain and his imminent death.

Lako doesn't sleep more than fifteen or twenty minutes, then we slowly work our way back to the main channel, keeping a sharp lookout for low-hanging wasps' nests. According to Lako, bumping into a wasp nest is probably the greatest danger in the rain forest. He says an unwary person can get a hundred stings in a heartbeat. Thankfully, we make it through the flooded forest without incident, and when we are finally back in the main channel he turns into the teeth of the current and guns the engine.

The constant roar of the outboard motor makes conversation nearly impossible, even if I were so inclined, which I'm not. Instead I lean back against a pack, pull my hat low over my face, and try to sleep. I doze off from time to time, but mostly I continue to wrestle with my tormenting thoughts. I struggle to understand what makes me do the things I do. *Am I a victim of circumstances, responding by rote to the capricious events that befall me, or am I the master of my own destiny? Do I have the power to choose how I respond, or am I helpless before the winds of fate?*

Gordon Arnold claims we are the masters of our own destiny. He says events and circumstances affect us, but they do not determine our response. According to his way of thinking, no matter what happens to us, we can still choose how we are going to respond. And how we respond determines our destiny. We will become either better or bitter. His reasoning produces conflicting emotions in me. On the one hand, it gives me hope. I can change if I want to. On the other hand, it makes me responsible. I can no longer blame anyone else for my self-destructive behavior.

I've always believed I am the way I am—angry and bitter—because I lost my father when I was just a child. But, as Gordon pointed out, Eurico lost his entire family—parents and siblings—when he was only six years old, and he is not bitter. He has lived as an orphan on the streets for the past three years, and yet he is one of the most optimistic people I have ever known. What does that say about me? Nothing good, I must admit!

And now look what I've done. I've run out on Eurico and Diana just when they need me most. What a cowardly thing to do. Thinking about it now, I am filled with self-loathing. Still, I can't bring myself to go back. I just can't. I want to, but I can't.

Sometimes I think I must be cursed. No matter how hard I try, nothing good ever comes of it. Look what's happening now. Just when things seemed to be falling into place—coming to the Amazon, finding Eurico, meeting Diana, learning about my father from his journal— and now Eurico's dying, and I've driven a spike into Diana's heart.

Belatedly, I realize that Lako has eased us out of the current and into the flooded forest. Moving slowly among the trees he guides the boat deeper into the stillness created by the towering trees. The sun is far down in the sky when we finally ease into a bank that rises several feet above the water. Climbing out, I secure the boat to a nearby tree. Even if the water comes up several feet in the night, we should be all right.

Moving quickly, I gather the driest sticks I can find and set about building a fire, thankful for any activity that takes my mind off the terrible thing I have done, an unpardonable sin if ever there was one. While I am preparing a simple meal of fried plantains, a slab of bacon, and some beans, Lako moves with practiced skill to set up camp. Quickly he stretches a tarp between four trees, making an effective shelter should it rain. Beneath it he hangs our hammocks and arranges our mosquito nets.

It is fully dark when we squat beside the fire to eat our supper. Already the forest is alive with a cacophony of night sounds—the bark of a spiny tree rat, the call of an owl, hoatzins hissing and huffing in a grove of mungubas, a dozen caimans croaking on the other side of the meander. Cocking his head to one side, Lako says, "Listen."

High overhead I hear a strange cry in the darkness, like the tearing of a piece of cloth. "Is that a bird?" I ask.

"A *rasga mortalha*," Lako says, swallowing a mouthful of beans. When he speaks again I have to lean close to catch his words. "Someone is going to die soon." After a moment he throws the remains of his coffee on the fire and walks into the night, wearing his sorrow like an extra shirt.

I give no credence to such things. They're just primitive superstitions and myths; still, I feel the hair standing up on the back of my neck, and a cold hand squeezes my heart.

Shortly thereafter I bank the fire and climb into my hammock, carefully closing my mosquito net against the ravenous insects that patrol the night. Through the trees I see a sliver of new moon and a few faint stars. Sometime later I hear Lako slip back into camp. I pretend to be asleep, and he crawls into his hammock without saying anything. Soon his snoring joins the night chorus, but as tired as I am, sleep will not come. Instead I hear Lako's words playing repeatedly in my mind, *Someone is going to die soon...someone is going to die soon...* And I cannot help but think of Eurico.

CHAPTER

50

WE SPEND THE NEXT two days on the river, finally heading up the Rio Azul late in the afternoon of the second day. Battling against the strength of the flood-swollen current has slowed us considerably and cut deeply into our fuel reserves, a fact that concerns me no little bit. Lako assures me that the current will carry us back down the river if need be, but I am not encouraged. Pushing such concerns to the back of my mind, I study the storm clouds that are piling up over the Serra Divisor, as they do almost every afternoon during the rainy season. Undoubtedly, the rain will hit before we stop for the night, drenching us before we can set up camp and get out of the weather. Lako seems oblivious to such discomforts, but they irritate me like an itch I can't reach.

Out of the current and into the flooded forest once more, Lako kills the engine and reaches for a long pole. With practiced skill he maneuvers the boat between the trees, gliding ever deeper into the silent glade. "Look," he whispers, pointing with his long pole at a young anaconda, yellow with black spots, sunning itself on a shelf of sticks. I find his fascination with the huge snake slightly unnerving as the stories I've heard about anacondas have given me a healthy respect for them.

Leaving the anaconda behind us, we move into regions ever more remote. I can't help thinking that it is like being in a vast cathedral, quiet and peaceful. But I'm not fooled. It may be quiet, but it is hardly peaceful. Even now the dance of death continues between predator and prey. In a patch of sunlight I see a yellow-breasted kiskadee catch a Morpho butterfly in mid-flight, and passing under an overhanging branch I spot a grasshopper impaled on a spider's horn. In the Amazon Basin every creature is either predator or prey, usually both, depending on the moment.

Most of my life I have felt like prey to the whims of a capricious deity or, if there is no God, to the winds of fate. Not anymore. I have decided to take matters into my own hands. As we move ever closer to the Amuacas, I find that I am taking on the mind-set of a predator. Each night I clean my guns, oiling them carefully to make sure they are in perfect condition. Should I discover who is responsible for my father's death, I have every intention of making them pay. If Lako suspects anything, he has been careful to keep it to himself.

As I review my plans, I sense my father's disapproval. Although he never went into the jungle without a gun, he would never have used it against another human being. On more than one occasion, I heard him tell my mother that he could never shoot an Indian, not even if his life was in danger. "Why," he reasoned, "would I send an Indian to eternal damnation simply to prolong my own Earthly life, especially since death for me is just the doorway into eternal life?"

As a small boy I did not understand his theology, but I did admire his courage. Having lived with the consequences of his choice the past twenty-two years, I no longer admire either his theology or his courage. I am more of an Old Testament kind of guy—"an eye for an eye" type. I will not hesitate to use a gun if the situation calls for it. A little voice deep inside of me, what my father called "conscience," reminds me that there is a difference between self-defense and revenge, but I ignore it.

To my surprise Lako nudges us into a high bank just ahead of the storm. Gusts of cold, dense air tug at our shirts, and I can smell the rain in the wind, but it is still some minutes away. Working swiftly we secure the boat, stretch the tarp, and hang our hammocks. We are just finishing when the first splatters of rain strike the tarp overhead. Grateful for small blessings, I roll into my hammock and prepare to wait out the storm.

I must have slept, for it is fully dark when I awake, and for a moment I think I am back at the mission station with Diana. *Eurico is asleep on a cot in the corner of the room, the picture of health, his breathing deep and regular. Diana tucks the flannel sheet around him and brushes his forehead with a kiss before sitting down at the table across from me. Taking a sip of her tea, she looks at me over the rim of her cup and smiles, her eyes the color of the Colorado sky and full of kindness. Reaching across the table, I take her hand in mine. This is the way I always hoped life would be, and I am content in a way I have never known. Diana is the love of my life, and Eurico makes our family complete.*

But it is just a dream, a figment of my imagination, and as I come fully awake I am assaulted by the memory of recent events. Nearly gagging on my grief I roll out of my hammock and stumble to the river's edge where I douse my face with water in a vain attempt to wash away my memories.

Coming back up the trail, I see Lako squatting by a small fire cooking supper. In addition to black beans and rice, I see two large fish cooking in the coals. All I want to do is crawl back into my hammock, fall asleep, and never wake, but I force myself to join him by the fire. Without a word he fills a tin cup with coffee, made from grounds boiled in brown sugar, and hands it to me. I blow on it to cool it before taking a sip, savoring the sweetness even though it makes my teeth ache.

"While you were sleeping," Lako says, "I located an oxbow lake about half a kilometer from here." Using a stick to poke at the fish baking in the coals, he continues. "That's where I caught these, using a drop line. After we eat, I'm going back over there and try my hand with a cast net. I could use your help with the canoe."

I grunt a reply, and he begins filling a tin plate, carefully extracting a fish from the coals. Picking up a second plate, I follow suit, and even as agitated as I am, I eat with relish, devouring everything including the fish head. Although I am a fast eater, Lako has already disappeared into the night when I finish. Taking a final gulp of coffee, I bank the fire and head to the boat to see if I can find him. Before I have taken more than a few steps, I see him coming up the path with the cast net, and we set off, being careful where we step on the boggy trail.

Once we reach the lake, he shoves a dugout canoe into the water and steps in. "Where did the canoe come from?" I ask, climbing in after him.

"I found it under some bushes over there," he says, picking up a paddle. A light rain has returned, and it is pitting the lake's surface as we work our way through the lily pads toward open water. I paddle in the stern, slicing the water sharply, doing my best to make no sound, pulling hard, and then using the blade as a rudder before lifting it out again. Once we are in position, Lako places the handle of his paddle to his ear while leaving the blade in the water. "What are you doing?" I ask in a hoarse whisper.

Motioning for me to be quiet, he continues listening. As best I can figure, he is using the blade of his paddle as a receiver in an attempt to hear the sounds made by fish below. Finally, he stands in the stern and positions himself to cast the net, all the while intently studying the dark surface of the water. He must have seen some-thing—a telltale bubble, a gulp of air, a ripple—for all at once he casts the net, utilizing centrifugal force to expand it full and round, at the same time shifting his hips and legs to counterbalance its movement. To my amazement the canoe holds rock steady. Lako repeats this performance half a dozen times, filling the bottom of the canoe with fish.

Back on the bank we work swiftly, gutting the fish and stringing them on vines for transporting back to camp. Once we arrive, I move quickly to build a small but smoky fire while Lako uses green bamboo, as thick as my finger, to construct a drying rack for smoking the fish. By the time we finally position the last fish on the rack, I am exhausted and only too happy to roll into my hammock, leaving Lako to tend the fire.

As I am nearing sleep, I note that it has been more than seventy-two hours since I abandoned Diana and left Eurico to his fate. A gut-wrenching pain doubles me up when I realize he may already be dead, but I will not allow myself to go there. If I did, I might never find my way back.

CHAPTER
51

HEARING THE GARAGE DOOR open, Helen makes her way toward the kitchen to greet Rob. It has been more than two weeks since the terrible scene in the living room, and nothing has been resolved. Although he has made no move to replace Rita, he has been on his best behavior, even bringing her flowers on one occasion, something he hadn't done in years. For her part, Helen has been painfully polite, which, in retrospect, may have been a mistake. Rob seems to have mistaken her patience for a lack of resolve.

The two days he has been away attending the quarterly meeting of the foreign mission board has given Helen time to think, and she has come to some decisions. Either Rob will replace Rita immediately, or she will take matters into her own hands. Though she has worked all her life to be a submissive woman, the truth of the matter is she has Whittaker genes. She is every inch her father's daughter, a fact Rob is about to discover, much to his chagrin.

Placing his briefcase on the bar, Rob hangs up his keys and brushes Helen's cheek with a kiss before sitting down on a barstool. Leaning on his elbows, he lets out a long sigh. "Boy, am I tired." Loosening his tie, he says, "I don't suppose you have any coffee, do you?"

"No, but I can make some," Helen replies. "It will only take a minute."

Moving to the sink, she fills the CorningWare® pot with water and carefully measures three scoops of coffee. Once she has the electric percolator going, she takes two mugs from the hooks under the cupboard and places them on the bar. "How were your meetings?" she asks.

Reaching for the evening paper, he says, "Tedious for the most part. I would like a bowl of ice cream, if you don't mind."

When the coffee is ready, she fills both mugs and places the bowl of ice cream on the bar in front of Rob. Wearily she sits on the barstool next to his and watches with growing irritation as he eats his ice cream while reading the paper, never looking up. Finally, she gets to her feet. "I guess I'll check on the boys and then get ready for bed."

"Okay," he mutters, still absorbed in his paper. "I'll be along shortly. On second thought, there's something we need to discuss before you go."

Returning to her barstool, Helen swings her foot impatiently while Rob folds his paper and takes a sip of coffee. Finally he opens his briefcase and extracts a letter. Without a word he lays it on the counter in front of Helen. Unfolding it, she sees that it is addressed to the director of the Department of Foreign Missions. Quickly scanning the letter, she readily identifies the pertinent parts.

We have an unusual situation at the mission compound involving a young man named Bryan Whittaker. He purports to be a freelance photojournalist on assignment for National Geographic. *Although he has done nothing improper to date, there have been some concerns about his identity. It has even been suggested that he might be the son of the late Harold Whittaker who founded this mission station. If that is the case, I cannot think of any good reason for him to hide the fact. He seems to be a nice enough fellow, but we would feel better if you could let us know if*

Harold Whittaker had a son, how old he would be, and what his name is.

Helen's mind is racing. Her first concern is for Bryan. What possible reason could he have for not disclosing the fact that he is Harold Whittaker's son? If he is interested only in learning what happened to their father, surely the other missionaries would be the first place to start. A dreadful thought is taking shape far back in her mind, and she shivers involuntarily as she considers it. Maybe what Bryan is seeking is not just information, but revenge. Maybe he plans on punishing whoever he feels is responsible for their father's death. Almost as quickly she rejects the thought, but she cannot rid herself of the lingering suspicion that Bryan is up to no good. Why else would he pretend to be a photojournalist?

Looking up, she sees Rob studying her intently. "What is it?" she asks. "Why are you looking at me like that?"

"What do you know about Bryan's reasons for going to the Amazon?"

"Nothing you don't know. You read the same letter I did. Bryan wants to find out what happened to our father so he can come to some kind of closure. Apparently he doesn't feel he can get on with his life until he makes peace with his past." Puzzled, she asks, "Why this sudden interest in Bryan's motives?"

Ignoring her question, Rob presses. "Have you received any other letters from him?"

"No, of course not. Why would you even ask me a thing like that?"

"What about Carolyn? Has she heard from Bryan?"

"Don't be ridiculous. She hasn't had any contact with Bryan since their divorce."

Agitated, Rob gets up and paces the room. Stopping in front of Helen, he places his hands on the bar and leans toward her. "Forgive me, but I'm having a hard time believing you haven't had any further correspondence with your brother."

"Are you suggesting that I'm not being truthful?"

"Well," he replies scornfully, "you do have a history of duplicity, especially when it comes to Bryan."

Disgusted, Helen retorts, "You're hardly the one to be talking about duplicity given your tawdry relationship with Rita. Which brings up another matter; have you given her her termination notice?"

Anger paints Rob's face a bright red, but with an effort he manages to control his temper. Taking a deep breath, he returns to the matter at hand. "Don't you find it a bit disingenuous on Bryan's part to hide his true identity?"

"I'll grant you that," Helen concedes, "but given Bryan's state of mind, nothing he does surprises me."

"My point exactly—Bryan's state of mind!"

"What are you suggesting?"

"I'm not suggesting anything, but I would like to remind you that Bryan has a long history of irresponsible behavior. If he goes off half-cocked and does something stupid, it could undo years of missionary effort, including your father's sacrifice, not to mention taint your family's good name and even embarrass me and our congregation."

"It's always about you, isn't it, Rob?" Helen says wearily.

"What are you talking about?"

"Listen to yourself, Rob. You're not concerned about Bryan or even the missionary work in the Amazon. All you're worried about is being embarrassed in front of all the bigwigs on the mission board."

Getting to her feet, Helen turns toward the bedroom. Grabbing her by the arm, Rob demands, "Where do you think you're going? We're not finished talking."

"Oh, we're finished all right," she says, glaring at him, "and not just with talking."

Releasing her arm, he says, "Well, before you storm out of here, there is something else you ought to know, something that might affect your precious brother."

"What? Is there something you haven't told me?"

"Not something, someone—Dr. Diana Rhoades."

"Let's not play this game, Rob. If you've got something to say, spit it out."

"Three missionary families are stationed on the compound founded by your father—Gordon and Eleanor Arnold, the senior missionaries; the Fergusons, who are home on furlough; and Diana Rhoades. She's a medical missionary from Minnesota who just happens to be single. Someone, I don't remember who, also mentioned that she is thirty-one years old and unusually attractive."

"So? What has that got to do with Bryan?"

Shaking his head in disbelief, Rob asks, "Do I have to draw you a picture?"

"Are you telling me that Bryan's involved with this woman?"

"Not as far as anyone knows, but if he's not, I have no doubt that he will be shortly. You know our Bryan—always the ladies' man."

"What are you suggesting?"

"Nothing, except given Bryan's penchant for beautiful women we may have cause for concern. If he becomes involved with a single missionary, nothing good can come of it, especially considering he's divorced, not to mention all the other baggage he's carrying around."

As Helen struggles to process this last bit of information, she cannot help noting that Rob seems to be taking a perverse pleasure in her distress. Seeing the meanness in his eyes, she finds herself grieving the tragic state of their marriage. Were they truly happy at one time? Was there really a time when they were in love? She thinks so, but how can she be sure? How does love turn into this charade?

Against her better judgment she finds herself blurting out what has been on her mind over the last few weeks. She has been undecided, but Rob's petty cruelty has pushed her over the edge. Now all she can think about is making him pay. She wants to shock him, to wipe that smug look off his face.

"I suppose I should tell you that I'm going away for a while. You will need to make arrangements for someone to look after the boys."

The transformation is priceless. One moment he is gloating, enjoying seeing her squirm, and the next he is speechless. Recovering, he blusters, "Going away? What are you talking about?"

Casually, she says, "I'll be spending several weeks in Cruzeiro do Sul."

"Where?"

"Cruzeiro do Sul. It's in Brazil. Not far from where Bryan is."

"Are you out of your mind?" Rob fumes. "You can't go traipsing off to some God-forsaken place. You've got responsibilities, for Heaven's sake. You're a pastor's wife; besides, who's going to take care of the boys?"

"Rob," she says, speaking condescendingly as if to a dull child, "you may not have noticed, but I am a grown woman, an adult. You may ask me to reconsider my decision, you can even ask me to pray about it, but you cannot forbid me to go. I am not a child, and you are not my father!"

"Can we talk about this?"

"What's there to talk about? My mind is made up."

"What about the boys? You can't just run off and leave the boys," Rob sputters.

At the mention of her children, Helen thinks her heart will break, but if there is to be any hope for their marriage she has to do something to bring Rob to his senses. Given her options, going to the Amazon seems like the best choice. It's a risky move, to be sure—Rob may do something stupid in her absence—but it is a risk she feels she must take.

"What about the boys?" Rob demands again. "Who's going to take care of the boys?"

"I won't be leaving for a couple of weeks. That should give you time to make arrangements. Maybe your mother can come." Pausing as if considering other options, Helen muses. "Perhaps Rita could look after them. That would be convenient, wouldn't it? Oh, I forgot; she still has a job, doesn't she? Well, whatever, I'm sure you will think of something."

Without another word, she turns and heads down the hall toward the bedroom. It is all she can do to keep from breaking down, but she must not let Rob see her cry. If he suspects how close she is to breaking, he will continue in the status quo, and there will be no hope for their marriage. No, as hard as this is, she has no other choice. *Thank God Carolyn is going with me. I don't think I could do this alone.* Closing the bedroom door, she retreats to the master bathroom where she stuffs a towel in her mouth to muffle her sobs.

CHAPTER

52

WE HAVE BEEN WALKING the better part of two days, and although I continue to be amazed by the wild beauty of the rain rorest, I am exhausted. More distressing is the fact that we haven't seen a trace of the Amuacas. Apparently spooked by Lako's initial contact, they seem to have abandoned their longhouses and moved deeper into the jungle. Lako thinks he knows where they have gone, but after a hard day's hike, without finding anything, I'm beginning to think it is just wishful thinking.

My boots are caked with mud, and the straps of my backpack are cutting painfully into my shoulders. Even worse are the sweat bees swarming around my head. Desperate for the excreted salt in my perspiration and saliva, they clamber over my face, crawling into my nostrils, mouth, and ears. They are stingless, but their sharp mandibles pinch, and it is all I can do not to swat at them continually. I crushed several before Lako could warn me, setting off a suicidal frenzy by their enraged sisters. "Leave them alone," he said, "and they will depart once they are satiated; but kill one of them, and the rest will go crazy."

A hundred feet overhead the treetops are alive with a troop of red howler monkeys, the air thick with their musk—a mix of body odor, urine, and feces. The smell is enough to gag me, but it is nothing compared to their screaming, which is not only loud, but also irritating; grating on my nerves and making my head ache. Dr. Peterson likened it to the sound of a demonic wind screaming through the rigging of a ship. He said it was their way of staking out their territory. Resting my hand on the butt of the pistol in my belt, I am sorely tempted to fire a shot or two to see if I can drive them away. Of course I don't, not wanting to alert the Amuacas, should they be anywhere near.

Lako has been walking about a hundred meters ahead of me, and now I see him coming off the ridge toward me. He holds up his hands, motioning for me to stop, and then disappears as the trail bends out of sight. Grateful for the break, I slide my heavy pack off and sit on it. Closing my eyes for a moment, I curse myself for having ever undertaken this madness. Eurico is undoubtedly dead, I've caused Diana unspeakable pain, and I've squandered most of my inheritance; and for what? I must have been crazy to think I could unravel the mystery of my father's death. Yes, death! Having spent the past few weeks in the Amazon, I realize that to consider any other possibility is insane. The only question that remains is how he died and why. And, of course, what I'm going to do about it.

Getting to my feet, I watch as Lako approaches, moving in and out of the shadows as he makes his way toward me. Without a word he picks up my pack and motions for me to follow him. Although I can't see anything even remotely resembling a path, he moves soundlessly through the undergrowth until we come to a small clearing, a good fifty meters off the trail. "The Amuaca village is just over that ridge," he says, leaning both packs against a nearby tree. "Not knowing their disposition, I think it would be wise to spend the night here. We can approach them at first light."

Night comes quickly in the jungle, and without further discussion we set about making camp. Already the light is fading, and if we are going to finish before dark we will have to hurry. Lako hangs our hammocks as I begin gathering dead branches to build a small fire on which to cook our supper. "Not tonight," he says. "We can't risk letting the Amuacas know we are here."

Tired as I am, I would give almost anything for a cup of Lako's coffee, but I don't argue with him. Instead I force myself to eat two pieces of smoked fish, which I wash down with a terrible-tasting beverage that he prepared a couple of nights ago. I might have handled it better if I hadn't watched him making it. After boiling manioc roots, he mashed them. During the mashing process, he put huge wads of the mash into his mouth to collect his saliva and then spat it back into a mixing bowl to start the digestive process. The object, according to Lako, is to create a food source that will provide quick energy.

Lako grins, watching me struggle to get it down, then drinks nearly a quart of it himself. Wiping his mouth on the back of his hand, he burps loudly. "You'll thank me for that tomorrow. You'll feel better, you'll see."

With a gratefulness I could not have imagined a few weeks ago, I roll into my hammock and secure my mosquito net, taking a perverse pleasure in knowing I am safe from the marauding insects. Lako seems impervious to the rigors of the jungle, but it is taking a frightful toll on me. As I relax, I realize that every muscle in my body aches, and my bum knee is swollen and stiff. Two days of hard hiking have worn me out, and in spite of the pain, I am out almost as soon as I close my eyes. For the first time in days, I sleep without dreaming, too tired to be tormented by the things I have done.

308 + Richard Exley

I awake four or five hours later, still exhausted, but my mind is racing. In a few hours I may be face to face with those who are responsible for my father's death, and I still have no plan of action. I can't decide if I should continue to pretend I'm a photojournalist, or if I should drop all pretense and start asking questions. Complicating everything is the fact that I will have to work through Lako. He's the only one who speaks the language, and who knows where his loyalties lie, seeing his mother was a full-blooded Amuaca? The fact that I'm still struggling with my Portuguese further complicates things, making communication with Lako a challenge.

The safest course would be to continue with my ruse. Posing as a photojournalist should allow me to poke around and shoot a lot of pictures, all the while keeping my eyes open for anything that might give me a clue about my father. That's the safest way, but it's also the slowest; besides, it's unlikely I will find any physical evidence after all these years.

The other option is to hit it head on, just lay all my cards on the table. We could get everyone together, and I could show them pictures of my father and explain what happened—that he responded to a plea for help and never returned. Then I could question them. The weaknesses in that approach are obvious. Since revenge killing is part of their culture, they would probably expect the same from me. So why would they tell me anything, especially if they had a part in my father's death? Such a course of action would likely get me killed, as it would be in their best interest to do away with me before I could take revenge on them.

I really have no choice but to continue in my role as a photojournalist and see what happens. It's a long shot, to be sure, but it's really the only viable alternative open to me.

Having decided on a course of action, I clasp my hands behind my head and try to imagine what it must have been like for my father to come alone to this wild place on the edge of the world. *Were the Indians hostile? Was the reported epidemic trickery, just a ploy to draw him away from the mission compound so they could kill him? Did he fall prey to the epidemic that was killing the Indians?* These and a host of other questions now flood my mind, but they no longer torment me. Thinking about them now, I feel close to my father. It may just be wishful thinking, but I can't shake the feeling that I'm very close to finding out what happened to him.

CHAPTER
53

THE SUN IS RINSING the last of the purple dawn out of the sky as we top the ridge and start our descent. Although the thick foliage makes it impossible for us to see the Amuaca village, the heavy moist air brings us the smoky smell of their breakfast fires. As we work our way closer, I hear a dog barking and the running laughter of children. Lako, who is a few meters ahead of me, stops and motions for me to join him. In the clearing at the base of the ridge, I see a longhouse. It is not nearly as big as the Kachinawa *maloca* where Eurico and I went with Diana, but it's still impressive. Oriented west to east, it is situated beside a stream running in the same direction.

On the far side of the clearing, I see several Indian women working with crude hoes, cultivating a small plot of ground. Nearer the longhouse, a group of men are sitting in the shade making arrows. Things look peaceful enough, but I know that could change in a heartbeat. Easing my Nikon to my eye, I focus through the telephoto lens. The whirring sound of the motor drive breaks the stillness of the morning, causing the Indians to look up in surprise. Grabbing their spears, the men spread out in a ragged skirmish line and advance toward us. The women move with practiced efficiency, gathering their children and hustling them inside the safety of the longhouse.

"You fool," Lako hisses, cursing me under his breath as he steps into the clearing and lifts his hand in greeting. I follow close on his heels, and in an instant we are surrounded. He speaks to them in their own language, but they pay him no mind. Poking and jabbing at us with their spears, they continue to mutter angrily in a language I do not understand. Once more Lako tries to speak to them, but a host of angry voices drown him out. As we are being herded toward an area directly in front of the longhouse, I see an old woman standing off to one side, studying us intently.

After shoving us to the ground, two of the spear-wielding Indians position themselves to guard us, while the others move off a short distance. Although their discussion is animated, we cannot hear what they are saying, not that I could understand them even if we could. I have no doubt that they are discussing our fate, and Lako's words return to haunt me: *What you are suggesting is dangerous. The Amuacas are fierce warriors who have been known to kill outsiders on sight.*

As the warriors continue their spirited discussion, life in the village drifts back to normal. The women have returned to their gardens, while the children squat in the mud a few meters away, laughing and pointing. We are no longer enemies to be feared but objects of curiosity, strange creatures from another world to be mocked and ridiculed. One of the young boys darts close and jabs me with a sharp stick.

Suddenly the children grow quiet, their eyes wide with fear. Following their gaze, I see an Indian in wild garb enter the clearing. He wears a necklace of jaguar teeth, pounds of glass beads, a magnificent corona with a halo of erect macaw feathers, and a long cape of parrot feathers that hangs down his back to the waist. His ears are pierced by the tail feathers of a scarlet macaw, and his wrists are decorated with leaves.

Turning to Lako, I ask, "Who is he?"

"The shaman," he says. "They've probably sent for him to decide our fate."

The way he says it makes my blood run cold, and I press him. "Can't you do something? Talk to them, tell them we're friends and that we come in peace."

"I've already tried. They're not interested in anything I have to say."

"What do you think is going to happen? Will they kill us?"

"Probably, but they won't do anything until they have gone through an elaborate ritual. They're big on ceremony; besides, they not only want to kill us but to destroy our souls as well, lest we attack them in the next life."

Apparently the shaman has made a decision, for the meeting is breaking up. In a few minutes a young warrior returns with several lengths of green vine. While one of the guards stands over me brandishing his spear, the warrior jerks my hands behind my back and secures them with the vine. Moving quickly, he also ties my feet. Going to Lako, he repeats the process, and then all three men move off, leaving us alone.

I scoot around until I am facing Lako. "Do you have any idea what's going on?"

"I figure they're preparing for some kind of religious ceremony, probably a *mariri* ritual."

"What's that?"

"The shaman prepares a secret concoction, which each participant drinks. Then they chant and dance until they pass out. While they're unconscious, they see visions and experience visitations from the spirit world. Only the shaman can understand the meaning of the visions, and his interpretation will determine whether we live or die."

Great, I think, *a bunch of Indians are going to get stoned on some kind of hallucinogenic concoction and decide our fate. That's like giving the jury LSD and then asking them to render a verdict in a capital murder case. Insane!*

We are sitting directly in the sun, and as it climbs higher in the sky the heat becomes unbearable. Even Lako seems to be suffering, and nothing ever affects him. But the heat may be the least of our discomforts. With our bodies drenched in nutrient-enriched sweat, we are attracting every mineral-deprived insect in the western Amazon Basin. A hoard of stingerless, *arapuá* bees swarm over my face, feasting on my salty sweat, while ravenous mosquitoes gorge themselves on my blood. With my hands tied behind my back, there is absolutely nothing I can do to relieve my torment. Now salty sweat runs down my forehead and into my eyes. In an instant half a dozen bees are contending for the salt on my eyebrows and eyelashes, forcing me to clamp my lids closed to protect my eyes from their sharp mandibles.

The hours drag on interminably, and when I am sure I can bear no more, a faint breeze ruffles the heavy air, birthing in me a desperate hope. Squinting against the sun, I see dark clouds piling up over the Serra Divisor, and I find myself praying for rain. In a matter of minutes the first scattered drops are rattling against the leaves overhead, then the sky opens up, and the storm comes with a rush. Closing my eyes, I turn my face to the heavens and let the downpour cool my sunburned skin. Greedily I gulp the rain, trying desperately to quench the thirst of my dehydrated body. Beside me, Lako is doing the same.

The onslaught of the storm only lasts a few minutes, then the rain settles into a gentle rhythm, which tapers off as darkness descends. When it is fully dark, the Indians begin gathering around a large fire that has been built in the common area in front of the longhouse. As they dance, firelight flickers off their painted faces, giving them a ghoulish appearance. From the darkness the shaman enters, shaking his rattles and chanting. Moving among the dancers, he places a gourd to their lips, and they drink. Now the chanting falls into a monotone, and the dancers are moving slower and slower. From time to time one of them will wander off into the dark, lost in a drug-induced stupor.

As the chanting goes on and on, I feel myself drifting. It's almost like I'm having an out of body experience or a vision. *I see my father the way he was the last time I saw him. He's young, hardly older than I am now. And he's here. In this very village, or one very much like it. Misery is every-where, and he moves among the sick and dying with tenderness I never imag-ined him capable of. Having exhausted his limited medical supplies days ago, he now offers only comfort. He holds the hand of a dying woman, cools the fevered brow of a suffering child, and weeps unashamedly as a grieving father sings the death chant, a mournful wail of excruciating sadness. In the wee hours of the morning the longhouse grows still, and in the smoky light of the dying fires I see my father cradling the rigid body of a convulsing child, his face a sorrowing mask, his lips moving silently in prayer.*

Suddenly a hand comes out of the darkness to cover my mouth, stifling my startled cry. Motioning for me to remain quiet, the old woman quickly cuts the vines binding my wrists and ankles. While I am rubbing my legs in a desperate attempt to restore the circulation to my feet, she moves quickly to free Lako. My hands and feet feel like they have a thousand needles in them, but hope is making my heart race. Following the old woman, we slip into the dark as silent as shadows.

She leads us away from the fire and the chanting, dancing Indians. Taking a circuitous route around the clearing, we move away from the village. Twice we stumble upon Indians in the brush, but they are so stoned they don't even know we are there; or if they do, they probably think we are part of their vision. At last we step out of the undergrowth onto a trail.

Talking rapidly in a language I do not understand, the old woman instructs Lako, gesturing with her hands and pointing from time to time. When she is sure he understands, she slips into the brush, disappearing into the night. I want to ask Lako what that was all about, but he is already heading down the trail at a rapid clip, forcing me to hustle to keep up. After about fifteen minutes we come to a small stream that crosses the trail. Motioning for me to wait, he turns into the brush. When he returns a few minutes later he is carrying both of our packs and my camera equipment. Without a word we cross the stream and begin the steep climb up the ridge, hurrying to put as much distance between us and the Amuacas as we possibly can.

CHAPTER
54

LAKO SETS A STIFF pace through the long night, and I am hard pressed to keep up. By the time we finally top the ridge, exhaustion has turned my long strides into a stumbling shuffle, and my knee is badly swollen. Dropping to the ground beside the trail, I gulp greedily from my water bottle, thankful that it is nearly full. Behind us, day is breaking, and I watch the sky change colors while trying to find the energy to rummage in my pack for a piece of smoked fish. Turning to Lako, I ask, "Do you have any idea where we're going?"

"According to the old woman," he says, talking around a mouthful of fish, "there is a man who lives alone in this valley who will give us sanctuary. He's an Amuaca, but an outcast, and the rest of the Indians steer clear of him. She says we'll be safe there."

Too tired to talk, we eat in silence, and when we have finished our fish we get to our feet and prepare to set off again. The sun is still low in the sky, leaving the valley steeped in deep shadows, the early morning mist lying like a gauzy membrane over the land. As I watch, fingers of light began erasing the darkness, revealing a palette of vibrant greens beneath the dome of the sky. Impatient to be on his way, Lako disappears around a bend several meters down the trail, while I remain transfixed by the beauty spread out below me. I linger for a moment more, enjoying the vista from the vantage of this high ridge, knowing that as I descend it will be swallowed by the rain forest. Almost as an afterthought I grab my Nikon and shoot several shots.

Reluctantly, I put my camera away and set out after Lako. I'm thankful to have the climb behind us, but descending the steep trail is just as hard, only in a different way. Now I have to brace my feet to hold myself back, being careful where I step lest I slip on the muddy trail. The pressure on my swollen knee is relentless, and the dull ache is rapidly turning into a stabbing pain, causing me to limp noticeably.

After a time, exhaustion lulls me into a stupor, and I move by rote, putting one foot in front of the other, while my mind drifts. Having long ago perfected the deadly art of self-flagellation, I return to it unconsciously, like a dog to his vomit. From some dark place deep inside of me I loose my demons, determined to punish myself even if no one else will. In voices that sound strangely like my own, they castigate me for Eurico's death. It's my fault. If it weren't for me, he would still be alive. I'm responsible, no matter that Diana calls the killer meningitis and blames it on a parasite. If I hadn't brought him to the jungle, he would still be alive.

Reason tells me I'm being ridiculous. Sickness and death is no respecter of persons; it comes to young and old alike, especially here in this God-forsaken place. But self-hatred is immune to reason, and even if I could forgive myself for Eurico's death, what I've done to Diana is unforgivable. An unspeakable act, so selfish, so cruel it leaves freezer burn on my soul. No matter how long I live, I will never be able to forgive myself, nor should I.

How unbelievably naive my earlier optimism now seems in light of the events in recent weeks. I must have been a fool to think I could find my father in this trackless wilderness, or even learn what happened to him. Still, if I've accomplished nothing else, I've convinced myself that there was nothing a woman with two small children could have done to save him. Any attempt to rescue him would have surely ended in disaster.

Admitting that I've failed in this, the most important endeavor of my life, invokes a nameless but familiar despair; not anger, but depression. I'm too tired, too broken to be angry. I'm finally coming to realize that, like me, my parents were flawed human beings doing the best they knew how. Even if I can't forgive them, I do accept them. It's God that I am most disappointed in. He demands our absolute allegiance, then He lets us down. He requires our unconditional trust, then He betrays us. But even that doesn't matter any more; nothing matters now.

Stepping into a clearing at the bottom of the ridge, I look up and address the heavens. *"God, if You're real, I hope You can hear me. I'm tired of fighting You; I want to call a truce. Please leave me alone and let me live my life. That's all I ask...just leave me alone..."*

Across the clearing Lako is staring at me with a strange look on his face. Hastily he crosses himself, and I realize he must have heard me railing at God, even if he couldn't understand exactly what I was saying. How he can still believe after all he has suffered is beyond me, but I guess that's between him and God. Straightening the pack on my shoulders, I limp across the clearing toward him. Parting the leaves, he motions for me to have a look. About sixty meters away, I see an old Indian, and behind him a thatched hut.

Tired as I am, I'm ready to throw caution to the wind, but Lako insists that we watch for a while to make sure he is alone. Two hours pass, and we see nothing suspicious. Finally, Lako hoists his pack and motions for me to do the same. Getting to my feet, I limp after him. By keeping to the edge of the trees, we are able to stay out of sight until we are within a few meters of the old man who seems to be dozing in the shade. Stepping from the trees, Lako calls a greeting, and the old Indian shades his eyes against the sun, studying us as we approach.

CHAPTER
55

AFTER WELCOMING US, THE old Indian—whose name is Komi—insists that we share a meal with him consisting of live tree grubs, large and wiggly, plus gourds of something very similar to the premasticated manioc drink Lako prepared a few nights ago. I am tempted to refuse, but the look Lako gives me convinces me otherwise. While we eat, Komi studies us, seeming to pay particular attention to me, a situation I find uncomfortable seeing I am doing my best not to be sick. There is one grub left, and Komi plucks it off of the banana leaf with his calloused fingers and offers it to me. It is an act of singular hospitality, and although my stomach is churning I place it in my mouth and force myself to swallow.

Reaching for his pack, Lako spreads a blanket on the ground and arranges the gifts we have brought—a spool of fishing line, several fish hooks, a machete, and an iron axe head, plus a leather pouch filled with salt. Komi seems pleased, particularly with the salt. Several times he licks a gnarled finger and thrusts it deep into the pouch, smiling with pleasure when he sucks the salt off.

I let my eyes roam over Komi's "homestead"—I don't know what else to call it. His house has only one room and a thatched roof. It's open-walled, built on a platform of split *buriti* with a few posts from which to suspend hammocks. Situated on a slight rise, it nestles up against a grove of banana trees, with a small stream about twenty-five meters away. Near the stream is a garden where it looks like he is growing beans, manioc, and papaya. I can't help noticing that it is carefully tended and appears to be thriving.

Lako explains our situation and asks Komi if he will be in danger if we take him up on his offer of hospitality. "I am an outcast from my people," he explains. "No Amuaca, other than my sister who helped you escape, has come to this place since I was sent into exile. Never fear, we will be safe."

The rain is coming, as it does almost every afternoon now, and we move our packs under the thatched roof. After hanging our hammocks, Lako rolls into his and closes his mosquito net. In minutes he is snoring softly. As tired as I am, I can't imagine sleeping without a bath. My clothes are filthy, and every square inch of exposed skin is raw with sunburn, insect bites, and scratches. Taking a bar of soap from my backpack, I walk through the rain toward the creek.

Stripping off my filthy clothes, I plunge into the cool water. After scrubbing the accumulated muck and grim from my abused body, I relax, letting the stream massage my sore muscles, hoping it will relieve the aches and pains. Depressed as I am, I can't help feeling that there is something providential about our being here. Why else would that old woman help us escape? Had things happened any other way, we would have never found this place.

Although I am eager to get back and discuss my feelings with Lako, I take time to wash my clothes in the creek. The few minutes it takes is a small price to pay for the comfort it will provide tomorrow. Pulling on my wet boxer shorts, I stuff my bare feet into my muddy boots, drape my wet clothes over my arm and head toward Komi's small hut, a faint hope struggling inside of me.

When I get back, Lako is still sleeping, and Komi is gone. Going to my pack, I extract my father's journal and carefully remove the oilcloth covering it. There is no furniture in the small room, so I crawl into my hammock. Opening the journal, I scan several pages at random. I'm not sure what I'm looking for, but maybe something will jump out at me. After reading for fifteen or twenty minutes without finding anything of interest, my eyes grow heavy, and I let the journal rest face down on my chest. In seconds I am asleep.

Sometime later I hear Komi return, but I can't rouse myself. I sleep fitfully after that, drifting in and out, vaguely aware of what's going on around me, but too tired to wake up. Lako and Komi are talking softly, but in a language I do not understand, so I turn over and go back to sleep. Finally, the smell of wood smoke and the tantalizing aroma of roasting meat, aided by my hunger pangs, coax me fully awake.

Komi has killed a monkey, which he is roasting on a spit over a small fire. From our rapidly dwindling food supply, Lako has contributed some rice and black beans. Squatting near Komi, Lako is frying plantains in a small cast iron skillet. I like fried plantains well enough, but I'm still trying to acquire a taste for monkey. Still, I can't help thinking it will be a big improvement over the grubs we had earlier.

While they cook, I try to decide on a course of action. I want to discuss my feelings with Lako, but I'm not sure how Komi will respond if we talk in front of him, considering he doesn't speak Portuguese. Maybe I had better wait until we are alone. I wouldn't want to do anything to jeopardize our relationship with the old Indian, especially since he may be the last chance I have to learn anything about my father. Not that I expect him to know anything.

Squatting around the fire, we fill the clay bowls Komi has handed us. As I'm shoveling a spoonful of rice and beans into my mouth, I notice he has bowed his head. Puzzled, I glance a question at Lako who just shrugs before stripping a stringy piece of monkey meat from the bone. Concentrating on our food, we eat with a purpose, without talking, and in a matter of minutes we have devoured every scrap. For desert, Komi cracks the monkey bones with his strong teeth and sucks out the marrow, sighing with contentment.

On an impulse I turn to Lako. "Ask him if he has ever gone down the river."

"What?"

"Ask him if he has ever been where the white man lives."

"I don't think we had better do that."

"Why not?"

"In the Amuaca culture it is not done."

"Ask him anyway," I say, growing impatient. "I want to know."

"To do such a thing, after we have accepted his hospitality, would be an insult."

"That's the dumbest thing I've ever heard," I retort. "Now ask him."

Still hesitating, Lako asks, "Why are you making such a big deal out of this?"

His stubbornness pushes me over the edge, and I scream at him. "Because he might know something about my father, you idiot!"

For a moment he glares at me, then understanding begins to brighten his dark features. "So Dr. Peterson was right. You're the missionary's son."

Komi has been listening to our exchange, his weathered face impassive. Now he leans forward and speaks to me in broken Portuguese. "I wait many year for you. You father tell me you come."

"You knew my father?" I ask in a strangled whisper, hardly able to speak. "You knew my father?"

"When first I see you, I know you be the one. Old woman know. You tall like father. Strong."

I can't breathe; I must be hyperventilating. My mind is reeling. Here is someone who knew my father. He may even know what happened to him, how he died.

"You not your father son," he says, speaking slowly and with great sadness. "Father have great heart, love many people. You have no heart. Just darkness…much anger. I be thankful you father no live to see. He be shamed, much shamed…"

I'm already emotionally wrought, and now Komi's words pierce my heart. Lunging to my feet, I stumble into the darkness, torn between denial and remorse. All my life I have blamed others, refusing to take responsibility for my actions. It was always someone else's fault—my father's fault for going away and never coming back, or my mother's for abandoning me in her grief, or Carolyn's for being too needy, or Helen's for being too "spiritual." Most of all I blamed God!

As I am stumbling through the night, choking on my sobs, my mother's words come back to me: *You blame others for too much, Bryan. When does it become your responsibility? When do you take your life into your own hands? When do you start accepting the blame for your own actions? When…*

Now denial gives way to remorse, to bitter regret. How I wish I could go back and undo the terrible things I have done. Only God knows the suffering I caused my mother, the tears she shed into her pillow, the wordless prayers she prayed on my behalf. Would to God I had forgiven her, her failings as a parent; but no, I sent her to her grave bearing my judgment. Even in death she wore her sorrow in her face, a suffering that only a wayward son could put there.

And poor sweet Carolyn, who loved me more than she loved herself. I can't even imagine the wounds I inflicted to her sensitive soul, the psychological damage I did when she needed me most, driving her into the arms of another. She was too needy, too hungry for love to resist temptation, but too full of love and goodness to live with her sin. I watched her die, day by day, hating herself for what she had done, yet I never lifted a hand to help her; I never spoke a word to ease her guilt.

Now the pain and the burden that is my life give birth to broken sobs of repentance. For the first time ever I cry out to God, not in anger but in brokenness. Using words I learned as a child, I pray. *"Have mercy on me, O Lord. Have mercy on me. I am a sinful man, broken and full of hurt and anger. I bring You my wounds and my bitterness. They have imprisoned me far too long. Heal my insecurities and deliver me from the anger they have birthed. Redeem my pain, turn it into loving compassion, the kind of compassion my father had. May even the tragedies of my life become tools in Your hands to make me the man You have called me to be, a man my father would be proud of."*

Having poured out my soul, I now sit in the darkness, emotionally exhausted yet renewed in a way I would be hard pressed to explain. For the first time since we left the Amazon more than twenty years ago I am at peace. The hurt and anger that have tormented me all these years are gone. The questions remain, as does the grief, but I am at peace in a way I have never known. I still don't understand why God allowed things to happen as they did, but I am coming to accept them. And as unbelievable as it is, I find myself yearning to know God, to have a relationship with Him.

Something Gordon Arnold said that day on the river bank now comes back to me. "Bryan," he said, "it seems to me that you need to forgive God."

I could hardly believe my ears. Surely I had misunderstood. Suggesting a mere mortal forgive God was blasphemy, and surely this good man would never do such a thing.

My shock must have been obvious, for he placed his hand on my arm saying, "Hear me out, Bryan. I don't mean that God does wrong and needs our forgivenss. Rather when bad things happen we some-times blame Him. We hold Him responsible. To forgive God means we let go of those feelings—all the hurt and anger, all the bitterness and distrust. It means we stop working against His purposes in our life. Instead, we yield ourselves to Him, we work with Him. And as a result, we experience His supernatural peace."

I had not been ready to let God off the hook that day; Eurico's health crisis was too fresh, his impending death too overwhelming. Without a word I had trudged back to Diana's mission house to resume my bedside vigil, railing at God in my heart. But now things feel different somehow, and I find I am willing to release the grudge I have carried against God all my life. In a voice that is hardly more than a strangled whisper I pray, *"God, I forgive You for not answering this little boy's desperate prayers. I forgive You for allowing my father to die. I forgive You for not preventing Eurico's illness and death…"*

When at last I finish, I realize that the anger I have felt toward God, for as long as I can remember, is gone. In its place is a stillness, a kind of holy quiet that now pervades my soul; and a tentative faith, a sense that God is at work in all of this. Wearily I get to my feet and turn toward Komi's small hut, feeling more hopeful than I ever have in my entire life.

CHAPTER
56

THE FIRST HINT OF daylight is just seeping into the valley when I roll out of my hammock and pull on my jeans. Early though it is, Komi is nowhere to be found. He has slipped away without waking us, as he has done each morning since our arrival. Stepping outside, I see Lako stirring up the fire before heading to the creek to wash. Already the coffee is boiling, so I pick up a banana leaf to use as a potholder and pour myself a cup, before walking into the morning. Near the garden, I see a faint trail leading into the forest, and on an impulse I decide to take it.

It rained most of the night, and even though the sky is overcast, the weak light is enough to make the water beads glisten on the leaves overhead. Most mornings I would be composing still shots in my mind or even snapping them into permanence with my Nikon and a close-focusing zoom lens. Not today, nor do I pay any mind to the sounds of the morning, although the forest is alive with them.

Today my mind is going a hundred miles an hour, and I need a place where I can sort through everything that has happened to me. Although my circumstances haven't changed, I have. The things that caused me so much distress—Father's death, my divorce, even the situation with Eurico—no longer devastate me. When I stopped looking for someone to blame and simply accepted things, I experienced a remarkable peace. I still grieve, and sometimes the pain is unbearable, especially when I think of Eurico, but I'm no longer raging on the inside.

I was ready to tear Komi's head off when he said I had no heart, only darkness. But he was right. Years ago my grief turned into anger, into a dark rage that was destroying everyone it touched including me, especially me. There's still much I don't understand, maybe I never will, but it seems to me that grief itself is not a fatal wound. It's the bitterness that kills, not the grief. Given time, our hearts will heal themselves. That's the way God made us; at least that's how it seems to me.

The trail has curved back toward the creek, and now it opens onto a tiny glade. Across the way Komi is kneeling, his arms resting on a stump, his back to me. As I draw near, I hear him speaking quietly in a language I do not understand. Belatedly, I realize he is praying, and although I have no idea what he is saying his passion is readily apparent. Not wanting to intrude on such a personal moment, I turn to go. He must have heard me, for now he looks my way, motioning with his hand for me to sit beside him.

Although there is much I want to ask Komi about my father, I have been avoiding him since that first night. Now I sit quietly, waiting for him to speak. He seems to be in no hurry, silence being familiar to him. As the minutes drag on, my mind returns to Diana, invoking a shame that stains my soul. It's not likely she will ever want to speak with me again, unless it's to give me a piece of her mind; nor can I blame her. I would give nearly anything if I could go back and live those fateful hours over. Instead of sneaking away while Diana slept, I would stay right there and never leave her side. When she nursed Eurico, I would help her, even knowing that our most determined efforts could neither ease his sufferings nor save his life. And when the inevitable time came, I would dig his grave under the *samaúma* tree, near the swing where Diana and I drank sweet tea. I would help her dress him in a new red shirt and tenderly place him in a mahogany casket that I would make with my own hands. After we had buried him, I would take her in my arms and comfort her as best I could, mingling my tears with hers.

Thinking about it makes my throat hurt, and I use the heel of my hands to wipe at my eyes. Komi looks at me, but he doesn't say anything. Regret tempts me to despair, but I strengthen myself with something I read in my father's journal just yesterday. He said "If only" are the two saddest words in the human vocabulary because they focus on the past, and the past can't be changed. He suggested replacing them with "Next time." *Next time I will be wiser. Next time I will be more courageous. Next time I will be more loving. Next time…*

Komi's broken Portuguese draws me back, and I turn, giving him my attention. His accent is thick, making it difficult for me to understand him. "I be with you father when he die. I bury him. He leave things for you. Say you come one day."

"Where is he buried?" I ask, speaking slowly, the thought of visiting my father's grave nearly too much for me.

"Two-day journey. Hard walk. I take you soon."

Wearied from the strain of conversing in a language mostly foreign to him, Komi gets to his feet and starts down the trail toward his home, but I remain where I am. After he has gone, I find myself thinking about my father, wondering how he died. Did the Indians turn on him when he failed to cure the fever that was decimating them? Maybe, but it now seems more likely he succumbed to the same sickness that was killing them. I wonder if he was afraid when he realized he was dying. Did he have any regrets? What was he thinking about during the last few hours when he knew he wasn't going to make it? Did he think about us?

Opening my father's journal, I thumb through it, thanking God for the hundredth time that Helen sent it to me. Although much of it was written before I was born, it speaks to me in a way few things ever have. Over the past few weeks, I've found myself going back to what I've read time and time again. To my surprise, I have come to realize that my father possessed remarkable powers of reason and that he was something of a deep thinker. He didn't have answers so much as insight—understanding.

As an example, I read the entry dated April 26, 1941. In it he is addressing the very issues that have plagued me my whole life—suffering, adversity, and feelings of abandonment. I have always seen these things as proof that God doesn't care what happens to us. Father turns my thinking completely upside down. He contends that God loves us too much to ever let us experience happiness and fulfillment apart from finding them in relationship with Him.

> *All which I took from thee, I did but take,*
> > *Not for thy harms,*
>
> *But just that thou might'st seek it in My arms.*
> > *All which thy child's mistake*
>
> *Fancies as lost, I have stored for thee at home:*
> > *Rise, clasp My hand, and come!*

All which I took from thee, I did but take. So what does God take from us—security, self-sufficiency, independence, peace of mind... things like that?

Not for thy harms... Not simply to make us miserable, but that in our misery we would turn to Him.

...but just that thou might'st seek it in My arms. Maybe that's what my father means by "severe mercy." Maybe God lets us hurt until our pain finally brings us back to Him.

Trying to relate all of this to my situation is making my head ache; I just can't seem to get my mind around it. I may not be able to figure out how it all works, but one thing I do know, I had to come to the end of myself before I was willing to call on God. And to my amazement He did not reject me. He did not reject me.

CHAPTER
57

RETURNING TO KOMI'S PLACE in the early afternoon, I find Lako restless and in a foul mood. He has moved inside to get out of the rain, but he cannot be still. Finally, he says, "I want to leave in the morning at first light."

Surprised, I respond, "What's the rush? I thought we had decided to stay a few days."

"The situation has changed. I backtracked up the trail to the top of the ridge, and I found a lot of fresh tracks. It looks like the Amuacas know we are here."

The possibility of falling into Amuaca hands again makes my blood run cold; still, I don't want to believe that they would follow us here. I don't want to believe that we are in any danger. Stubbornly I insist. "Komi said they never come here. They believe this valley is haunted."

"That's what he said all right," Lako snaps, "but I know what I saw."

"Have you talked this over with him?" I persist. "What does he think?"

"Who knows? He's been gone since early this morning."

My mind is racing. It is obvious that Lako thinks the risk is real, and he's not easily spooked. That being the case, we could be in deep trouble. If there is not another way out of this valley, we will have to go back through Amuaca territory to reach the river where we left our boat and the rest of our supplies. Reluctantly I ask, "What's the plan? Is there another way out of here?"

"Komi says there's a back way, an ancient trail that very few know about, but he will have to guide us. According to him it's steep and dangerous, especially during the rainy season."

"That's a relief," I mutter, kicking off my boots and rolling into my hammock. "I'll take my chances in the jungle any day rather than risk being captured by the Amuacas again."

Unable to be still, Lako puts on his hat and walks into the rain, leaving me alone. Once he is gone, I find myself pondering our return to the mission station. Going back to face Diana and the Arnolds will be one of the hardest things I've ever done. In times past when I found myself facing a tough situation I always adopted the fight or flight response, either raging in anger or skipping out. Although I'm sorely tempted to bypass the mission station and go directly to Cruzeiro, I won't allow myself to do that. No matter how hard it is, I'm going to come clean about everything. I owe Diana that much.

There's no way to explain my walking out on her when Eurico was dying, so I won't even try. In my mind, it's the most indefensible thing I've ever done; an act so cowardly, so cruel, that I can hardly bear to think of it. I don't expect her to forgive me—how could she? No matter, I won't be able to live with myself if I don't take responsibility for what I did. It's the least I can do.

Then there's the whole matter of my deception—hiding my identity and pretending to be a photojournalist with *National Geographic* magazine. While I don't expect either Diana or the Arnolds to understand why I did what I did, I do hope they can find it in their hearts to forgive me. They are good and decent people, and their opinion is very important to me. Even though I will probably never see them again, I want them to remember me kindly.

Surprisingly, the rain has ceased, and for the moment the late afternoon sun is bright, laying broad bars of yellow light between the trees. Getting up, I shove my feet into my boots and head outside. Thinking about what awaits me at the mission compound, not to mention the ever-present danger posed by the Amuacas, has made me restless.

Stepping into the sun, I shade my eyes and watch Komi make his way across the open area toward me. He is naked except for a loin-cloth. A lifetime of exposure to the sun has made his dark skin coarse and left his face a web of wrinkles. In his hands he carries a stained canvas satchel that is strangely familiar to me. The careful way in which he handles it makes me know that it is special to him.

Stopping directly in front of me, he hands me the satchel, and my heart begins a slow heavy beating in my chest. The first thing I notice is the dark stains on the canvas, and then my eyes are drawn to a leather patch that is stitched to the flap between the buckles. Although the leather is old and stained, there is no mistaking the initials carved into it.

Swallowing past the fist-sized lump that has lodged in my throat, I run my fingers slowly over the *H* and the *W* on the leather patch, squeezing my eyes tightly closed to shut off my tears. Hugging the canvas satchel to my chest, I turn blindly toward the creek, seeking a place where I can be alone. I sense Komi staring after me, but wisely he does not follow, and in a few minutes I find myself in the glade where he and I talked this morning.

With trembling fingers I work the leather straps free of the rusty buckles and open the flap. The damp smell of mildew and old canvas is nearly overpowering, and once more I struggle to control my emotions. Finally, after all these years I am going to learn what happened to my father. Taking a deep breath, I look inside. The first thing I see is an alabaster cross on a sweat-stained leather string. Now I know, beyond all doubt, that my father is dead. I can never remember seeing him without his cross. He wore it at all times, whether waking or sleeping, and more than any other single thing it is a symbol of who he was—a man of God and a missionary! If he were still alive, he would have never let anyone remove it.

Without really thinking about what I am doing, I find myself kissing the cross, the imbedded dirt gritty against my lips, the taste of my father's sweat still pungent these many years later; or maybe it's just my imagination. Once more I'm a little boy, and I hear myself calling his name. "Daddy, I love you! Daddy, I love you!" And now I'm sobbing, grieving in a way I've never allowed myself to grieve. Not in anger and bitterness, railing at God, but in honest grief, richly seasoned with gratefulness to God for allowing me to be Harold Whittaker's son.

After awhile, I compose myself somewhat and look inside the satchel again. There are a couple of fishhooks, a spool of fishing line, a pocketknife, and a stub of a pencil, plus two books wrapped in oilcloth. One is my father's Bible, and the other is his last journal. Carefully I remove the oilcloth, thankful for the protection it has afforded; preserving not just his writing but also the only portrait I will ever have of the man who was my father. A portrait far more valuable than any ever captured on film or painted on canvas. Not a portrait of his physical likeness, but a glimpse of his heart and soul, a picture of the man himself, and what a great man he was, although he had feet of clay as we all do.

It's growing dark now, and the night birds are calling; still, I can't bring myself to return to Komi's. I need a few minutes more to be alone with my father. Opening his journal, I see he has folded down the corner of several pages together. The first page is for my mother, and although I hunger to read it, the light is fading, and I am anxious to see if he has any last words for me. The next page is addressed to Helen, and then I come to one with my name on it.

Dearest Bryan:

Death is not far away now, and I could welcome it with open arms, knowing that to be absent from the body is to be at home with Christ, were it not for you. I hate the thought of you growing up without your father. There are so many things I wanted to teach you, but I never got around to it. I wanted to teach you to throw a ball and how to make a yoyo out of a block of wood. I wanted to show you how to tie a dry fly and catch cutthroat trout high in the Rockies on bright sunlit mornings. I wanted to teach you to use a square and a level so you could build your own house if you ever needed to. Most of all I wanted to teach you to be a man of God, a husband, and a father.

I could grieve away these last hours, fretting over all the things I will never get to do with you, but instead I choose to thank God for all the special times we've shared. Most of them you won't remember, but I will never forget them, not in this world or the next. I thank God for the moment of your birth, and the first time I ever held you in my arms. I thank God for all the times you chewed on my knuckle while cutting your baby teeth, and the exquisite joy of rocking you in the wee hours of the morning when you couldn't sleep. I thank God for the canoe trip we took to Cruzeiro to fetch supplies, just the two of us. I will never forget the first time you returned thanks at the table, or the first time you read the Scriptures for family devotions, or the time you were "preaching" to all the little Indian kids.

My time with you was far too short, but it was also rich, and it is the richness I remember as I prepare to meet my Maker. I have no houses or lands to bequeath to you, no Earthly wealth with which to endow you, but I have something of far greater value— my faith! It has sustained me all the days of my life, and now in the hour of my death I find it sustains me still. By faith I know God will not leave you comfortless. He has promised to be a Father to the fatherless, and so will He be. By faith I know the plans He has for you, Bryan Scott Whittaker. Plans to prosper you and not to harm you, plans to give you hope and a future. He has promised that the children of the man who fears the Lord will be mighty in the land, and so will you be. You will be mighty in the land, and your righteousness will endure forever.

I leave you my alabaster cross, the Earthly symbol of my eternal faith. Wear it all the days of your life as a symbol of your covenant with the Lord. I bequeath you my Bible, for it is the Word of the Lord. Hide it in your heart, and it will keep you wherever you go. And last of all I leave you my journal. Through it I can still speak even though I am dead.

Never forget how much I love you, and always remember that even though I am physically absent, I will always be with you in my spirit. Be a man of God, Bryan Whittaker, my precious son, be a man of God.

> *With all my love now and forever,*
> *Father*
> *January 1949*

I hug my father's journal to my chest the way I would hug him if he were here. Tears are coursing down my cheeks, and I am not ashamed—tears of both grief and gratefulness, and that's the way it should be. If I've learned anything the past twenty-two years, I've learned that unshed tears turn into bitterness, and bitterness kills.

It is almost fully dark now, and I carefully wrap my father's journal in oilcloth before returning it to his satchel along with his Bible. His pocketknife goes into the pocket of my jeans. Picking up his alabaster cross, I study it for a long moment, contemplating all it meant to him, and then I humbly slip it over my head and tuck it inside my shirt. *I will be a man of God; I will be.*

CHAPTER

58

IT IS STILL AN hour before first light when we slip away from Komi's thatch-roofed hut and into the forest, being careful to make no sound. It's not likely the Amuacas are close enough to hear anything, given their aversion to this valley, but we don't want to take any chances. Behind us we have left a small cooking fire that should burn for a while. If they're keeping watch from the ridge, they may spot the smoke rising through the trees and assume we are going about our daily routine. It's a long shot, but anything that buys us a little time is worth the effort.

Komi is in the lead as we move out, slipping through the night as silently as ground fog pushed by the wind. I can't hear him, but I know Lako is somewhere behind me, bringing up the rear. If we push hard, Komi assures me, we should be well up the far ridge by the time day is breaking. Once we are out of the valley, the Amuacas will be hard pressed to overtake us even if they are so inclined. The biggest obstacles from there on out will be the terrain and the weather. Now that we are moving into the heart of the rainy season, the rain will be almost continual, making both the rivers and the trails dangerous and nearly impassable.

It's so dark I almost bump into Komi before I see him. He has stopped at the edge of the trail, listening. I strain to hear what might have caused him concern, but I cannot distinguish between one noise and another. They all sound alike to my city-bred ear. After a moment he seems satisfied, and we move out again. Adjusting the backpack on my shoulders, I can't help noticing how light it is, a sobering reminder of the depleted condition of our provisions. In fact, if it weren't for my father's satchel, my pack would be virtually empty. Instead of fretting, I remind myself that a light pack will make the steep climb easier.

To the east a weak sun is finally pushing its way above the rim of the Earth, and just in time too, for we have left the valley floor, and the footing is treacherous as we begin the steep climb up the muddy trail. The air is thick, heavy with humidity, making it hard for me to breathe. Ahead of me, I can see Komi clearing the way with his machete. Beneath a sheen of sweat, the scars lie like jagged ridges on his back, clearly visible. The story of his life is written there, and a tragic one it is, but with a remarkable ending.

Komi was just nine years old when the batedores attacked from ambush, their Winchesters booming, the tree line surrounding his Amuaca village ablaze with the muzzle blasts of their rifles. In seconds, the area before the longhouses was littered with the dead and dying, the screams of terrified children filling the night. Seeing his father gunned down, Komi tried to flee into the forest, but before he could escape, a batedor scooped him up and deposited him with a group of young women and children who were huddled together on the far side of the village. As the long night played out, they were forced to watch as the wounded were massacred and the longhouses torched.

At first light the batedores tied their hands behind their backs before threading a long rope between the bound wrists, effectively stringing them together. For two days they were given neither food nor water, arriving at the rubber estate late the second day after a cruel march through the rain forest. Life was brutal on the seringal, and by the time he was thirteen Komi had escaped and been recaptured a number of times. He was brutally beaten each time he was returned to the seringal, but no matter how cruelly his captors punished him, they could not break his spirit. Each failed attempt left him wiser and more determined.

He was nineteen years old but with the body of a grown man when he finally made good his escape. Returning to his people, he found that he was an outsider, distrusted and isolated. Only his sister welcomed him back, and she suffered for it. When an outbreak of yellow fever struck some years after his return, the shaman blamed him for it. There was talk of banishing him or even killing him to appease the gods.

While enslaved on the seringal, he had seen my father treat the patrão, effecting a remarkable cure, so he now set out downriver to see if he could find him. Arriving at the mission station some days later, he used the broken Portuguese he had picked up on the rubber estate to relate the situation and beg my father to help. The following day they set off for the Amuaca village, finally arriving five days later after battling incessant rains and floods. By that time yellow fever was epidemic, and the dead and dying were everywhere. Although my father labored tirelessly, he had no cure for that deadly disease.

As the fever spread, the shaman incited the Indians against Komi and my father. Learning of the plot, Komi's sister warned them, and they escaped under the cover of darkness, taking refuge in the haunted valley. Almost immediately my father fell ill, spending days flat on his back suffering from high fever and chills, as well as a blinding headache and vomiting. Thinking he was going to die, he wrote the letters in his journal. After several days he began to recover, and although he was weak he seemed to gain a little strength each day. Through all of this Komi nursed him, and he in turn told Komi about Jesus, the Savior who could heal the sickness in his soul.

Having gained a little strength, my father insisted on returning to the mission compound. Against his better judgment Komi agreed to help him, and they set off over this very trail. My father was weak but determined, and they made surprisingly good time. By the end of the second day, however, his strength was failing, and they had to stop before they reached the river. That night the fever returned, and the next day my father was unable to travel. Each day he grew weaker, the whites of his eyes turning a dull yellow, as did his skin. His kidneys were failing, as was his liver.

As the end drew near, my father removed the alabaster cross from around his neck, kissed it, and placed it in his satchel. By then he was so weak he fumbled with the buckles, trying to fasten them, but when Komi tried to help he brushed his hand aside, insisting on doing it himself. When at last he finished, he handed the satchel to Komi. In a voice no more than a ragged whisper, he said, "Keep this for my son Bryan. One day he will come for it."

Those were the last words he spoke, falling into a coma shortly thereafter. He died sometime later that night, and Komi buried him the next morning. His grave bears no name, its location known only to Komi and to God.

My father was not a great man as the world counts greatness. He founded no organizations, amassed no wealth, made no discoveries, left no inventions, and wrote no books, but in my heart I know he was a special man. He was an imperfect man, to be sure. His parenting skills were sadly lacking, but, in his defense, he was a product of his times. He grew up when men were stern and unexpressive, and children were to be seen and not heard. On occasion his heavy-handed ways bruised my tender soul; but all things taken together, I can only conclude that he was a special man—a man of God and a missionary!

Komi has topped the ridge, and now he waits for us to join him. He has moved under some trees, being careful not to silhouette himself against the skyline. He is studying the valley below, and when I step up beside him, he says, "They come." For a moment I don't see anything, and then a faint movement catches my eye, and as I watch a line of Indians moves stealthily toward Komi's thatch-roofed hut. For a moment I grieve for him, knowing he will never be able to return.

Then I remember he has no reason to go back for he has fulfilled his promise to my father.

When I have caught my breath, he begins the descent, setting a stiff pace. Though the sun has climbed higher in the sky, the day is dull, the rain seeming to soak up the weak light. We walk for hours, climbing and descending, crossing flood-swollen streams and fighting our way through tangled underbrush. The rain never stops. As relentless as death, it varies in intensity—sometimes hardly more than a damp mist, at other times a blinding torrent, as if the sky has cracked open—but it never stops.

The pace is grueling, but when I am tempted to complain I remind myself that my father was dying with yellow fever when he made this trek. Desperate to return to the family he loved, he fought his way up and down these cruel ridges, refusing to allow his illness to stop him. If he could do that, then I can do this.

As the day wears on, I grow feverish, and my knee tries to lock up with every step, but somehow I keep going. Doggedly, I put one foot in front of the other, and in my mind I hear these words playing over and over like a mantra: *I am my father's son. I am my father's son. I am my father's son...*

When Komi finally stops for the day, I want to kiss him, but of course I don't. Instead, I shed my backpack and set about gathering the driest sticks I can find, no easy task in all this rain. When I have a small fire going, I cook the last of our rice and a little corned beef. We eat in silence, too tired to talk. As I crawl into my hammock, I encourage myself with the thought that tomorrow we will reach the river where we left our boat and the rest of our supplies. If all goes as planned, we will arrive at the mission compound a few days after that. I can do this, I can. I am my father's son!

CHAPTER

59

WE ARRIVE AT THE Rio Azul late in the afternoon, after hiking all day in a steady rain. The Azul has risen considerably in the last ten days, but our boat is high and dry, just as we left it. Another day or two and the floodwaters might have reached it, but for now we are okay. Lako has gone directly to the boat, and I can hear him cursing. "What is it?" I call, leaning my backpack against a nearby tree before going to join him.

Holding up an empty pack, he fumes. "It looks like the Amuacas beat us here. The dirty thieves have taken all our supplies." Slamming the pack down, he continues to rant. "They must have backtracked us to here as soon as they discovered we had escaped."

Picking up an empty five-gallon gas can, he hurls it against a nearby tree. "Dumped our fuel too!"

Having exhausted his anger, he now joins Komi and me in setting up camp. Once that is done, I turn to him. "Why don't we take the cast net and go to the oxbow lake and see if we can get some fish."

"Can't," he mutters. "The Amuacas took that too!"

"What about a drop line? Isn't that how you caught the first fish?"

Growing impatient, he glares at me. "You don't get it, do you? They took everything—food, cast net, fishing line, hooks...they got it all!"

Komi looks at me and then at the backpack containing my father's satchel. When he does, it hits me. Along with the other things, there were some fishhooks and a spool of line in his satchel.

"All's not lost," I say to Lako as I remove the satchel from my backpack. Opening it, I rummage around until I locate what we need. Holding up the spool of line and the fishhooks, I announce, "We're in business!"

Lako just grunts, but he does start up the path that leads to the lake. On the way he stops to collect some wiggly tree grubs for bait. After offering me one, which I refuse, he pops a couple in his mouth. I may be hungry, but I think I'll wait for the fish.

At the lake another surprise awaits us—the canoe is gone. We spend fifteen or twenty minutes looking for it, but to no avail. It's hard to believe the Amuacas would have taken it, but they may have. At any rate, it is gone. When I suggest fishing from the bank, Lako just looks at me and shakes his head in disgust. The shoreline is covered with huge lily pads, extending out into the lake for several meters, making fishing impossible. Discouraged, we head back to camp, our stomachs growling with hunger.

Hunger, however, is just one of our problems. Without fuel the outboard motor is useless, and without it we have no way of steering the boat. The current will propel us, but we have to figure out some way to control the boat or we will be just an accident looking for a place to happen. Long into the night, we sit around the fire trying to design a rudder system without coming up with anything that looks very promising. Exhausted, we finally turn in, hoping we'll do better in the morning when our minds are fresh.

Awaking with the first hint of light, I slip down to the river where I decide to try my hand at fishing. Swinging the baited hook over my head, I cast the line out about five or six meters. I haven't even had time to take up the slack when it's jerked taut. In an instant the line is quivering in my hand, and I know I have hooked a good-sized fish. Carefully I play out some line, praying that it won't break. When the fish seems to tire a little, I quickly retrieve the line. Sensing what I am doing, the big fish explodes with a burst of energy, striping the line from my hand. My fingers are raw and burning, but I must keep the line tight or risk losing a fish we desperately need. Gritting my teeth against the pain, I keep the pressure on. Suddenly the fish tries a different tactic; reversing directions, it swims directly toward me. Frantically I take up the line hand over fist, nearly sick with the thought that I might lose this fish.

We continue this desperate battle for at least fifteen minutes before the fish finally begins to tire. As I ease it toward the bank for the last time, it rolls over on its side, exhausted. When it is close enough for me to reach, I drop the line and, using both hands, I grab it under the gills and heave it onto the bank. It's a catfish, probably weighing more than twenty pounds, and I can't help thinking that we will eat well today.

Using my father's pocketknife, I gut the fish and carry it up to camp. Hardly able to contain my excitement, I hold up my catch and announce, "Breakfast is served!"

Lako skewers it on a green stalk of bamboo and ties it in place. Having done that, he arranges a forked branch on either side of the fire and hangs the fish between them. Slowly he rotates the fish, its fat dripping into the flames. When it is finally ready, we eat it greedily, burning our fingers as we pull the tender meat from the bones being careful to peel away the skin. When we have eaten all we can hold, there is still enough left for another meal.

While I was fishing, Lako finally figured out how to build a rudder system for the boat, and now he attempts to explain it to me.

"If we tilt the outboard motor forward and lock it in place," he says, "we can use it as a base for our rudder. We'll tie a stout piece of limb—about one meter in length—on either side of the casing that houses the driveshaft. That will serve as the frame to hold the handle for our rudder. From a second branch we'll make the handle. It should be about five meters long and as big around as a man's arm. We'll lash one of the oars to the end of it to make the rudder itself."

Having never been very good at anything mechanical, I'm having trouble grasping the concept. Impatiently, he grabs a pointed stick and proceeds to draw a crude diagram in the mud. It still makes little sense to me, but I pretend to understand, nodding my head with enthusiasm. Satisfied, he and Komi set to work carving and whittling the various pieces we're going to need, while I head into the rain forest in search of green vines about the size of a man's finger. These we will use to lash the whole thing together.

By late afternoon we have all the parts, and with Komi's help Lako sets to work assembling it. After collecting some fresh grubs, I make my way back to the river to see if I can catch our supper. I fish until dark, but I don't have a single bite. Disappointed, I stow my gear in my backpack and make my way back to camp.

The morning is grey, the air dead still and heavy with moisture as we make our way to the Azul for the last time. Near the river the ground fog is so thick we can hardly see our boat. As we stow our gear, Komi stands watching, his arms folded, his face impassive. It grieves me to think that my coming has resulted in the loss of his home and the valley he loved. I would like to invite him to return with us to the mission compound, but that is not my place. Instead, I take what comfort I can by reminding myself that the rain forest is vast and that he will surely find another valley. Who knows maybe his sister can join him there? Still, thinking of him living out his last days in isolation hurts me in ways I would be hard pressed to explain.

When we are ready to cast off, I make my way to him and place my hands on his shoulders. In a certain sense he, more than any other single person, is responsible for my father's death. If he had not come to the mission compound seeking help, my father might still be alive. He is the reason I came to the Amazon. I wanted to find the man responsible for my father's death and make him pay; yet all I feel now is a profound gratefulness. The anger and hatred that brought me here is gone. In its place is a newly found peace, a peace richly seasoned with sorrow.

In my throat there is a lump the size of a man's fist, making it nearly impossible for me to speak. "Thank you, Komi," I manage to say, my voice breaking. "Thank you."

For a moment he says nothing, and I wonder if he understood me. Then he places his gnarled hand on my chest, and in his broken Portuguese he says, "You have great heart, Bryan Whittaker. Much light."

I have a nearly overwhelming urge to hug him, to crush him to my chest, but of course I don't. I am, after all, my father's son, and expressing our emotions does not come easy for us. Without another word, I turn and step into the boat, shoving us off as I do. Picking up a long pole, Lako begins pushing us out of the river margin toward the main channel of the Azul. Looking over my shoulder, I see Komi wrapped in wisps of river fog. As I watch, he turns and disappears into the forest, never looking back.

CHAPTER

60

THE FOG HOVERS JUST above the surface of the water as Lako poles us toward the main channel of the Rio Azul. The rudder makes poling the boat awkward, but we have no other means of propulsion until the current takes over. As Lako fights the boat, I can't help thinking that I will probably never see any of this again. Having learned my father's fate, I have no reason to return. He gave his life doing what he loved, and his grave is here, among his adopted people—the Indians of the far western Amazon Basin. His spirit is with the Lord he loved more than life, but his memory belongs to me, and now I find myself reliving our final good-bye.

After descending one final stretch of steep trail, Komi pauses in a small clearing. Impatient to push on to the river, Lako complains under his breath at the delay, but Komi will not be hurried. Taking me by the arm, he walks me to a towering samaúma tree. Carved in the base of its enormous trunk is a crude cross. Slowly it dawns on me. This is where my father is buried. Now my throat is tight, and I cannot speak. When I look at Komi, he nods solemnly and turns away. After a moment, I realize I am alone, he and Lako having gone a short distance on down the trail.

My legs are weak, and I sink to my knees on the soggy ground. I know my father is not here—his physical body decomposed and returned to the Earth long ago, while his spirit is with Christ—still, I feel closer to him in this moment than I have at anytime since he left us more than twenty-two years ago. Through his journals he has communicated with me, but I have not yet spoken to him. It may be crazy, but I think that's why I'm here. It's time to make peace with my father.

So where do I start? What do I say?

Feeling more than a little foolish, I begin. "Dad," I say, already choking up. "I don't know how to talk to you. You were always too busy or too preoccupied to talk. Do you have any idea how many times you said, 'Not now, Son. Can't you see I'm busy?' At mealtime it was always, 'Don't talk with food in your mouth,' or 'Don't interrupt; your mother and I are talking.' To tell you the truth, Dad, I almost expect you to sit up in your grave and tell me to be quiet."

I pause, trying to collect my thoughts while a lifetime of tears swim in my eyes. This is harder than I could ever have imagined. I'm a grown man, and my father is dead, yet I feel just the way I did when I was a little boy—intimidated and tongue-tied. Forcing myself to take two or three deep breaths, I try again.

"I've always had a love/hate relationship with you, Dad. I idolized you, and I feared you. I hungered for your approval, but I never knew how to get it. The few times you were affectionate stand out in my mind even these many years later. I've never forgotten the touch of your hand on my shoulder or what it felt like when you tousled my hair. The sense of well-being it generated in me lasted for days, sometimes weeks, and it always left me wanting more. When it wasn't forthcoming, I thought the fault was mine—maybe I had done something wrong, or I just wasn't good enough. Those feelings cast a dark shadow over my childhood and torment me to this day, and I hate it!"

I'm sobbing now, but I push on, saying the things that I've needed to say for so long. "You were not physically abusive, but you were indifferent, and that's just another kind of abuse. Your indifference robbed me of my dignity; it caused me to doubt my value as a person; it made me feel worthless. Your death was just the final blow, a loss from which I never recovered. Indifference had become abandonment. I was angry with you, but I blamed myself. If I had been a better son, you would not have gone away, you would not have died and left me to grow up alone. It seems silly in retrospect, but that's the way it was, and I carry the scars with me to this day."

"For years I could hardly look back on my ruined childhood, and yet it haunted me every waking moment. It made me a terrible son to my mother, it estranged me from my sister, and it ruined my marriage. It wounded me, turning me into an emotional cripple; and worst of all, I grew up to be just like you— unable to express any emotion except anger!"

The guilt I feel at saying these things nearly gags me. I love my father, and I have no desire to hurt him, but I can't pretend these things never happened. Yet they are not the whole truth either, as I have mistakenly supposed they were. For years I believed only the worst about him, holding his human foibles against him and defining my childhood by his parental mistakes. Yes, he was a flawed man and an imperfect father; but as I am only now learning, he was also a giant of a man—a missionary legend. The truth is never one-dimensional. It's a many-sided thing, and only when we embrace the whole of it can we find healing and peace.

Using the heels of my hands, I wipe at my eyes and take a deep breath before continuing. "Dad, without your journals I may never have been able to forgive you, but through your writings I became acquainted with another side of you. The feelings you could never show, the things you could never say, were all there. To my surprise, I discovered that you were not indifferent only inarticulate and probably a product of your own rearing, just as I am a product of mine."

"So I want you to know that I forgive you. I forgive you for not giving me the affection and affirmation I so desperately needed. I forgive you for not taking the time to be a daddy to a little guy who needed his daddy more than anything in the world. I forgive you for turning my mother into a clone of *yourself and for making her repress her natural affections in order to please you. And most of all, I forgive you for dying and leaving me to grow up lost and alone."*

Totally wrung out, I kneel in silence for several minutes before getting to my feet. In a way that I would be hard pressed to explain, it feels as if a great weight has lifted off of me. I had carried that grudge against my father for so long I had no idea how heavy it was. Forgiving my father has given me hope and a new lease on life. Who knows, maybe some day I will even find the grace to forgive myself.

Turning to go, I pause one last time. For a moment I study the crude cross that Komi had carved into the base of the tree at the head of my father's grave. More than any other symbol, it defined my father. "Harold Whittaker," I say, my voice choking with emotion, "you were a man of the cross—a true follower of Jesus Christ!"

At the edge of the clearing, I glance back one final time, knowing I will never see the place of my father's burial again. "I love you, Daddy. Rest in peace."

We are nearing the main channel, and I can feel the strength of the current. As it seizes our boat, Lako stows the pole and grabs for the rudder. In seconds we are hurling down the Azul, being carried along like so much flotsam. The power of the river is amazing, but with the rudder Lako is able to direct the boat using the force of the current to our advantage. At this rate we should reach the mission compound some time late tomorrow.

For two days we ride the river, enduring the rain while trying to ignore our empty bellies. Lako managed to get us into the river margin late the first day, just after the Azul connected with the Moa, and we were able to spend the night ashore. It was good to stretch our legs, but without a fire camp was wet and miserable. After getting the tarp up, we crawled into our hammocks, but trying to sleep in our wet clothes made for a long night, and we were only too happy to get back on the river at first light.

As the morning of the second day wears on, I find that I am growing increasingly apprehensive. Eurico's death is never far from my mind, and a heaviness has settled in my soul. Although I no longer blame myself, I find it hard to imagine a world without his infectious smile and buoyant optimism. And it grieves me to realize that although I loved him like a son, I never once told him so. If I could do things over again, I would do them differently. I would wrestle with him and tickle him until he begged me to stop. And whether he liked it or not, I would tuck him in at night and tell him how much I love him. But that will never be, so I steel myself for what awaits me at the mission compound.

By mid-afternoon the rain has ceased for the first time in two days, and the sun is trying to push its way though the low-hanging grey clouds. With the river this high, things look different; nonetheless, I am starting to see some familiar landmarks. A couple of hours later, the mission compound comes into view as we round a wide sweeping bend in the river. Thrusting the rudder all the way over, Lako expertly guides the boat toward a sandbar deposited by an earlier flood. As the bow runs aground, I leap out and begin hauling the boat ashore. With Lako's help we drag it completely out of the water and tie it securely to a tree well back from the river.

Gathering my camera equipment and my backpack with my father's satchel in it, I head up the trail toward Whittaker House. All I can think about is Eurico, and in spite of my resolve to be strong, I am sorely tempted to get back in the boat and head for Cruzeiro. I don't know if I can do this. I can't bear the thought of visiting Eurico's grave or enduring Diana's rejection. Unconsciously, I find myself whispering a prayer. *"Help me, Lord Jesus. Help me."*

Being burdened with neither the guilt nor the grief that is holding me back, Lako has shouldered his gear and gone on ahead. Twice I start up the trail only to stumble to a stop, overcome with sorrow. This is the hardest thing I have ever had to do, but I have got to face it or I will be running for the rest of my life. Taking a deep breath, I force myself to put one foot in front of the other. *I can do this. I will take a shower and clean up, and then I will visit Eurico's grave. After that, I will face Diana…*

The *samaúma* tree is still blocking the trail, but someone has cut a new path around it. As I turn toward Whittaker House, my eyes play a cruel trick on me. In my imagination I see Eurico running toward me, smiling as only he can, his face full of joy. He is wearing a bright red shirt, and now I hear him calling my name. "Bryan. Bryan."

In an instant my legs turn to rubber, and I drop to my knees to keep from fainting. Through the haze of my imagining, I watch Eurico running toward me in wild abandon. When he is about a meter from me, he launches himself and crashes into my chest, knocking me over backward. His arms are around my neck, and we are wrestling in the wet grass. I am covering his face with kisses and tickling him. He is begging me to stop, but I can't. Now I am flat on my back, and he is sitting on my chest. Grinning, he puts both of his hands on my cheeks and says, "You're back, Bryan, you're back."

Over his shoulder I see Diana standing on the porch of the clinic. She is leaning on her crutches, her blonde hair blowing in the wind. When she sees me looking her way, she turns and limps back inside. For a moment I am crushed. It's what I expected and what I deserve, but it still breaks my heart. Eurico continues to pull my hair and punch my chest, and I resume our wrestling with renewed vigor, nearly mad with wonder. *How can this be? How can Eurico be alive?*

Chapter

61

AFTER A SHOWER, A change of clothes, and a hearty meal, I am feeling better than I have in days. Eurico is sitting across the table from me, the picture of health. I'm still in shock, and I can't take my eyes off him. I never expected to see him alive again. The last time I saw him, he was in excruciating pain, suffering with a raging fever and a cruelly bowed back. Diana had said he couldn't live more than seventy-two hours. *What,* I wonder, *brought about his remarkable recovery? Did Diana find some medicine she forgot she had? Maybe her diagnosis was wrong, and his disease wasn't fatal after all? Who knows? The important thing is he is alive!* Every couple of minutes I reach across the table to tousle his hair or to give his shoulder a playful punch. Only by touching him can I assure myself that he is real and not just a figment of my imagination.

Life, as I am learning, is a mixed bag, and human beings can feel more than one emotion at once. A part of me is nearly giddy with joy at Eurico's recovery, while another part of me is sorely grieved by what I've done to Diana. By running out on her during the crisis with Eurico, I hurt her deeply and wounded our relationship in ways from which it may never recover. If, by some miracle, she can forgive me for what I did, there is still the matter of my deception. Our whole relationship was built on lies, either of omission or commission.

Considering the magnitude of my deceit, I don't know how she can ever trust me again.

Getting up from the table, I make my way to the window. Of course it is raining again, and the weak light is fading as the sun slides far down in the sky. Looking toward the mission house where Diana lives, I see that it is still dark. Apparently she has not yet returned from the clinic, but she should be getting home any time now, and then I will go to her and do what I can to heal the wounds I have caused. Eurico comes to stand beside me, and I slip my arm around his narrow shoulders and pull him close. Seeing a dim light appear in the window across the way, he announces, "Diana's home."

The warmth in his voice gives silent testimony to their relationship. How right that seems to me—the single missionary doctor with no children of her own and the orphan boy making a family together, each meeting a heart need in the other. "Hey," I say, "where did you get that bright red shirt?"

"Diana made it for me," he says proudly. "She made me a blue one too."

Dropping to one knee, I put my hands on his narrow shoulders and look him in the eye. "Eurico, I did a very bad thing when you were sick. I went upriver and left Diana to care for you by herself. It was a heartless thing to do, and it hurt Diana deeply. I don't know if she will ever be able to forgive me."

Silent tears are sliding down my cheeks in spite of my most determined effort not to cry. "It will be okay, Bryan," Eurico says, as he wipes at my tears with his shirttail. "Diana loves you, I know she does."

How can this be? How can this little orphaned boy, who has lost so much, give me more comfort than I have ever known in my life? Pulling him close, I hug him tightly against my chest. When he slips his thin arms around my neck, I think my heart will burst, and I hear myself whispering, *"Thank You, God, for allowing Eurico to live!"*

"Bryan," Eurico ventures, "maybe we should pray before you go see Diana. She says God answers our prayers, and I'm living proof."

"So you are, Eurico, so you are."

We bow our heads, and while I'm trying to find the right words, Eurico blurts out a simple prayer. *"Lord Jesus, help Bryan know what to say to fix Diana's heart so she won't cry any more. Amen."*

Amazed, I ask, "Who taught you to pray?"

"Diana did," Eurico says matter-of-factly. "We pray together every morning and every night."

Giving him a kiss on the top of his head, I get to my feet. "You stay here with Lako while I go talk with Diana. This is something I need to do by myself."

Ignoring the rain, I make my way slowly toward Diana's place. Stepping on the porch, I hesitate before knocking. I'm nearly sick with apprehension. Will she speak to me, or will she just ask me to leave? I don't expect her to forgive me, how could she? But I do hope she will give me a chance to apologize and take responsibility for what I've done.

Against my will, memories of the evening we spent together come rushing back. I don't want to remember, not now. It will only make things harder, but I seem powerless to stop them.

I'm sitting on the floor beside Diana's chair in the living room of her small mission house. Leaning back, I rest my head against her leg. She runs her fingers through my hair, and although I know it can never be, I try to imagine what it would be like to spend the rest of my life with her. Maybe Eurico could live with us and be a part of our family. I know Diana loves him, as I do.

Interrupting my reverie, Diana says, "Bryan, look at me."

Simple though her words are, they throb with emotion, and I scoot around so that I'm now facing her. Looking at me intently, she takes my face in her hands. "I love you, Bryan Scott Whittaker," she says, her voice sounding breathy in the still room. "It makes no sense, but I can't deny my feelings. I truly love you."

I am stunned! Why would she say such a thing? There can be no future for us, surely she knows that. Our lives are far too different. She's a missionary doctor who loves God passionately. I'm a wandering man, a lost soul, who doesn't even know if he believes in God. Nonetheless, her declaration moves me to examine my own feelings, something I've been studiously avoiding.

Finding my voice, I finally manage to say, "I love you too, Diana Rhoades, but there's no point in saying it. There's no future for us, no—"

Putting her finger on my lips, she hushes me. "Not now, Bryan. Not tonight. Just hold me."

Taking her in my arms for the very first time, I cradle her head against my chest, her hair smelling as clean and fresh as rainwater. Almost without realizing what I am doing, I find myself kissing her hair, her eyes, the tip of her nose, and finally her lips. Her arms are around my neck, her fingers in my hair. Her joy, it seems, is as great as my own, but when I kiss her face I taste her tears, and my heart hurts.

"Are you sad?" I ask.

Pursing her lips, she nods. "Yes, I'm sad, but it's okay, because I'm happy too. I'm happy for tonight, for us. If this is all we ever have, just this one kiss, this one night, I'll treasure it forever."

With a determined effort I push those memories from my mind and steel myself for what's ahead. Taking a deep breath, I knock firmly. After a moment, I hear the noise of her crutches on the floor as she moves across the room toward the door. When she opens it, neither of us says anything for a moment. "I thought it might be you," she finally manages. "But then again, I didn't know if you would have the courage to face me after what you did."

Her voice is flat, her words emotionless, and my heart sinks. I expected her to be angry, to rage at me in her fury, to tell me what a sorry excuse for a man I was, but never, not even in my wildest imaginings, did I think she would be beyond caring. Whatever faint hope I had brought to this moment is now gone. Still, I am determined that she knows how sorry I am for hurting her. And I want her to know the truth about me, no matter if it causes her to despise me all the more. I can't live with the lies; they're killing me.

Clearing my throat, I ask, "May I come in?" When she hesitates, I hasten to add, "There are some things I think you should know before I go. They will in no wise excuse what I have done, but they may help you to understand."

Raising her eyebrows skeptically, she turns and limps across the room. Assuming this is my invitation, I follow her into the small living room. Taking a seat, I can't help noticing that the room has been transformed. In one corner she has created a living space for Eurico complete with his cot, a wooden crate—sitting upright to serve as both a nightstand and a storage space—and a kerosene lamp. Colorful throw rugs now adorn the rough plank floors, and she has even put out a few family photos. The room lacks Eleanor's touch, but it's a far cry from what it was. If she notices my surprise, she doesn't comment on it.

Nervously I blurt out, "What happened to Eurico? I thought you said he was going to die, that he had less than seventy-two hours to live."

At the mention of Eurico's name her eyes light up, and the deadness goes out of her face. It's obvious that she loves the little guy, and I am encouraged to see that she still has feelings, even if she has none for me. "After you left," she begins, "he grew worse over the next twenty-four hours. His suffering was unbearable, and I thought my heart would break. I felt so helpless; there was nothing I could do."

Reaching for a tissue, she dabs at her eyes before continuing. "If Eleanor hadn't stayed with me, I don't think I could have made it. Late the next afternoon Gordon came, and we anointed Eurico with oil and prayed for his healing. There was no immediate change, but by the morning of the second day I noticed a slight improvement. By the third day it was apparent he was going to make it."

I want to believe that God healed Eurico in response to their prayers, I really do, but my skepticism is too deeply ingrained. Although I hate myself for doing it, I ask, "Isn't it possible that you made a wrong diagnosis? Maybe Eurico would have recovered whether you prayed or not."

The hurt in Diana's eyes grieves me, and I kick myself for being such a jerk. Wearily, she says, "Anything is possible, Bryan. I could have made a wrong diagnosis. Eurico might have recovered on his own, but I choose to believe God healed him. You can believe or not believe. It's up to you."

"I want to believe, Diana, I really do, but it's hard for me. I've had a lot of disappointments with prayer, that's all."

"We all have," she replies, her voice sounding terribly sad. "In fact, disappointment is almost inevitable if you put your faith in an outcome rather than in the person of Jesus Christ. We pray for an outcome—in this case Eurico's healing—but our hope is in God! It can't be any other way."

To my way of thinking, she's splitting hairs, but I don't want to risk offending her again, so I just nod. Sensing my continuing skepticism, she just looks at me and shakes her head. Finally, she says, "Bryan, could we get on with it please? I've had a long day, and I'm tired."

Gathering my courage, I plunge in. "Sneaking out and leaving you to care for Eurico alone is the most disgusting thing I've ever done. It was cowardly and indefensible. I don't think I will ever be able to forgive myself, and I certainly don't expect you to forgive me. But I do want you to know how much I regret what I did and how sorry I am for hurting you."

Diana struggles to control her emotions, but the memory of my betrayal is too much. Sobbing, she asks, "How could you, Bryan? How could you leave me when I was depending on you?"

Her words are like daggers piercing my heart. Dropping my eyes, I study the floor between my feet. Finally I mumble, "Diana, I've asked myself that same question at least a hundred times, and I've yet to find an answer. All I can say is that watching Eurico die was more than I could bear. I had to get out of there before I fell apart and did something crazy. It's no answer, but it's all I've got."

She has turned her face from me and is staring at the wall, weeping silently as though her heart is breaking. More than anything, I want to take her in my arms and comfort her, but I can't. I am the source of her pain, the one who broke her heart.

Swallowing my own grief, I now proceed to recount the story of my life, leaving nothing out. I tell her things I've never told anyone, things I'm just now admitting to myself. It's not a pretty story, and I spare no detail; not about my dysfunctional childhood or my failed marriage, not about the loss of my faith or the real reason I came to the Amazon. I admit my duplicity and my lies, making no excuses, and when I am finally finished, I am completely wrung out, drained of all emotion.

Finally, I tell her about Komi and finding my father's satchel. Reaching inside my shirt, I pull out the stained alabaster cross and show it to her. I tell her about my father's journals and the letter he wrote to me from his deathbed and about visiting his grave. Taking the alabaster cross completely off, I hold it in my hand and tell her about making peace with my father, the rebirth of my faith, and my desire to be a follower of Christ and a man my father would be proud of.

By the time I finish, it is completely dark outside, and has been for a couple of hours or more. The only light in Diana's small living room comes from the kerosene lamp sitting on the wooden crate by Eurico's cot. Even in the dim light I can see that her face is full of conflict, and her blue eyes glisten with tears. To me she is the most beautiful woman in the world, and I long to hold her in my arms and dry her tears with my kisses, but of course I don't. By my selfish and irresponsible behavior I have forever forfeited that right. I should go, but I can't bring myself to leave, knowing this may be the last time I ever see the woman I love.

I would have to be blind not to see the turmoil in her soul, so clearly is it written in her face and in the way she hugs herself, rocking back and forth. To punish me, to withhold her forgiveness, obviously goes against everything she is, but the thought of forgiving me must be terrifying. I betrayed her trust and hurt her deeply, surely she is asking herself what will keep me from doing it again? I don't blame her. I don't even trust myself. Given the opportunity, I might even counsel her against forgiving me, against taking the chance on being hurt again.

"Bryan," she says at last, her voice trembling, "please hold me."

For an instant I don't believe my ears. It's too good to be true. It's like the first moment I saw Eurico running down the path toward me. I thought I was imagining it.

Then she says it again. "Please, Bryan, would you hold me?"

It's not my imagination. As unbelievable as it is, Diana wants me to hold her!

I am forgiven. Even knowing I might hurt her again, she has chosen to trust me with her heart, with her life. There's no good reason why she should, not after what I've done, but she does.

Kneeling beside her chair, I take her in my arms and hold her head against my chest. Her thick hair is soft against my face as I kiss her head and whisper, "Diana. Diana." Turning, she lifts her face toward me, and I kiss her full lips, pouring out all the love and gratitude that is overflowing my heart. Her fingers are in my hair, and now she leans back in order to look me fully in the eye. "I love you, Bryan Scott Whittaker," she says, "I love you!"

Epilogue
September 1971

I AM LIVING ALONE in an old farmhouse just outside of Fort Collins, Colorado, nestled up against the foothills of the Rockies. As I write this, I am sitting at a makeshift desk that I have constructed out of two sawhorses and a sheet of plywood. It sits before the west window in the front room, facing the mountains. To my left is a framed black-and-white family photo taken in 1946. We are standing in front of the mission house and behind it the towering trees of the Amazon rain forest block out the sky. Helen is clutching a homemade doll while looking shyly into the camera. I'm glaring up at my father who has a firm grip on my shoulder. Of course, both Mother and Father look severe. It's the only picture I have of my family, and I treasure it.

To my right there are two framed photos in vivid color. In the first, Diana and Eurico are sitting side by side in the swing beneath the *samaúma* tree. She has her arm around his narrow shoulders, and he is smiling up at her, his red shirt bright against the green background. In the second, Diana is sitting on the porch step in front of her small house on the mission compound. Her hair, the color of new honey, is streaked by the sun. She is smiling bravely, but there is sadness in her blue eyes, and I cannot look at her without getting a lump in my throat.

My father's Bible and his journals are sitting between two book-ends at the front edge of my desk, in the very center. Next to them there is a coffee cup full of cheap ballpoint pens, a pair of scissors, and a letter opener. I'm writing in a lined journal with a kerosene lamp at my elbow and a cup of coffee that has now grown cold. This is where I come when I need solitude but cannot bear to be alone.

When I first returned from the Amazon, I considered going back to college to study photojournalism. But after thinking about it, I realized that while I have a good eye, there's no art in my photography, nothing to set it apart. Truthfully, I'll never be more than an amateur shutterbug. I love it, but I have no talent for photography.

Much to my surprise, I have discovered that I have a gift with words. Like my father, I am mostly tongue-tied, but with a pen in my hand all the inarticulate yearnings of my soul seem to find their voice. For me, writing is like coming home. It's like I have finally found what I've been searching for my whole life. I want to be published. I want to write novels that tens of thousands of people will read, but what fulfills me is the writing itself. When I write, I feel alive, and it seems that God smiles on me.

I've enrolled at Colorado State University with a major in creative writing. Classes start in about ten days, and as hard as it may be to believe, I'm actually looking forward to it. I was always a poor student, but I think that was more a reflection of my lack of interest than any lack of intellect. For the first time ever, I'm excited about going to school.

Never a day goes by that I don't think of Diana, Eurico too. They continue to live together in Diana's small house on the mission station. The adoption is finally official, much to the consternation of the foreign mission board. Who knows what kind of disciplinary action they might have taken if Gordon Arnold hadn't interceded on Diana's behalf? To their way of reasoning, it only takes one exception to set a bad precedent. Be that as it may, Diana and Eurico are a family, and I couldn't be happier. Yes I could—if I was also a part of the family—but that can never be.

Leaving Diana and returning to the States was the hardest thing I have ever done. It ripped the heart out of me, but even worse was the knowledge that I was breaking Diana's heart once again. I wasn't being selfish; not this time. In fact, it may prove to be the most selfless thing I will ever do. I can only liken it to a mother giving up her beloved baby for adoption. She denies herself, risks her child's misunderstanding, maybe even her child's lifelong animosity, to do what's best for the child. I did it for Diana, and it nearly killed me.

During those final days in the Amazon, we discussed every possible scenario, left no option unexplored. Late into the night we planned and schemed and argued, but when all was said and done, there was no way we could make a life together. Diana could not marry me and continue to serve as a missionary, even had I been willing to live in the Amazon. Her denomination has a prohibition against ministers or missionaries marrying someone who has been divorced. If she were to marry me, the Department of Foreign Missions would rescind her appointment, and her denomination would defrock her. No matter how much we love each other, I could never permit her to suffer such a loss or the inevitable public humiliation that would accompany it. Nor could I let Diana give up her call and return with me to the States. God has first claim on her life, and whether she realizes it or not, turning her back on her call would kill something vital inside of her. In time she would come to resent me, to blame me for the loss of her life's purpose, and then her love for me would die. It was better, I reasoned, to suffer a clean break, painful though it was, than to slowly destroy each other, as inevitably we must.

So I sit here late into the night, a kerosene lamp my only light, and remember. I remember the way she looked the first time I saw her and how beautiful she was sitting in the swing beneath the towering *samaúma* tree. Her eyes were the color of the Colorado sky, and her face was full of laughter, the afternoon sun highlighting her blonde hair. I remember her gentle touch when she cared for me while I had malaria, and the terror I felt when she plunged down the mountain. I remember the soft pinging of a gentle rain against the corrugated tin roof, creating what will always be in my mind a kind of music, a love song. I fixed those images in my mind, carefully noting each detail. Even then I knew it would be important later when all I would have are the memories, and so it is. When I look back on my days in the Amazon, this is what I remember—the soft glow of a kerosene lamp, the murmur of rain on the roof, and Diana's fingers in my hair. And no matter where my life's journey may take me, the drumming of rain on a tin roof will always sound like love to me—Diana's love.

ACKNOWLEDGEMENTS

With special thanks to the following:

Brenda Starr Exley, a wife for all seasons, who read my work each day and shared in the creative process.

Debbie Justus, of Emerald Pointe Books, who had the vision for this book long before anyone else did. Without your vision it would not have been birthed, and without your dedicated efforts it would not have become reality.

Leah Starr Baker, my beloved daughter and a novelist in her own right, who planted the seed for this story in my mind.

John and Evelyn Looper, special friends who read the early drafts and gave me unflagging encouragement. Your comments were invaluable.

Craig Butler, who suggested using a journal to "flesh out" the character of Harold Whittaker.

The wonderful men who serve on the Richard Exley Ministry Board who prayed for me faithfully during the writing of this book. Robert Exley, PhD, Kurt Green, Jack Ingram, Keith Provance, Barry Tims, and Bill Tims.

The wonderful friends whose prayers and encouragement sustain me: Bob and Susie Arnold, Eddy and Claudia Brewer, Keith and Carol Butler, Mike and Pam Buie, Frank and Linda Cargill, Greg and Donna Davis, Max Davis, Don and Dana Duke, Ed Jones, Mike and

Jeanie Kruger, Roger and Debbie Lewis, Greg and Marilynda Lynch, John and Ruth Merrill, Curt and Karol Neimeister, Randy and Sandy Phillips, Ken Revell, Jerry and Barbra Russell, Ron and Dee Siegenthaler, Elaine Wells, Paul and Aileen Wynkoop.

My parents, Dick and Irene Exley, and Brenda's mother, Hildegarde Wallace, whose faithful prayers I value more than I can ever say.

Don Exley, my missionary brother, who is my hero and whose faith in me enables me to be whatever I am.

Sherry Echols, my sister, who reads everything I write.

Several books and their authors opened the Amazon Basin for me and enriched the lure of the rain forest and the missionaries who serve there: *End of the Spear* by Steve Saint, *Jungle Pilot* by Russell T. Hitt, *Through Gates of Splendor* by Elisabeth Elliot, *Land of Ghosts* by David G. Campbell, *The Lost Amazon* by Wade Davis, and *Heart of the Amazon* by Yossi Ghinsberg.

Aldeia—Missionary village.

Arapuá—Stingless bee about the size of a housefly.

Aviacáo—Grubstake provided to a rubber-trapper by his *patrao* (see definition below).

Bairro Fluntuante—Cruzeiro do Sul's floating waterfront neighborhood built on pontoons and stilts above the mud flats.

Batedor (plural, *batedores*)—Professional Indian-hunter.

Bola—Ball of smoked, coagulated rubber latex.

Botfly—Fly with parasitic maggots.

Buriti—Common fan-leafed palm.

Caapi—Vine.

Caboclo—Amazonian of mixed descent but culturally Indian (Native American).

Cachaça—Cheap white rum.

Coreira—Hunting party intended to kill Indians.

Cruzéiro—Brazilian coin.

Estrada—Rubber trapper's trail.

Maloca—Native American communal house or longhouse.

Mariri—Indian (Native American) ceremony in which hallucinogenic *caapi* is drunk.

Mateiro—(1) Woodsman. (2) Manager of a *seringal*.

Patrâo—Boss of a rubber estate.

Peixote—("little fish")—Street urchin.

Pico da jaca—Bushmaster snake.

Pistoleiro—Hired gunslinger.

Pium—Biting fly.

Rasga mortalha—("shroud-tearer")—The name refers to the nightjar's rasping voice.

Rio—River.

Samaúma—Silk-cotton tree. It is one of the tallest trees in Amazonia, growing to two hundred feet.

Seringal—Rubber estate.

Seringueiro—Rubber tapper.

READING GROUP DISCUSSION QUESTIONS

1. Bryan was only seven years old when his father disappeared. How do you think growing up without a father affected him? What does his experience portend for the millions of children in America who are growing up without a father in their lives? How can we address this sociological crisis?

2. Initially Bryan blamed God for his father's disappearance (death). Why do you think he blamed God? How did this action affect him? How did it affect his relationship with Helen? With Carolyn? With God?

3. Why do you think Bryan's mother insisted on grieving alone? Was this a significant factor in Bryan's anger, or did he just use it as an excuse to blame others for his personal problems? How would you have liked to see his mother respond to the loss of her husband? At what point does a person stop blaming others and take responsibility for his or her own life?

4. Helen told Carolyn that there are three basic ways we can respond to tragedy. We can curse life and look for some way to express our grief and rage. Or we can grit our teeth and endure it. Or we can accept it. Do you agree? How do you respond to tragedy in your own life?

5. Rob and Helen appeared to have a strong marriage until Bryan disappeared and Helen became depressed. Over a period of weeks

their marriage became strained almost to the breaking point. What do you think happened? Who was to blame? How could they have restored their marriage and moved on?

6. Why do you think Bryan and Eurico responded so differently to the tragedies in their lives? Most of us have known people who have gone through great tragedy. As you think about them, try to identify the ways they responded and how it has affected them and their relationships. What can you learn from their experiences?

7. When Bryan was in danger after falling down the mountain and injuring himself in the Amazon Basin, Carolyn was awakened with concern for him although she had no way of knowing he was in danger. What do you think awakened her? Was it extrasensory perception? Or was it the Holy Spirit? Do you think her prayers played a part in his rescue and safe return to the mission compound?

8. Although Diana was a missionary doctor serving selflessly in the Amazon Basin, she continued to battle condemnation for having an abortion while still in college. Why do you think she continued to struggle with this issue? Was her guilt punishment from God, or was it self-induced? How could she have been freed of her debilitating condemnation?

9. *The Alabaster Cross* is filled with providential events—Bryan met Eurico who introduced him to Lako who just happened to be part Amuaca. Lako just happened to be one of the few people who spoke both Portuguese and the Amuaca dialect, enabling Bryan to communicate with Komi and learn what happened to his father. Were all these events blind luck, or did God have a hand in them? Was God orchestrating these events to bring about Bryan's spiritual and emotional healing, or did they just happen? Do you

believe God is involved in our personal lives, in your personal life? If so, how?

10. In the process of making peace with his deceased father, Bryan finally came to realize that the truth is never one-dimensional. What did he mean when he said, "It's a many-sided thing, and only when we embrace the whole of it can we find healing and peace"? What was the "whole" truth about Bryan's father? How did his understanding of this truth affect Bryan's memories of his father? How did it affect his view of life and his future?

11. Upon returning to the mission compound, Bryan discovered that Eurico had unexpectedly recovered from his illness. When Diana told him that prayer had healed Eurico, Bryan had trouble accepting it. Why do you suppose he still doubted, considering all that God had done for him? What do you think Diana meant when she said, "We pray for an outcome—in this case Eurico's healing—but our hope is in God! It can't be any other way."

12. Why do you think Diana was able to forgive Bryan considering the horrible thing he had done to her? It has been said, "Our ability to forgive is only limited by the depth of our love." What do you think that means? Do you think it was true in Diana's case?

13. Bryan chose not to marry Diana and build a life with her even though he loved her. Do you think he made the right decision? Why or why not? Do you think he was acting selflessly in her best interest, or do you think he was thinking only of himself?

An Interview with Author Richard Exley

1) **When did you first realize that you wanted to be a writer? Was there anything in your childhood that influenced you to become a writer?**

I didn't actually "decide" to be a writer until I was twenty years old, but I believe the desire was born in me while I was still an infant, long before it became a conscious thought. My father was an avid reader, and I am told that when I was just a baby, I would sit in his lap for hours while he read. Quite likely my own love for books, and thus my desire to be a writer, were born right there in his arms. Even today I think of a good book as a trusted friend, and I associate them with happiness and love. The positive feelings that books evoke in me is most likely a carry-over of the love and security I found in my father's arms.

2) **Although you have written a significant number of books, *The Alabaster Cross* is your first novel. Why did you decide to venture into fiction?**

Actually I began writing my "first" novel when I was just twenty-five years old. Unfortunately, or perhaps I should say fortunately, since my early efforts were so clumsy, I never finished it. I actually finished a second novel in 1980 but I never submitted it, so I think it is safe to say that fiction has always been my first love.

Opportunities for writing nonfiction began coming my way, and I responded; but I never stopped dreaming of the day I would write a novel. When Debbie Justus, vice president of marketing and product development for Emerald Pointe Books, approached me about writing a novel in December 2004, I knew the time had finally come. I can say without reservation that writing *The Alabaster Cross* was my most rewarding writing experience. Nothing I've ever written fulfilled me so completely.

3) **Knowing that you are an avid reader, which novelists have influenced your writing and in what ways?**

To my way of thinking there are only two ways to become a writer—by reading voraciously and by writing. Everything I know about my craft I learned from the writers I read. I couldn't begin to name all of the novelists who have influenced me, but I will name those who come immediately to mind. Pat Conroy's use of language and his ability to plumb the depths of his personal experiences, in order to bring to his novels the hauntingly poignant reality of life, never ceases to both inspire me and challenge me. Anita Shreve's ability to develop her characters and make the ordinary fascinating set a standard I am always striving for; not to mention the unique ways in which she structures her novels. No one does research better than the late James Michener, unless it's Michael Creighton. Their research is so comprehensive it can be intimidating. I also have a profound appreciate for John Steinbeck, Leon Uris, and Herman Wouk. I owe each of them, and so many others, a debt I can never repay.

4) **Why did you write *The Alabaster Cross* rather than some other story?**

When Debbie Justus approached me about writing a novel I didn't have any idea what I would write. Immediately I began brainstorming with my family and friends, and out of that came several ideas. Over the next several weeks the idea for *The Alabaster Cross* began to take shape in my mind. Having been involved in both family counseling and grief counseling for a number of years I was well aware of the dynamics at work in those situations. I was also concerned about the number of children growing up without fathers, thus I crafted a novel around issues I knew and understood. I wanted to write a novel that would be entertaining and interesting—a good read—but I also wanted it to address issues critical to so many.

5) **Your novel is set in the Amazon Basin in far western Brazil, and many of your characters are missionaries. Why did you select the Amazon Basin, and why did you write about missionaries?**

I needed a setting where the culture of the Stone Age and the culture of the twentieth century were in conflict. Although there were several possible locations, having a brother who is a career missionary in Latin America provided the inspiration for setting the story in the Amazon Basin and for making the experiences of a missionary family a core part of the story. From my many conversations with him I have gained considerable insight into the special challenges missionaries and their families face, and I knew their experiences would provide a unique twist. Let me be quick to point out that *The Alabaster Cross* is not a missionary story per se but a novel set in the wilds of the Amazonian Rain Forest using the missionary culture as a backdrop.

6) **Your characters are complex, multi-dimensional, and true to life. The way you have developed them reveals a profound**

understanding of human nature. I can't help wondering where your insights come from. How do you know human nature so well?

Having lived nearly sixty years I think I can safely say that life is the great teacher. I've either experienced or walked with others through all of the experiences described in *The Alabaster Cross*. Of course it is possible to live without learning and to experience without understanding, but I have and will continue to work hard not to waste my life experiences. By temperament I am a student of human nature. I am constantly studying people, trying to figure out why they do the things they do. In addition I have served as a minister and a counselor for nearly forty years, and that in itself is a graduate course in human nature.

7) **One of your strongest skills is your ability to transport the reader into your literary landscape—in this case the Amazonian Rain Forest. What kind of research did you do to make your locale so real? Did you go to the Amazon Basin as part of your research?**

Although I have been privileged to travel in all fifty states and twenty-two foreign countries I've never been to the Rain Forests of the Amazon Basin. Since I could not afford either the time or the expense to travel to the far western Amazon Basin I had to rely on the information I could glean from books and the internet. All told I read more than one thousand pages. In many ways it was probably more educational than actually going to the Amazon, but I still want to experience it in person someday.

8) **How do you develop your plot and your characters?**

In a certain sense the plot and the characters develop themselves. I start with an idea and work out the ending. Then I build tall fences on either side to keep me on track, and then I start writing without knowing all of the details. For instance when I started writing *The Alabaster Cross* I didn't know that Dr. Peterson or Eurico would be part of the story, but they both became key characters. I like to say that writing a novel is kind of like watching a child grow up. You set boundaries and you guide their development, but they are always doing something unexpected. Within the boundaries of the story I let the characters grow and develop on their own as long as they don't get out of character. Sometimes what they do or say comes as a total surprise to me, and yet I realize it is the right thing for the story. I sometimes think of myself as a kind of midwife. I help with the birthing, but I am not really the source of life. The best stories have a life of their own.

9) **How would you describe your writing style—not your literary style—but the actual writing itself? What kind of techniques do you use?**

I'm a painfully slow writer. I rewrite as I go, laboring over each sentence until I have it as good as I can possibly make it. Brenda (my wife) says I write out loud because I sit at my computer and mutter all day long. I guess that comes from my years in radio. If something doesn't read well out loud it's probably not written as well as it should be, especially dialogue. I warm up for each day's work by rewriting all I have written the previous day. By the time I finally submit my manuscript to the publisher I have probably rewritten it at least eight or ten times.

10) **Many novelists say ending the novel is the most difficult part of writing. Why do you think that is and how do you know when you have reached the end of your story?**

Let me answer the last part of your question first. I knew *The Alabaster Cross* was nearing the end once Bryan resolved his issues with his late father and with God. Although there were several other issues in the book this was the main theme and once it was resolved I knew I had reached the end of this novel.

As rewarding as writing a novel is, it is also an emotionally draining task, and by the time an author is approaching the end he or she is often exhausted. I think that's one of the reasons ending a novel well is so difficult. Also many readers want the author to "wrap things up" and if the author is writing about real life that is seldom possible. Life is messy and it doesn't lend itself to neat endings. For instance many readers expected Bryan and Carolyn to get back together, or they thought Bryan would take up his father's mantle and become a missionary. Neither scenario is very realistic. Instead I left the relationships unresolved. I did that for a couple of reasons. First it was more realistic, that's the way life is. It also lends itself to a sequel.

11) **There's obviously more to a novel than just an entertaining read. What do you want the reader to take away from *The Alabaster Cross*?**

In a word: hope! No matter what your situation is, no matter how sorely you have been wounded or how hopeless your situation may look, God can turn it around. Years ago a wise friend gave me a word of encouragement that I have never forgotten. He said, "There's no broken heart that God cannot mend if we will just give Him all the pieces."

12) **We've talked about the novelists that most influenced you as a writer, so now let me make the question a little more personal. As an adult what one person has been most influential in your life?**

I am indebted to so many people who have enriched my life that limiting it to one person is not only difficult but impossible. As a child my Grandma Miller and my parents were the most influential figures in my small world. Even now their fingerprints are all over my life. Through the years several people have played significant roles in my life—Ben Roy and Hildegarde Wallace, Jim Calhoun, Tex Groff, Roy Williams, Keith Provance, Jack Ingram, John and Evelyn Looper, and John and Ruth Merrell. My brother Don is the most godly person I have ever known, and his selfless commitment serves as a constant challenge to my own faith and commitment. Although we are separated by continents, and see each other no more than once or twice a year, his influence continues to make me a better man than I would otherwise be. Having said all of that I must now tell you that the single most influential person in my life is Brenda Starr, my wife of more than forty years. Her love for me and her faith in me are a constant source of strength and encouragement, enabling me to take risks and live life in ways that I would never attempt alone.

13) **In conclusion, tell us something personal about Richard Exley that most people may not know?**

Most people probably don't know that I accepted Jesus Christ as my personal Savior when I was only six years old. Although I was reared in church until that night I did not realize that I needed a personal relationship with Jesus. My family was driving cross country, and it was late at night. My brother and I were supposed to be asleep in the back seat, but I was awake listening to my parents' conversation. They were discussing the fact that a number of young people who attended our church appeared to have no personal relationship with Jesus. Although they weren't talking about me, I knew what they were saying described me perfectly. Rolling over, I buried my face against the back of the seat and called on the name of Jesus. That night He became my Savior, and I have endeavored to live for Him all the days of my life.

RICHARD EXLEY is the author of twenty-nine books, many of them best-sellers, most recently *Man of Valor* and *Encounters with Christ*.

Richard is known as a master storyteller—a gift he utilizes with consummate skill in his first novel, *The Alabaster Cross*.

His rich and diversified background has included serving as senior pastor of churches in Colorado and Oklahoma, as well as hosting several popular radio programs, including the nationally syndicated *Straight from the Heart*.

When not traveling the country as a speaker, Richard and his wife, Brenda Starr, spend their time in a cabin overlooking picturesque Beaver Lake in Northwest Arkansas.

Richard enjoys quiet talks with old friends, kerosene lamps, good books, a warm fire when it is cold, and a good cup of coffee any time. He's an avid Denver Broncos fan, an aspiring bass fisherman, and an amateur photographer.

For additional information on seminars, scheduling speaking engagements, or to write the author, please address your correspondence to:

Richard Exley
P.O. Box 54744
Tulsa, Oklahoma 74155

Or visit: www.richardexleyministry.org

OTHER GREAT READS FROM EMERALD POINTE BOOKS

0-98751-371-1

Luke Hatcher is the pride of Magnolia Springs, Louisiana. The perfect kid, he's the star of the high school baseball team and is on his way to LSU after graduation on a full scholarship—destined for the big leagues. Little did he know that a simple dare from his high school sweetheart would change his whole life.

A riveting novel that celebrates the God who gives second chances. If you've ever looked back on your life, feeling you threw away a golden moment, you will walk away from this passionate story cheering and with a renewed outlook on your own life.

0-97851-372-X

Following the Civil War, Juliana, a beautiful, young abolitionist, seeks to help the South heal and repent of its past, when she meets a former Confederate naval officer, Andre, who swears never to forgive the North for the devastation to his family. The question is whether these two strong-willed individuals will be able to swallow their pride and discover a common path to rebuilding the city—and their own lives.

A story about the North and South, a man and a woman, courage and resilience in the face of fierce opposition, and the triumphant dignity of the human spirit.

Additional copies of this book and other titles by
Emerald Pointe Books are available from your local bookstore.

If you have enjoyed this book, or if it has impacted your life,
we would like to hear from you:

Please contact us at:

Emerald Pointe Books
Attention: Editorial Department
P.O. Box 35327
Tulsa, OK 74153

Emerald Pointe Books